'The undisputed queen of crime writing'
Erwin James

MARTINA COLE

Author of 23 novels – and counting...

15 No. 1 bestsellers

4 screen adaptations

3 stage shows

Over 15 million copies sold across the world

Celebrating 25 years of record-breaking bestsellers

Stay in touch for film and TV news,
book releases and more...

🐦 @MartinaCole
f /OfficialMartinaCole
www.martinacole.co.uk

*Martina Cole's 23 bestsellers (so far) –
in order of publication.
All available from Headline.*

Dangerous Lady (1992)
The Ladykiller: DI Kate Burrows 1 (1993)
Goodnight Lady (1994)
The Jump (1995)
The Runaway (1997)
Two Women (1999)
Broken: DI Kate Burrows 2 (2000)
Faceless (2001)*
Maura's Game: Dangerous Lady 2 (2002)*
The Know (2003)*
The Graft (2004)*
The Take (2005)*
Close (2006)*
Faces (2007)*
The Business (2008)*
Hard Girls: DI Kate Burrows 3 (2009)*
The Family (2010)*
The Faithless (2011)*
The Life (2012)*
Revenge (2013)*
The Good Life (2014)*
Get Even (2015)
Betrayal (2016)*

On Screen:
Dangerous Lady (ITV 1995)
The Jump (ITV 1998)
Martina Cole's Lady Killers (ITV3 documentary 2003)
The Take (Sky 1 2009)
Martina Cole's Girl Gangs (Sky Factual documentary 2009)
The Runaway (Sky 1 2011)

*Martina Cole's No. 1 bestsellers – at time of press she has
spent more weeks at No. 1 than any other author

MARTINA COLE
THE LIFE

HEADLINE

First published in Great Britain in 2012
by HEADLINE PUBLISHING GROUP

First published in Great Britain in paperback in 2013
by HEADLINE PUBLISHING GROUP

This edition published in paperback in 2017 by
HEADLINE PUBLISHING GROUP

12

The acknowledgements on pages 594–596 constitute an extension
of this copyright page.

Every effort has been made to fulfil requirements with regard
to producing copyright material. The author and publisher will be
glad to rectify any omissions at the earliest opportunity.

Cataloguing in Publication Data is available from the British Library

ISBN 978 0 7553 7559 2

Typeset in Galliard by Avon DataSet Ltd, Bidford-on-Avon, Warwickshire

Printed and bound in Great Britain by Clays Ltd, St Ives plc

Headline's policy is to use papers that are natural, renewable and recyclable
products and made from wood grown in well-managed forests and other
controlled sources. The logging and manufacturing processes are expected to
conform to the environmental regulations of the country of origin.

HEADLINE PUBLISHING GROUP
An Hachette UK Company
Carmelite House
50 Victoria Embankment
London, EC4Y 0DZ

www.headline.co.uk
www.hachette.co.uk

Foreword

After books, my big love is music. As I'm writing of a night time, I listen to the sounds of the eras I am writing about. It's a perfect way to get into the characters' minds and, as everyone knows, a certain record can transport you back to a particular moment in time. If I hear 'Mama Weer All Crazee Now' by Slade, I can remember with stunning clarity one of my oldest friends, Graham Petherick, air-guitaring to it as a crowd of us watched his silhouette through his bathroom window! When I listen to 'Woke Up This Morning' by Alabama 3, I can see my daughter Freddie Mary and my grandson Lewis, both four years old at the time, singing along to it as we travelled down to my caravan in Eastbourne. Wonderful memories, captured in time by music. Music can do that to you, bring back a memory and make you smile even on your saddest of days. After I buried my mum, I played Bowie, and even in my grief I had to smile as I remembered her asking me to turn up 'Rock 'n' Roll Suicide' on my record player; she loved that song, she loved Bowie. She died in the early eighties, eight months after my father's death, and I still miss them both very much.

As I wrote *The Life*, I listened to a lot of Alabama 3 – one of my favourite bands of all time – and I have used their lyrics in this book. They are the band I listen to most these days. I have seen them live, and they are a really visual band, whose music seems to encompass the thoughts of many different generations. I look forward to seeing them again soon. I was very lucky to be asked to be a part of their latest album, *Shoplifting For Jesus*, and I am now pretending to be a recording artist! Thanks, guys, especially Ian Gough and Larry Love.

I can't believe it has been twenty years since the publication of my first book *Dangerous Lady*. To celebrate, *Dangerous Lady* is going to be performed as a play at the Theatre Royal Stratford East, in East London. This theatre is very close to my heart; if we lose the local theatres *and* the libraries, the whole heart of local communities will be gone. It's a disgrace, and something that needs to be addressed because we will never get these things back. Without my local library when I was a child, I don't know what I would have done, and our local theatre also played a big part in my quest for knowledge.

Dangerous Lady was a big milestone in my life, and I'm very proud of it. I would never have been published had it not been for my agent, Darley Anderson, who is not only my agent but a wonderful friend to boot. I can't thank him enough for everything, especially his friendship and support. Darley is that rare breed – a man who genuinely understands women! He is also my daughter's godfather, and a close member of my family, loved by us all. His wisdom is unique, and his friendship means the world to me.

Susan Fletcher, my first editor and a terrific person, who believed in me from her first glance at *Dangerous Lady*; a big thank you once more. Sadly, Sue is retiring from publishing this year, and she will be greatly missed by everyone.

Tim Hely Hutchinson, always so good to me, and who, along with Sue Fletcher and Sian Thomas, built Headline up into the wonderful publishing house it is today. I have been with Headline for over twenty years now, and everyone I have ever dealt with has always been wonderful. Thank you, Tim, for everything.

Clare Foss – my editor for many years – another person I can never thank enough for her support, and her kindness. Go, Clare!

Jane Morpeth – who is now my editor – a really lovely lady, and someone I truly admire and respect. Thank you, Jane; I look forward to the next twenty years! You've been a great friend, and a fantastic editor. Thank you again.

Martin Neild, the loveliest man on earth, thank you so much. You have been a great influence, and I appreciate your friendship very much. (Pink Floyd in a Bentley is a memory I will have for ever.) Good luck for the future.

I'd also like to thank Amanda Ridout. She was very good to me when she was at Headline, and I will always be grateful for all that she did for me. Great girl; and I'll never drink five bottles of Montrachet with anyone else – she knows what I am talking about! (PS, Amanda, we are still welcome at the OXO Tower!)

I want to say a big thank you to Kerr MacRae; he was always so very nice to me when he was at Headline and, even though he has moved on to pastures new, we have stayed good friends. He is possibly one of the nicest people in publishing, and he played a big part in my success. Now I wish *him* every success for the future.

Louise Page – what can I say? She is fantastic – not only a good person and a wonderful friend, but the best PR in the land! Thanks, Lou, you have been a star over the years. Me, you and Peter – otherwise known as The Waberthwaite Three – have travelled the length and breadth of this country, and had some good laughs along the way. Thank you, once more; you always find the best venues, and you can throw one hell of a party!

Now on to Peter Bates. You have driven me for many years now, Pete, and we have both seen our share of ups and downs. One thing never changes though: your friendship and your humour. I love you, Pete, and I can't thank you enough for being there beside me since time began! We have had some screams along the way, and without you those journeys would not have been half as much fun. I wish you everything that is good for the future. I still don't know how Rita puts up with you; she is a lovely lady, and a saint!

I would like to thank everyone at Headline, old and new. It's been a second family to me, and I know how lucky I have been to be a part of it. It's been a privilege, and it's been a lot of fun – and hard work! So, thank you all again, especially a certain Irishman! Darragh – driving through Spain listening to good music is a memory I will never forget. Thank you.

I'd also like to thank Peter Newsom, who was another good friend to me. I remember meeting him at a Morrissey concert a few years ago and I don't know who was more surprised! But thanks, Peter – I had some great times in Oz, New Zealand and South Africa. I wish you well for the future.

A big thank you to Martin Booth, a really good man who was responsible for my first ever pay cheque for writing! He was at the BBC in the early nineties and he took up a script I had sent in. We became good friends and he gave me the confidence I needed to look towards writing as a career. So thank you, Martin, very much.

Last, but certainly not least, I would like to thank Lavinia Warner. She made *Dangerous Lady* into a TV series many years ago. Since then we have become close friends and business partners, going on to make three more series together, along with other projects we have in the pipeline. Thanks, Vin, you have been a real star, and you're a big part of my family, we all love you dearly. In New York earlier this year, we watched her cousin on Broadway in *Venus in Fur*. It was one of the highlights of my life; thank you for making me a part of it. I love you, girl.

Now, to my readers – you know who you are! I've met so many of you over the years, especially at Pat Fletcher's stall on Romford Market. Pat gave me my first book signing, and I will always be very grateful to her for that. We have become good friends, and even have houses near each other in Northern Cyprus! So thank you to Pat and Harry Fletcher, and I will see you soon, mate, at Kybele restaurant in Bellapais.

So thank you, once more, to you all, my loyal readers, who have been there since *Dangerous Lady*, all those years ago. I hope you enjoy *The Life*. I have been living with the Bailey family for a year now, and I plan to finish Tania's story off in a few years' time! So I hope you enjoy her ups and downs – and, believe me, there are a lot of those! I hope to meet many of you at my signings, and I look forward to saying hello to you all.

Take care and God bless,

Martina

x

Prologue

1997

I'd grown up in the Life, but I'd never really been a part of it – my mum had made sure of that. It all changed the day she died.

On the day we buried her, I looked around the church. My whole family was there, and we were a big family, the Baileys, and a well-known family to boot. My nana, Theresa Bailey, the matriarch, was sitting beside me, holding my hand. She was good to me, always. I could depend on her – she would never repeat my secrets. She knew more than any of them, and she kept it to herself. But then, if she had opened her mouth, there would have been another murder – we needed to keep the secret no matter what, and that is exactly what we did. I knew that I could never have coped without her, especially not that day.

My four brothers – all big, handsome, honourable men – sat on her other side and my father, broken by his wife's death, and completely unaware of his only daughter's shame, sat by me. It was *how* my mum died that was affecting him even more than just the loss of her. She had been taken in a heartbeat – those were his words, not mine.

I sat beside him, his youngest child and his only daughter, small-boned like my mother and with my paternal grandmother's thick auburn hair. But I had his eyes – the deep blue Irish eyes that showed every emotion and told the whole world what I was thinking, especially him and my brothers. I learned quickly to never let anyone know my true feelings and that is a sad testament to the life I live now. Knowledge is power and even the smallest slip can be enough to bring you down.

We were the Baileys – the most talked about and revered family in the East End – the foremost family in England, actually, for many a long year. We led charmed lives, we had everything – and I mean *everything*. My father, Daniel Bailey, saw to that.

As I held his hand on that cold bleak day, he slipped it into his coat pocket as he had when I was a small child. Even at nearly eighteen, I still appreciated the warmth and kindness behind the act. I knew my father was dangerous from the time I was a child, but I had not known just how dangerous he really was until recently. He had only ever done what he felt was needed; I understood that and, on that day, unhappy and devastated at the loss of my mother, I depended on him more than ever to bring me comfort.

My world had changed overnight. With my mum gone there was no one to shield me from my family's real way of life. My mum, God love her, had done her best to make sure I never knew the real deal, but however hard she tried, I overheard more than was good for me. My family were murderers, liars, people for whom violence and intimidation were literally their daily bread.

My brothers were years older than me – I was my mum's last hurrah, as she would say with a big grin on her face. God had sent me to her as a gift – I was all hers. She talked about God a lot, she set great store by Him and His son, the Christ who had died on the cross to take away the sins of the world. When she died, they just didn't know what to do with me, this female left in their predominantly male world, but they loved me all the same and would do anything to protect me, I knew that. And I'll never stop loving any of them, as bad as they are. They love me, and they care for me. And, at this time in my young life, that is enough.

I suspect my mum knew more than she let on about her husband's and sons' activities and it must have been very hard for her to hear so much that was bad about them, and still believe in them. She was a decent woman in her own way – God fearing, and with a strong belief in the afterlife. She put up with the men in her life because she had to. She was a mother after all, and these were her little boys. But deep inside she had to have condoned what they were.

I remember smiling at my eldest brother Danny that day, knowing he would always be there for me. Danny, despite his blond hair, was my dad's double, like the spit out of his mouth, as the old fucking shawlies – as my nana called them – would say. He and my other brothers, Davey, Noel and Jamsie, had each received Confession, made a good act of contrition, so they could take Communion at their mother's funeral without fear or favour – my father had made sure of that. Hypocritical, I know, but it was for her more than for him, and I loved that he had done that for her. He had loved my mother with a vengeance.

Years later, when I remembered seeing him cutting a man's fingers off, I would also see him as he was on this day. The two sides of Daniel Bailey.

I watched his face contort with emotion as his brother Peter Bailey and his wife Ria entered the church with their remaining children. He gritted his teeth, and I saw in his eyes that it was hard for him to forget his brother's part in this terrible day.

My Auntie Ria, Peter's wife, had always been good friends with my mother – they were very close, and she looked unbearably sad.

I smiled at her, and at my cousins as they followed their parents to the front of the church. My cousin Imelda, a beautiful woman with long, dark, relaxed hair, who exhibited more Jamaican heritage than her brothers, walked over to me and my father. Smiling sadly, she hugged him first, then me, her eyes wet with unshed tears. I was pleased and so relieved when my father had hugged her back; she had always been a favourite of his. No one really knew then how much the Life had affected her.

I looked at my Uncle Peter, a big, handsome black man, and at my father, so like him in many ways, even though he was what would be called white. They had the same mother, but different fathers, and were so close they were like pages in the same book, united now in their grief. It was a grief that transcended feuds.

The church full of people were wondering who the bastard was that had set the car bomb that had blown my poor mother all over Soho. But, unlike them, *we* knew who was responsible for planting the bomb which had caused this carnage. And we also knew that the bomb hadn't been meant for my mother. If the intended recipient had died maybe, just maybe, things would never have turned out like they did. Hindsight really is a fucking wonderful thing.

I still had a lot to learn about my family. On that day I knew nothing about guns, and the murder of a baby, an innocent child tragically drawn into this world of violence as easily as my mother had been. I would find out about these things eventually. You name it, my family had done it. But they couldn't have foreseen how deep they would get into the quagmire of revenge, and how they would lose all semblance of reality, forgetting about the real world outside of *their* world.

The loss of my mum had opened my eyes to the truth of the Life. In the last month I had seen and done things which would change me for ever. And, despite everything my mum did to protect me, she didn't prepare me for how seductive the Life could be.

There was an old Irish saying of my nana's – she always said you get the life you deserve. I hope against hope that there was no truth in that. But only time will tell.

Book One

She shakes the blues off then she tries her luck
Makes a little bet, hopes her horse comes up
Pickin' pockets for some easy money
'Cause she blew the goddamn lot on the National
Lottery

Alabama 3, 'Mansion On The Hill'
Album: *La Peste*, 2000

Flip, baby flip my switch
Blow my head off
If you're gonna cry, keep your shades on

Alabama 3, 'Keep Your Shades On'
Album: *Outlaw*, 2005

Book One

Chapter One

1979

'You and whose fucking army? Listen to yourself! You're threatening *us* with your cunt of an uncle? You're talking utter shite.'

Daniel Bailey was fuming, and everyone in the factory knew that this was not going to end well.

Michael Lanson, or Micky L as he liked to be known, was trussed up like a chicken, and he was seriously regretting opening his big trap. He had heard the Baileys were a law unto themselves but he had not really understood the seriousness of their outfit until he had been abducted off the street two hours previously.

He worked for his uncle, a man called Jed Lanson, and he had believed he was invincible because of that. Jed was an old-time Face; he had his creds, and no one, until now, had ever had the nerve to take him on. It seemed that Daniel and Peter Bailey were the exceptions to the rule.

Peter Bailey sat quietly, sipping on a glass of white rum, watching his brother with interest. Peter understood the logic of his brother's methods even if he didn't follow them himself. It was why they were such a good team – they each had different strengths. Peter liked to do things quietly, with the minimum of fuss. He liked privacy. But he was also known to be a man who would seriously harm anyone who crossed him. Long and slow was Peter Bailey's retribution. It was rumoured he enjoyed the whole gamut of emotions his victims were put through, from fear, pain and agony, to begging for their lives to be finally ended. But there was never any evidence; the person would disappear, and all that would be left of their ordeal would be rumours.

Daniel, on the other hand, was happy to take out anybody who crossed him with as much melodrama as possible. He believed that if you were going to take someone out you should do it in such a way as to make it a lesson of sorts. Make sure that people understood what would happen to them if *they* pushed it too far. Daniel knew the value of a decent reputation. It kept mouths shut, and kept the 'hoi polloi', as he called them, in their place. He believed that reputation was everything; there was time enough for the down low when you were properly established – until then you had to build your rep and you had to make it a good one. The brothers were in their thirties now, and this was the time to take what they wanted. No more fucking about, working for other people, being taken for cunts left, right and centre. It was time to take what was rightfully theirs.

Daniel and Peter were starting with the Lansons. Micky's uncle was a seriously big fish, in a very, very small pond. So small, in fact, that it was easy for the Baileys to walk in and take it away from him. Jed Lanson didn't have an eye to the future: he still thought he was hard enough to keep a hold of what he had created. But the fact that this boy – his own nephew – was confident enough to mug him off, spoke volumes to the Baileys. It was time for Jed to disappear. First, though, the kind of disrespect Micky L had shown his uncle had to be dealt with. It was a diabolical fucking liberty and, to the Bailey brothers, it was tantamount to fucking mutiny.

Daniel picked up a ball-peen hammer and, motioning to his men with his chin, he said angrily, 'Hold his fucking hand out. I'm going to teach him a lesson about loyalty he won't forget in a hurry. You should have known that family is worth more than strangers, boy. You mugged off your uncle, your mother's brother, your own flesh and blood. You're a fucking Judas, in every sense of the word.'

Daniel watched as his men did his bidding without hesitation. Micky fought them with all his might. A ball-peen hammer had that effect on people. It was a legal weapon you could put in your boot without worrying about a tug from the Old Bill, unlike a shotgun or a machete, both of which could lead to a serious nicking. A hammer, on the other hand, was like a screwdriver or a chisel – a legal tool for legal business – even though it could inflict serious and personal damage in the right hands. In *his* hands anyway.

Micky was sweating with fear, and Daniel grinned at him, before taunting him, 'You thought you could take us for cunts, did you? Call my brother a fucking coon, and me a coon's asswipe, and you really thought we would let that go?'

He brought the hammer down on the boy's hand, as it was held on the concrete floor. Everyone heard the crunch as the bones were shattered, the blood splattering everywhere.

The pain was excruciating, and Micky, feeling the bile rising in his stomach, knew he was going to black out. He finally understood the enormity of what was going on, just as Daniel Bailey had intended. He had been seriously harmed, and he could die in this stinking factory, on this stinking floor.

Daniel shook his head at what he perceived to be the sheer skulduggery of the man before him. 'Fucking look at him, will you? Fainted, like a fucking little girl. Hold his head up, boys. When he finally decides to rejoin us, I'm gonna take the wanker's teeth out. He won't be fucking smiling at anyone for a few years.'

'You're letting him get out of here? Seriously?' One of the crew voiced what they were all thinking, incredulous.

'Course I'm letting him out! This ponce is the reason his uncle is going to come after us.' He pointed to the man on the floor. '*This* is the reason his uncle is going to get his fucking ugly big head caved in, the treacherous bastard that he is too.' Daniel walked back to where his brother was sitting. 'Like fucking nuns these days – a bit of pain and they faint like virgins on a stag night.'

Peter Bailey laughed. 'He's not the first person to call me a coon, and you know it.'

Daniel shrugged. 'It always bothered me more than it did you, Peter, even when we was kids. But if he insults *you* he insults *me* and, more to the point, he insults *our* mother. But you're right – this time it's just another excuse for having a go. Fucking wanker. Thinks he can short-change us? I don't fucking think so.'

Peter nodded. 'A fucking liberty all right.'

'Well, bruv, we've worked long and hard for this, and tonight we'll take it. Be like the fucking black and white minstrels just took over East London. After all, that's what they are calling us, according to that ponce anyway.'

Peter smiled, showing his expensive white teeth. 'I always liked them myself. Remember when we were kids and we used to tap dance on the lino, copying them? After tonight we will tap dance all over the Smoke.'

'Fucking right we will, Peter, we've fucking earned it.'

'Well, after this little lot, we'd better be prepared because this is not going to go down too well.'

Daniel laughed. 'I should hope not, or this was all in vain! Fuck them! Me and you, bruv, are on the up.'

A groan from the floor interrupted their conversation, as Micky came round. Daniel knew he was in terrible pain and bewildered as to why this had happened to him, but he said delightedly and in an exaggerated pseudo-posh voice, 'Oh, Peter, I do believe our guest is finally back with us. Where's my fucking manners?'

He walked slowly back to where Micky was being held upright on his knees by his men and, looking into the young man's eyes, he said jovially, 'I hope you've got a good dentist, son, you're going to fucking need one,' before taking out the boy's jaw, and the majority of his teeth, with one swipe of the hammer. Then, throwing the hammer on to a nearby bench, he said offhandedly, 'Drop him off at his uncle's pub, right outside the public bar. We don't want people thinking that we don't look after our guests, do we?'

Chapter Two

Lena Bailey was always worrying about something – it was part of her everyday life. But tonight was different. She knew in her heart that something was going to happen – what that was to be, she had no idea. Daniel was keeping very quiet, but then she never asked him about his business dealings.

Trying to put her worries out of her mind, Lena turned to her mother-in-law and smiled. 'Theresa, that smells fantastic. You're too good to us.'

Theresa Bailey was still a good-looking woman, with traces of her youthful beauty in her eyes and her smile. She was in her early fifties, but with her make-up on, and in the right light, she could still pass for early forties. Peter and Daniel were so proud of her. Her boys both adored her, she was everything to them, and so she should be. She had borne them against the odds, and she had brought them up against even harder odds. Never having married, they had her maiden name; neither of their fathers had stayed around long after the births.

Theresa shrugged good-naturedly. 'Ah, I was always the good cook. My mother, God rest her soul, she taught me feck-all about life, but she taught me good, basic Irish cookery.'

They both laughed at that.

'Leave it to cool, it will be gorgeous tomorrow. And it will feed your whole fecking bunch for two days!'

She glanced at the clock on the kitchen wall; Lena could tell that her mother-in-law was as worried as she was, otherwise she would already be down the pub. She liked her nights there – she had good friends, played bingo, and enjoyed her life such as it was. She had given birth to her two sons in the forties, one by a Jamaican soldier, the other by an East-End wide boy. She had brought them up on her own, and she had made a life of sorts. She had never gone back to Ireland, her home-land, knowing that she would have had no welcome there considering the circumstances she was in. But she was still a devout Catholic, and she loved both her sons with a vengeance.

Theresa often said that life was for the people who were prepared to live it, and she had lived her life, and she didn't regret a second. She had two handsome sons, and they had provided her with enough grandchildren to keep her busy into her old age. Lena often wondered who Theresa was trying to convince – herself or her sons. It had not been an easy life for her, and she respected her mother-in-law for the way she had brought the two of them up, and the wonderful way she had stood by them. Not an easy life in those days, or these days, if they were honest. Theresa had been sixteen and eighteen respectively when she had given birth to her sons. Her sister, who had begged for her to come over to England and help her out after marrying an English soldier, had thrown her out after the first one had arrived, and stopped talking to her altogether after the second. But she had never really let anyone know that she cared what they thought. Lena knew from things Theresa said that it had hurt, deep down, but she had too much pride to let other people's narrowmindedness ruin her days. Consequently, she had worked her fingers to the bone, and given her two sons the best she could afford. Now, they tried to repay her by making sure she wanted for nothing.

Both Lena and Peter's wife Ria adored her. Ria, like Theresa herself, had faced prejudice to be with her Peter, but she had won the battle and married him anyway, although her father had never accepted it. He had seen her marriage to a black man as a foolishness which could only bring trouble. Ria's mother had come around eventually, and visited her on the sly as often as she could. Even so, she would still be loath to acknowledge her son-in-law in the street, or her grandchildren for that matter. Ria had understood her mother's prejudice in her own way. It was the way of the world. But to the Bailey family, colour meant nothing, and any prejudice they encountered just made them all stronger and tighter.

Lena's husband Daniel had always looked up to his elder brother, had always been close to him – they were like twins in many respects. It hurt Daniel more when people were racially prejudiced than it ever hurt Peter. Peter felt that it was their problem not his; Daniel felt it was a slur on them all, the whole family. He took it as a personal insult to him and his mother, and Daniel Bailey did not like people insulting him or his. Theresa always said that Daniel would be his own worst enemy. Peter rose above people's pettiness, whereas Daniel let himself be dragged down to their level.

Lena could see Theresa's logic but, as Daniel's wife, she also knew how much he loved his brother, and how people's words could wound him. He idolised Peter, and Peter idolised him. True, they were as different as chalk and cheese personality-wise. But together they were a formidable team.

'You feel it too, don't you, Lena? It's like one of those humid and stormy summer days when you could cut the air with a knife. Something's going on with the boys and, as always, we will be the last to know what it is.'

Lena nodded. She wondered sometimes if her mother-in-law was fey; she often knew exactly what you were thinking. Unlike her mother-in-law, though, Lena preferred not to know too much about her husband's business dealings – as far as she was concerned, ignorance was bliss.

Chapter Three

Jed Lanson looked at his nephew, a boy he had never really found it in his heart to like. He was too much like his mother. Jed's sister Adelaide was a miserable fucking bitch and, like her son, she took the piss at every opportunity. All animosity aside, though, *this* was a fucking liberty, and it was something not to be taken lightly. Jed was an acknowledged Face; this was clearly the work of someone who wanted to challenge him. And he had a good idea who that might be.

The fucking Baileys. The trouble was, deep down, he liked them, respected them inasmuch as they were decent men. Peter, certainly, was a man of his word, and he was also a good earner. Daniel, on the other hand, was a hothead; it was Daniel who would have done this, he was the drama merchant. Jed had used that very quality many times himself, and paid Daniel Bailey handsomely because of it. He was like the BBC. All drama, but no real substance. But he knew that Daniel and Peter wanted a bit more, and why wouldn't they?

If his idiot of a nephew had not felt the urge to berate them, humiliate them and, in short, fucking aggravate them, Jed would have offered them an in sooner rather than later. Now it would have to be a fucking lesson – he would have to make sure that everyone knew he would not countenance any kind of insubordination. He would have to go after two of his best earners over this useless boy, who couldn't find a golden fiver without a detailed map and a candle shoved up his arse! It was so unfair. But Micky was family, and if Jed swallowed this he would lose all face.

'Sling him in a motor and get him to hospital. He's had a battering, but he'll get over it. If the Baileys wanted him dead, I think we can safely assume that would be the case.'

He had said it now, said the name Bailey out loud. Everyone had guessed who the perpetrators were anyway, so it was pointless trying to pretend otherwise.

Jed Lanson looked around him, saw the faces of his workforce – good men, loyal to him – but they were getting on, were paunchy having lived the good life for far too long. Always a mistake, getting too complacent; after all, this was how he had got to where he was now. Taking out the old guard. He should have retired ten years before, quit while he was ahead. But it was hard, so hard to admit you were past it. That it was time to step back and enjoy the fruits of your labour. But, then again, unlike the Baileys, he had three daughters, no sons to bring up in the Life; that's why his sister's son had thought he was the dog's knob. For all the good it had done him – done any of them come to that.

He looked around him once more, at the men he

had grown up with, worked with all these years, and he smiled wryly to himself. He had a feeling that they didn't stand a fucking chance. The Baileys would have thought this out down to the last second. This was going to be a well-planned and well-executed coup.

He sighed heavily. Twenty years ago they were the cream of the crop. Now they were more like *Dad's Army*, and he, it seemed, was Captain fucking Mainwaring. He knew instinctively that this night was not going to end well for any of them. And all over that useless ponce Micky. He would lose everything he had worked for, over a man he had never really liked, or indeed never even respected. It was life taking the piss all right.

Two hours later the last thing he ever saw was Daniel Bailey's face as he shot him through his right eye.

Chapter Four

'Where have you been, Dan? I've been worried out of my mind.'

Daniel Bailey grinned that roguish smile that had attracted Lena so many years ago. It was strange really, even after all this time and giving him four strapping sons, she still felt the same pull that she had felt the first time she saw him. He had looked like an even more handsome Rhett Butler to her – taller than most men, with thick dark hair, and deep blue eyes. She had been bowled over by him then, and she still was.

He slipped into the bed beside her and, pulling her into his arms, he said quietly, 'I was working. You know me, Lena, there'll never be no one else for me.'

She did know that. If he had strayed she would have heard a whisper, their world was like that. Anyway, her husband was a stickler for fidelity. He saw it as his yardstick for decency and morality.

'I know that! But I do worry about you sometimes, Dan. If anything happened to you . . .' she trailed off.

Daniel Bailey smiled in the darkness; he had chosen well with his Lena. She was a good woman, and still gorgeous too, with her rich chestnut hair and soft green eyes. She never asked for too much information about his lifestyle and his decisions either. He respected her enough to say in honesty, 'I swear, Lena, on my mother's life, you have *nothing* to worry about, darling. Everything is fine. In fact, it's hunky fucking dory.'

He felt her relax in his arms, knew he had allayed her fears, and he hugged her to him tightly. As she drifted back to sleep he sighed in contentment. Jed Lanson had died well, he had accepted the inevitable, realising that he should have given the Bailey boys their due before they took it.

He lay in the darkness, listening to the church clock as it chimed the hours away, planning the next few weeks. It was the aftermath of their coup that would be the hardest, and both he and his brother knew that. Taking out the Lansons was the easy bit; it was waiting to see who would crawl out of the woodwork for revenge that was going to cause them headaches. And Lanson had a boss. *He* was a shrewd man, who had let Lanson take the accolades and earn the poke. This would be the hardest part of their coup, and they would have to plan their next move carefully.

Chapter Five

Peter Bailey knocked on the door of Kevin O'Neill's house at four thirty in the morning. As he waited for the man to answer, he looked around him with genuine respect. O'Neill had left the East End, bought a large farm in Essex and had reinvented himself as a gentleman farmer.

Jed Lanson had just been a mouthpiece – O'Neill's. And now that Lanson was well out of the way, Peter Bailey was determined to make sure that Kevin O'Neill knew where *he* stood in the grand scheme of things. He felt in his pocket for the Stanley knife he had brought with him. He had come here without telling Daniel because he wanted this over as quickly as possible, and because he had a personal grudge against O'Neill.

Kevin opened the door with a genuine smile, and a cavalier attitude. O'Neill was a man who knew the importance of change and, as far as he was concerned, he didn't give a fuck who worked the Smoke for him, as long as he got his poke. He was glad it was Peter Bailey who had come to give him the hard word. At least Peter had a reputation for doing things quietly, unlike his brother Daniel. *He* was a drama queen of Olympian standards, which was why Kevin had more often used Daniel for jobs rather than this one. He began to realise now he'd overlooked the more dangerous Bailey brother.

'Well, I was expecting you at some point. Come on in.'

Peter went into the house, impressed despite himself at the sheer size and opulence around him. This was the good life all right and he wanted a bit of it for himself. In what was obviously an office, he waited for O'Neill to pour them both a drink before he said quietly, 'We've taken them all out, Kevin, but you already know that, I'm sure.'

Kevin O'Neill looked at the huge black man before him. He had to admit he was a formidable opponent – both he and his brother were hard fuckers, the hardest he had ever come up against if he was honest about it.

'I heard.'

Peter smiled. 'I don't think you really get this, do you?'

Kevin O'Neill laughed, half impressed with the man's front, but aware that he also needed to be taken down a peg, sooner rather than later. 'What's to get, Peter? I couldn't give a fuck who works *my* pavements, whether it's *you*, fucking Jed Lanson or King Street fucking Charlie. As long as my name is kept out of it, I couldn't give a toss. You had a swerve tonight because Lanson was getting too old. I've been wanting a younger, keener, hungrier crew, and if you and that moron of a brother had waited a few weeks I would have offered it to you on a plate.'

Peter raised an eyebrow sceptically. 'I have never heard anything remotely like that and, believe me, I hear fucking everything.' He downed his brandy and placed the glass carefully on the mantelpiece, watching O'Neill intently. He had admired him once, many moons ago, when they were much younger, but now he saw him for what he had become. 'Do you know what you are, Kevin? You're a fucking leech. You have lived off everyone around you since day one – you live off a rep that you got in the fucking Dark Ages. It's the seventies, mate, people don't doff their fucking caps no more because you shot someone once. All that's long gone. You're a mug, no more and no less. It's a new order now. You could have had another five years if you had used your fucking loaf. But you have no real intelligence. You're a fucking fool.'

Kevin O'Neill looked at the man who had the audacity to walk into his home and insult him and, shaking his head in disbelief, he said quietly, his anger now bubbling to the surface, 'You stupid black cunt. I was willing to swallow your outrageous fucking behaviour, because I believed you and your brother were worth me taking an interest. But you walk in here like you are fucking important, and have the nerve to talk to me like *I'm* a cunt, and you think I'm going to swallow my knob like that fucker Lanson? Well, I fucking well won't.'

Peter said seriously, 'I should hope not.'

Then, taking out the Stanley knife, he sliced O'Neill across the face, opening the man's mouth from ear to ear. He disabled him in the worst way possible, making it impossible for him to say a word. It was an insult worse than anything he could have experienced and they both knew it.

'No one's coming to *your* aid, mate – we've already nobbled your little boys, I'm afraid. They deserted this sinking ship hours ago. And one last thing before I slice you up good and proper. Don't you *ever* call my brother a fucking moron. He's worth a hundred of you.'

Peter Bailey took his time, and he made sure Kevin O'Neill was still alive when he finally left him. He wanted him to die slowly, knowing exactly who had killed him, and why. He looked around the room, noting everything. He would call his men to clean up later.

As he drove home he looked at the sun rising and smiled to himself. Today was the dawn of a new age and the Bailey boys were exactly where they deserved to be.

Chapter Six

'All right, Mum?'

Theresa nodded, smiling at Peter. Her eldest son was so like his father. In fact, she marvelled at how both her sons had so little of her in them. 'I'm fine, son. I hear you two have been busy?'

'Oh, leave it out, Mum, you know our Peter is a man of few words!' Daniel followed his brother into their mother's kitchen.

He was still stunned at how Peter had gone after O'Neill alone. He admired him for it but, if he was brutally honest, it still rankled. He hated that he hadn't been there for the moment of triumph. He feared that Peter would always have the edge over him because he was known to even his scores on the QT. It might be good for them as a crew, but Daniel resented that it gave his brother a better rep than him, an advantage, if you like. They were brothers and they were *partners*.

Pushing Peter outside into the back garden of their mother's ground-floor flat, Daniel was determined to say his piece but Peter held up his hand.

'I had to iron him out, Dan, it was a personal score that needed settling.'

Daniel looked into his brother's deep brown eyes and said honestly, 'But we were going to do it together, Pete, and, in future, that's how I expect it to be.'

Peter nodded, contrite. 'I know, bruv, but there were many times when he overlooked me for you. We both know that, and we both know why. Well, I ain't putting up with it anymore. I ain't playing second fiddle to fucking *anyone*.'

Daniel nodded, understanding his brother as he always had. 'Fair enough but, in future, we either do it together, or give the other a heads up before we make a move. We have fought long and hard for this, and the only way we can keep on top is by working together.'

'I know that, mate, and I apologise. I know *you* don't see my skin, but they all do.'

Daniel sighed heavily. 'Who cares what they see or think? It's us against them. As it has always been, bruv.'

Peter nodded.

'I hate that you went there alone, Pete, that you didn't bring a crew. Kevin O'Neill was a slippery bastard. Anything might have happened. We're a team, always were, since we were kids.'

Peter had tears in his eyes as he looked at his brother, his blood. 'We're there now, we're where we wanted to be. It's all ours, Dan. We can take whatever we want.'

Everyone who had ever worked for Kevin had already pledged allegiance to the Baileys and were glad to do so. Who needed the aggravation? And, more to the point, all the old Faces were long gone, either banged up or living in Spain. It wasn't a difficult decision; the Baileys were formidable and no one was willing to iron them out. Why would they? They weren't people you made an enemy of.

The Bailey brothers hugged and, as their mother watched them through the French doors, she smiled to herself. She had always told them that the only thing that mattered was each other; she had brought them up to be closer than most brothers could ever hope to be, and she was glad to see that, all these years on, they were as close now as they had been as children. She was proud of her sons, and she knew they would look out for each other. She also knew they were dangerous fuckers, and that was all right too as far as she was concerned. She was well aware that these two sons of hers were never going to be nine-to-fivers.

Chapter Seven

'You're really pregnant?' Ria Bailey was thrilled for her friend and sister-in-law. 'That's wonderful news, Lena. I hope it's a girl!'

Lena was grinning from ear to ear. She was shocked at the news of her pregnancy, but now that it was confirmed she hoped against hope that it would be a girl. She already had four sons – Danny, the eldest, was sixteen, and his brother Davey, at fifteen, was like his elder brother's shadow – the two were always together. Noel and Jamsie, at twelve and eleven, had been her babies until now. 'So do I, it would be nice to have another female in the house. Well, you'd know that better than me, you've got a daughter.'

Ria laughed delightedly. 'Too fucking true, but I warn you now, Lena, girls are lovely as little kids, but once they hit their teens, you could lay them out on a daily basis, believe me. But, all that aside, they're still worth every hormonal fucking minute!'

'Oh, knowing my luck it will be another boy. I'll believe it when I see it.'

Ria poured the tea into two expensive china cups. Ria liked beautiful things and she surrounded herself with the best that money could buy her. Lena liked nice things but, unlike Ria, she always felt the need to save. Lena had too recent a memory of poverty, and she was terrified of ever going back there again. Sometimes she hated herself for it; at other times she congratulated herself on her thriftiness. The downside of the Life was you could have seven lean years or seven fat years. She would never say it out loud but her fear was always the lean years. She had known what it was to be truly poor, and she never wanted that for her own kids. Ria, on the other hand, lived for the moment, and Lena envied her that.

They both had lovely homes, but Lena knew that Ria bought real quality, stuff that would always make its money back – antique chairs that looked like jumble sale items, which Ria would have re-covered, often costing more than Lena would pay for a new three-piece suite, and they would look fantastic. Ria had what her mother-in-law called a 'good eye', and although Lena balked at how much Ria would spend on a single item, she had picked up quite a bit of knowledge about antiques along the way. Ria was like that, she drew you into her world, and you were grateful to her for making you a part of it. With her shiny blond hair and lively blue eyes, Ria was a real live wire, and she had a knack of making you believe, for a few hours anyway, that you were a live wire too.

Lena had grown up in a council flat in Hackney. Her mum and dad had been nice people, but they had never had any ambition, not for themselves or for their only child, and Lena had resented them for that. All around her had been large families squeezed into a few rooms, and she had seen those people scrimp and save to see their children better themselves. But not her mum and dad, they had never once asked her what she wanted to do with her life, what dreams she might have had. They had fed her and clothed her, but never once really talked to her.

What she had really craved was security, to be taken care of, and to be part of a real family – one which looked out for its own and where you were always surrounded by people. When she had met Daniel Bailey it was as if Christ Himself had climbed down off the cross and answered her prayers. Daniel had swept her off her feet at fifteen years old, and she had loved him since that day, loved him with a passion that no one would ever have believed her capable of. Daniel adored her just as much and, when their kids came along, Lena felt that all her dreams had come true – she had the family life she had always craved. The only dark spot for Lena, if she was truly honest with herself, was the lack of stability. She never asked too many questions about her husband's lifestyle and where the money came from. She wasn't naïve enough to think it was all legit but she adhered to the principle of what you don't know can't hurt you. That didn't mean she wasn't afraid it would disappear one day. She was determined, therefore, that if it fell out of bed, she would have enough put by to weather any storm. Ria never thought their lifestyles would end, but Lena was terrified in case that did happen one day. She hated seeming as though she didn't trust her husband, but she never voiced her fears – she just squirrelled away, and prayed for the best.

Chapter Eight

Imelda Bailey looked at her reflection in the mirror and was pleased with what she saw. At eighteen, she was tall, willowy and high breasted, and she knew she looked good. She also knew that her father was not too thrilled about her recent marriage to Delroy Parkes. Delroy had been her boyfriend on and off for four years – even *she* admitted it was more off than on. But, for all that, she loved him, and she believed that he loved her. She was young, but she knew that Delroy was the love of her life. Sadly she realised that Delroy would always be a man who needed more than one woman – that had, after all, been the cause of so many of their bust-ups. But she had decided that if she would be his 'number one girl', as he referred to her, then she could live with it, and the fact that he had married her proved *something*. She knew it was impossible for her to live without him anyway. She also knew that he was scared shitless of her father and his brother, so if push ever came to shove she could strong-arm him if needs be. Whatever her family had said, she had not been able to help how she felt about him. He was a very dark-skinned Jamaican and he talked with the Jamaican lilt. He was everything she wanted in a man and the sex was incredible – not that she would ever tell anyone *that*, of course. Her father would see Delroy in the ground if he thought he had taken any kind of liberties with her before he put a ring on her finger!

Now they were finally married and Delroy had got a job on the doors of one of the Brixton clubs. She knew her father would not be that impressed, but she also knew that, now he was part of the family, he would see Delroy's potential as a rent collector or similar. Delroy was a big lad – a very big lad in more ways than one. Once he was working for the family, she would be able to monitor him much better; after all, he would be part of the crew, wouldn't he?

She sighed with happiness and, as she went to meet Delroy, she prayed to God that He would grant them both a good life. Grant them happiness, and give them both the opportunity to make something of themselves, make a life that was worth living. Tonight they were getting together with the family at their pub to celebrate her Auntie Lena's big news. And she hoped with all her heart that Delroy Parkes, the love of her life, didn't get stoned or drunk, and did not fuck up in any other way.

She was still praying as the taxi drove them towards the pub two hours later.

Chapter Nine

'Oh, Lena, what great news, I hope it's a girl this time!' Peter kissed his sister-in-law on both cheeks, and hugged her to him. He genuinely cared for her, and he knew that both Daniel and Lena were thrilled at the prospect of another child. Personally, he wouldn't want all that again, and neither would his Ria. They'd had three boys after Imelda – Peter Junior, or Petey as they called him, Liam, and Jack. Jack was already thirteen so the days of taking care of a baby were long behind them. But this wasn't about them, and he was happy for his brother and his wife.

'How lucky are you two, eh, at this stage? I'm almost jealous!'

'You liar! You and Ria would rather shit a rugby ball than go through another pregnancy! But me and Daniel are thrilled.' Lena was glowing.

Peter laughed. 'I got to admit, at this point, I wouldn't fancy it. But I know you, and this is exactly what you need.'

Lena sighed. 'I am pleased, Pete. I was a bit surprised, but you know me, God is good.'

'Well, we'll see how good God is. Imelda's bringing her new husband tonight. I've got to be honest, I still think he's a fucking waster of the first order but, as Ria keeps pointing out, it's not about what we think or want for her, it's about what she wants. I want my little girl to be happy, but I don't think she will be with this muppet.'

Lena grinned. 'I bet Ria's father said that about you!'

Peter Bailey laughed then, a deep belly laugh that caused everyone in the pub to look his way. 'I think all Ria's father saw was my colour. I'm dark, even for a half-caste, but her mum and dad just wanted shot of her, I think, when they realised there was no changing her mind. And lucky me, because I got her.'

'True, but lucky all of us, eh? We've come a long way, and we've raised our families together. We are very fortunate. Hold up, here comes your mother, looking like the poor man's Diana Dors. You got to give it to her, she scrubs up fucking well. I'm going to go say hello.'

Peter smiled in agreement as Lena walked away. Theresa had always looked after herself. It was a shame really, because if he had been white she would probably have been married by now. Men overlooked a lot for a beautiful woman and, in all fairness, she had been a beauty in her day, but no one had overlooked *that*.

His thoughts were interrupted by Imelda's entrance; she looked gorgeous, bless her, and far too good, in Peter's opinion, for the Rasta on her arm. Delroy had a lot to prove to win Peter's trust and tonight they would find out if he was worthy of it.

'So what do you think, Pete?' Daniel joined his brother and passed Peter a full glass, easily reading his brother's thoughts.

Peter shrugged. 'Let's see if he's come through for us, shall we? See if we can trust him.' Catching Delroy's attention, he raised an eyebrow speculatively.

And Delroy, knowing exactly what was being asked of him, nodded back.

'Well, well, it appears, bruv, that our little problem with Jonny Bryant has been well and truly taken care of.' Daniel was clearly impressed. 'Now are you going to give him a break?'

'I still don't trust him, Dan. He's a fucking waster, a Jamaican jumper, all smiles and no bite.'

Daniel Bailey shook his head ruefully. This side of his brother bothered him. Daniel saw Delroy as a potential asset to the family, but Peter had taken umbrage and it annoyed him.

'He's all right, for fuck's sake, he's taken out fucking Bryant and, be fair, asking him to do that was an insult. But he's done it. He knows you were testing him, and he's come up fucking trumps. Your trouble is you don't like your daughter with a man, any man. Well it was going to happen sometime, especially with a girl as good-looking as her. For fuck's sake, Peter, she is a grown woman. Get over it. Delroy is her choice, and I like him. He is well liked by his peers, he's a grafter.

And we need another good man on-side until our boys are old enough to do the business. Anyway, love him or loathe him, he is now your flesh and blood. Imelda will breed with him, and his kids will be your grandchildren.' Daniel laughed out loud then. 'It's the cycle of life, Peter. Give him a chance, for fuck's sake. He put a ring on her finger. We were all there, remember? He even swallowed the Catholic service. Now I don't know about you, but that screams dedication to me. If you're not careful you will push him away, and that will mean she will go with him. She's mad about him and, from what I can see, he is mad about her. Give him the benefit of the doubt, eh?'

'I know you're right, but a daughter is different to a son, Dan. If this baby is a girl you will understand where I am coming from. Believe me, a daughter makes you see men for what we really are, see the womaniser we once laughed at as an enemy, the friend who had a mistress or a one-night stand as a disloyal bastard. Daughters make you look inside yourself and you will not like what you see. It's totally different to having a son. When daughters are put into your arms you feel a protectiveness that borders on paranoia.'

Daniel nodded his understanding. 'I can imagine, I feel like that about Imelda too. In me own way, of course. But you are going to lose her if you don't accept Delroy.'

Peter knew his brother was making sense. Delroy was making a name for himself, a good name, and he could be useful to them all – certainly until Petey Junior, his eldest, and Danny were old enough to join the family firm.

But no matter the logic, Delroy irritated him; he knew a fucking useless ponce when he saw one. He might have been loyal to Imelda until now, but Peter felt it was all an act. Delroy had more sides than a fucking tetrahedron; he hated himself for thinking as he did but he couldn't help it. His baby, his daughter, was worth more than Delroy Parkes, and if she didn't know that, then it was a good fucking job that her old man did.

Chapter Ten

Delroy Parkes was on his best behaviour. He knew he was on probation, as it were, with his father-in-law. He knew he had been used, but he wasn't too bothered about it – he had wanted to prove himself, and he had done it. He had seen the sceptical look on Peter Bailey's face when he had casually requested that his son-in-law should take out Jonny Bryant. Well, he had done it and proved he had his own creds.

Delroy had been offended at his reception into the Bailey family; after all, his own father-in-law was also black; he could have understood the animosity if the man had been white with a white daughter.

Delroy was determined to make a life for himself and Imelda and their children; a good life, that was worthy of them. He had been willing to take out Bryant if it would help his relations with his father-in-law, but he hated that he had been used, and that Peter Bailey thought so little of him. He was determined to show that fucker that he was a man in his own right. He had a plan and he hoped that his wife's father would see the logic in it, and that it made good business sense. If he didn't then it would be time for Delroy to do his own thing.

Chapter Eleven

Daniel Bailey was a happy man. He knew that he was a winner; he had what he wanted in more ways than one.

He sensed, though, that his Lena was less than happy these days. Maybe it was the pregnancy hormones making her jumpier than normal. He knew about her hoarding money; she always had, and he allowed for that, realised that it made her feel secure. He also knew where the money was which, as far as he was concerned, was all that mattered. He was impressed actually at how much she had salted away, and he understood how important it was for her to think that she was in control of that part of her life. The money came out of her so-called 'housekeeping' and, though they still lived it large, he knew they could live much larger than they currently did.

He allowed her the leeway he did because he wasn't always as honest with her as he should be. But he was also well aware that she was not a woman who could cope with the reality of their situation in life. And now that the boys were growing up, she could see, he knew, that they were never going to be accountants or fucking suits. They were never going to be anything other than what they were: Baileys. And, as such, they were always going to be part of the firm.

He understood her fears. If he was to get a capture by the Old Bill, she would feel much better if she didn't have to rely on other people to see her all right. She had money everywhere, and he loved that she was determined to look after not only herself but the kids as well. He didn't take her hoarding as an insult, as if she didn't trust him, because he knew that she did trust him – with her life. But she was from a background of people who didn't make allowances for a rainy day. He remembered her mum and dad and how, after the first meeting, he had thanked God that his mother had been the woman she had. Reviled for her lifestyle and her two illegitimate children, his mother had, nevertheless, worked her fingers to the bone. It was strange really that her sons had both chosen the criminal lifestyle, because throughout their lives they had witnessed their mother working in real jobs, paying her taxes, and never claiming a penny from the state.

Theresa had always drummed it into her sons that other people working to keep you or yours was wrong – that was for the ponces of the world. The dole was there to see you over a bad patch, until you could find another job – it was never meant to be a way of life. Theresa had been known to have three or four jobs at a time to make ends meet.

Peter and Daniel had been good boys, they had never brought the police to her door, or been involved in anything that might cause her trouble. They had been too shrewd to get involved in the futile petty crime that abounded on the estate where they lived. Instead, they had observed, studied and made sure they never went into anything before they had sussed it out. They would no more shame her than they would shame themselves. Although both of them had ducked and dived to put money on the table, neither of them had ever been caught.

But he guessed, rightly, that their mother knew far more than she let on about her boys and their lifestyles. She had always said, if you are going to nick, nick big time, and never nick off your own. She accepted what they did, as she had always accepted them.

Chapter Twelve

'You all right, Mum?' Davey Bailey was worried and it showed. His mother looked awful, she was white-faced and without her usual energy.

'I'm pregnant, son, it does tend to take it out of you!'

She was smiling at him, but he wasn't convinced. 'Is Dad back yet?'

She shook her head. 'No, he'll be back later today, and don't you tell him that I'm feeling rough. He's got a lot on his mind.'

Davey nodded, but he was angry at his dad. He should be here, but he was always out 'on a job' these days. He took a deep breath. 'Come on, Mum, sit down. I'll make you a cup of tea. I wish I had known how you were feeling.'

Lena sat back down and smiled quietly to herself. Not one of her sons had given her condition a second's thought, and why would they? They were only boys themselves – none of them understood pregnancy and what it entailed. She had not wanted to burden them with it, but if she was honest she didn't feel good. It was all the worry. She knew her husband was doing some important business with his brother and that always made her nervous.

As he placed a cup of tea before her, Davey berated his dad silently once more. And where was his fucking nana? Normally she was never off the bloody doorstep.

'The baby's kicking, Davey. Feel.' Lena took her son's hand and laid it on her swollen belly. She saw the surprise on his face as he felt the strength of the child within her.

'Must be another boy there, Mum! A footballer, do you reckon?'

She smiled. 'You were the real kicker in the family, Davey. You kept me up night after night.'

Davey looked at his mother, at her heavy belly, at her face so drawn and white. He saw the thinness of her arms, and the swelling around her ankles. He suddenly realised that she had borne all this discomfort for him too, and for each of his brothers. He felt the love she had for them, and he knew, despite his youth, how much they took her for granted. He also saw the enormity of what having a child really entailed. His mother was stoic and uncomplaining, despite having a living, breathing human being inside her. The miracle of childbirth hit him like a freight train.

He laid his hands once more on her belly, and the child kicked again, a strong kick that made his mother wince, but made his heart soften towards the child inside her.

'That's amazing, Mum. That's a real person in there. You're growing a real person!'

Lena smiled happily. 'I've grown four of you already. Honestly, Davey, it's not a chore. I enjoyed every one of my pregnancies. It's just today I'm feeling more tired than usual. I'm not as young as I was!'

Davey grinned. 'I tell you what, Mum, shall we have a night in, just the two of us?'

Lena really laughed then. 'I must look rough, Davey! Honestly, son, I'm fine. You don't need to baby-sit me.'

'That's OK, Mum, I don't mind staying with you.'

Lena smiled. She was under no illusions that her sons wouldn't follow their father to becoming hard men, but for now she decided to make the most of any time she had with them. She wished things could have been different, but her Daniel had carved the path for them all, herself included.

She caressed her belly, and she swore to herself that, girl or boy, this little one would never be a part of the world that her husband inhabited and which her sons would one day join. As much as she loved them, she was determined that this child would not be a part of it. Daniel had brought the boys up to be with him; they would be beside him, follow him, and she had never questioned that before. As they approached manhood, though, the reality was beginning to hit home.

Daniel would introduce the boys to, and expect them to be part of, the Life. They would have no choice. But what would their lives be if they were nicked? The thought of her lovely boys locked away for years on end tortured her. Unlike Ria, who was at peace with the paths chosen for her sons, Lena didn't want it for her boys. She didn't want them to be villains. Deep down, she hated that she had never had any real say in their lives.

She hoped this intense worry was all down to her hormones, because she didn't like feeling like this. She had lived through her married life secretly anxious that her husband might get a tug, but her husband and her boys were two different things. The thought of her sons banged up was anathema to her. A woman she had known for years had just seen her son get what amounted to a life sentence. He was a bank robber, a nice lad, but he had been caught with the guns and the money. He had been served up at the Old Bailey by the Serious Crime Squad, and they had made him look worse than a fucking murderer. They had arranged police outriders to follow his paddy wagon, so he looked far more dangerous than he was. The jury had seen them and before they had heard a word said in the actual courtroom the impression that he was dangerous was cemented. He had been handed down an eighteen stretch – he would not have got that even if he had raped and murdered someone!

But money and property – that was what the courts cared about in this country. If you opened the paper, sex offenders were getting away with all sorts on a daily basis. Young girls were cross-examined in court about their sex lives as if *they* were on trial, not the piece of dirt that raped them. And, even if the man *was* found guilty, he didn't get a real lump – four to seven years for ruining a girl's whole life. But rob a Post Office and you were sent down for the duration. It was a scandal. Eighteen years for a robbery meant at least fourteen years before he was eligible for parole. He would have been better off if he had killed someone – then he would have been out in seven.

The whole thing with her friend had thrown Lena Bailey; no one in her world had ever got a real sentence, a real lump. Fourteen years was a serious amount of time out of a young man's life and it had really hit home that soon that could be one of *her* sons. Suddenly she saw the lives they could be aspiring to in stark contrast with what Daniel wanted for them, and it bothered her.

This child, she would make sure, would know nothing about the Life. *This* child would be brought up outside of it all; she would make sure that one of them at least would have the chance to escape it. She only hoped this was a girl, because she knew that a boy would be too hard to control, would look at his brothers and want what they had.

She sighed. 'Davey, would you do me a favour, son?'

'Course I will, Mum; what do you want?'

'Can you phone your Auntie Ria and your nana? Then can you please track your father down? My waters just broke.'

Davey Bailey went whiter than a sheet. 'Are you sure?' he stuttered.

Lena laughed. 'I'm sure, son.'

Chapter Thirteen

'It's a girl, Pete!' Daniel had just called home to check on Lena and been given the news.

Peter Bailey was genuinely pleased for his brother; he knew that he'd wanted a girl this time, for Lena as much as for himself. Ria had a daughter, and he was glad about that. In their world, sons were their father's ammunition – and they were always on their side. If they were big, handsome lumps all the better. Seven boys between him and Daniel made the Baileys a formidable family. Peter and Daniel were just biding their time until they could bring their sons into the business, introduce them properly to the Life.

Daniel was back in the car now, and they were speeding along the M1 towards London. They had been up to Liverpool, brokering a deal which would cement their standing in London, and make sure that there would be no chance of anyone allying themselves with the North without them knowing about it first. 'Good job I phoned! She was early. Tania, Lena's calling her. And you will never guess what, Pete – Davey was there when she was born! He helped bring her into the world. Fucking rather him than me!'

Peter grinned. 'Poor Davey. Be enough to put him off women for life! Well, let's get back and meet this new daughter of yours.'

Daniel shook his head. 'I want to finish what we started, Pete; let's stick to the original plan. We go and see Alfie Clarke and sort him out once and for all. If he *is* giving our friends in the North grief then we have to show willing, don't we? Otherwise this was a fruitless exercise.'

Peter sighed, but he nodded in agreement. Daniel was hyped up, determined to make his mark, create another legendary bust-up to be talked about in the years to come, and all to placate the Northerners. He understood that on one level, but he wondered how he could put such a minor job before the birth of his only daughter. But since they had taken over, Daniel had really grown into his own reputation. They were like good cop, bad cop now; Peter was the level-headed one, the voice of reason, whereas Daniel was the hothead, the one people were really wary of. It worked for them, just as it always had, but Peter felt that now all eyes were on them Daniel should tone the violence down a notch – at least stop the public displays if nothing else.

A few weeks earlier, Daniel had kneecapped someone who owed a debt. Peter felt it was beneath them to do such a task themselves – they should give those jobs to the men who they employed. As his mother always said, why have a dog and bark yourself?

But Daniel felt it kept them on top, made people

realise that they were still very involved and knew what was going on. He didn't allow for the fact that, if he got his collar felt, he would end up going down for what amounted to no more than what a local thug would be tried for. Plus, it would bring all sorts of Old Bill down on their heads, from the Serious Crime Squad to the Sweeney themselves, as well as other newly formed task forces that, as yet, no one had managed to penetrate.

It was a new world, and they had to work out how to live safely and securely within it. It wasn't the sixties any more, and the police were suddenly acting like they knew what they were doing. The newspapers didn't glamorise the underworld now, Princess Margaret didn't fraternise with them – not in public anyway – and the Krays were a distant memory. The tabloids asked questions these days, wanted to know why certain people were not being nicked. The front pages of the Sunday papers demanded to know why certain people were still walking about even though they were almost certainly living off criminal proceeds – usually immoral earnings. It was an anomaly to him how newspapers that made their poke off sex scandals involving vicars and politicians could have the cheek to talk about living off immoral earnings, but there you go. That was the new world, the new order.

This should be the era of the low profile for men such as themselves, but Daniel couldn't or wouldn't accept that as a fact of life. Since they had become the new Faces, he seemed more determined than ever to be known, to be lauded – to be feared. And Peter felt that was wrong; they should be content simply with everyone in their world knowing their status. Outsiders meant nothing to him personally, and they should mean nothing to Daniel. What the fuck was he trying to prove? If he wasn't careful they would have their collars felt and, like the Krays, they would be over before they were even really getting started. They had worked so hard for this. Peter was not going to sit back and let his brother destroy it all before they had even really begun.

Peter could see how the world was going, he could see that these were dangerous times for people like them. They were sensible in that they had enough legitimate businesses to explain away their lifestyles, but there was no reason to attract too much attention to them as people, as personalities. They had enough creds – they didn't need any more. Plus, if they kept their violence quiet, so only the people who were in their world knew about it, he believed they would get a much better profile anyway. Times were changing, people were much more aware of how they were perceived these days, the Filth had so much more at their disposal, so why play into their hands? Why put yourself in the frame, when you could quietly and calmly take out your enemies with the minimum of fuss and the maximum of terror? If a person just disappeared, never to be heard of again, Peter felt that was a much more sinister ending than a gun shot in a car park, or a battering in a public place. He wanted a low key takeover of the Smoke, not a fucking remake of *High Noon*. He felt instinctively that the lower the profile, the better the earn. The days of bursting into a place waving a sawn-off shotgun, or kneecapping an enemy in full view of a crowded pub, were long gone. He believed, strongly, that this was the era of the quiet disappearance, of the 'Reported Missing'; no one these days drew too much attention to themselves unless they had to. Even then you used someone else to do your dirty work, making sure that when the skulduggery occurred, you were out with at least fifty people who would happily swear on oath that you were in their company should it all turn pear-shaped, and a court hearing ensue.

Daniel needed to get this point through his head and, after they had seen Alfie, Peter was going to make sure that Daniel understood that, if he wasn't careful, his actions would eventually be the cause of their demise. Already his brother was pissing him off, making him nervous, jeopardising everything they had worked towards, but this wasn't anything new; he had always pushed it to the hilt – it was part of his so-called fucking charm. Whereas Peter was the voice of reason, Daniel was the voice of absolute chaos. He relished the drama of the fight, never allowing for the fact that the more people who knew what they were up to the more chance there was of a fucking serious capture.

Even the birth of his only daughter had not scratched the surface of his arrogance; he was still too involved with what he saw as his personal crusade to wipe out the competition. Peter could not help wondering when that would include him and his boys. Daniel was not a man to take kindly to criticism, and Peter was criticising him left, right and centre at the moment.

Daniel continued, 'I want to be there when we tell him the score. I don't think you understand how important it is for us to show a united front, Pete. You seem to think this is cut and dried.'

Peter sighed heavily. 'It *is*, Dan. You have got to lighten up, mate. We have achieved what we set out to achieve – now we can play the good guys. You acting like *A Man Called Horse* ain't going to earn us any creds. Calm down, will you? We don't need the blatant violence any more, Dan. Alfie's a good earner, let's keep him onside.'

Daniel was annoyed at his brother's interference, even though he knew he had a point. 'What are you trying to fucking say, big bruv?'

Peter bit back his anger, and instead said reasonably, 'What I'm trying to say is, Dan, we don't need the bully-boy tactics any more. We have sorted everything out perfectly well so far. We need to establish a new order, a new way of handling things. You have to see that taking everyone out at a second's notice will only cause upset and distrust. We have worked long and hard for this, I'm begging you, don't let's fuck it up by generating bad will. We don't need to prove ourselves any more. We've arrived, mate. Let everyone else take the chances – *we* need to be here to oversee everything. To make sure it goes in our favour.'

Daniel grinned. 'So it's all right for you to do things off your own bat but not me? Is that it?' He was still upset with his brother for taking out Kevin O'Neill behind his back, and Peter knew it.

He smiled, and held his hands up in mock surrender. 'I'll give you that one, Dan. But this isn't about now, this is about the future. We have always been very different in our approaches to our work, and up till now that has been one of our strengths. No one knows how to handle us, not separately and definitely not when we are together. We are like chalk and cheese, but now we have to pull together properly, and we have to keep a low profile.' Peter could see the scepticism on his brother's face and it angered him that Daniel could not see the danger he brought to their daily lives with his violence and his pettiness.

'You think you know everything, Pete, you always have, since we were little kids. And I love that about you, but you can't sit there like the fucking Angel Gabriel spreading your glad tidings at this late stage in the game. We took all this with our front, and only our front will keep us in the running. You need to remember that.'

Peter shook his head then. He had dropped the rest of the crew off at a pub, making sure that there were only the two of them for this conversation. He was aware that Daniel would fight him on this – on every

57

level. Daniel always acted first and thought it all out afterwards. When they were on their way *up* the ladder that had been less of a problem. Now, though, they needed to pull back a little, keep a low profile for a while. In short, they had to wait and see how their new status was received by the general populace.

Daniel seemed to think they faced no opposition. Well, it wasn't the case. They had trodden on more than a few fucking toes and, even though they were convinced they were big enough and tough enough for the job in hand, it would not hurt either of them to wait and see if there were going to be any reprisals.

'We don't know, Dan, what the upshot of this is yet. We have done our best, but we have still fucked a lot of people over. I believe we need to step back and see what the future holds. Alfie is a good earner and, as lairy as he is, he has his creds. All I am saying is, let's see what he has to offer.'

Daniel Bailey looked into his brother's eyes; he was sorry for him in some ways. Peter always believed the best of people if he could – he got that from their mother. He also thought that because he did things on the quiet they didn't count. But they did. Peter was paranoid these days. Since they had made their move Peter seemed convinced they were going to get their collars felt. Daniel wondered at how he was going to convince his brother of his way of thinking. He saw their next moves as pivotal in their conquering of London and the Home Counties. Daniel felt they should be rattling the cages of everyone within their orbit, making them see just how dangerous they were, whereas Peter wanted to tiptoe in, like fucking burglars, creepers – the lowest of the low where they came from.

Daniel thought they should remove all the old guard, and replace them with their own people. He could not see the logic of keeping people employed who had worked closely with the very people they had annihilated and he said as much. 'For fuck's sake, they don't trust us, Pete, they see us as their fucking enemies. They are wondering what we are going to do to them.'

Peter smiled. '*Exactly*. And we can work with them. They'll work with whoever is running the show, Dan. We can use this as our chance to recruit more of the real workers. We already have the bully boys and the fucking romancers. What we should be concentrating on is the real earners. And we should be making sure that they are working for *us*. They don't give a shit who they answer to as long as they still get their money. We were the same, Dan – if you remember, we worked with whoever guaranteed us a wage. Now, I know you have a fucking problem with Alfie, but you have problems with everyone, and I want Alfie on our payroll. He's a shrewd fucker, and he can sniff out a serious earn in his sleep. People like him are few and far between.'

Daniel knew his brother was talking sense. But Alfie had never been a favourite of his. He looked down his nose at everyone around him.

Ultimately, though, Daniel had a different agenda to

Peter. Daniel had always seen their eventual rise to the top as an opportunity to pay back old debts, insults, fucking piss-takes and, more to the point, he had seen himself paying them all back in a public arena, had pictured himself taking out certain men in front of audiences of his choice. He was well aware that his penchant for petty anger and his ability to hold a grudge was not conducive to the world his brother wanted them to inhabit. He should not let things bother him as much as they did, but that was his nature.

Peter, who he loved, was more than capable of overlooking slights about his colour. Peter was, in many respects, the bigger man because of that. Whereas Daniel saw any slights, whether towards him or his brother, as something warranting a personal vendetta. He saw anything – no matter how trivial – as a reason to prove how hard he was and show his personal disgust at the treacherous bastards around him. And he enjoyed it. He *liked* to make people see that he was not a man to be messed with, he *wanted* people to fear him. Still, he saw the sense in his brother's words, knew that Peter was trying to keep them on an even keel until they were properly settled in. He would swallow this time; after all, if Alfie Clarke pushed his luck, then that was his fucking lookout. Daniel would then take him down like a rabid dog.

'OK, Peter, but if he says one fucking detrimental thing to me, or he fucking dares to treat me like a cunt, he's fucking history.'

Peter couldn't argue with that – it was more than he had expected. 'Let's pick the lads up, and go to the meet then.'

'As you wish, bruv. But I'm telling you now, we *need* to establish our-fucking-selves in more ways than one. You and me need to make sure we are seen as capable of *anything*. And, let's face it, we *are*, Pete. Look at some of the fucking stunts we've pulled over the years. But I swear to you now, no one is ever going to disrespect me or mine. I ain't worked my bollocks off to be made a fucking mug of. Not by anyone.'

Peter nodded because he didn't trust himself to speak. They *were* established, if only Daniel could see that. They didn't need to prove anything to anyone. But he kept his own counsel, and hoped against hope that Alfie Clarke had the sense to keep his mouth shut, and his sarcastic comments to himself.

Chapter Fourteen

'She's beautiful, Lena. A real little heartbreaker.' Ria's voice was choked with emotion. 'Seven pounds, and a month early. Sure you never got the dates wrong?'

Lena smiled wearily. 'No, she was early. Just like a woman, afraid she would miss something. Boys are lazy bastards. All mine were late, too settled in the womb, only came out for the football season.'

They laughed together.

'I bet your Davey nearly had a seizure! Is it true he almost delivered her?'

Lena shook her head in abject disbelief at what had happened. 'Bless him; my waters broke, I told him to get you, his nana and locate his father, in that order and, before I knew it, this little one was here. Within fifteen minutes of my waters going, she was out. It was so quick. Poor Davey saw it all, he was in a right two and eight. But he was a trooper, Ria, he looked after me.'

Lena would never forget the shock on his face as his sister slid into the world. It was a mixture of wonderment and disgust. He was only fifteen and the mystery of birth was as alien to him as knitting himself a crash helmet. But, in fairness, he had been good, he had done everything he was asked to do and with the minimum of fuss.

Holding his new little sister in his arms Lena had seen the look of pure love in his eyes, and she had also seen the natural way he had held the child to him. He had grown up in that moment. Her Daniel, after four children, had never once held any of them with such confidence. Davey had looked at her with tears in his eyes and said huskily, 'It's a miracle, Mum.' He seemed utterly overwhelmed.

Lena was glad to know that one of her boys had a heart in there. She worried that her sons might only have inherited their father's worst characteristics: the tendency towards the dramatic, the anger that was never far from the surface, the aggression that emanated from him at times. But she knew now, and she blessed herself unconsciously as she said thanks be to God and His Holy Mother, that Davey, at least, had the same capacity for loving as his father did.

It was a revelation to her, and she felt a calmness come over her because of it. She knew that the boys were Daniel's, were his from the day they could follow him around. She had only had her sons to herself until that point. Oh, they loved her, she knew that, but they all idolised their father. Danny Junior was a good lad but, like his father, capable of great violence, and already strong as an ox to boot. Her Davey had proved today that he was capable of great emotion but she was well aware that that could translate into hatred and anger as well as love. Noel and Jamsie were still only boys, and they would follow where the elder ones led. They already had the makings of hard men – it was in their genes. Oh, yes, all four of her sons would be men of substance – her husband would make sure of that. And there was nothing she could do about it.

But now Lena had a daughter, and she would be all *hers*. She would see to it that she didn't become a part of that world, and Daniel would not have any sway over her little girl's life at all.

Ria watched as her sister-in-law gazed down at her daughter, and she knew exactly what she was thinking, because she had been there herself. True, daughters belonged wholly to their mothers in their world, but she had found out, as the years went on that, unlike the boys, girls grew up fast. They were harder to rein in and, one day, they fell in love and, if this little one was anything like her Imelda, she would want a man who was her father and brothers personified. *That* was when the real worry started. But Ria kept her own counsel; after all, Lena had plenty of time to find that out for herself.

'You thought of a name yet, Lena?'

Lena nodded. 'Tania. I think this little one looks like a Tania.'

Ria grinned. 'With that hair and those Irish eyes, she'll be a beauty, our Tania. She looks like her nana, don't you think?'

They smiled as Theresa Bailey bowled into the room; she was excited and worried all at the same time. 'I can't believe it, Lena! I was in the pub when they came and got me. Let me have a look at her then.'

Lena passed the child to her mother-in-law, and watched happily as the woman expertly snuggled the little child into the crook of her arm.

Theresa stared down at the child for long moments then, nodding as if answering a question, she said softly, 'She's a Bailey all right, from the eyes to the hands. She has my mother's hands – long fingers. She'll play the piano, and she'll know love.'

Lena and Ria didn't say a word. Theresa, they knew, missed her mother and her sister so badly it was a constant pain inside of her. But they had turned their backs on not only her, but on her two children, and that, she could not – *would* not – ever forgive.

'She'll be a comfort to you in your old age! That's what the old shawlies used to say in Ireland about a late child, especially a daughter. Oh, God love her, she's gorgeous.'

Lena sank back into her pillows, and sighed happily. She would be just that, a comfort to her in the years ahead. She was thirty-three years old, and she finally had the daughter she had always wanted. She wondered when Daniel would arrive to greet his only daughter, but she knew he would come as soon as he could. Until then, she would do what she had always done and wait patiently for him to come to her.

But, as time wore on, Lena began to feel uneasy. Where was her husband? He knew she had given birth, knew he had a daughter, he should have been here by now, should have been beside her. He should have come straightaway, and she knew that Ria and her mother-in-law both thought the same, even though neither of them had said it – not in front of her anyway.

She looked at her daughter's tiny hands, curled up into little fists, at her heart-shaped face, and she saw the long eyelashes that would one day attract a man, and she felt the panic rising inside her.

She breathed as deeply as she could, knowing that she had to stop this feeling before it got out of control. She had to swallow it down, as she had swallowed it down in the past. She had to be strong, had to put her brave face on for the world. She had to gather her strength, because this little child would need her to be strong. But, as she fought against the terror rising in her breast, she felt the first stirrings of discontent inside her. Daniel had let her down, and badly. As ever, he had more important things on his mind. There was always something more important than his wife or his family. And until now, until this second, she had never before admitted that to herself.

She hugged her daughter to her so tightly she made the child cry, and as she soothed her daughter she wondered at how she was ever going to make peace with herself again.

Chapter Fifteen

Alfie Clarke was an ugly man, but he had a funny personality; he could, as his own mother said, make a cat laugh. This was his secret with not only the ladies – who he was sensible enough to spend money on as well as giving them his undivided attention – but also with the men around him. He was always smiling, always in a good mood.

And he was in an especially fantastic mood since the birth of his only child eighteen months previously – a son, Alfie Junior. He loved that boy with a vengeance. No one would ever have believed he could feel as he did about his son, least of all Alfie. The boy's mother, Annette, was a young girl he had picked up with two years ago – pretty, with a killer body and the personality of a lettuce. Just his type – no real conversation. But she had been a virgin, a fact that had shocked and thrilled him all at the same time. He liked her well enough; she was like a pet – he rang and she came round. He had never heard of her being with anyone else, and she didn't frequent the clubs. He had met her on one of her first jaunts out on the town for a mate's birthday, otherwise he would never have laid eyes on her, or she him. He had liked that she was greener than the proverbial grass, and he had quite liked that she was not a chatterbox. Annette expected *him* to do the talking and, after years of Essex girls and East-End birds who could talk the hind leg off a fucking camel, that was quite a novelty. So he had seen her again and again.

When she had told him she was up the duff he had been sceptical to say the least. But he had asked around and, in fairness, no one could say a word against her. So he had seen her all right, looked after her and, when the child was born, he had been amazed at the feelings that seeing the boy had awakened in him. He was his double, in every way. If you put his baby photos beside his boy's, there was no difference. It was uncanny. He was an ugly baby, as he himself had been, but Alfie didn't care.

For the first time in his life he understood what family meant. What blood meant. He had looked into that boy's eyes and he had seen the future, his future, seen his name being carried on by another generation, and he had been compelled to give him his name. And give the boy's mother a house. He had found that inside him somewhere was a nice bloke.

Alfie was aware that the boy made him vulnerable; he now had someone in his life who he cared for more than he did himself. He also found that he cared for Annette – something he had not expected. She was nineteen years old and a born mother, a great little mum, in fact. She was only interested in his boy and him. Thick as shit she might be, but she knew where her priorities lay. He respected that, and there was no way his boy would ever be outside of his orbit. Annette was *his* now, and she would never be able to walk away from him. He would see her dead first.

He was a good businessman; he could turn a profit easily, and with the minimum of fuss. If he had been born into a different class he would have been a well-heeled legitimate businessman instead of a rich criminal one. He dreamed of the day he could school his son in the intricacies of ducking and diving. People came to him when they wanted to invest money and make a profit; Alfie knew every scam that was going at any given time. He also collected money for the people who had a good scam and needed investors. It was a win-win situation for all involved. But he had a bad habit of keeping a higher percentage for himself than originally negotiated. Especially when it concerned the Northerners. He hated them – it was a gut reaction. He had a cockney disregard for anyone north of the Watford Gap and he had made his feelings plain. Those choice remarks and his jokes at their expense were coming home to roost. He had seen them as cash cows; they got a good deal, but he squeezed them, and they knew it and, because he had the edge where investments were concerned, he let them know he was squeezing them. He was a broker and, like all good brokers, he knew his own worth.

He had a new deal coming up and he was going to give it to the Baileys, just them, and he knew they would fall on it like a junkie on a needle. It was easy money, with little or no risk; all they had to do was put up the finance. It was so sweet he knew it was a winner. Consequently, Alfie was feeling very confident as he waited for them to arrive.

He was in his pub, surrounded by his cronies, and telling jokes at a shotgun pace. He had good reason to be pleased with himself. He knew he held all the cards, and because of that he could do what he liked. The Baileys might be the new kings of East London, but kings needed princes, and they needed him far fucking more than he needed them. Villainy was like a river or a sea – it moved constantly, changed with the tides, and it eventually had the power to destroy everyone who sailed on its waters. He had seen so many Faces come and go, it was like a fucking merry-go-round; one day they were the dog's gonads, the next they were banged up for the duration. That is what taking control did to people. In his opinion, you were far better off as a well-respected soldier. Who needed the aggro of being in charge of the kind of people he dealt with on a daily basis? They were scum, thieves, liars. But such good money spinners. No, he was happy as he was, in the upper echelons, but never the top dog. It was too much like hard work, watching your back twenty-four seven, wondering who you could trust – dealing with people like himself! People out for their own ends, not yours – never yours.

Now he was expected to arse-lick the Baileys, and so he would. Let them take the flak – he couldn't give a flying fuck. Peter was a sensible head, Daniel was a loose cannon. He gave them six months – a year at the outside – before they imploded. Then he would work with whoever came out on top. Alfie Clarke held enough cards to hold his own in any game the Baileys might decide to play.

He slipped into the back room of his pub and looked at his son sleeping in his mother's arms.

'You need anything, Annette?'

She smiled happily and shook her head. 'I'm fine, Alfie, thanks.'

'He's a good boy, ain't he?'

'Course he is, he's a happy little soul.'

Alfie caressed his son's head with a tenderness which would have shocked his enemies, looking forward to the day when it would be him and his boy taking care of business, together.

He made his way back into the main room, and caught sight of Delroy Parkes, Peter Bailey's son-in-law. He had a decent rep, and now, thanks to his marriage, a very good pedigree. He wondered what he was doing here.

Delroy nodded amiably, and Alfie sent him over a drink. He was feeling magnanimous today, and why wouldn't he? He had the scam of scams.

When the Bailey brothers finally arrived he was full of good-humoured bonhomie, and Courvoisier brandy.

Chapter Sixteen

'Promise me, Dan, you won't do anything until we have heard him out.'

Daniel sighed in annoyance. Why was his brother so worried about a fucking nonsense like Alfie Clarke? 'Let it go, Pete, OK? We've been through this; get a grip.'

Peter saw Delroy as soon as they entered the pub. He was alone, and clearly well out of his comfort zone. Despite himself he felt a twinge of respect for his son-in-law. He guessed rightly that Delroy had heard whispers that there could be aggravation at this meet and he had come to watch their backs. Peter walked over to him as if he was a long-lost child. Taking Delroy in his arms he hugged him, making a big production of it. Everyone was watching expectantly. Word on the street was that these two were not the best of friends, but they seemed to be happy enough in each other's company now.

Daniel looked around the pub. He guessed there were twenty or so people in there, just the usual hangers-on, nobody to worry about. He allowed himself to relax. The fact that Alfie did not have anyone there who might be a handful went in his favour.

He joined Peter in greeting Delroy, understanding that the man must have heard something on the grapevine or he would not have been there. He appreciated the man's loyalty, and he knew his brother did too.

The atmosphere was genial enough, and he smiled his best smile as he said loudly, 'A large Scotch! My old woman gave me a daughter today. I'm celebrating.'

Alfie Clarke smiled. 'A child, eh? Until my boy was born, Dan, I never understood the importance of family. He is the light of my life, bless him.'

Daniel grinned. 'Well, wait until you get three or four of them! They grow up and go to school, and they are always in trouble, always costing you money. And, to top it all, they end up twice your fucking size!'

Alfie laughed at the thought; he couldn't wait. He was picturing a life with a son by his side, imagining comforting his boy, making him into a good man, teaching him all the scams, every con available. He was eager to start the child's education. For the first time in his life he was part of a unit, a family unit, and he was loving every second.

Peter watched as Daniel acted like the man's new best friend; it was what he was good at. He could lie to a person's face, and they would never suspect anything was amiss. Daniel was volatile, and he was at his most dangerous when he was like this, playing the fool, acting the goat. He could laugh and joke, and ten minutes later cut your throat.

'So, Alfie.' Daniel's eyes glittered dangerously.

'What's this my brother and I hear about you upsetting our Northern friends?'

The time for pleasantries was clearly over.

Chapter Seventeen

Daniel looked down at his new daughter and felt a fierce protectiveness wash over him. As drunk as he was, he knew that this feeling was real. She was perfect, this new baby, so small, so delicate. Not like the lads; they had been huge lumps and noisy babies from the off – masculine from the day they were born. None of them had ever been this frail, this tiny. They had each been born with the Bailey scowl; by six months they were already their own men, and they had been a handful from the day they could walk.

He knew his mother was watching him, knew she was not impressed with him at this moment in time. She was clearly disappointed with him for not coming home sooner. Well, fuck her. Tonight, he'd had serious work to see to and the sooner she understood that the better. They were real Faces now, finally top of the fucking heap. He smiled at her anyway – she was his mum after all. The alcohol was making him maudlin. He'd been so hyped up after the meet with Alfie Clarke, Peter had taken him to their pub to calm down. But once the news of Tania's birth got round, the drinks had been overflowing. He felt the tears stinging his eyes, and he tried to wipe them away before anyone saw, unaware that every movement he made was overdone, too forced.

Daniel was not a good drunk. Drink made his temper flare up faster than usual, it made him overly confident and, worse, it made him cry. He could break down at a record, a memory, or a thought, and the majority of the people he rolled with saw that as a weakness.

'Give me that child before you drop her on her fecking head, and she ends up a fecking moron like her father.' Theresa Bailey did not like this son of hers when he had been drinking; he irritated her and she hated that the drink made him foolish, made him forget that he was a family man. She took the child gently.

Lena watched the exchange and smiled despite herself; for all his big talk, Daniel was still scared of his mother, no matter how much he tried to pretend he wasn't.

She actually thought she understood her husband in a way his mother never could. She got angry with him – anyone would, he could be such a prat at times. But she knew the real Daniel Bailey. His upbringing as a fatherless boy, with a brother who was black and who he adored, had made an indelible mark on him. He had spent his whole life proving he was better than everyone, that the *Baileys* were better than anyone. He worked hard for them all. Just as she had her mania for saving money, her husband had a mania for making himself successful.

Yes, she was terrified he would get his collar felt, and she was equally terrified that he would lead the boys into things that would result in them going away. But, when all was said and done, she loved him. And she knew that, no matter how misguided he might be, he would always do his best for them.

'She's a diamond, Lena. You've given me a treasure, girl.'

He was sitting on the bed beside her now, and she could see the tears forming in his eyes again. As tired as she was after the birth, she would have to comfort her husband as the drink made his emotions erupt into a bout of prolonged weeping.

She held out her arms and, as he grasped on to her and cried noisily on her shoulder, she saw her mother-in-law shaking her head in annoyance, as she walked the child out of the room. Even the slamming of the bedroom door was lost on Daniel Bailey. As Lena knew from experience, it was all about him now.

Chapter Eighteen

'Come on, Pete, he's always been over the top.'

Peter Bailey grinned. He had just aired his worries to his wife. He needed someone to confide in, to say out loud what was bothering him and Ria was a good listener. He knew he could trust her. 'You're preaching to the converted, love. He's me brother, but this is too important for him to nause up. He's going too far too soon.'

Peter sighed. Life was getting more and more difficult by the day; whoever said it was lonely at the top knew exactly what they were talking about. It had been a hard road; they were finally where they wanted to be, but the cracks were already showing.

Daniel was acting like Al Capone on speed, and Peter didn't trust him as far as he could throw him at the moment. True, they were at the top, but they were still waiting for any pretenders to the throne to make themselves known. This was when they needed their wits about them twenty-four seven.

Ria was sad that even though her husband had finally achieved everything he had wanted to, he was not a happy bunny. She knew Daniel was not the easiest of people to be in partnership with, but then Peter had known that from the off. After all, they were brothers, it wasn't like they didn't know each other. And they had always said that it was *because* of their differences that they were so successful.

But in the last year she could feel the tension growing between them – everyone could. Not that anybody mentioned it, of course. As bad as the relationship between the brothers was, they would still cut the throat of anyone who tried to come between them.

She knew Daniel was drinking a lot these days and Lena was worried about it. Daniel Bailey and drink was never a good combination. When he wasn't maudlin, he was a violent drunk – not towards his wife or family but with people he didn't know very well. He saw a slight where none existed. He'd always been the same but until this last year he had never been a bully. Now he was getting a reputation as a troublesome pisshead.

For the moment, his name and his standing were enough to keep him safe; Peter saw to it that he was watched and he smoothed over things that might otherwise grow out of proportion. But Ria knew that there would always be someone who could not be placated. One day, Daniel would push his luck too far. That concerned Ria insomuch as it affected *her* husband, *her* family.

She also knew that it worried Lena, though Lena thought the sun shone out of her husband's arse, and would stand by him no matter what. Ria respected Lena for that, but she also felt that it was time Lena put her foot down, and told her husband the truth about his behaviour, and how it was affecting the whole family. But that would never happen. Lena still feigned ignorance – and Ria did think it *had* to be feigned.

Even so, she was not as involved with the family business as Ria was. And these days, Lena was far too wrapped up in the new baby to pay much attention to what was going on around her. All Ria could do was support her husband, as she had always done, and thank God she chose the better brother.

Chapter Nineteen

The DJ was playing Edwin Starr, and the music was so loud it seemed to make the walls move with the reverberation from the bass. All around, the young people were dancing, gyrating, shouting to be heard above the noise. The place was packed to capacity, the smell of cheap perfume and sweat heavy in the air. Half-naked girls were dancing around as if their lives depended on it, determined to pull or be pulled. They wore brightly coloured make-up, and were dressed in the height of fashion. This was Ilford, Essex, bordering East London; these were the girls who set the fashions for the rest of the country. These were the girls who decided what was in, and what wasn't. They were like exotic birds, so young, so lovely. Ilford had several major nightclubs, all well known, well frequented, and always packed. Now there was a new club, just off Green Lane, called The House. It was open later than the others, and it was always guaranteed to have the best DJs and the best live music on a Friday and a Saturday.

Peter and Daniel Bailey had opened this club and watched as the money rolled in; for with the clubs came the drugs, both of which were earning them fortunes.

Peter was happy for Daniel to run this side of the business. Personally, he didn't like it, but he was sensible enough to know it was a necessary evil. Peter prided himself on providing the best that could be procured, from the DJs to the live music. And so, despite his dislike of them, he also insisted on the best quality of narcotic. Peter believed that if you offered the best, you would have the edge over the rest.

As he walked into The House, he saw the bouncers on the door searching two young men, and he nodded at them, pleased. No one dealt in here, unless they had the permission of the head doorman. It was not just so that they were the only game in town – it was to make sure that no one was sold anything that could kill. So much of the speed that was sold around and about was cut with everything from Ajax, a kitchen cleaner, to strychnine, a bona fide poison. Peter accepted they had to *sell* the stuff – along with the LSD, the marijuana: the home-grown sinsemilla, Afghan Black. That was without the Valium, the Mogadon, the uppers and the downers that went hand-in-hand with the stimulants that were in such high demand.

Oh, they were like a fucking pharmacy, but Peter had made peace with that. As Daniel said, if they didn't provide the drugs, somebody else would. The money to be made was too quick and too easy to overlook, and he knew the truth of that statement.

As he walked through the downstairs bar, Peter wondered at the money that would change hands in here this night. He pushed his way through the crush of bodies, looking around him, as always, still watching for the errant knife, the lone gunman. He knew that to survive you could never get complacent. Especially with Daniel pissing more people off by the day. Well, Daniel was a fucking idiot as far as he was concerned. He admired his brother's confidence, in a way. But Peter was a man who believed that the worst *could* happen, and frequently did. Therefore he was always on the lookout for the nearest escape route, the hidden assassin or the fucking drunk trying to prove themselves.

The last of these was the worst worry of all; nothing was worse than an old has-been just released from stir, who still pledged allegiance to the old Faces, trying to settle a score that was not only pointless, but was also completely without provocation. That was the trouble with a long sentence, if the person wasn't careful they got caught in a time warp. They stormed out of the nick, all pumped up with adrenalin and hatred, determined to right old wrongs, twenty years too fucking late. The world had changed too much for them, they had no idea how to fit in any more; they were fucking dinosaurs who still thought you could buy a pint, go to the pictures, have a meal and still get change from a fucking groat. He was sorry for them, understood their dilemma, but he also knew how dangerous they were, not only to themselves, but to the people around them. Because of that, Peter had made a point of contacting all the old Faces who had found themselves proud possessors of long sentences. He made sure they had a few quid, and that they were well looked after. He felt they deserved respect. These men were often forgotten, and that was wrong.

Peter Bailey was a man who always looked at every angle, even when he was at home in his bed, cuddling his wife. He still made sure that no one could penetrate his home. He was overly careful, but believed he had to be. The bigger you got, the more you had to lose.

As he slipped into the office he sighed with relief. 'What a fucking racket! Call that music?'

Daniel laughed. 'Well, *I* don't, but the youth of today, who spend a good wedge in here, think it's the dog's bollocks. This place is a fucking money machine, I tell you.'

Peter nodded. He was pleased. This was actually Delroy's brainchild. The boy had come up trumps. He had said this was a good investment, made a convincing argument and he had been right. He had also made sure they had a good DJ, cheap drink, and late licences. All in all, he had given them a seriously good – and legal – earn. His son-in-law had really come into his own because of this and Peter was impressed. The place was perfect for meets; it was a large building, with front and back access, four floors and, more to the point, it was always packed so it made it much harder for the Filth to infiltrate – bearing in mind the undercover police stuck out like a fucking pork chop in a mosque. You could see them a mile off, from their newly pierced ears, to their brand new leather jackets. It was embarrassing really. They couldn't fit in just anywhere – they were the Filth, for fuck's sake – they only fit in with their own. Ten years out of date in their clothing, they were so uncomfortable in the discotheque surroundings, they were easier to spot than a leper at a poker game. Peter had noticed more than one Filth on his foray into the offices tonight; it was laughable really.

'You see those Filth dressed up like real people?'

Daniel laughed. 'It's awful, Peter, we know them all by name! Our new boy at the Met, Smith, has furnished us with all their details. Like we need them! They look like spare pricks at a wedding. But, in fairness, he's come through for us.'

Peter nodded, then, going to the small bar in the corner of the office, he poured himself a large Scotch. He sipped it before saying quietly, 'So, what's the problem with Alfie Clarke now, Dan?'

Daniel shrugged nonchalantly, but he was wondering who had given his brother the nod. He was hoping to take Clarke out before his brother even realised there was a problem. Peter was too fucking gullible as far as he was concerned. He trusted the wrong people; he thought that his associates were as honest and loyal as he was.

Daniel squared up to his brother, pushing his shoulders back, taking a deep breath. It was a completely unconscious gesture. He was not happy about being caught like this, on the hop as it were. 'You know my feelings about him, Pete. I have never hidden my contempt. I worked with him for you, but I have never trusted him.'

Peter finished his drink, and poured himself another before saying quietly, 'You have to stop this, Dan, and you have to stop it now. Alfie is earning us serious money. He's a cunt, granted, but he is also *our* cunt. You have this fucking mental haze – you take against people for no reason. I know you have been goading him. If I was him I would have taken you out, even if it meant I was shot dead in the street. I would not let you make a fucking mug of me like you have him. You're out of order, and you did all this behind my back.'

Daniel had known it would come out eventually, but it had never occurred to him that his brother knew what was happening but had chosen to let it go. Peter had been repairing the damage on the quiet. Daniel decided the best way forward was to go on the offensive.

'Come on, Peter, you and I both know that bastard is not trustworthy.'

Peter Bailey smiled despite himself; if there was one thing he loved about his brother, it was that he never changed. He was always constant, ignorant as shit, but stoic in his opinions.

'This is not about Clarke, is it? Not really him, personally. It's about you, as usual. Well, do you know something, Dan? This is one time I am putting my foot down. You have got to stop this, all this petty fucking stupidity. I'm sick of it. Sick of clearing up after you.

You're getting the reputation of a cunt. No one trusts *you*.' Peter Bailey poked his finger into his own chest as he said angrily, '*I* don't fucking trust you! You cause upset everywhere you go. You take offence at every little fucking opportunity. You have to prove yourself to people who mean *nothing* to us, to people so beneath our radar they might as well be dead. Come on, bruv, enjoy this, enjoy what we've created. Please, Dan, it's like we don't know each other any more.'

Daniel looked into his brother's brown eyes; this was the only person in the world who he really loved – he sometimes thought that this man might actually take precedence over his wife and kids. But he couldn't back down this time. Clarke was like a cancer to him; he ate at him every minute of the day. He knew it was irrational, but that didn't bother him. He truly believed that if this brother of his had felt like this about someone, he would not dare to question him about it, he would just accept it. Accept the fact that his brother must obviously have his reasons for his strong dislike of a person, no matter what the score. Daniel would just have stepped back and allowed for the inevitable. He expected the same support.

'Look, Pete, I loathe him. He looks down his nose at us. And what the fuck have we really achieved with him on our payroll? I've heard he's mugging us off. So are we going to take that? Come on, you tell me.'

Peter shook his head in abject disbelief; he knew that Daniel was drunk – he was always drunk lately – but he had heard rumours he was not averse to a line or two of coke. That had to be the reason for this paranoia. He had always been a bit paranoid had Daniel, but lately he was completely out of it.

'What we have achieved, Dan, is all this –' he opened his arms wide – 'this and much more. If you can't see that then I'm wasting my fucking time here, ain't I? Clarke is no more than a fucking drone, a worker, and he delivers. He delivers regularly, and he is well respected. Now, I am asking you for the last time. Don't rock the boat, we have a lot of money riding on him.'

Daniel looked at his brother, then around the office. He liked it here, it was a nice room, big enough to accommodate up to ten people, and smart enough to feel you were on the up. There were no windows, so no fear of a petrol bomb, or a shooting. He felt the same need as his brother to feel safe. Unlike his brother, he knew he didn't always have his eye on the ball. He was easily sidetracked, he was not a man who really embraced the nitty-gritty, whereas for Peter all that kind of stuff came naturally. Peter always read the small print, he saw the little things, things that to most people meant nothing, but were often the cause of a major problem, mainly because the person concerned didn't bother to look for them, or didn't understand the importance of them. Peter was the voice of reason.

Now Daniel could see that Peter had no trust for him any more, that he saw him as a liability. He knew at that moment, with stunning clarity, that Peter had every right to feel that way.

He had made the cardinal mistake; he had succumbed to the worst thing men like them could succumb to.

He was taking his own drugs.

Chapter Twenty

Daniel was sweating, but he was not going to let that bother him. He looked down at the man on the floor and, smiling craftily, he began laying into him once more.

His two eldest sons watched as their father carried out the attack. He'd said that the man owed them money, and had brought them with him so that they could see what happened to anyone who mugged off the Baileys.

Davey looked at his older brother and held his arms out in a gesture of bewilderment; he wasn't sure what this was about really. It seemed so over the top.

Danny Junior sighed and said quietly, 'He loves a fucking audience, so get used to it.' It wasn't the first time he'd seen his father out of control. 'Uncle Peter is going to go fucking mad when he finds out. He's already warned him about making scenes like this.'

Davey shook his head in consternation. Surely his father was going too far now? He looked at the man on the ground. Lenny Jones was a good bloke, with a decent reputation, everyone knew that. He was a diamond geezer. Now he was lying on a cement floor, and he was suffering the humiliation of being beaten up and accused of all sorts. It was wrong. The boys, young as they were, knew it.

Lenny Jones was a hard man in his own right. He had felt he had enough creds to be approached calmly for the money he owed – not chased as if he was a fucking shank. He had the money, and he was willing to give it up, but he felt he should've been asked respectfully and privately. It was six grand, for fuck's sake, not a fortune. He'd only needed it to tide him over until he could unlock his capital, which was his proceeds from a robbery that he had undertaken with the full knowledge of this man and his brother. He had assumed he would be treated with the same respect that he had shown the Baileys; he had requested permission to knock off a bank on their turf, had negotiated the six grand up front, and had happily agreed to their terms and conditions if the loan was not paid back within the specified time. He had the money well in advance of the due date, so he had not expected this shit.

He deserved respect – he was not a fucking muppet. He still believed in the old-school values, in the old-style manners. He had done a ten stretch without a murmur, had kept his mouth shut, his head down and found it in his heart to be glad for his colleagues who had swerved that particular bullet. He had been in the game for a long time, and had a reputation for paying his bills. He had thought, wrongly as it turned out, that the Baileys would have given him the credit he was due.

Lenny realised he had seriously underestimated the

whole situation. He'd forgotten that Daniel Bailey was an animal, a thug, a man who had no real regard for anyone or anything. He already had a bad rep because of his insistence on using violence at every available opportunity.

Lenny looked squarely into Daniel's eyes as he leaned over him and Daniel saw the hatred there. In his heart Daniel knew he was out of order. This man was more than worth his time and effort, and deserved his goodwill. This was a man who was respected throughout their world. But knowing that just made Daniel dislike Lenny even more. He was like all the old Faces, thinking they were fucking better than everyone else, just because they had done a stretch, or worked with the old fucking has-beens.

That cut no fucking ice with him. It might with his brother; Peter was in awe of these old boys, listened to their stories of days gone by, laughed in all the right places, talked to them as if they were fucking oracles or suchlike. Peter treated them with kid gloves, as if they were important, as if they were celebrities or something. Well, Peter was soft, and Daniel was done with listening to him.

Taking his leg back, he kicked the man with every ounce of strength that he had left. He saw Lenny's body rise up off the cement floor, and knew that it had to hurt.

Daniel also knew that Peter was going to hit the fucking roof when he found out about this latest debacle.

Chapter Twenty-One

Theresa Bailey looked down at her little granddaughter and secretly marvelled at the child's likeness to her. Theresa was the image of her own mother, and little Tania was the living image of *her*. It was amazing really how seeing yourself in your children or your grand-children made you aware of your own roots, brought to mind people, and events, that you had not thought about for years. Tania had done that to her. She felt the rejection of her family all over again, as if it was new, had just happened. She saw her sister's face clearly, the shock and disgust when she saw that Peter was black. Theresa smiled sadly to herself as she remembered.

'You know, Lena, this little girl is my mother's double. It's uncanny. But I suppose that's the circle of life. Anyway, this little one is the last we'll see from either of those boys of mine. Imelda will produce now. She's sensible that one, she'll have them in her own time. Sure, girls are lucky as shite these days; they can control everything if they use their noggins.'

Lena laughed out loud. 'I suppose so. But then again is there *ever* a right time to have a baby? All this planning and deciding *when* you will have one! It seems to me as if they are trying to fit childbirth into their lives, but they are still completely unaware of just how powerful having a child actually is. They spend so much time planning everything, they don't allow for just how fucking intrusive a baby can be. Kids are like a bomb going off in your life. They are all different, with different personalities, and you can't plan for that. You have to just go along with them when they arrive.'

Theresa laughed with her daughter-in-law. She was so glad to see her happy at last. She knew these past months had been a nightmare, with all the worry about Daniel. That eejit of a son of hers! He'd shamed her more than anything in her entire life. Her boys had worked so hard for so long to get where they were, and Daniel had crumbled under the pressure within weeks.

He'd always had a temper, an irrational streak, even as a child. But he was her son and she loved him. It was seeing him weak, dependent on alcohol, using drugs, which she could not, for the life of her, understand. He had left this woman basically all alone after she'd given him a child, and Lena had never once brought him to task. The foolish bitch! Theresa would have felt happier if Lena *had* torn him out a second arse, *that* she would have applauded. But her acceptance of his behaviour, her complete and utter refusal to even acknowledge it, she could not fathom. Daniel had left her to mind the child, mind the house, the boys. *His* needs were, as usual, of paramount importance, and Lena had just rolled over for him.

She was, all in all, very fond of her daughters-in-law. Theresa felt blessed that her sons had each found wonderful women, decent women – who were, in reality, far too good for the men they had chosen. Not that she would ever say that out loud, of course. Consequently, she was finding it very hard to forgive her Daniel his treatment of Lena. In fact, she found herself biting her tongue not only with him, but with Lena too. She wanted to shake her so hard she had to physically restrain herself at times. She never interfered with the boys' private lives; if the girls came to her with a problem, she tried her hardest to be fair. She was amazed that, more often than not, she found herself coming down on the girls' side. She loved her sons, but she was not blind to their failings. If she had one criticism of Lena it was that she acted as if nothing was amiss. Theresa, ever the realist, found this was driving her demented. But saying it out loud was tantamount to criticism, which couldn't be tolerated.

'There is never a right time for having children, you're right there, Lena. Look at me, I had two men in my life and, through them, two children. If I had stayed in Ireland, I would probably be married now, a respectable married woman, and surrounded by an army of fecking children. I'd look years older than I am, would have lost all me teeth before I was thirty, and would live my life by the church bells, say the rosary every night, and thank God every day for the life I was living. Instead I came over here, got into trouble – as they called it in them days – and now I have a great life, sure Jaysus, out and about, and still able to enjoy meself.'

Lena laughed again. 'You're still gorgeous, even at your age now.' She'd always envied her mother-in-law's bright sovereign-coloured hair and porcelain skin.

Theresa smiled. 'This girl here is gorgeous. I swear I have never seen a child so contented. But don't say that to Ria – Imelda was a fecker of a baby. She cried for the first two years of her life – miserable as fecking sin she was.'

Lena grinned. 'I remember. She screamed if anyone even looked at her. I hope little Tania will have a happy life – I really want her to be somebody, you know? I want her to follow her star. I don't want her to be a part of this life, not when she grows up. I want her to be outside all this. Imelda's just married her father – or as good as – she is one of us now, and I'm not putting her down, but I want this little one to be able to *choose* what she wants from this life.'

Theresa nodded sadly. 'That's exactly what I want for her as well. For all the lads' hard work, and as far as they have come, I don't think they are any happier. They thought it was the Holy Grail, that getting to the top would miraculously make them happy. If only life was that easy.'

Chapter Twenty-Two

'Daniel, talk to me. Are you sure you're all right?'

Daniel Bailey sighed heavily. His blue eyes were tired-looking, and his mouth was set in a grim line. He had just arrived at their new offices in East London. He poured himself a coffee and sipped it carefully; last time he'd nearly welded his lips together it had been so hot.

When he was finally settled he turned to the question in hand. In his most aggrieved voice he said plaintively, 'For fuck's sake, Pete, what do you want from me? What can I do to make you feel better, eh? I'm tired, I admit that. But I have been out on the earn. You know – taking care of business?'

Peter Bailey could feel the anger boiling up inside him. 'Is that what you call it, Dan? Beaten up any more old men recently?' Peter was still fuming at Daniel's vicious attack on Lenny Jones, a man who he had been friends with for years, who had never given either of them anything other than his loyalty and respect. A man who was now half crippled, and unable to button up his own shirt. A man who, thanks to his brother, had nearly been the cause of a fucking war, whose friends had seen to it that *he*, Peter, had been held responsible for making sure this brother of his not only apologised, but saw to it that Lenny was given the best treatment available. Peter had done this without a second's thought; he would have insisted on that anyway. The upside was that Daniel had understood – finally – that his actions had consequences.

It had been a learning curve for Daniel. He could see now just how fucking precarious his position actually *was* – especially when you offended just about everyone within a fifty-mile radius. It had taken all that before Daniel had understood just how much damage he had done to their reputations with his arrogance and his temper. He had taken out Lenny Jones on a whim, and look what had happened.

No matter how hard you were, no matter how high you might have risen, without the goodwill of the people on your manor, you had nothing of any worth. Oh, the Baileys were still up there, still on top but, thanks to Daniel, they now had to claw back not only the trust, but also the respect, of the people they dealt with on a daily basis – the people who should have been their allies from the off.

Peter was all right; *he* had been assured of his place in the world. It was Daniel who needed to swallow, who needed to show willing. But as his brother and his partner, Peter was under no illusions that until Daniel proved himself they would both be suspect. If any other firm decided to push for the top right now, Peter knew that there would not be too many people rooting for the Baileys. Daniel had seen to that.

Daniel allowed his brother that remark. He understood that he needed to keep his head down and regain his footing with not only his brother, but the whole of East London. He had shown his hand too soon; he should have waited a while, allowed them to get deeply rooted before he started paying back old scores. But that didn't mean he wasn't gathering new ones; he would pay back every one of the fuckers who had questioned his actions and seen Peter as the man in charge of everything, the man who could rein Daniel in.

They were supposed to be the fucking new kings, for Christ's sake – *both* of them. And they were not supposed to be questioned about anything. But East London was only available for rent – provided the people renting it were seen as acceptable and did not step out of line.

Peter had understood that from the off, whereas Daniel had not cared one way or the other. He had been forced to swallow his knob now, and he had done it because he knew that if he had refused, his days would have been numbered. He'd had no other choice, but it would never be the same for him now – no matter what he achieved in the future, people would always remember his failures, would repeat this story behind their hands.

The worst thing of all for Daniel was that his brother had no real time for him any more. Peter saw him as a burden these days. He was too loyal to aim him out of it completely, and had stood beside him when other men would have walked away. Peter had guaranteed his safety when more than one man had been baying for his blood over Lenny Jones. Peter had smoothed all that over, and let it be known, on the quiet, of course, that if anyone went near his brother he would feel within his rights to distribute his own revenge. Seeing just how well respected and how well liked Peter was had been the hardest blow for Daniel. Peter's reputation for settling his scores quietly, with the minimum of fuss but the maximum of violence, had given him a certain mystique. Peter's secrecy made him an enigma. And that gave him an aura of power which Daniel did not share.

Daniel had thrown away his chance to shine, had brought about his own demise and he knew it. He hated that he was now seen as less than his brother. He was the man who had crippled Lenny Jones for no real reason. Lenny Jones, who had had more creds than him, had been the cause of his downfall. Lenny Jones, it seemed, had, inadvertently, been Daniel's nemesis.

Peter Bailey, his own brother, suddenly seemed like a stranger to him. Daniel watched him as he stalked around the office, wishing with all his heart that they did not have this wedge between them. But *he* had caused this rift, and he hated that the longer it went on, the more he resented this man and everything he stood for.

Chapter Twenty-Three

Davey held his little sister in his arms, laughing at her as she attempted to grab his hair. He never ceased to be amazed how much he loved her. He loved his mum, he loved his nana – they were very important to him – and he loved his brothers and cousins, but Tania seemed to evoke feelings that were even stronger. She smiled up into his eyes, and he felt his heart melt with an overwhelming love. He wondered if it was because he had seen her born, although when he thought about *that* it made him feel ill. He had never felt right about that; his mother was a diamond, but he had seen a bit too much of her for his own good that night.

Whatever the reason, Davey knew that, out of the boys, he had a special bond with Tania. They all loved her, but it was a haphazard affection, just because she was there. Now she was starting to become a little person, and Davey knew he was already wrapped round her little finger.

Lena watched her big, handsome son holding his sister and she smiled happily. Davey adored the child, he was a good lad and he'd grown up a lot since Tania's birth. She liked to see them together – the other boys were not as enamoured with their little sister, they just accepted her as part of the family. To them Tania would only ever be someone they felt the need to protect; none of them would ever really know the girl. Except Davey, of course – he already knew her, already understood her, in fact.

'She loves you, Davey.'

He smiled. 'Why wouldn't she, Mum? She knows I'd do anything for her.'

Lena laughed. As she poured out the tea she heard the back door open and, smiling widely, she said loudly, 'Might have known you'd smell a cuppa, Delroy. I'm sure you can hear a kettle boil from fifty paces!'

Delroy grinned. He looked like a young Harry Belafonte when he smiled, and his grin had got him out of many a scrape through his life. He did not underestimate its power. 'I do love a cuppa – you know that, Mrs Bailey – never refuse one!'

He was telling the truth; Delroy Parkes loved a cup of tea. Even in his youth, when he had been arrested then released, he wouldn't leave the police station if a cup of tea was in the offing. He enjoyed his tea more than anything else in the world. He drank, but not as much as people would think; in reality, he could quite happily be teetotal. He drank to be sociable, that was all.

As he sipped his tea, he looked down at the little girl in Davey's arms and marvelled at just how beautiful she was. He was not a baby person, but no one could deny the attraction of this little girl; she was like a fucking poster baby for health and beauty. The Pears' baby looked like a fucking freak in comparison! She had such a good nature too – all that combined made her a special little kid. She held her arms out for a cuddle and he took her without hesitating. She snuggled into him, and he marvelled at how comfortable she was with everyone who came into her orbit.

'Hello, you!'

She was laughing at him, and he liked that she was happy in his arms, that she trusted him, felt safe. He turned to Davey. 'You ready for the off?' Daniel and Peter wanted to start getting the older boys involved in the day-to-day running of the business, and Delroy was helping to show them the ropes.

'Sure, Del.' Davey was all eagerness. 'I'll get me coat.'

Davey left the room and Lena said quietly, 'How is everything, Delroy? Are Peter and Daniel all right?' She was smiling but she could see the tension in her face. He knew she asked him the questions she couldn't ask her husband or any of her family, even Ria. She couldn't ask anyone else because it would be tantamount to treason as far as she was concerned. She would never betray her husband, never make him feel she was checking up on him. If she questioned him or his actions he would never forgive her. Their whole world had turned its back on him, and this woman knew that her husband had overstepped the mark, had somehow fucked up big time. She also knew that as long as he thought she was ignorant of that fact, Daniel could look her in the eye. Delroy really respected Mrs Bailey for her loyalty, even though he believed it was misplaced.

'Yeah, they're cool, Mrs Bailey.' He hated lying to her but what could he do? He couldn't tell her the truth, he couldn't tell her that her husband was a fucking imbecile who had nearly caused the early demise of not only himself, but his own brother. He could not tell her that her husband was right now one of the most hated men to ever walk the streets of London Town. She had to be aware of it anyway; after all, it wasn't like it was a big secret or anything.

Davey came back into the kitchen putting on his leather jacket and Delroy breathed a sigh of relief. He passed the baby to her mother and, gulping the last of his tea, he was happy to finally leave the house.

Chapter Twenty-Four

Ria was thrilled. Her daughter was finally pregnant, and she was so pleased for her. If ever a girl needed a child in her arms it was her Imelda. She needed more in her life than her husband, who she loved with a passion so intense it was a wonder it didn't burn them both up.

Ria was heart-sorry for her at times. Imelda's feelings for Delroy were not healthy; she was consumed by him twenty-four hours a day, seven days a week. Ria could almost smell the fear that he would leave her. It was hard for Delroy because she knew he loved this girl of hers, but Imelda could not bring herself to believe it. For the life of her, Ria could not understand why.

Imelda had been given every chance in life – she had been brought up to believe she was loved and cherished, not just by Ria and Peter, but by her brothers too. Imelda had been literally worshipped from the moment she had entered this world. So why, Ria asked herself on a daily basis, did her daughter have no confidence in herself at all?

'You'll be a great mum, Imelda. You can't even imagine what it's like to grow a child inside you and then bring it into the world. From the second you feel it stir inside your belly, and feel the strength of it, you change. Suddenly no one else in the world can ever replace that child in your affections. It's like you suddenly understand what this life is really about.'

Imelda smiled, but she had the feeling that her mother was warning her about something, and she didn't like it. She put her hand instinctively on to her belly, and wondered what the child she held within her would bring into her life. Until now she had seen it simply as the glue that would keep Delroy by her side, his own flesh and blood, his own kin. She realised that she had not once thought of the baby as hers too, only as an extension of her husband, and an invisible tie between them. Now, though, the enormity of what was happening hit her; she was going to produce a real live human being, who was going to need her for the rest of its life. And she knew that she would need it too.

She looked at her mother then, and knew that her mother saw that she was not just in love with Delroy, she was consumed by him.

'I can't help it, Mum. I just know that without him I would die.'

Ria smiled sadly. 'Listen, love, we all felt like that at the beginning, but I can tell you now, if you don't learn how to manage your emotions, he will run for the hills, baby or no baby. He is not stupid, Imelda. Eventually he'll know that he can never live up to your expectations – no one could, darling. You want him within your eye-line day and night. I've watched you, seen the way you watch him, and my heart has broken for you. But I am finally saying what I've wanted to say for so long. If you don't learn to step back, you'll drive him away from you. You knew he was a ladies' man, you knew he was a villain, you knew *everything* about him, and you *still* wanted him anyway. Fuck knows, you were determined to have him. You got what you wanted, now you need to learn-to be content with that. Because I'm telling you, darling, there ain't a man on earth, or a woman for that matter, who could take that much loving. Marriage is a partnership, and to keep it going you have to look away sometimes, make a point of not asking the questions you want to ask. And you have to be honest with yourself first, and ask only if you really want to know the answers.'

Imelda knew that her mother was right. She was warning her, was trying to tell her what she already knew – that she had to somehow control these feelings that she had for Delroy, and stop the overpowering love she had for him, before it destroyed their marriage completely. 'I know you're right, Mum, and I know I need to calm down, and I will try. But it's like I'm possessed sometimes. I can hear myself shouting and raving, and I know it's wrong, I know I am irrational. But it's like someone else is doing it, and I hate myself for it.'

Ria hugged her daughter, and wondered again at how this girl who had always been a sensible head, who had always been the most reasonable, albeit the most strong-minded of her children, had turned into this jealous, insecure woman. 'Listen, love, all the children in the world won't keep him beside you. Children put more of a strain on a marriage than anything else. All that shite about it bringing you closer is just that – shite. For the first few years you won't sleep enough, you won't eat properly and your sex life will be almost non-existent. But if you can get through it all, I promise you, *that* is when you finally bond together. And, remember this, when you have a baby in a cot, *you* can't walk out of the house. *He* can, but you can't. You're stuck there no matter how angry you might be or how murderous you're feeling. *He* can walk out, go down the pub, whatever. You are trapped like a bloody rabbit, and I can tell you now, it is one of the most frustrating feelings you will ever experience. But I can also tell you that if you learn how to calm yourself down, learn how to channel your anger into the home, or the washing, you will eventually come out the other side, frazzled, but with your marriage in one piece. Your father was out all hours of the day and night – that was his life, and I accepted that. We ain't married to nine-to-fivers, love – you picked Delroy knowing he was like your dad. You can't expect him to change now. So, listen to me. Get a grip, accept your life, accept his lifestyle, or run a mile now. Because he ain't ever going to change.'

Imelda knew her mother was offering her the chance to walk away from her marriage; she was telling her that if she wanted to, she could come back here with her baby and start again. But she couldn't. She could no more leave Delroy than she could cut her own throat.

Knowing that her mother understood how she was feeling was a relief in itself, though. She could come to her now, she could ask her advice, she had a sounding board and she had a feeling that, without this conversation, she would eventually have lost her mind.

'I love you, Mum.'

Ria smiled sadly. 'I love you too, poppet.'

She glanced at their reflection in the mirror and she saw how old she was getting, and how this daughter of hers was ageing too quickly because of her constant scowl. She already had the beginnings of lines around her eyes and her mouth. But she was still a truly beautiful girl, and she deserved much more in her life than she had now.

Chapter Twenty-Five

'Come on, Peter, I've held me hand up, I've swallowed about as much as I can without a fucking stomach pump. So I'm asking you nicely, with a pretty please, and a cherry on the top: can I have the debts back?'

Peter Bailey looked into his brother's eyes. They were a real blue, just like his mum's. She had the same big eyes, the same deep blue colour. All Daniel's kids had inherited them as well. Peter's kids were brown-eyed like him; he had hoped years ago that one of them would get those blue eyes, but it had never happened.

Now, looking at Daniel's eyes, seeing how much he resembled their mum, and knowing that, deep down, he had always secretly envied his brother because of that, he wondered how this state of affairs had ever come about. 'I am willing to give you the debts, Dan, but you have to promise me you will not give any unnecessary grief to the people you come into contact with.'

Daniel closed his eyes in genuine consternation. 'Don't you think I've been shamed enough, Peter? Do you think I don't know what people think of me? Do you really think I am that fucking stupid? I want the debts because I am good at collecting, and I want to prove that I am ready to take on some of the responsibility again. After all, we are supposed to be partners, ain't we?'

Peter knew how hard that was for his brother to say out loud. Daniel would never get over the shame of being blackballed by those he had seen as no more than his workforce. These were men who liked Lenny Jones, but who also knew that if they did not do something about his treatment, they could well find that they were next. Peter got that; he really could see their point of view. Daniel, though, believed he was the victim of jealousy and grudges.

Daniel was convinced he had already paid his penance ten times over. As far as he was concerned, Lenny Jones was a fucking old man; he should have had more sense than to mouth off to him and treat him like a cunt. He had got no more than what he deserved, and not before time either.

Peter sighed. 'I'm saying, Daniel, that I will bring you back into the fold, but only on the debts. I can't justify having you back on board in any other capacity unless you can guarantee to me that you will toe the line. I have to listen to the people I'm working with now. They don't want *you*. They see you as a liability; you bring too much attention on not only yourself, but everyone you are associated with. I have argued your case, believe me. But your reputation, as always, precedes you. It's a different ball game, Dan. You can't just do what you like any more.'

Daniel didn't answer his brother. He didn't trust himself; all he could see was the complete and utter disloyalty of it. How could his brother, who had been closer to him than anyone in the world, allow him to be treated like this? Could treat him like this himself? It was an outrage. He felt a murderous rage rising inside his chest at the utter shame his brother had put on his shoulders.

He had to get out of this place, and soon. But first he had to negotiate a settlement of some kind. He was not leaving here empty-handed; without him his brother wouldn't have had a pot to piss in and they both knew that.

'OK, then. Whatever you might think of me now, Pete, I've *always* had my fucking creds, mate. Now, I have been good enough to swallow my knob over Lenny. I know I overstepped a boundary. But do you know what? Fuck it all, mate. Stick it up your arse.'

Peter didn't answer his brother. He just stood and waited for him to say his piece.

'I want the debts, but I want them all. I want every last one of them, Pete, and you know as well as I do that I've earned them. If anyone needs money brought in, *I* get the call. You see to that. I also want the betting shops, North as well as East London. I want my fucking fair share. I also want a percentage of the other businesses, and I will promise you now I will not interfere in any way, shape or form provided I get my poke. You fucking think I'm a mug! I can't believe you have the gall to treat me like this, your own brother, the only person you have ever really been able to trust, and you know that's true, Pete. No matter what you think now, you will always be the fucking coon, the outsider, and I hate that you have made me say that to you.'

Peter Bailey looked at this man, his brother, his closest kin, and he knew he was speaking the truth. It had taken a lot for him to say what he had said, because Daniel had never once seen his colour, only that he was his brother, and he loved him for that. Daniel had always had his back, of that there was never any doubt. What was in question was Daniel's ability to make enemies without discrimination, to cause upset and discord without thought for the consequences. Peter shook his head sadly as he said seriously, and against his better judgement, 'I'll give you what you want, Dan, but on one condition.'

Daniel didn't answer him, he just stared at him, and Peter saw that his eyes were wet with unshed tears.

'You can have the debts and the bets – all the bets across London – and we will work side by side. I don't want to row with you, Dan. I just want you to see that we have to box clever, make you understand that we can't be seen to be weak in any way. I *want* you beside me, for fuck's sake, Dan! You're my brother. But we have to be on the same page. You have to be seen as a sensible head. No more fucking mindless violence; we have to be men who are seen as trustworthy, reliable, to be seen as able to work in tandem, so people know that we are a real partnership. If we can't achieve that, Dan, then you can go your own way now. You have to see what's at stake here. You have to make sure you do not fuck up again.'

Now he had tears in his eyes too, and he knew that Daniel could see them. He hoped against hope that tonight had cleared the air, and they could both move on.

'You can rely on me, bruv.'

Peter hugged his younger brother, could smell the aroma that was so peculiar to him: Acqua di Selva and Palmolive soap. And prayed that he had done the right thing. As much as he loved his brother – and that had never been in question – Daniel was not a man who could be trusted to make sensible decisions off his own bat. He needed guidance, and Peter would have to watch him like a hawk because of that. They would start with the debts and the bets; let Daniel prove himself there and everything else should fall into place. After all, they were brothers, bonded by blood, and nothing would ever change that.

Chapter Twenty-Six

Peter Bailey was uneasy. It seemed that his brother was running true to form. He'd only been back in the fold a couple of weeks and already people were on the blower complaining about him, his attitude, and his aggression. Luckily, the people who were complaining were not people he had any real interest in. And, anyway, he had bigger fish to fry. Like Alfie Clarke, for example. Alfie, so the gossip went, was double dealing. He was still supplying the Baileys with drugs, but he was also supplying the very people they themselves were selling on to. He was going straight to the dealers, and side-stepping the middle men. Peter would see it as a good move if *he* wasn't the middle man. Not only had the earn gone down considerably – a fucking irritation in itself – but the principle of it really offended Peter Bailey.

He had thought Alfie Clarke far too shrewd to think he could get away with something so fucking basic; he had not believed it at first because it was so fucking outrageous, and so blatantly a piss-take, he had been hard pushed to accept the truth of it. But then Daniel's words came back to him: *I've heard he's mugging us off. So are we going to take that?* It seemed his brother had been right about Alfie Clarke all along.

Delroy had brought him the news; he'd been as dumbfounded by it all as Peter was. Delroy, though, had noticed the gradual slide in the weekly take, and he had decided to investigate. It had not taken him long to find out the score, and then he had made it his business to pay a late-night visit to a certain Essex wide boy by the name of Robbie Jennings. Robbie had been only too pleased to tell Delroy the whole sorry tale.

Robbie Jennings was a young man, and a foolish one at that. He had not understood the seriousness of his offence, though Delroy had apparently disabused him of that notion. He would be drinking his food through a straw for the foreseeable future.

What to do now, though, was the real melon scratcher. Alfie Clarke had to be reprimanded, and he had to be reprimanded in such a way that people would remember it, and know that it was because he had pushed his luck with the Baileys. Delroy had suggested giving the job to Daniel, believing it would give Daniel a chance to prove his worth. Furthermore, knowing Daniel as they did, Alfie Clarke would get his comeuppance in a spectacular fashion.

Peter nodded to himself, his mind made up. Delroy was right. *This* was where Daniel really shone; he loved any reason to prove himself, and this would be perfect for him. He would make sure that he was in a public place when it all went down; after all, if Daniel went too far, there was no reason for them both to get a capture.

Chapter Twenty-Seven

'I can't believe we're off to Spain, Ria; it's like a dream come true. And just what I need before Tania's christening. All the arranging has worn me out! Shame the boys can't come out with us though. I was looking forward to all of us being together, like old times.'

Lena was packing Tania's case as she chattered and Ria was glad that she couldn't see her face. Peter had no intention of going away with Daniel, and he had said as much. They were still not right, and she knew from what Imelda had gleaned from Delroy that it was not going to get better any time soon. She lifted Tania up and hugged her; she was a dear little thing. 'I tell you what, Lena, we'll have a nice girly one, eh? *I'm* glad the boys aren't coming – we can just relax and do what we like without them. Let's face it, when they come all we ever do is cook or go out to bars so they can have their meetings; at least we can do what we want if we're on our own. Anyway, Peter wants me to look for a bigger villa, and we can do that in our sleep! I know exactly what I want – an older place with an orange grove, you know? Somewhere really beautiful with a bit of land, room for a pool, a real Spanish hacienda, with marble floors, big hardwood doors, shutters . . .'

Lena laughed at her friend's excitement; if she knew Ria she would already have a place picked out! She'd have been furnishing it in her mind for months. 'You are a case, Ria! How often are you out there? You've already got a villa, and it ain't exactly small, is it!'

Ria shrugged in annoyance; it irritated her that Lena never saw the big picture, but was happy to just jog along. 'It's an investment, Lena. Spain is already a big holiday destination – people are not content with a week in Bognor any more. They want guaranteed sunshine, and Spain is as cheap as chips once you get there. They pour your drink straight out of the bottle – no optics, no fucking weights and measures like here! Marbella is beautiful with the sea and the beaches. You should talk Daniel into buying a place. I tell you, Lena, you will make your money back on it. I love waking up to the sun, looking out at the sea while I'm eating my breakfast, and then walking into the town for a bit of lunch. It's what we have worked for, mate; for me it's my reward for all those years of child-rearing. I go out there and I relax completely.'

Lena closed Tania's case. She understood what Ria was saying, and she quite easily had the means to buy a villa out there if she wanted to. But she was still tortured by the fear that their lives could collapse around them at any moment. Her fears were in no way assuaged by the fact that Daniel and Peter seemed to be permanently at loggerheads these days.

No, Ria was an amazing woman, and she loved her dearly, but Lena knew that her expensive lifestyle wasn't for her; she would never be able to rest if she didn't have her nest egg. But she decided to be amenable to the idea – on the face of it at least. 'You're right, Ria, I should have a nose around for a little place. I think it would be lovely to have somewhere to take Tania for her holidays.'

Ria smiled. She really hoped that Lena *would* buy a place of her own – if ever anyone needed a bolt hole, she did.

Chapter Twenty-Eight

Alfie Clarke had a set routine these days. Every morning he put his little son into the passenger seat of his Mercedes, and together they visited his different businesses. He loved to show him off, loved people to remark on his boy, how handsome and strong he was already. Every accolade heaped on Alfie Junior was a compliment to him. Everyone talked about his devotion to the lad, and they were a fixture now in the urban landscape that Alfie ruled.

As he pulled up outside their regular café on Ilford High Street, he was feeling very happy. They had a drink and a snack here every day. He unbuckled his son and lifted him into his arms and, as he went to open the car door, he felt the first prickle of fear.

A dark-coloured car had pulled up beside him, and all his instincts told him that something was wrong, that there was a problem. He turned to look at whoever was driving the offending motor, and he saw Daniel Bailey grinning at him.

As Alfie finally understood what was happening, he tried to shield his son with his own body, but he knew in his heart that it was too late.

It was all over in minutes – Alfie Clarke and his little son were both dead. Daniel Bailey had pumped eight bullets into them.

Chapter Twenty-Nine

Peter Bailey was waiting for the tragic news about Alfie Clarke's demise at one of his favourite pubs in Dagenham. He was holding court with a group of friends, and enjoying a few beers when Delroy came into the bar with a face like thunder.

Leading Delroy outside to the car park, Peter looked at his son-in-law askance, and waited patiently for him to deliver the news.

'You're not going to believe this, Peter. *I* can't fucking believe it.'

Peter frowned. Assuming it had all gone wrong, he said quickly, 'Is Daniel OK? Has he been nicked or something?'

Delroy shook his head slowly. 'If only. The fucker did the deed all right, but he didn't only take Clarke out – he took his little boy out as well. The mad cunt killed them both. Shot the fuck out of them.'

Peter Bailey was silent. He knew his son-in-law was telling him the truth; Delroy wouldn't lie, and certainly not about something as serious as this. What on earth went on in Daniel's head? What the fuck was wrong with him? This would cause fucking murders – literally.

How could Daniel even *think* that what he had done would be remotely acceptable to the people in their world? He had to know that he had crossed a line, had to understand that this would be seen as an outrageous affront to everyone who knew them.

'I'll fucking *kill* him. I will fucking kill him myself.'

Delroy grabbed his father-in-law's arms and, as he tried to stop the man from jumping into his car and making a bad situation worse, he was reminded of just how strong he was. It was taking all his strength to stop Peter getting away from him.

'Listen to me, Peter! You can't go near him – not like this. We have to think this through, we have to box clever.'

Peter knew Delroy was making sense, and he willed himself to calm down, but his heart was pounding in his chest. He could not for the life of him understand what his brother had done.

'Daniel didn't only take Alfie and his little boy out, Peter. He also made it his business to take out both of the Menendez brothers, the dealers who were skimming us. He took them out in a pub on Brixton High Street in full view of the regular clientele. He made sure that everyone saw him. From what I've heard he was alone, though – none of his lads were with him, so that's something, I suppose. But fucking hell, Peter! He is one mad bastard.'

Peter was nodding his head, but he knew that they had to do some serious damage limitation, and do it fast. The Menendez brothers were nothing to worry about – they were both fucking accidents waiting to happen. They were going to get murdered eventually, it was just a case of when, where and by whom.

And Alfie Clarke wasn't exactly popular – no one he knew would be willing to right any wrongs for him, dead or alive. But his little lad was a different kettle of fish. It was a fucking nightmare. Even the Filth would feel honour-bound to solve this one. Once it hit the news, it would cause untold aggravation for everyone.

A shooting was newsworthy enough in itself, but a child being shot? Being part of what was, to all intents and purposes, a hit? That would be national news. It would be the first story before the bongs on *News at Ten*, make the front page of all the papers. And so it should – it was shocking. This would bring the Filth out in droves, there was no getting away from that. It would cost a small fortune to keep them out of it.

'This is fucking going to cause ructions, Delroy.'

Delroy shrugged. 'That, my man, is the under-statement of the fucking year.'

Chapter Thirty

Daniel Bailey knew *exactly* what he had caused, and he was glad. He'd felt that he had to make a fucking splash, and he had done just that. The Menendez brothers were gone, and no one would say a word about that so he was as safe as houses there. It was a genuine grievance that would be understood by everyone in their world; they were a pair of fucking wasters, who had believed that they could scam the very people who had been good enough to give them a fucking good earn in the first place. He shook his head at the utter front of some people.

As for Alfie Clarke, that fucker had only got what was coming to him and Daniel had been thrilled to be the one to finally give him his comeuppance. And he had no real care for Alfie Clarke's son; he was collateral damage, that's all. True, he could have waited for Alfie to put the child down, but he didn't have the patience to fart-arse about all day. He had known when he had pulled up beside the Merc that he was going to take the child out too. It was his way of letting everyone know that he was capable of literally *anything*.

He looked around his front room; it was too quiet

without little Tania careering all over the place. He looked fondly at her toys, packed neatly into a wicker basket. Lena had always been good like that, she had never let the kids take over the living room. She always said that once they were in bed, the toys were to be put away, and it was the grown-ups' time.

He hoped they were OK and that their flight had been on time. She was a nervous flier, his Lena. She was always convinced they were going to crash! He smiled at her foolishness; she was a real worrier, but that was part of her charm as far as he was concerned.

He went into the kitchen, and poured himself a large Scotch. The back door opened and he turned quickly, expecting his brother, but it was his mother.

'You filthy bastard.'

Daniel could feel the animosity emanating from his mother; she was looking at him as if he was a piece of dog shit she had just found on the bottom of her shoe.

'You are a wicked fecking man, Daniel. A murdering bastard. I wish I had never set eyes on you.'

Daniel let her have her say, knew from years of experience that it was pointless to interrupt her – the best way to deal with her was to let her vent her spleen.

'A fecking little child! An *infant*. Jaysus, Daniel, how could you? An innocent little child. Imagine if it was little Tania? And as for the poor child's mother! She must be off her fecking head with the grief.'

She was crying now, and Daniel made a suitably contrite face. 'Listen, Mum, I hold my hand up to taking Clarke out, but he was the one who used the kid as a shield. I couldn't believe it . . .'

Theresa Bailey stared at her youngest child, her Daniel, and she knew he was lying to her. He could lie to your face, this one – even as a child he'd told bold-faced lies always. She had laughed at him then, never dreaming that she was rearing a man who would one day be capable of a crime such as this.

She accepted a long time ago that both her sons had chosen to make their mark on the world through villainy, and she had known from the start that nothing she could have said or done would have made any difference to them. She had stood by them through it all, but this was something she could not let go; it was a step too far. She knew that Peter would not have been involved in it – this was wholly Daniel's doing. Turning from him, she left him without another word.

Daniel sipped his drink, and he felt sad. He hated that his mum was so upset, but she would get over it.

Chapter Thirty-One

'Are you winding me up, Delroy?' The disbelief in Daniel's voice was evident.

Delroy shook his head so hard that his dreadlocks seemed to take on a life of their own. Daniel should be well aware of how his actions would be viewed by the majority – how could he honestly believe that what he was guilty of could be overlooked? These weren't his usual bully-boy tactics, this had gone much further and he had stepped over the imaginary line. The Krays, the Richardsons, they understood how far you could go with the general populace. Wives and children were a no-no, in anyone's books.

'No, I'm not winding you up, Daniel. Peter has told me to tell you that he wants *nothing* more to do with you. In future, you are to get your share, and that's it. Over with, done. He is absolutely finished with you on any kind of personal level.'

Daniel was genuinely flabbergasted, and it showed; he honestly couldn't believe what he was hearing. He had always been the lairy one, the exhibitionist – it was his role. Peter had then been seen as the voice of reason, the calmer of the two – that was their strength as far as he was concerned. For fuck's sake, if it was left to his brother everything would be done so quietly no fucker would *know* their strengths, know what they were really capable of! Rumour was all well and good, but it proved nothing. For all his bravado, Daniel had always believed that his brother accepted his actions because they were the reason people were so fucking wary of them.

'That's bollocks! I did him a fucking favour, mate. I am not going to stand here and listen to this shite. Where is he?'

'Daniel, he is now as far away from you as he could possibly get. You have to accept, mate, you crossed a line. Not just with your brother, but with a lot of other people as well. You killed a little *kid* and, no matter how you try to put a spin on it, the fact is you fucking shot a man with his kid beside him in his motor.' Delroy was incredulous that he was having to spell this out.

Daniel was reeling from the shock. He looked at Delroy intently, as if waiting for him to deliver the punch line to a joke that he didn't understand.

Delroy shook his head once more. 'It was wrong, Daniel. As always, you fucking had to go too far.'

Daniel nodded then, unable to speak for a moment, his brain whirling, and his anger rising. 'So where's he gone then? Where's he fucked off to?'

Daniel was suddenly struck by fear. He had genuinely believed that, no matter what he did, his brother would stand by his side, as he always had done. Even after the

Lenny Jones incident, Peter had come around soon enough.

'Listen, Daniel, it's all over with him. He's fucking livid, he had to get away – otherwise, I think you would have had real trouble on your hands.'

'So he's fucked off, has he? Left me on me tod. The treacherous cunt. Well, Delroy, I got to admit, I never saw this coming.'

Delroy looked at Daniel and he could almost feel pity for him. The realisation that his brother had really turned his back on him finally appeared to be sinking in. He had gone too far; his actions were not going to be tolerated this time. He was snorting coke like it was going out of fashion and, for a man who was seriously paranoid anyway, that was never going to end well. He had wanted to make his brother see that he was prepared to do anything he felt necessary to make them be seen as invincible, show him that he was without conscience where retribution was concerned. Only he had really fucked up this time.

Delroy shook his head. How could Daniel have believed that *anyone* in their world would agree with his actions? It was as if he lived on another planet to the rest of the criminal underworld. As Peter Bailey had cut his ties with this man, it could have been as good as a death sentence, but Peter had put out the word that his brother was not to be challenged. Delroy believed, personally, that that edict had more to do with their mother than brotherly love.

Delroy sighed in annoyance. 'He's on his way to Spain, Daniel. He can't be around you now, surely even you can see that? You wiped out a man's child. All your bollocks about him using the child as a shield! That's *shite*. You should never have been anywhere near that kid with a fucking firearm. What fucking planet are you on? You shot a baby, Daniel – he couldn't even talk. It wasn't like he was going to pick you out of a line-up, was it?'

Daniel suddenly saw with stunning clarity that this was one outrage too many. He would never admit it, but a tiny thread of shame was there, at the back of his mind. After he had pulled the trigger a part of him had known that he was in the wrong, but it was far too late. Perhaps he was just continually six seconds behind everyone else – it seemed he never saw the big picture till it was too late. Now his brother's reaction would be the yardstick for every other fucker in his orbit. And if his own brother was going on the trot, where did that leave him?

Delroy could see utter dismay cross Daniel's face as he realised the enormity of what he had caused. It was as if a light bulb went on.

'So you're his fucking errand boy now, are you? He sent you to fucking give me a message, did he? He ain't got the fucking guts to come himself, see me face to face.'

Daniel's temper clearly wasn't abating and Delroy couldn't help but feel wary, knowing what he was capable of. At least he had good back-up with him – he had made fucking sure of that much.

'He didn't come, Daniel, because I don't think he could trust himself not to fucking take you out once and for all. You being his brother is all that has kept him from fucking removing you permanently. Honestly, Daniel, if you weren't blood, you would be dead now. And it's not just Peter – there are plenty who see what you did as a fucking diabolical liberty.'

Daniel smiled coldly, keeping a lid on his emotions. 'Spain, you say?'

Delroy nodded. 'Yeah, and he told me to tell you that he won't say a word to Lena, not because of you, but because he respects her. But she will find out, Daniel, you know that. You might get a swerve because Peter hasn't taken it on himself to fucking reprimand you over your fucking stupidity, but everyone knows that's because you're brothers, and he loves you. But if you fuck up in future, he will not raise a hand to defend you. You can look after yourself from now on, mate. He thinks you're a fucking liability, a fucking scumbag. You are not to approach him or ring him – you are not to ever share the same space as him. You're out, Daniel, you're on your own.'

Daniel Bailey's arrogance came racing to the fore, his sorrow at his actions long gone. This was personal now, this was a piss-take. Who the fuck did Peter think he was? Laughing, he said mockingly, in an upper-class accent, 'Well, I'm shocked and appalled, old chap!' Pushing his finger into Delroy's face, he said viciously, 'I took that cunt out because he needed to be fucking taught a lesson. I showed everyone that we were serious, that we would not be made fucking cunts of. If you lot can't see that then you're fools. You're fucking weak. You don't get where we got by being fucking nice to people. All we've done over the years, and you're vilifying *me* over a fucking shooting?'

Delroy was bored now. Daniel Bailey was a lunatic, a fucking nutcase. Any dialogue with him was utterly pointless.

'It wasn't the shooting, Daniel, it was *who* you fucking shot. You murdered a kid. Now every Old Bill in the Smoke is gunning for you. Even those on the take won't fucking lift a finger. You stepped over a line and you single-handedly fucked it up for everyone.'

Daniel didn't say anything for long moments, then, shrugging, he said gaily, as if he didn't have a care in the world, 'Well, do you know what? Fuck him, and fuck you. I don't need Peter. I don't need anyone, mate. And you can tell him that from me.'

Delroy laughed sarcastically. 'Oh, don't worry, Daniel, I will. And before I go, word of advice from someone who once thought a lot of you as a man and as family. Get off the fucking coke, Daniel, you ain't got the temperament for it. You're enough of a fucking headcase without it. Everyone knows you're a cokehead, and that little child's death happened because you think snorting gives you the edge. Coke is a mug's game; you use it to sober up on a night out, no more and no less. So think on that.'

Chapter Thirty-Two

'I wonder why Peter's coming out and not Daniel. Did he say why, Ria?'

Ria was heart-sorry for her friend; Lena had no idea just how serious the situation had become, and she was not going to be the one to tell her. She knew that Lena had guessed that something grim and serious had occurred between her husband and his brother but, being Lena, she wouldn't dig for an answer. Ria wondered what she saw in Daniel Bailey to inspire such unstinting loyalty; he must have something going for him, because Lena was still as besotted with him now as she was when they first met. But then Daniel was the same – he worshipped her.

'I expect Daniel's working as usual.' Lena smiled tightly.

Ria shrugged lightly. 'I don't know; Peter never said much to be honest.'

Tania was lying on a sunbed in the shade of a large lemon tree. Watching her mummy and her auntie closely, she picked up on the underlying tension between the two women. She felt a tiny shiver of anxiety. She got up, went to her mother and, climbing on to her lap, she snuggled into the warmth and safety of her body. She was suddenly frightened again, but what of, she didn't know. She felt her mother's arms tighten around her, but instead of that making her feel better, it worried her. She understood somehow that her mother was trying to gain comfort from her, not the other way round.

It was a hot day. The sky was a bright blue, without a cloud in sight, and the only noise was the high-pitched whirring from the cicadas. Even so, Lena felt a chill inside her. Something was very wrong, but she was determined to stay out of it. Experience had taught her that ignorance was bliss. And with the christening coming up, surely everything would be back to rights? 'I'll be glad to get this baptism over, Ria! It's taken long enough to find a date. I'm so pleased that you and Peter will be Tania's godparents, like you are to the boys. I hope it all goes well.'

Ria smiled tightly. She knew that her husband would have to be worked on; he had to go no matter what had happened – she owed Lena that much.

Chapter Thirty-Three

'It's my Daniel, he wants to talk to you, Peter.'

Ria watched warily as Lena passed the phone to Peter, and sighed heavily as she saw the distress on his face. Ria knew her husband didn't want to speak to him, but Daniel had used Lena, his wife, as the go-between, knowing that Peter would never have told Lena the truth of the situation. She hated that Daniel could be so sneaky, even though she had always known he was a fucking Judas deep down.

'Come on, Lena, I can see a business call coming on. Let's go outside and have a drink on the patio.'

Peter waited until the women were gone before he put the phone to his ear. 'You know my thoughts; Delroy has relayed them to you. I have nothing else to say to you. You're dead to me, Daniel.'

Replacing the receiver gently, Peter felt as though the great burden of Daniel Bailey had been lifted from his shoulders.

Chapter Thirty-Four

Lena felt sick with apprehension. She had waited so long for Tania's christening day to arrive, and now she was wondering if it was even going to happen. She'd wanted it to be the family occasion it deserved to be, but now, in all honesty, she just wanted it over with.

Peter and Daniel's work had initially been the cause of its delay, and she had accepted that as she always did. She wondered at times like this if she was *too* bloody accepting, but she had never *wanted* to know too much about her husband's work life. That would mean she might actually have to admit to what he was capable of. She already had more than an inkling – she didn't need it thrown in her face. Daniel certainly believed that she was an innocent where he was concerned, and that suited them both. She would stand by his side no matter what. That was the main reason she avoided the truth because, no matter how bad it might be, she could *never* find it in her to berate him or walk away from him.

There was clearly trouble between the brothers right now, and she didn't want to know the basis of it all. She had weathered this kind of thing before, many times. But, deep down, she feared this time was different.

Daniel had obviously caused some really serious aggravation. Peter and Ria had not crossed their front door for weeks, Theresa was tight-lipped and didn't have a decent word to throw at her youngest son, and the tension was getting too much for Lena. The boys could sense it too and she suspected the older two at least probably knew more than she did. She hated it when there was any kind of discord, and she could feel the atmosphere all around her like a heavy weight, draining all her strength.

Ria sounded like a bundle of nerves when she called her, and Imelda, who was ringing her regularly, was the same. She was close to Imelda, and she loved Ria – she loved them all – but she would always put her husband first. Before anyone, except her little Tania, but that was natural. Tania was her baby, her last born, her heart.

Ria, Theresa, and even young Imelda would understand that; they were cut from the same cloth, even though like her they would never admit it out loud. To love men like the Baileys, to be a part of the Life, you really had no other option.

Everyone had labelled her weak, a fool, because she had never ever involved herself in the daily grind. But to Lena's mind it had made her much stronger because, when you were tied to a man like Daniel Bailey, the less you knew the better for all concerned. Lena knew, from experience, that the truth could be a very dangerous thing. In the Life the truth didn't set you free, the truth just hurt you. It just made you reassess your morals, boundaries and guidelines; it made you rework them, so that you could eventually condone literally *anything*.

All she wanted now was for her daughter's baptism to go well, and for her husband and his family to find some kind of common ground, and come together again. She knew that it was an important day in more ways than one. It was the only chance to get her husband and his brother in the same room, and that was all she wanted.

Chapter Thirty-Five

'I'm telling you now, Peter, we are the godparents, and you will not fucking boycott that child's baptism. I don't give a flying fuck about yours and Daniel's big drama, all right? I promised we would be there, and we will. The whole family.'

Peter Bailey was genuinely astonished at his wife's vehemence, considering she knew the score. She wasn't like Lena, a fucking moron; his Ria made a point of knowing everything, that was Ria's way.

'Are you having a fucking mad half hour, woman? You know the score, you fucking coated me over it! Gave me grief, accused me of not fucking having my eye on the ball. Telling me I should have stopped Daniel going after Alfie and his little boy. Now you're telling me I have to be the godfather of little Tania, because I promised when she was born? Before her father fucked up everything around him?'

Ria was staring at him angrily. 'You're going, and that is the end of it.'

'Oh no, I ain't. Daniel can hang as he grows. I've washed my hands of him.'

Ria snorted in derision. 'Oh, stop it, you tart! This is

for *Lena*, and her child. You promised you would be the godfather, and you *will*, Peter. I swear to Christ Himself you will do it – you can't fucking renege on something like that, no matter what. This is about *religion*, Peter, about family. Not about fucking skulduggery. Lena asked you and you agreed. You can't fucking back out now – not if you ever want to be welcome in this fucking house anyway! I don't ask for much, boy, but when I do actually ask you for something, you know I won't take no for an answer. Whatever Daniel's done – and I know what a fucking looney he is – he's still your brother, and Tania is still your niece.'

She left the room then, slamming the door noisily behind her. She knew how to make a dramatic exit, she was the world's expert in them when the fancy took her. In fairness to her, these were very rare occurrences, but all the same, they were a warning as well. Ria was feisty; she could cause a fight in an empty house when she wanted to. Every now and then she was known to put her foot down, and once she did that, there was no arguing with her. As Peter had often got his way over the years – without a whisper from her – when she *did* force the issue, he generally gave her whatever she wanted. But he was not about to humour her this time.

Daniel had gone too far: he had nearly ruined everything for them. It was solely Peter's damage limitation that had kept not only his brother's death from occurring, but also kept his own place as the head of the Bailey clan. It was only *his* fucking diplomatic skills – and he had really had to dig deep for them – along with his own obvious outrage at his brother's actions that had stopped what could have been an international incident. He had put the word out that he would deal with Daniel himself, and that anyone else who felt the urge to chastise his brother would eventually have to answer to him personally. That wouldn't be a good thing for anyone concerned; after all, whatever Daniel was, he was still Peter's brother.

Sending Delroy to tell Daniel he wanted nothing more to do with him had been the hardest thing he had ever had to do. Delroy passed on Daniel's response – in detail – but Peter knew that was just a front. Daniel would be more devastated by Peter's anger and disappointment than anyone else's.

Peter blamed a lot of this on the fact that his brother was on the old Persian rugs. Daniel taking drugs was a fucking anomaly in itself, as he had always hated them. Daniel was a drinker – he liked a few bevvies, end of. Now it seemed he was the fucking coke meister. He had only recently understood just how religiously Daniel had embraced the fucking snort. He had a line himself occasionally – they all did. It sobered you up, countermanded the drink, it allowed you to tear the arse out of the night. But for someone like his brother, a paranoid fuck at the best of times, it just exacerbated his natural inclinations, and his brother's natural inclinations were always fucking violent.

He could hear Ria and his mother in the kitchen, and he wished he could, just once, wave a magic wand and strike the pair of them dumb.

Five minutes later, his mother and his wife were standing in front of him, demanding that he keep his promise.

Theresa looked into his eyes and said quietly, 'He needs this, Peter, and you know that as well as I do. He is a fecking idiot, but he is still your brother. Nothing you do or say can ever change that.'

He didn't answer her; she had always insisted that they kept together, that they were closer than close. He *knew* that.

She touched his arm gently, and he put his large hand over hers. Looking into his eyes, she said forcefully, 'You *have* to be there, you *have* to show some kind of solidarity. His sons will need to know that they are still part of the family – for the future. You're as arrogant as he is in your own way. But you and I know that all this is killing him. He knows he did wrong. Wipe your mouth and stand godfather, and remember that whatever he is and whatever he's done, he is still your little brother, and he is still my youngest son, and together you will always be stronger than anyone around you. He needs you to pull him back, rein him in, tell him the truth. I'm not asking you to take him back into the fold, I'm asking you to remember that Daniel *needs* you beside him. No matter how we feel about him and his actions, he is still our flesh and blood. He can't even contemplate a life without you beside him – without you somewhere in his world he will wilt. I will not let you do that to him. I have stood beside you both, no matter what. I know you have more than a few bodies on your conscience, but I accept that like I accept Daniel. You know I never ask either of you boys for anything, but I am asking you now, Peter – give Daniel a fecking lifeline, tell him to sort himself out. Only *you* can tell him that. You're the only person he has ever listened to.'

Peter sighed. His mother *would* stand by her boys no matter what and, as much as her words annoyed him, he knew she was right. Daniel would only listen to him now. Daniel would be so distraught about their estrangement that he would gladly take any criticism from Peter if he thought it would get things back to normal.

So he would go to the child's baptism; his mother was right – they had to be seen to be back on track, even if, in reality, they were not. But Daniel had to play his part – admit that he was wrong and change his ways. Daniel had consistently refused to work as a team, never accepting that Peter was the person people wanted to deal with, who had the creds needed. Daniel had always gone out of his way to prove a point, push his luck, force an issue, settle a score.

His mother was asking the impossible. She was as disgusted with Daniel as he was himself but she was still pleading that he give his brother – a child killer –

another chance. She was their mum, and as a mum she was trying to build a bridge between them. Peter wasn't sure that Isambard Kingdom Brunel could build a fucking bridge big enough to span their differences.

Daniel's murder of that little child was something that no one would ever forget, and very few people – including himself – would ever forgive.

Chapter Thirty-Six

The church was packed out with people and Lena looked at her little daughter proudly. She looked gorgeous. The christening gown was old now – it had been used by each of them – but it was all the more important because of that. Theresa had handsewn it all those years ago, and it made her proud to know that it was still in use.

As she passed her daughter gently to her mother-in-law, Lena smiled. 'She is so like you, Theresa, it's uncanny, especially when she frowns! I'm having Theresa as her middle name, in honour of you and all you mean to us. It was your mother's name as well, wasn't it?'

Theresa looked at her granddaughter, and she nodded, touched. 'It was, but I hope this Theresa has more luck in her life than we have had. Doesn't make the same mistakes. When you're young, you never see the pitfalls, or the foolishness of your actions, do you? You make people into what you *want* them to be and, then, when they break your heart, you have to find the strength to carry on. I think you know that as well as I do, Lena.'

Lena understood her mother-in-law was trying to warn her about Daniel and what had happened between him and Peter, but this was not the time or place. Lena had rewritten the commandments so many times. She had made allowances for her husband over and over again; she had convinced herself that as a Catholic and a wife she was honour-bound to stand by her husband no matter what. She had spent so much time at Mass, praying for his salvation, along with her own, but the bottom line was that she knew she would actually walk away from everyone if that meant it would keep her husband safe. Even after all these years, Theresa *still* didn't understand that she would never, *ever* betray Daniel.

Smiling gently, she said complacently, 'I think this little one will be all right, Theresa; she has us. I know you will always look out for her – they all will.'

Theresa smiled, but Lena could tell she was irritated. She just didn't seem to understand that there were certain things that once voiced out loud could never be taken back. Look at poor Imelda: she ferreted out everything she could about Delroy even when she knew that most of it would not be good. As a result, Imelda, God love her, was the most unhappy person Lena knew.

In the Life, knowledge wasn't power. In the Life, knowledge was no more than added aggravation.

She saw the priest beckoning to her, and she felt a second's shame at her distraction. She was in the house of God for her daughter's baptism, and she was thinking all these terrible things. Plastering a smile on to her face, she walked to the altar, and she began to pray, asking His forgiveness, and asking Him to make sure the rest of the day went off without a hitch.

Chapter Thirty-Seven

Peter Bailey had renounced the devil, done all he had been asked, and was now watching his brother's reaction to his daughter's screams of distress as the holy water was poured over her head.

Tania was not impressed in the least – that much was obvious. As Peter saw his brother scoop the child into his arms and try his hardest to placate her, he wondered once more at a man who was such a mass of contradictions. Daniel appeared genuinely worried about his daughter's distress, and he was jiggling her up and down in an effort to calm her. It was only when Lena took her from him, and nestled the child into her shoulder, that she quietened down.

Peter closed his eyes, and allowed himself to become immersed in the Mass. He knew that it was the only way he could ignore his brother. He didn't like this priest – he was a ponce. Father Mahoney always took the weddings, the christenings and the burials – he knew the earners. There was always a drink for the priest after those, unlike after the daily Masses. Peter knew his mother revered Father Mahoney, as all the women did; he made a fuss of them, and they loved it. Even his Ria was not averse to his charms. He flirted with the females in the congregation, and they loved it, lapped it up.

He repeated the Mass without thinking. 'We lift them up to the Lord.'

He felt his brother come to stand beside him; he knew it was him before he even heard him repeat the Mass with him, something that they had done all their lives.

They had often gone to the six o'clock Mass with their mum, before they went to school. She still went to early Mass most days and, years ago, her two boys had stood beside her, both of them repeating the liturgy without a thought. It was something they had always listened to, was already a part of them. Both of them scrubbed till they shone, so young they didn't question any of it. Theresa had held their hands in hers as if her life depended on it, sure in the knowledge that God was looking out for them. They didn't know then that their mum was looked down on because she had them both – one black and one white – and no husband to boot. They had not known then that their mum had had to be brave to walk into the church with her head held high, and her two little boys dressed like princes, and that she had to run the gauntlet of public opinion every time. That she was looked at with disgust, and treated with disdain. They had only realised that much later, and she had told them that she did not give a flying fuck about a crowd of dried-up old fucking bitches who looked down their noses at her, and that she was proud of her boys. She said she knew that if God Himself had seen fit to send them to her, she was not going to let a few old bags, who had never had a real fucking shag in their lives, dictate to her how she should act in public. Christ Himself was fatherless, Joseph was His foster father, for fuck's sake, and poor Mary was one of the first unmarried mothers!

Peter kept his eyes closed, but he was smiling as he remembered her anger. He had understood a lot sooner than she realised that his colour was the main bone of contention with the women around them. She had been abandoned by her family because of him, and he loved her for keeping him and loving him like she had.

Peter turned his attention back to the Mass, aware that they were being watched; everyone around them was more interested in *them* than the actual baptism. His appearance had guaranteed a lot of the guests turning up – not for Daniel, but because they wanted to keep in with Peter.

His mum had been right; as bad as Daniel was, this was about more than the two of them. It was about Lena, and the lads, little Tania, and his own Imelda too. It was a real family affair and Ria was over the moon; she loved little Tania dearly.

Peter looked at his own daughter, and her swollen belly. He would be back in this church soon, welcoming his first grandchild into the Catholic faith. He hoped his Imelda calmed herself down sooner rather than later; he could already feel Delroy's irritation towards her and, in all honesty, he could understand the man's feelings. Delroy had more than proved his loyalty and Peter had slowly changed his tune about his son-in-law. Now he saw him as a man he could trust. In fact, he saw a lot of himself in Delroy. And Imelda was far too insecure for a man like him. His Ria, who he worshipped, had always had the sense to turn a blind eye when necessary, she knew he would always come home to her. But his Imelda was so aggressive and so insistent about working in the business, all to keep an eye on her husband.

Peter sighed. The Mass was ending at last. He just wanted it all over now.

Chapter Thirty-Eight

As the family filed out of the church after the ceremony, Daniel caught up with his brother. 'I appreciate you coming, Peter, I know you didn't want to.' He was smiling as he said it.

Peter didn't answer him, letting the anger at his brother's stupidity wash over him. Daniel clearly believed that his attendance today meant they were once again back on track. He still thought that he could do whatever he wanted and that, if he acted contrite, Peter would welcome him back with open arms.

Peter Bailey stared into his brother's face, and he saw the handsome man he had loved, the blue eyes so like their mother's, the genuine affection for Peter in them, and the total lack of comprehension at the situation they were in.

'I came for Mum, Lena and Ria. *You* don't ever make any kind of contact with me again, Daniel. You baptised *your* baby today all the time knowing you fucking murdered a child. I know, Daniel, that you planned that. You knew you were going to kill that little boy, you knew he was the apple of his father's eye, you *wanted* Alfie to know his boy would die with him. That's you

153

all over, Daniel. You're a vicious, wicked cunt. Now, leave me *alone*. I can't look at you without seeing that little child, bloodied and dying and innocent. You get off the coke, and you sort your fucking self out, but you don't come near me, you hear?'

Chapter Thirty-Nine

Theresa was drunk as a lord, and she knew that it was the only way she could get through this day. Peter and Daniel, her boys, her *babies*, were now further apart than ever.

She could see her Daniel's distress. She hated what Daniel had done, but in her drunken haze she couldn't help blaming Peter. *He* should have monitored his brother, *he* should have looked after him. How could he not have known that Daniel was a few sandwiches short of the proverbial picnic?

She sipped her whisky, watching as Ria and Lena fussed over little Tania, and her grandsons laughed and joked with each other. At least *they* were still getting along. But what would the fallout from all this be? What would be the future of the Baileys? She sighed, wondering how the feck her sons had come to this, standing as far away from each other as possible, yet more aware of each other than either of them would ever care to admit.

Chapter Forty

Lena was lying in bed with her daughter, but she was unable to sleep. She didn't know where Daniel was. Today had just proven how drastically wrong the situation between him and his brother was. They'd all tried to act like nothing was amiss, but the tension had been impossible to ignore.

She hugged Tania, felt the warmth of her child's fragile body and knew that, no matter what happened in the future, she had to protect her little girl. She had to make sure she never knew the truth of her family's lives. Lena was her daughter's only real cushion against the Life, and she was more determined than ever that Tania would never have to be a part of it in any way. She was an innocent, and Lena would move heaven and earth if necessary to make sure she stayed that way. As her mother, it was all she could do. After all, if she didn't protect Tania from the Life, who would?

Book Two

You lost the plot again, where you are now ain't clear
It's a misty morning memory, the road that took you
here

Alabama 3, 'You Don't Dance To Techno Anymore'
Album: *Exile on Coldharbour Lane*, 1997

Shoot me up
Every damn day with a hypo full of love

Alabama 3, 'Hypo Full Of Love'
Album: *Exile on Coldharbour Lane*, 1997

We can't wait, can't hesitate, they're picking the
padlocks at the gate
Smell the violence, blind suckers on the side of silence
Are smiling, giving the eye

Alabama 3, 'The Night We Nearly Got Busted'
Album: *Exile on Coldharbour Lane*, 1997

Book Two

Chapter Forty-One

1987

Father Brendan Murphy watched warily as Lena Bailey crept into the church with her husband. She had the grace to be ashamed even though she was too loyal to admit to anything that might show her husband in a bad light. She deliberately overlooked all the talk about him. In a way, he admired her for it; she took the Catholic sacrament of marriage seriously, and he had to give her credit for that. But knowing what he did about this man meant he loathed being in his company. He knew he had no choice about this meeting, but that didn't mean he was looking forward to it. He was, Christ forgive him his sin, dreading it.

Daniel Bailey was a hard man – that was common knowledge – but it cut no ice with him. Father Murphy had been a boxer in his day, and seen his fair share of hard men. He had grown up in Dublin, the son of a bare-knuckle fighter, a drunkard and one of the hardest men he had ever come across. Michael Murphy had been a legend in his own lifetime; if only he had had the brain capacity to use the money he had earned sensibly, he could have been a man of means. Instead, he had

159

squandered his hard-earned cash in the nearest pubs, buying drinks for the hangers-on, slipping money to anyone with a hard-luck story.

His mother, God love her and keep her – Father Murphy blessed himself then, as he always did when he thought of her – had been drawn to an early grave trying to raise eight children. Along with feeding them and cleaning for them on a pittance, she had worked tirelessly to make sure that they were good Catholics and decent men and women. He had entered the priesthood, having known from an early age that it would eventually become his calling, but he had returned home and looked after his mother and sisters after his father's untimely death. The drink had taken him quickly in the end, and it had been a relief to them all.

His older brothers had gone to America, never to be heard of again, his younger brother was doing life for murder, and his sisters were all married with families – and problems – of their own. Good women, but laden down by the men they had settled for, and wondering why they had not listened to their mother instead of taking the first men who had shown any interest in them.

He knew the cut of Daniel Bailey all right and, even though the man worshipped in his church, knelt for Communion at his feet, and made his confession regularly, he knew he was a fraud, a liar and, worst of all, a hypocrite. Daniel Bailey was the worst kind of liar because his lies were rooted in fact, and he used that to keep a decent woman beside him, even though, these days, so the rumours went, his own children were not so easily fooled.

Father Murphy was a man of many sides. He had learned years ago that there were plenty of sinners inside the church itself, from the vicious gossips, who stood cleaning the altar while destroying someone's reputation, to the drunks, the gamblers and the wife-beaters, who confessed their sins, and who he knew would be back within the month, confessing the same sins again. He knew the women who were having affairs, knew the young ones who were promiscuous, or were taking drugs. He tried his best to be a good priest, a good man, not to be too judgemental.

But Daniel Bailey made his skin literally crawl. He had joined the parish six years ago, replacing Father Mahoney, who had been moved elsewhere – he never knew exactly why. Not long after, Daniel Bailey had come to him, and confessed to the murders of a man and his child, and Father Murphy had never been able to forgive him. He had done his job, had given him a good act of contrition; after all, as he was forever reminding himself, he was only the go-between, the emissary of God on this earth. It was not his job to judge anyone, but he couldn't help how he felt.

Daniel, he knew, only went to confession to appease his wife, not because he ever felt any kind of remorse for his actions, and Brendan Murphy the man, not the priest, had known that from the off. Daniel Bailey looked at him with what bordered on defiance at times, knowing that they shared a terrible secret – a secret that he could never reveal. It felt as if Daniel believed he had something over Father Murphy; he acted as if they were in league somehow, as if his confession had given Bailey the upper hand in their relationship and, in many ways, it had done just that. Because Daniel Bailey had known instinctively that his confession had not only shocked Father Murphy, but had also disgusted him to his very core.

As a priest, he was not supposed to let anything he heard in the confessional colour his relationship with his flock and, until Daniel Bailey's bombshell, he had never felt this kind of repugnance for a parishioner in his life. His own brother had once confessed his sin of murder to him, and he had been genuinely sorry for his actions, had understood the enormity of what he had done. He had taken a man's life in a bar fight – drunk and belligerent, he had beaten a man to death, hit him so hard the man had never even regained consciousness. A terrible tragedy for all concerned, and he was serving a life sentence for it.

But this man came to him regularly, and confessed to all sorts of violent behaviour, sharing his hatred in the privacy of the confessional, and Brendan Murphy knew that he *enjoyed* telling him. This was East London, and he had heard his fair share of villains' confessions over the years. He wasn't a man who dwelt on people's situations, he was only there to hear them confess, and assure them that, as long as they were truly sorry, they would be forgiven. Bailey, though, saw it as some kind of game, as a way to demean him, and everything that he believed in, and thereby assert his own authority over him. Daniel Bailey was a bully of the worst kind, because he enjoyed it.

Lena was a regular at early morning Mass; she made sure the boys attended at least once a week, and she met up with Ria Bailey, Peter's wife, along with Peter himself, and their own children.

Now Peter Bailey, Father Murphy had a lot of time for, which was strange inasmuch as he knew he was just as big a villain as his brother. Peter Bailey was not a man to cross unless you were on a death wish of some sort, but, for all that, he was a different entity entirely from his brother. Whatever Peter Bailey might be, he wasn't a hypocrite.

Father Murphy knelt before the cross of Christ for fifteen minutes, knowing that Daniel would not dare to interrupt him at prayer, and enjoying the fact that keeping him waiting was making him angry.

Standing slowly, he blessed himself once more and, forcing a smile on his face, he turned to Lena and said as brightly as he could, 'Sure, Lena, I forgot you were coming.'

Daniel Bailey watched as his wife practically bowed in reverence to the priest, and he had to fight the urge to punch him as hard as he could in the face. He knew this man drank with Peter, visited his brother's house regularly, and worked with him closely for charities. Peter had given the money needed for a boxing club and for a trip to Lourdes for the poorer parishioners, had seen to it that the people who couldn't afford it had been able to go and pray to God to ease their suffering. All bollocks, as far as Daniel was concerned. His brother did it for personal gain, no other reason. Saint fucking Peter, his mother's golden boy, and all-round fucking good guy. When *he* gave money for the various causes – and he gave serious money – no one said a fucking word about it! Except Tania's school that is – the nuns there knew which side their bread was buttered on. Tania had been Mary in the Nativity play, he had made sure of that.

But this ponce here looked down on him. At least Daniel's presence unsettled him, that was something. Unlike Lena, he wasn't enamoured of the Church – he saw it as another fucking business, a scam. But his mother and his wife saw it as a way of life, and he understood that he had to swallow because of that. He knew how to play the game, and at least this man afforded him some pleasure inasmuch as he got the satisfaction of taunting him with his presence.

He held his hand out and, smiling, he said pleasantly, 'Good day to you, Father; we are so looking forward to our little Tania's Communion.'

Father Murphy shook the man's hand, and prayed that this meeting would be over quickly.

Lena beamed with happiness; she loved to see her

husband in the church, it helped calm the fears she had for his eternal soul. Father Murphy understood her feelings, she was convinced of that. She knew that he was a man who saw a lot more than he let on, and was willing to go the extra mile for the people in his care. He was a man not only of good values, but also of discretion. He heard her Daniel's confession regularly, and knowing that helped her sleep at night.

Chapter Forty-Two

'Tell me you're fucking joking, will you!'

Davey Bailey shrugged. At twenty-three, he was now a big man and, like his brothers, he was firmly entrenched in the family businesses. 'I'm not joking. For fuck's sake, Danny, you of all people must have seen it coming?'

Daniel Bailey Junior sat down heavily, jarring his spine with the action. He looked around the office as if he was trying to find an escape route.

'He's a fucking nutcase, Danny, I was fucking gobsmacked. Couldn't believe what I was witnessing.'

Danny dropped his head into his hands and groaned theatrically. 'I saw it coming all right, I just didn't think he would fucking actually do it – he knows how we feel about it.'

Davey lit a cigarette and, pulling on it deeply, he said quietly, 'Like what we think means anything to him. He battered the fuck out of him. Derek Thomas is now fighting for his life in hospital. All over three grand! Talk about going over the top. I'm fucking sick of it, Danny. He's out of control again. He acts like he's in the right, and he ain't.'

Danny didn't answer his brother. He knew *exactly* what was eating at his father; he had been expecting something like this, even though they were all on a good fucking wedge. Daniel Bailey Senior, his father, was still regarded with suspicion by everyone around them and, even though he had tried to regain the ground he had lost over the Clarke debacle, it had never really been an option without Peter's support. It was a miracle he had not had his collar felt for it, a miracle that Danny suspected had a lot to do with his Uncle Peter's desire to protect the family business, and the man's knack for finding the people best placed to do him favours, or to smooth his paths, depending on what he required, and who was available for a fee. His father could never get his head round the fact that friendly negotiations and goodwill were far more lucrative in the end than brute force or intimidation could ever be.

Peter Bailey, on the other hand, had always understood that. Consequently, he had branched out into all sorts of different spheres, and he had also managed, in his own inimitable way, not only to muscle in on other people's earns, but ensure that the person he went into partnership with actually earned *more*. Therefore, the people concerned were understandably happy with the new arrangements. Unlike his father, who just took and, in the process, managed to make even more enemies than he already had. And his enemies, as the Bible would say, were fucking legion.

His father was a taker, and that was what was causing

so much trouble. Danny had spent a lot of time building up *his* family's side of the business. He had painstakingly attempted to make sure that his brothers, as well as himself, were seen as fair, were seen as trustworthy; he treated people with respect, made sure his brothers did too. He was the antithesis of his father in that respect, though his father's presence in the background made sure the people they dealt with toed the fucking line.

He had learned from his Uncle Peter the wisdom of making people feel they were appreciated, and that it was easier when you were already at the top of your game to make friends of the new Faces, of the up-and-coming generation, that it was much more sensible to use the talents of the people who worked for or with you, than it was to make them into enemies.

His father had seemed to be finally understanding that as well, had seemed to be pleased at the way they were now treated as a family unit by their peers. His father had four huge sons; they were not little kids any more and were working hard to portray an image of familial solidarity – they dealt with their cousins on an almost daily basis after all. Now, Daniel Bailey Senior had, in one afternoon, destroyed it – he had once more shown himself as nothing more than a common thug.

He had ruined his sons' graft for a poxy three grand, had sacrificed them because he had heard that his brother was opening another nightclub, and he hated that he wasn't a part of it, or of anything that would require his active involvement.

'Did he use his fists, or a weapon?'

Davey looked into Danny's eyes, and the brothers were both so disheartened and so angry that it was like looking into a mirror. 'Both. He started out pounding him, then he picked up a fucking spanner that was lying on his desk. He finished him with that, all the time screaming and cursing. It was a fucking embarrassment.'

Danny groaned again. 'Were there many people in the betting shop?'

Davey sighed. 'Ten, eight, I wasn't taking the fucking register, was I? Enough to make sure it gets talked about anyway. Oh, and on the way out of there, he emptied the tills like a fucking schoolboy robber – stuffing the money into his pockets. I tell you, Dan, he's a waste of time. He has no fucking care for how that looks to people, he really believes that it all makes him look big or something. He's such a cunt . . .'

Danny stood up then and, taking a deep breath, he said seriously and against his better judgement, 'Look, Davey, whatever he is, he is still our father, and we have to be seen to be on the same page as him, no matter what. We can say what we like to each other, but outside the family we say *nothing*, do you hear me? That's the worst kind of betrayal – you know that as well as I do.'

Davey sighed and said sarcastically, 'I know that, bruv, but in reality, it's getting harder and fucking harder.'

Davey stood before him, running his enormous hands through his thick hair, and Danny saw how big he was, how powerful he had become; they were both the image of their father. They all had the Irish blue eyes, inherited from their grandmother, and passed down from generations long gone.

Danny also knew that it was getting more difficult to control his brothers; they were men now, and they had their own thoughts and opinions, which they were entitled to express. Sooner rather than later their father was going to have to accept that as a fact of life. Danny had a modicum of control over his father. Daniel had known for a long time that his eldest son was not in any way amenable to him, or his bullying.

Even before Alfie Clarke, Danny had been appalled by what his father had done to Lenny Jones. He was a fucking saint, and Danny had taken to visiting him at least once a week. Lenny could talk now, but he would never walk again. Even after all this time, Danny hated to see the man so broken, hated that his father had done it.

Lenny told him stories of the old days that were as thrilling as they were outrageous; he brought the East End alive, the old East End before the slum clearance and the tower blocks. And Danny had got an education from him as well, learning how the scams worked, how you weighed up situations, how you worked out the odds. He had never really thought about situations as a mathematical problem before, but Lenny had explained it to him in language he understood.

Lenny didn't know he was Daniel's son, at least he

didn't think he did. Lenny had lots of visitors, and Danny wondered if any of them had said who he was. He didn't think so, because Lenny was always nice to him; he liked Lenny a lot. He was a good bloke.

Young as he had been at the time, Danny had only visited at first to see who had been the cause of all the grief, and he had found himself going back again and again. Now, though, he went because he wanted to, not because of any ulterior motives.

His Uncle Peter had found out about his visits. He had got him on his own and asked him how Lenny was faring; he had told him he was a good lad to go in and visit him. Said he thought he was growing up to be a good man, and he was keeping his eye on him. Danny liked that, had liked hearing it, even though he felt a twinge of disloyalty to his dad.

It was his Uncle Peter who had asked him to look out for his brothers' interests and, even though his father's name had not been mentioned, Danny knew that he was also asking him to try and work by his father's side, and keep his eye on the family businesses. His Uncle Peter did not want to be given any reason to chastise his father; Danny knew if *that* happened it would not end well for any of them. His father, for all his talk and bravado, was still heartbroken over the rift between him and Peter.

Danny wondered how on earth he was supposed to smooth over this latest outrage, but he had to try. It was another step back for them all as a family, when he and his brothers had worked so hard to get this far. Damage limitation, that was what was needed. He almost smiled at the thought; he was becoming an expert at it.

Chapter Forty-Three

Peter Bailey was in the offices of his new nightclub; it was noisy and the DJ was not his cup of tea – give him Etta James or a bit of Bob Marley any day – but he knew the clientele were loving it and that was all that mattered.

He was quietly fuming. Daniel had once more caused a fucking scene, which he would, yet again, have to clean up. He had scarcely laid eyes on him in the years since the Alfie Clarke drama; they saw each other in church and that was it. But Peter kept close tabs on his brother – especially as far as the business went. He knew Daniel's every move.

He sipped his brandy, savouring the burn and, as his eldest nephew came into the room, he held his hand up, enjoying the last few moments before he had to deal with the aftermath of his brother's actions.

'Is he dead?'

Danny shook his head. 'No, but let's just say Derek won't be back in circulation for a good while. I've sorted him a private hospital with the best doctors. I've paid his wife off, and guaranteed all her bills are covered, including the school fees for the kids.'

Peter nodded, it was what he had expected. 'You've got to sort him out, Danny, once and for all. If you don't, I am going to have to get involved personally. I've covered his arse once too often and this has got to stop.'

Danny nodded humbly. 'I know, Uncle Pete. We'll take care of it.'

'I know you will, son. Now, what's this I hear about you, my Petey, and some problem with the debts?'

When Danny slipped out half an hour later, Peter sat in his chair and, pouring himself another large brandy, he closed his eyes. He was tired tonight, tired and worried. He had so much riding on the next few years. He had invested in numerous new enterprises, from the drugs trade – which was so lucrative it was fucking outrageous – to gentlemen's clubs with private dancers and guaranteed privacy. He had more clubs opening for this new generation of youngsters who were convinced that the only thing that mattered was getting out, getting drunk, and having a good time. He envied them being born into an era when responsibility was something from a bygone age, and where nothing really mattered except doing what the fuck you liked. The sixties had started the drug culture, the seventies had cemented it into the public psyche – thanks to pop stars who had glamorised it – and now the eighties were all about money, clothes and chemical highs. It was almost like printing money, it was so fucking lucrative. But, by the same token, it was also about keeping that part of the business as low profile as possible.

Now his brother was not only attracting unwanted attention, but Peter was facing problems with his own sons. In particular Peter Junior – or Petey as he was known – who, it seemed, had more of his uncle in him than his own father. Petey believed he was more important than his father, his brothers, his uncle, his cousins – in fact, anyone else in his orbit. Peter had always perceived this weakness in his eldest son, this snide side to his personality; Petey had such an inflated opinion of his own worth it was frightening. But it was the lack of loyalty that was the real worry. Loyalty was paramount in the world they inhabited – it was what kept them out of stir, what kept them on the street. Petey was basically a bully, just like his uncle. He needed to be taught a lesson that he would not forget in a hurry, and tonight Peter intended to have it out with him.

He sighed. Might as well get this over with. He knew Petey was down in the club and he picked up the phone to get him sent in. When Petey came in, looking decidedly sheepish, Peter let rip.

'You had better explain yourself, boy. I know you have been claiming money in *my* name, and I will fucking take you out, seriously harm you, son or not, before I let you fuck up me, my brother or his family.'

Petey looked at his father; he guessed his cousin had told his father the story. Even though he was ashamed of his actions, he still felt there was a justification. 'I didn't expect Danny to get the flak, I was supposed to go there myself. But Danny took it on himself to collect all the rents . . .'

Peter closed his eyes in distress. Nothing could justify what had happened, what this son of his had done. He held his hand up to stop the flow of treachery in its tracks. 'Are you trying to justify having me over? Are you that fucking stupid?'

Petey didn't answer. He knew when to keep a low profile.

'Danny was trying to do you a favour and, because of *you*, he nearly got stabbed. Why would you rob your own, eh? You were taking money off me *and* my brother. Two earns, you jammy fucker, and it still wasn't enough for you, was it, eh? If you weren't my son, Petey, you would be a fucking dead man.'

Petey was a realist and he knew when he was beaten. He was aware that his father knew *exactly* why he had done this. He was just waiting for him to come clean and throw himself on his mercy. It was pathetic. Petey was a grown man, and his father still treated him like a fucking child. 'You know why, Dad. I owe money.'

Peter looked at his eldest son, his namesake, and felt sick with shame. 'You owe gambling money again? Have you learned nothing at all? I have earned off weak people like you all my life, and a gambler is the weakest of the weak. You know what gamblers are, don't you? Fucking fools, mugs. They are the reason we own betting shops. We can't fucking lose, you imbecile! If gambling was such a fucking doddle, don't you think bookies would be few and far between? They're on every high street in the country, waiting for fucking mugs like you to throw your money at them. Well, this is your last warning. You can't go to any of the card venues around here. I'm making you persona non grata, my son. I'm making this personal to *me* and, believe me, there ain't a person living who will give you a fucking chair anywhere. I'm giving you six months to get your act together. If you don't sort yourself out, me and you are finished. You need a wife, a family – you need responsibilities, son. You need to fucking grow up!'

Petey saw that his father was right, but he resented that his father did not pay his boys anywhere near what Daniel paid *his* sons. His father felt that they should live within the means he provided for them, yet he, himself, lived like a king.

'I have listened to you, and I accept what you're saying, Dad, but me and my brothers need to be paid the same as Uncle Daniel's boys. You control everything about us – you always have, Dad, and we don't like it. So, while we are being honest, let me say my piece. I want to be paid my due, and then maybe I wouldn't have to scam for it. As for a wife and family, how could I keep anyone on what you weigh out to us? I can't even keep myself. And, as for my cards, I'm a grown man, and that is my prerogative. I'm twenty-four, Dad, not a fucking teenager. So, you think on what I'm saying, as I will on what you have said. I could get work anywhere and you know it.'

Peter Bailey saw the truth in his son's words but it didn't mean he trusted him, weak fool that he was. Gamblers would always look for the quick buck, the easy money; they only saw money as something you got in a win, not something you worked for. This son of his, his own flesh and blood, was everything he loathed in other people. That Petey had been the cause of trouble for one of Daniel's sons weighed heavily on his mind. To know that he had bred a Judas like this was anathema to him. How could this have happened? How had he produced such a fucking loose cannon? He hated to think it, but this lad had a lot of Daniel in him; he had the same arrogance, the same need to be noticed. Except Daniel knew the strength of an earn, whereas this cunt wanted it on a plate.

Petey looked at his father, and he knew exactly what was going through his mind. He realised he had to rein himself in, but it rankled. He wanted to break out on his own, he wanted his own crew. He wanted everything, and sooner rather than later. His father was the past and Petey wasn't willing to wait for years to take over the family business. He wanted it *now*. He didn't have the firepower yet, but he would wait, and he would watch. Until then, he would toe the line – outwardly at least. For now, it was all he could do.

Chapter Forty-Four

'She's gorgeous, Lena, look at her beautiful hair!'

Tania could hear the compliments coming her way, and she preened with delight. All her life she had been told how beautiful she was, how clever she was, and how loved she was. Despite that, she still felt frightened when she was alone. It was only when she was surrounded by her family that she felt secure. She was learning to dance and she loved showing off what she'd learned.

Lena watched her little daughter with absolute delight; this child was her life, the reason she got up in the morning. She was wholly Lena's responsibility and, consequently, they were as close as they could possibly be.

'She's going to look a beauty in her Communion dress! We'd better get that sorted soon – you'll help won't you, Ria?'

Ria nodded, and smiled at her friend kindly. 'Mad really, ain't it? My grandson's making his Communion at the same time as Tania! They will look a picture together.'

Lena nodded in agreement, but Ria knew she was dreading the actual day. Peter and Daniel would both be in the church together, and Ria knew that Peter would not acknowledge his brother in any way. Before the latest aggro it might have been a possibility, but now it was never going to happen.

Ria had never been that fond of Daniel, whereas Lena had become a close friend from day one. Ria loved the boys – they were their father's sons in looks, but none of them had inherited their father's strange outlook on life, thank God. Daniel Bailey was a walking fucking psycho as far as she was concerned, and he was never going to change – Ria knew that as well as she knew her own name.

Peter had always felt the need to defend his brother, but even he had finally had to admit defeat. She was pleased about that. She hated herself for it, but she had to be honest with herself if not with anyone else. Daniel being out of the picture was something she had celebrated. He was a liability and she was convinced he would be the eventual cause of the Baileys' downfall, if they were not careful.

'I wish we could enjoy the day together, Ria. You know, celebrate as a family.'

It was the first time Lena had ever acknowledged the rift, which meant that Peter never visited this house now. Ria was so shocked at her words she didn't answer her straightaway.

Lena continued, 'It hurts, Ria. Holy Communion is

a big day in a child's life – accepting the body of Christ for the first time, making their first confession. It's a big step for them, and I wish we were going to celebrate it together.'

Ria grasped her friend's hand. Lena was looking older than her years lately; she still kept herself nice, but the weight of her worries had taken its toll. 'I know, mate, and I wish it could be different too.'

Lena held her friend's gaze as she said quietly, 'He ain't right, Ria, he's worse than ever. I'm worried about him.'

Ria was absolutely dumbfounded at Lena's words. In all the years they had known each other, Lena had never once discussed her husband in any way other than to praise him. For her to admit there was a problem of any kind was unheard of. If Daniel Bailey had murdered his neighbours with an axe, in front of an audience of fifty people, Lena would say, 'Well, they must have upset him.' She had never once said anything even *remotely* critical about the man she was married to. Now here she was, admitting the truth of the situation out loud. Ria knew it was her way of asking her to talk to Peter about it.

Tania watched the exchange between her mother and her auntie. Even though she didn't know what the problem was, she understood enough of the conversation to know that the problem could only be solved by her Auntie Ria. And Tania, as young as she was, could see from the way her Auntie Ria was shaking her head slowly, that she wasn't going to do anything to help at all.

Tania slipped her hand into her mother's and, holding on to her tightly, she wondered why she was suddenly feeling frightened again.

'It's between them, Lena, you know that as well as I do, mate.'

Lena nodded; she had expected nothing more if she was really honest. Looking down at her daughter, she smiled sadly, as she said with forced gaiety, 'Who fancies a Wimpy, then?'

Tania nodded in agreement, but she could see the glimmer of tears in her mother's eyes. This must be about her dad, but she couldn't for the life of her understand what was wrong because her daddy was the nicest man she knew.

Her Uncle Peter was a nice man too, she thought. She knew that he was her father's brother, even though she had never seen them talk to each other. She only ever saw them under the same roof at Mass, when they did not even look at one another. When she had asked her mother why that was, her mother had told her quietly and seriously – almost angrily – to never ask her father or her brothers that question.

She had said it was something that was for the adults to know, and for children to mind their own business about. It was the one and only time her mother had seemed to be cross with her, and she had learned then not to ask *any* questions about the family.

There were so many things she didn't understand, and she accepted that she was too young to have them explained. But it didn't stop her from taking in what was happening around her, and wondering what was going on. She was frightened of the unknown, but she knew that her mum would never let anything happen to her and neither would her daddy or her brothers. They were so much older than her but she knew they adored her – and they treated her like a princess. She worshipped her brothers – especially Davey – and she loved it when they were all around the house for their dinner, making a big fuss of her and her mum.

But any happiness at the prospect of the treat in store was lost as Tania could feel the tension in the room. It was clear that her Auntie Ria was feeling as bad as she was, and that just made it seem ten times worse.

Chapter Forty-Five

Daniel poured himself a large Scotch and, as he sipped it, he looked around him at his offices. They were a far cry from Peter's upmarket domain, but he'd decided he preferred being in the heart of East London. He felt he could see to things much easier from here. That they were in a scrapyard, and the offices consisted of two Portakabins berthed side by side, meant nothing to him. All he saw was the fact that they were well guarded, not just by guard dogs, but by a large metal fence and electric gates. No fucker was coming in here without his knowledge, and that was just how he liked things.

He heard the cars that heralded the arrival of his sons, and he watched warily as they parked up, and walked slowly towards his lair. He wondered what had brought them all to see him – together. They looked as miserable as sin.

'What the fuck is the matter with you lot?'

'You know what's wrong with us, Dad. Davey told us what you did to Derek Thomas, and we've come to tell you that none of us is going to put up with your fucking stupid behaviour any more.' Danny spoke for them all.

'Hang on a minute, are you fucking threatening me?' Daniel Bailey's voice was bordering on the incredulous, and as he looked at his four sons it occurred to him that he was actually outnumbered. For the first time ever, he saw that his boys were not kids any longer.

Davey, Noel and Jamsie were sitting together on the black leather sofa that had cost an arm and a leg. It was a huge piece of furniture, but still not big enough to hold his three youngest boys comfortably. They were seriously big lumps, grown men, and they were now, it seemed, prepared to front him up. Danny, his eldest, was standing by the doorway, as if he was keeping guard, making sure he couldn't leave. It was fucking ludicrous! No one could stop him doing anything he wanted, surely they knew that by now?

'No one's threatening you, Dad. But we have to sort this out, once and for all.'

Daniel Bailey looked at his eldest son; his words were so outrageous he was sure that he must have imagined them. He laughed incredulously. '*What* did you just fucking say?'

Danny sighed heavily before repeating the words once more. 'I said, no one's threatening you, Dad – not yet anyway – but we have to sort this out, once and for all.'

Daniel Bailey looked at his sons again, warily now. He licked his lips slowly, contemplating how best to deal with the situation he was in, and wondered how he'd reached the point where his own kids felt they were within their rights to question him as if he was a fucking romancer, a fucking no one. He shook his head in disbelief.

His sons waited, on tenterhooks, aware that if he went off they would need their wits and their combined strength to subdue him. He was a hard old fucker – there was no doubt in any of their minds about that – but he was also a liability, and they were all agreed that this was something they had to address, no matter what the result might be.

Noel raised his right hand instinctively to his chest. Daniel was stunned to see the boy caress the outline of what was obviously a gun.

He challenged him. 'What, you going to fucking shoot me, son? Is that what this is about?' He was almost laughing as he spoke to him.

Danny sighed. 'We all carry guns, Dad, remember? You were the one who *insisted* on it. No one wants to have a fucking row about this, but we will if that's what it's gonna take. You nearly killed Derek, and there was no fucking need for any of it. Now we are back to square one; you wiped out in a fucking afternoon everything we have achieved over the last couple of years. All our credibility has disappeared, Dad. No one will want to deal with us in the future, because they won't feel fucking safe, they will think you will fucking take umbrage over fuck-all, and they will be the next person you decide to batter senseless. This is about *us* working together as a team and about *you* giving us the respect we give you.'

Daniel Bailey was looking at his sons as if he had never seen any of them before in his life. A detached part of him realised that they were boys to be proud of. They were trying to talk to him as men – as men who saw themselves as his equal. But it was a shocker because it occurred to him just how much he had taken them for granted; somehow along the line he had missed them growing up, growing away from him. They had all grown closer to each other and now they were a formidable team. He had never truly appreciated them, and that was a mistake he was now paying for big time.

Daniel Bailey had only ever shown real affection to the women in his life and, of course, his brother Peter. He had only ever seen his boys as a potential workforce who would, one day, run his businesses alongside him. And, as his flesh and blood, he had assumed that they would always be as easy to manipulate, to manage, as they had been as children.

Well, he had certainly fucking got that wrong! They had become great big lumps who he now saw he had seriously underestimated. He had to diffuse this situation, he knew that much.

'Are you going to answer me, Dad?'

Daniel Bailey nodded, his whole demeanour changing in an instant, as he attempted to appear contrite. 'Derek fucking mugged me off, and you know me, boys – I don't take kindly to people who think they can take advantage of my good nature.'

'Look, Dad, it's not just us who have had enough of

your fucking antics, right? Uncle Peter has asked me to tell you that he is not impressed with your behaviour either. He makes sure you have your earn, and we, my brothers and me, *your* sons, are trying to keep up with Uncle Peter and his lads. We could be earning a lot more if you weren't hanging round our necks like a fucking albatross. So you think twice before you threaten us in the future, because if we walk away, you won't have fucking no one.'

Daniel Bailey saw that if he wasn't careful he would lose them once and for all. They were good earners, he knew that better than anyone. His eldest lad had a flair for negotiating with people, and he was fair. He had a lot of Peter in him actually, had his brother's understanding of people's weak spots, and how best to utilise them to his own advantage.

But the mention of his brother's interference was the final humiliation for Daniel as a man. That his own sons were willing to use Peter as a bargaining chip was not only an outrageous act, but also a seriously treacherous and humiliating one. It showed him just how far apart they had been driven. That they had already discussed him with his brother was demeaning, was wrong, all fucking wrong. The fact that Peter had not even bothered to talk to him personally was the final insult. But even feeling as he did about the whole situation, Daniel saw that he had no choice any more, he had to toe the line. The days of him demanding his sons' obedience were long gone.

He looked once more at his sons, saw their handsome faces, knew he should be proud of them, knew that most men in their world would be patting themselves on the back, thrilled at having produced four fine sons who were savvy, respected and, best of all, loyal to their own flesh and blood. But, instead, Daniel felt betrayed.

Chapter Forty-Six

Peter Bailey was happy. He was in one of his own pubs, relaxing with his wife, kids and grandson. He had bought this pub a few months earlier. It was in the heart of Essex, and the countryside surrounding it was stunning. It was a real family place, and he loved that he could go there with his nearest and dearest, have a nice meal, a few drinks and, more to the point, conduct certain parts of his businesses in peace and tranquillity. The beer garden was packed, and he was pleased to see the children playing in the small playground he had recently had installed. It was a perfect Sunday afternoon – the weather was good, the gardens looked well tended, and the punters were nice people with smart cars and money to spend.

Ria had been the one to suggest getting a decent chef in, and she had been right – it was more than paying off. Word had spread about the quality of the grub and they were now getting so many bookings they were considering extending the premises.

As he sipped his beer, he sighed contentedly. Delroy grinned at him, and he shrugged nonchalantly. 'What? What's so funny?'

'You, sitting there like a day tripper, all relaxed and full of bonhomie.'

Peter laughed himself then. 'I suppose that's just what I am really – today anyway. I'm just out with my family, having a few beers, and enjoying the good weather. What more could I want?'

Delroy nodded in agreement. 'Good fucking investment this – people have money to spend, and somewhere like this is perfect. Look at them. Smiling, contented and, above all, willing to weigh out for a meal as well as their drinks. Whoever coined the term "family pub" should be knighted.'

'Too right.' Peter picked up his pint and sipped it once more. This was the first time in ages he had felt so relaxed. Since the trouble with his brother, he had been on edge, knowing that his silence over the debacle had not been appreciated. He was aware that people felt he should have chastised Daniel to show that he did not condone his brother's actions. But, as much as he had wanted to, he just couldn't do it to him. There were too many people waiting their chance to settle old scores with Daniel; if *he* turned his back on his little brother publicly, it would be like finally admitting to everyone that he was finished with him for ever.

His nephews were growing up into decent men, good earners and, more important than anything else, they were loyal right down to the bone. They worked hard, and they were up against it with their father's natural lunacy fucking it up for them!

Peter pushed the thoughts out of his head; he was sick of still having his brother invading his life. He was out with his family, he wanted to enjoy the day.

He watched as Imelda came out of the pub with a tray of drinks. She was a good girl and, as much as it had pained him to admit it, Delroy had been a good husband to her. Oh, Peter knew he took a flyer occasionally, but then that wasn't a big deal. It was when a man had a regular bird that the trouble started. No, all in all, he was pleased with Delroy, he had proved his loyalty, and come up trumps with the idea to buy the clubs. And now he was a Face in his own right, so he had nothing to prove.

Delroy got up and helped Imelda with the tray of drinks and, as Ria walked back to the table holding her grandson's hand, Peter realised what a lucky man he was. He had so much – it was time to start enjoying it properly. His boys were old enough to take over the lion's share of the business, and that would give him and Ria the opportunity to spend some time together before they were too old to really enjoy themselves.

'Uncle Peter?'

'Hello, lads.'

It was young Danny and his brother Davey. Peter smiled widely at them both, pleased to see them and, as they sat down at the table, gratified to see their obvious pleasure in their surroundings. It was the first time they had been to this pub, and he liked that they were immediately impressed with it. They were good lads.

They had never come to him complaining about their father's behaviour – they had enough loyalty to try and sort out any creases by themselves. They were clearly relieved though at his intervention over Derek; he knew better than anyone how awkward his brother could be when the fancy took him.

Delroy went off to get them drinks, and Peter said quietly, 'How did he take it?'

Danny shrugged his shoulders. 'Better than I thought but, to be really honest, he was only swayed when we mentioned you. He's a strange man, Uncle Peter.'

Peter sighed heavily, the joy of the day deserting him. 'How are things on the street?'

Danny sat back in his chair, his blond hair golden in the sunlight. Peter had to admit just how good-looking his nephews were – they were really handsome.

'We've smoothed most of it over, but the bookies are fucking antsy now, as you can imagine, after the old man's latest escapade. Typical fucking bookies! Rob each other blind, but cut one of the bastards and they all bleed.'

Peter Bailey put his head back and laughed loudly. 'Never a truer fucking word spoken, but they'll get over it. What we need to do now is ensure that it never happens again. I have swallowed about as much as I can, and you know that. I could have rowed him out a long time ago, but I didn't. Now I am telling you all, you can have your share, but if he steps out of line once more, I will fucking take him out myself.'

Danny and his brother both dropped their heads in embarrassment.

'Do you know the worst of it, boys? Your father doesn't even think he's done anything wrong. When he attacks like that, it means nothing to him.'

No one said a word then. They just sat back in their chairs, and waited patiently for Delroy to bring out their drinks.

Chapter Forty-Seven

Lena was excited because today her Noel was bringing a girl home to meet her. It was the first time any of her sons had officially invited a girl round to the house. Oh, she knew they had snuck girls in – she wasn't stupid – but the boys had always made sure they were gone by the morning. And now here was her Noel bringing home a girl he was obviously keen on, and she was really thrilled at the prospect.

She had knocked up a nice sponge cake and some sandwiches, and she had also made a quiche and a huge bowl of salad. She looked around her kitchen and, for the first time, wished she had as nice a house as Ria. Not that they couldn't have afforded it, but Lena would rather have the cash. Most days she felt her home was more than adequate, if not exactly luxurious.

She wiped the worktops down for the twentieth time, and looked out of the window to check on Tania. She smiled to herself as she saw her daughter sitting on the grass, playing with her dolls while chattering away to herself. Tania had a great imagination, and she was not a child who was constantly demanding attention – unlike the boys who had driven her mental from the moment they had opened their eyes, until she had finally got them back into their beds.

She heard the front door open and, plastering a wide smile on her face, she waited for her son to bring in the girl he was obviously really keen on.

Noel came into the kitchen and, looking decidedly sheepish, he introduced the girl who was standing behind him in the hallway. All Lena could really see was that the girl was tiny, but as she walked into the kitchen, Lena smiled in delight. She was an angel; she had a thick head of auburn hair, and green eyes – it was a startling combination. She was very fine-boned, with cheekbones you could cut paper on, and a trim figure that was in perfect proportion.

'This is Christine Marks. Christine, this is my old mum.' Noel's voice was full of pride as he made the introductions.

As the girl held out her hand, the front door banged open noisily and Theresa Bailey burst into the kitchen, all excited and looking at Christine Marks as if she was a prime cow on sale at the auctions. She said loudly, 'Jaysus, Noel, she's fecking gorgeous.'

Noel laughed with a mixture of delight and embarrassment. 'This is my nana, Theresa Bailey. Just about as Irish as you can get and, Nana, this is Christine Marks. You'll be pleased to know she's from good Irish stock!'

The women took to each other immediately and Noel, seeing that, was deeply relieved. Sitting down at the kitchen table, he watched quietly as they chatted amongst themselves. He was madly in love with Christine, and he had prayed like a Benedictine monk all day long that she would get on with his mother. If they had not taken to each other, he knew he would have had to out her, and that would have been hard. But the fact of it was, you could have fifty birds and five wives in your lifetime, but you only had one mother.

Daniel Bailey came home to find his wife and his mother entertaining a young girl, and his son Noel sitting in the kitchen watching it all like some kind of fucking imbecile. He was the first of the boys to go looking for a wife, and she was a nice-looking girl, no doubt about that but, as he was introduced to her, and feigned interest in what was going on around him, his mind was on other things.

Tania came in from the garden and she slipped on to his lap. As he hugged her to him, he felt the loneliness of his life envelop him. He had once had it all – everything he had ever dreamed of, had ever wanted, and now it was ruined. First, his brother had abandoned him and now, it seemed, his sons had followed in their uncle's footsteps. He was still a man to be reckoned with, was still a man who was known as somebody you didn't mess with, but he was also now a man who was afforded no real respect. He had finally realised, at this late date, when his own sons, his flesh and blood, had confronted him, that everything he had ever believed in was a sham. Especially where his boys were concerned.

Chapter Forty-Eight

Petey Bailey was watching the poker game with interest. His father was testing him by putting him in charge of the gaming clubs, that was clear enough – seeing if his son had the strength to resist the lure of the tables. So far, Petey felt he was doing pretty well; his urge to gamble was somewhat assuaged by the fact that he was creaming at least twenty per cent of the profits thereby ensuring himself a nice little earner on the side.

It was in his nature to want a sideline of his own. His father would see it as a weakness but, even knowing that, Petey still felt the familiar thrill as he pocketed his ill-gotten gains. He had the gambler's need to earn money for nothing, and he knew that he would always need that rush. He wondered how long it would be before his father found out he was on the rob. He knew he had to be careful if he was to regain the trust of the family and that made him hate them all the more.

Chapter Forty-Nine

Lena and Imelda were both laughing at Theresa as she described her latest beau. Ria poured wine for them all as she marvelled at the older woman's lust for life.

Theresa was the first person to admit that she had no interest in a relationship, but she still liked to be chased and, in truth, she did seem to be chased on a regular basis. At nearly sixty, she still had more than a vestige of her youthful good looks, there was no denying that. Lena knew her own daughter had inherited them, and she was glad; Theresa had been a beauty in her day.

Ria was more pleased about Lena's easy laughter; it was good to see her sister-in-law so relaxed. Ria knew the situation between the brothers was harder on her than any of them. Lena had said nothing to Ria about it since she'd asked her, in a roundabout way, to speak to Peter. Ria feared that Lena had taken a step backwards into her own world since she'd refused to help. But it was only a matter of time till it all came to a head and what was Lena going to do then?

Ria turned her attention to Theresa. 'So, come on, who is it this time?'

Theresa laughed loudly. Her eyes were a beautiful

deep blue, and her laugh was as deep and husky as ever. 'Well, he's an old Face from years ago. Tommy Barker's his name, done a serious lump in his youth, came out and earned his coin, as you do. Now he's well set up with his own house, a nice business. I like his company. He makes me laugh.'

Ria grinned. Theresa was a real character; she lived life to the full, and good luck to her as well. She had always gone through men like a hot knife through butter. 'What was he away for, then?'

Theresa shrugged her shoulders, and said sotto voce, 'Murder, but it was a long time ago. It wasn't a civilian or nothing like that. He ain't an animal, it was just business.'

Lena appeared genuinely shocked at her mother-in-law's words, and Ria wondered at the woman's ability to play the ingénue with two women who knew she *had* to be aware of at least some of Daniel's lifestyle. No one was that fucking green, not in their world anyway.

'You be careful, Theresa. Who did he murder?'

Theresa smiled sadly. 'It was a long time ago. Tommy was a gangster in the fifties and he killed a man who owed him money and respect. I remember it, actually. His wife died while he was banged up, and his kids were brought up by his sister. Sad, for *everyone* concerned. But, anyway, I like him. He's a laugh, and good company to boot.'

Lena was tight-lipped, and Theresa could see the disapproval on her face, as if she was above it all, not a part of the life they were living. Sometimes Lena's insistence on acting as if her husband was a fucking saint really stuck in her craw. Who the hell did she think she was? Turning to her daughter-in-law, she said angrily, 'Why the shocked face, Lena? You're married to Daniel Bailey, *my* son. He has more than a few fucking bodies on his conscience – that's if he actually has one, which I doubt very much and I'm his mother! So, in future, I would appreciate it if you didn't act shocked at the men I have in *my* life. I have *never* answered to anyone and, Lena, my darling, I am not fucking starting now. So don't you dare try and make me feel bad about the life I live. At least I'm not a fucking hypocrite!'

Ria was so shocked at Theresa's words she actually laughed – it was her nerves, she knew. But no one had ever said the like to Lena Bailey. It had always been the unwritten rule: Lena Bailey was never to be reminded of her husband's deeds. Lena was always to be looked after, shielded from her husband's actions. Lena was never made to face the truth and, if Ria was completely honest, it had often irritated her in the past.

Ria saw Lena lick her lips slowly, saw the look of abject horror as it passed over her face. Her mother-in-law saw it too and sighed, busying herself with lighting a cigarette.

'I'm sure I don't know what you mean, Theresa.'

Lena's voice was loud, and Ria could see the anger in her eyes.

Theresa pulled deeply on her John Player Special,

before saying seriously, 'But that's just it, love. You *do*, Lena, you know *exactly* what I mean, so let's stop this fecking charade, shall we? You're a grown-up – get over yourself and face up to the real world for once in your fecking life.'

Lena looked at the woman she loved like her own mother, unable to comprehend why, after all this time, she would finally decide to force the truth on her.

'He's my son, Lena, and I love him – and it's hard to love that fecker at times, believe me – but *you*, Lena, are the only person he will listen to. You could have reined him in years ago if you had used your fecking loaf. You need to get your head out of your arse, and start looking out for those boys of yours; they are going to need you in the next few years, and you had better understand that, lady. He is pushing everybody around him away, and I know my Daniel – that means he will keep pushing with all he's got. So, for once in your life, take a fecking interest, will you, before your sons are wiped out before your own eyes. Because you know as well as I do what Daniel is capable of.' Theresa took another deep drag on her cigarette before saying sadly, 'You had a good run, Lena. You kept out of it, but now it's time to start taking an interest in what's going on around you.'

Lena was white-faced, absolutely distraught at the turn of events, unable to believe that her mother-in-law could be capable of such treachery, not just towards her, but towards her own son. 'I will not be spoken to like this, Theresa. I think it's best if I leave now before we all say things we might regret.'

As Lena stood up and collected her belongings, Theresa said loudly, and with obvious sarcasm, 'You can't run away for ever, Lena – even you must know that much, darling. Eventually you are going to have to accept the truth of your situation. You live the Life, just like we all do. You know I'm telling the truth. Use your intelligence, girl! Use your influence to rein Daniel in – if not for his sake, then for his sons. *Your* sons.'

Ria watched as Lena battled the urge to swipe her mother-in-law across the face. It was a real eye-opener for Ria to see Lena so angry and strong. Gone now was her usual quiet demeanour; she had pulled herself upright, her fist was clenched and she looked more than capable of fighting her own corner. Theresa had hit a nerve all right – that much was plain to see – but Ria felt it was a good thing. Lena did need to get her head out of her arse, and start living in the real world with everyone else. She had swerved the Life for too long, and it was time she admitted that the money she spent came at a price, especially for women like them, who lived at the very top of the food chain.

Lena slammed the door behind her, and Theresa raised her arms in annoyance. 'I could cheerfully swing for her at times, Ria! She wanders through life like Dilly fecking Daydream and, you know something? Deep down, she's stronger than any of us.'

Ria nodded in agreement. Whoever said that the truth hurt didn't know the half of it.

Chapter Fifty

Peter Bailey looked at his eldest son for long moments, then he barked at him angrily, 'Did Daniel and the lads collect the money or not?'

Petey nodded warily. 'Yeah, he started with Lance Porter and finished with Graham Black. Why the big fucking third degree all of a sudden? You know the boys were on to it. Who's rattled your fucking cage?'

Peter sighed loudly. 'It's not the fucking boys I'm worried about, is it?'

'Well, the boys have put the hard word on their old man, and he seems to be toeing the line, so I don't know what else we can fucking say, Dad.'

'I can never trust him, he's such a fucking Looney Tunes. Radio Rental, as they say. This is what I hate, wondering how far he's gone. I am not sure the boys can handle him . . .'

Petey smiled. 'I think they can, Dad. He knows they ain't kids any more, he sees the sense of what they say. Danny reckons he has finally come around to their way of thinking.'

Peter laughed. 'Oh, he thinks that, does he? Then he is an idiot. My brother Daniel is not a man who is easily thwarted. For example: when we were kids, a neighbour stole a pint of milk off our step. Daniel cut two of the fucker's fingers off with a pair of secateurs. As far as he was concerned, the punishment fit the crime. The thing was, though, he waited ten fucking years to take his revenge. Do you see where I am coming from now? Daniel Bailey will never swallow his knob, and you need to take that onboard. He would cut his own sons' throats if he thought they were mugging him off, and he would burn his Lena alive if he thought she had betrayed him. *That* is what we are dealing with. So you watch him like a fucking hawk, and you make sure he never has the opportunity to right any of his wrongs, real or imagined. You tell the boys he needs to be monitored, OK?'

'I know what you mean, Dad, but I feel sorry for the lads. They work so hard, and they love him – he's their dad after all.'

Peter laughed then. 'You're preaching to the converted, son; he's my fucking *brother* remember. What I want to make sure of now, however, is that he don't fuck up any of the new earns. The lads have got to keep him under some kind of control, and make sure he is never, and I mean *never*, allowed to mix with people we are dealing with unless he has a fucking minder.'

Petey could hear the threat in his father's voice and he respected that. 'I have made all this crystal clear, Dad. Danny is determined to see that it goes smoothly from now on, and I trust him. He is backed up by his brothers, and they know the seriousness of it, I promise you.'

Peter Bailey shook his head in despair. 'Real, ain't it, son? The fact I even have to have these conversations is bad enough, but I know it's a necessary evil . . .'

Petey could see the weight of responsibility on his father's shoulders, and he genuinely wanted to help. He also wanted to earn his father's trust again, be allowed a bigger part in his operations. 'Look, Dad, I need to ask you something serious.' He wiped his nose and, taking a deep breath, he said nervously, 'Do you want me to take Uncle Daniel out, Dad? I can do it on the quiet – no one would *ever* know it was us. Let's face it, most people wouldn't even fucking care either way. I reckon even his sons would breathe a sigh of relief in private . . .'

Peter Bailey looked at his son, saw how sincere he was. A part of him was impressed; after all, it took a lot to suggest something like that, especially to him. He gave nothing away as he asked, 'So, young Petey, you want my permission to kill your uncle, do you?'

'No, no, Dad, I just want you to know that if it ever comes to it, I would do it for you. Happily do it, in fact. I hate him; he's like a fucking leech. He sucks the life out of everything and everyone around him. He's a fucking tosser.'

Peter Bailey held his hand up, he didn't want to hear any more. 'You remember this, son, for all Daniel is – and he is a fucking handful, granted – *he* would never take a halfpenny off me that he hadn't earned. *He* wouldn't skim a pound that wasn't his, and *he* would *never* think that I wouldn't suss him out if he had tried it on. I know, better than anyone, what a fucking handful he is, but he is still my brother, and *if*, and I mean this with all my heart, *if* and when I feel that he needs to be taken care of on a permanent basis, I will do it myself. I owe him that much.'

Petey was well aware of his father's underlying message. His dad knew *he* was skimming off the clubs, and he was telling him that. He felt the shame wash over him, more so because his father had not accused him outright. Instead he had given him the opportunity to address the situation, reminding him along the way that, for all Daniel's faults, he had never taken a penny that he wasn't entitled to. He was also reminding him that he was more than capable of sorting out his own problems.

'I appreciate the offer, though, son, but you know there's an old saying: Get your own house in order.'

Petey nodded, ashamed, but also impressed with his father's acumen. Nothing, it seemed, got by him. Why was he not surprised?

Chapter Fifty-One

'Hello, Mum.'

Theresa looked at her younger son as he popped his head round her back door. 'I assume you're here to have a row?'

Daniel laughed. 'No.'

Theresa smiled then; she could see that her Daniel was not in a fighting frame of mind, so she guessed he was here to build bridges. She assumed that Lena had mentioned the conversation they had had.

Daniel sat down in his mother's kitchen. He felt so comfortable here. It reminded him of his childhood: the smell of lavender polish, the gleam of her sink, and the feeling of safety she had always tried to give her sons. Daniel knew how hard her life had been, but there was no denying she had really grafted for her family and he would forever respect that. She had the arse with him over Peter – he knew that much – but she still loved him, he could feel it. Like his Lena, it was unconditional love, as it should be with mothers and wives.

'So, to what do I owe this pleasure, son?'

Daniel grinned. 'I hear you're knocking about with Tommy Barker.'

Theresa narrowed her large blue eyes and, looking at her son with obvious suspicion, she said, 'And what if I am? What the feck has it got to do with you?'

Daniel raised his hands in a gesture of surrender. 'Calm down, Mum! What's your problem? He's an old-time Face – I just wondered if it was all right to meet him, that's all. Fucking hell, Mum, anyone would think I was trying to cause you problems or something . . .'

Theresa knew then that Lena had not said a word to her husband after their row, and that annoyed her; Lena needed to do something before it was too late. Daniel would have let on by now that he knew what she had said to his wife. He would have given her his opinion, all right, and she would have happily given him her own opinion back. Unlike most people, he didn't scare her.

'I'm meeting him tonight actually, at the Irish club in Ilford. You'd like him, Daniel, he's a lot like you – what you see is what you get. Bring Lena and Tania; it's a good night there on a Thursday.' Theresa wanted things to get back to normal with Lena. She might annoy her but she was still her daughter-in-law.

Daniel shrugged happily. 'OK then, Lena could do with a night out, she's too insular really, she needs to get out more, Mum. I reckon Tommy Barker could do with an earn, don't you? And I could do with someone who has a good rep with the public as such. I hear he's honest and trustworthy.' He knew his mother understood exactly where he was coming from. That was one of the reasons she was so well respected – she saw the crux of the matter in seconds and age had not dampened that skill at all. 'You know what, Mum? I think little Tania will enjoy it as well. She's doing so well with her Irish dancing, she's a right little performer. Also, you can talk to Lena about the Communion. She's nervous about it, you know what she's like. I would also appreciate it if you could see yourself fit to sit with my Tania at the actual Communion do. Lena will need someone to take her mind off the underlying aggro.'

Theresa shook her head at her son's obvious skulduggery. He wanted her sitting with his family, not his brother's. 'You're a slippery fecker, Daniel.'

He laughed and, making as innocent a face as possible, he said jovially, 'I had a fucking good teacher, didn't I, Mum?'

'I'll do it, but only because of Lena and the situation between you and Peter. You might as well know, I told your wife to open her fecking eyes, and see what is going on around her, especially where *you're* concerned. It's ridiculous, Daniel! She's still acting like a fecking teenager. Well, her sons are part of it now and she needs to make sure they are protected, like I did with you and your brother.'

Daniel shrugged; he made sure his mother did not see the anger she had caused in him. Lena had not said a dickybird about it.

'You know my Lena, Mum, she will never have a word said against me. The less she knows the better, as far as I am concerned.'

Theresa looked into his eyes as she said seriously, 'That is where you are wrong, son. Now *her* sons are in the equation, and that changes everything. The sooner you accept that, the better off you'll be. She's a fucking grown woman, not a young girl any more, Daniel. She needs to act like the adult she is, and you need to fecking see that she understands the reality of the rift between you and Peter.'

Daniel could feel the heat washing over his body, could feel the anger that his mother's words caused rising, knew that he had to keep a lid on it. 'Lena doesn't need you or anyone else to tell her anything, Mum; she knows the score but, unlike you and Ria, she doesn't need to advertise that fact to the whole fucking world. She just chooses to keep her opinions to herself and, with all due respect, Mum, that is her prerogative. She ain't you, and she ain't Ria, thank Christ.'

Theresa sighed heavily. 'You're a fool to yourself, Daniel Bailey. I don't know what it is with you. There's a kink in your nature, always has been. You never see the things around you like everyone else. Peter understood that and, in his own way, he tried to guide you, as I always did. But you are determined to go your own road, and what has that got you, eh? You have caused so much heartache, son. Always caused trouble and, when you go off on your own you never think it through. That's why you're in the situation you are in now. You know, deep down in your guts, that you have no moral compass whatsoever. You act before you think

211

of the consequences. I know that you honestly don't see what you've done is wrong, you can't understand why everyone is so cross with you, but then, you never did, Daniel – not even as a little kid. But I know you better than you know yourself, and I am telling you now that you have to start thinking everything through, and let your boys in on what you're doing. They love you, but they need the chance to prove to the world that they can be trusted to deliver. You have to start thinking of them, and their futures.'

Daniel knew that for his mother to say what she had just said she must be genuinely trying to help him. She had always had his back, both her sons' backs. He also knew she was right – he was devoid of this so-called moral compass, even if, in all honesty, he felt that was a contradiction in terms. But he knew she was right – there was a morality in the Life, and he had never really understood that fact. He did now though – he knew he had to learn just what the boundaries and guidelines were. His sons were more than aware of how they should all conduct themselves, so he had them to use as a yardstick. Despite all this, his mother's words hurt, even though he knew she had the best intentions.

He smiled. 'I'll see you later then, Mum. The Shandon Bells, eh? I bet Father Murphy will be there. He does like a drink, the old ponce.'

Theresa grinned at her son, but she was aware that he had listened to her advice; whether or not he would choose to use it was anybody's guess. 'Don't we all, son! Eventually, when you get to my age, the drink is all you've got to look forward to.'

Daniel Bailey looked at his mother and, sighing sadly, he said gently, 'You're a good 'un, Mum, and I love you very much.'

Chapter Fifty-Two

'Well, are you going to show me or what?' Jack Bailey was laughing as he spoke, and his cousins Noel and Jamsie, who were with him, laughed too.

George Theodopolis, however, wasn't laughing; he knew he was in serious trouble. 'Come on back to my office, boys, I've got your envelope waiting.'

Jack Bailey shook his head angrily, and replied in a sarcastic yet humorous tone, 'Bollocks to you, George! This is the third week we have requested our due. Now, me and my cousins have had to come in person, take time out of our busy lives to collect from you. I ask you, is that fair on us? I mean, in reality, who the fuck are you? You're a cunt who believed we would overlook the insult.' He looked around him with wide eyes, the eternal innocent. Then, grinning nastily, he said viciously, 'So, I ask you again, cunt, show us your club. If you don't, we will take it down around your fucking ears. Brick by brick, punch by punch.'

George knew what was going to happen now. It was his own fault, but he'd had to try; after all, no one paid out without a good reason. Now he was backed into a corner – once they saw his premises he would have to pay more than his usual wage; unfortunately, this was the way of the world he lived in.

Jack knew all this; he had already done his research, and he had been looking forward to taking this Greek ponce down a few pegs. He had a natural bent for this type of work. He researched his marks without being told to, and he had known instinctively that they were not getting their due from this one. His cousins had both stood back and let him run the show, recognising his talent for the job. But this place was not like the pubs or the cab ranks he usually dealt with – this was a different ball game altogether. Jack liked the idea of an all-day drinking club, a place to hang out, where girls were in abundance, and where he was not liable to be treated like a kid. He saw the potential here.

Jack was a ladies' man – he had a permanent erection and he preferred faceless sex. The girls who worked here were on an earn, so they would not be too fussy. At twenty-one he was shrewd enough to know that, if he played his cards right, the possibilities were endless.

'Please, boys, I can pay. I promise you.'

Jack smiled at his cousins; they were not yet *au fait* with his way of working, but they soon would be. He would see to that.

As he walked into the club, Jack could smell the cheap perfume, the stink of old lager and could see the stains on carpets that only looked good late at night. He saw the interest on the girls' faces, and he responded to them instinctively, drinking in their fake smiles and their fake cleavages. This was shag central to him; this was what he had been dreaming of for years. Jack Bailey felt like he had finally come home.

His two cousins were impressed with his confidence; if they followed his lead their lives would be enriched in more ways than they had ever imagined. Jack Bailey was born to spread it about; this job made it all the easier for him to do that, and he embraced it with every bit of energy he possessed. He grinned at his cousins and, winking, he said pleasantly, 'Noel, Jamsie, follow the man, and count the money. I have to acquaint myself with the premises, and the females within it, as I am sure you both understand.'

As he sat down with the girls, and saw them smiling at him as if he was a male model or a movie star, he knew his father had inadvertently given him the world on a plate and for that alone he would always be thankful.

'All right, girls? So what're your names, then?'

The girls, for their part, knew a mug when they saw one, and this mug was obviously someone of note. They gave him their best smiles, and invited him into their group without a second's thought. This was, after all, a hostess club.

Chapter Fifty-Three

'She is a fucking stripper, Liam! Will you get a grip!' Imelda Bailey was clearly annoyed; she didn't like that her brother was being taken for a fool. What was it with her brothers and strippers?

'I don't care; I like her.'

Imelda rolled her eyes at the ceiling. 'Strippers are like pros, Liam, they just see the money. You go out with her, do what you like, but you do *not* treat her as a real girlfriend. I'm trying to help you here. You are a fucking complete idiot where women are concerned.'

'She's nice.'

Imelda grabbed him by the shoulders and shouted, 'She's nice to everyone, you idiot! She flashes her clout for a fucking living! For fuck's sake, Liam, don't let anyone see that you really care for her, or you will be slaughtered! All I'm saying is, have a bit of discretion, OK?'

Liam nodded. But he couldn't help his feelings. Mandy, as she was called, rang every bell he possessed. Nice tits, tight snatch, and she treated him like a king. He couldn't help it – he went through the girls like water, was always on a love job of sorts.

'Your job is to run this club, Liam, with me. And you do a good job. Then a new stripper arrives and you fall in love! It's not right, Liam – you need to differentiate between the strippers and real birds. That's all I am saying.'

Liam just grinned and Imelda sighed in frustration – she knew she was wasting her time. Liam, who was a good guy, had a weakness for women in him. He was attracted to the strippers and, unlike the other boys, he actually dated them. Handsome fucker he was, so she could understand the girls' interest in him, but she was determined that not one of them would ever get a foot in his doorway. Not on her watch anyway.

Imelda actually liked this Mandy Wright; she was a genuinely lovely girl. The hardest part was that, since Imelda had taken over the Soho clubs, she had seen a different side to it. She'd become a part of the girls' lives and seen the reality of their situations. Mandy had a two-year-old boy, a nice little kid called Bernard who she worshipped, and who was the reason she stripped for a living. She had no real education, no real family in the background to help her out, and she was doing what she had to, to get by: stripping for a living. Through that, she paid her rent, and fed and clothed her boy. But she was still a fucking stripper, a Jack the Ripper as the slang went, and Liam needed to understand that there was a fine line, and once you stepped over it, you lost your credibility.

'Look, Liam, I like Mandy, she is a nice girl.'

'I'm glad to hear it, sis, because this time it's for real. I love her.'

Liam laughed at his sister's expression. She was fantastic, his Imelda, but she had no idea how his mind worked. He didn't give a toss what his bird did for a living – he thought she was the proverbial dog's knob, and that was enough as far as he was concerned.

Chapter Fifty-Four

Daniel looked at Tommy Barker with genuine interest. He had picked up on the fact that his mother really did like him and, from what he could see, he liked her. He had done his homework, and it seemed that Tommy was a straight arrow. He had murdered someone, granted, but it seemed he was well within his rights, and he had done his time – and a serious fucking lump at that. He had come out, was still on licence, he had a bit of an earn – a good earn in fact – and he had more or less kept his nose clean. He was well respected by his peers, and it looked as if he genuinely liked his mother's company.

His mum was notorious for outing her paramours within a few weeks; she had always had her diversions, but she had never brought a man into her sons' lives. Both Peter and Daniel had appreciated that. Ironically, at this late stage, it now seemed to be a distinct possibility.

Daniel was surprised that he didn't really care either way. Years before, he knew that if she had brought a man into their home, he would have felt honour-bound to see that he was removed, would have seen his presence as a fucking insult. As a rival almost, he supposed, shocked at the thought. Now, though, he didn't really care. She was old and he was a grown man with his own family. She still looked out for him – as today had proved – but she was entitled to her own life now. He wondered briefly if that was a good thing, and found he couldn't answer that question.

Lena seemed wary of the old fucker, but Tania had taken to him straight off. She seemed to like him, and they said that kids had a built-in radar. This Tommy Barker was a big old lump. In his day he would have been someone to respect, he would have been – in fact, from what Daniel had heard, *had* been – a man who people were wary of, who had a decent reputation. Even now, as old as he was, he still had a certain air about him; you could see he had been a serious fucking handful in his day.

Daniel stood up. 'What can I get you, Tommy? The drinks are on me.'

Tommy Barker had his arm around Theresa. He inclined his head. 'I'll have a large Scotch, Daniel, thank you very much.'

When Daniel eventually placed the drink on the table in front of Tommy Barker, he leaned towards him, and said quietly into his ear, 'You hurt my mother and you will have to deal with me.'

Tommy downed the Scotch in one swallow before he answered seriously, 'I wouldn't expect anything else from you, son. It's your mother. But remember this, I'm an old hand, and I don't take kindly to threats.'

Daniel Bailey laughed out loud. He liked this old boy; he was one of the old guard. 'I'll drink to that, mate.'

Lena watched it through frightened eyes and, even when Theresa squeezed her hand, grateful that she was that they had made up, she still felt the terror inside her. She didn't want to be a part of this world, and she was determined to make sure, no matter what her mother-in-law said, that she was not going to become a part of the Life, and neither was her daughter.

Chapter Fifty-Five

Mandy Wright looked at the man asleep beside her in her bed and marvelled at how this had all come about. She had sworn that she would not get involved with another man, and now here she was lying in bed with Liam Bailey. She had been determined to keep herself to herself, and just take care of her little boy. Now she had to admit that she had completely ignored her own advice – and she had allowed herself, once more, to fall for a man who she knew would hurt her.

Liam was handsome, kind – everything she wanted in a man – but she also suspected he was not a man who was looking for a partner for life. He had an eye for the ladies and why not? He was young, and he had the looks and the money to chase whatever and whoever he wanted. He came from a powerful family, he could write his own ticket. But it had only taken one look and, even though she knew he was a player, she couldn't stop herself; once he had shown an interest in her she had melted. She had given herself to him without hesitation. This time, though, she was on the pill; now she knew more about life and all its pitfalls, so at least there would not be another child.

Mandy had been in care on and off for most of her life. Her parents were upper middle class; her mother was a drunk, who self-medicated with tranquillisers, and her father was a lawyer. He was also a drunk, but a very violent one who, along with her mother, believed that his education and his background meant that they didn't have to live by the rules of normal people.

It was only when she was eight – and her mother had beaten her unconscious – that Mandy had finally been taken into care; a broken arm and fractured skull had been too much for her parents to explain away. A new social worker, Janice Carter – all love beads and afghans and still so new to the job she wasn't intimidated by the Wrights' pedigree – had removed her from them immediately. Mandy had been so grateful; for the first time in her life she had slept in a clean bed, had eaten three square meals a day, and attended school regularly. She had felt safe for the first time in her young life.

Over the years she had been reunited with her mother and father many times, but it had never been a success for any of them. Her mum and dad were so self-obsessed, and they had only fought for her for appearances' sake and then, when they got her, all they saw was their biggest failure. They knew their daughter saw them for what they were, not as the people they tried so desperately to portray.

Both sets of grandparents had washed their hands of their offspring long before she had arrived on the scene and, on the few occasions she had met them, they had not shown any real interest in her. Going into care had been her salvation; as bad as it was, it had at least afforded her a degree of security, something she had never before experienced in her young life.

She had eventually left the care system at sixteen, and immediately fallen for a young man who lived in the same bed and breakfast. He had been the product of the care system himself; he had given her a child and promptly disappeared. Amanda hadn't really expected anything else, if she was honest; everyone in her life had let her down up till then. But she had kept her little boy, and she loved him with a passion. She had been determined that she would give him the love that she had never had, and that *he* would never feel unwanted or inadequate.

She had ended up stripping, because she knew she had a good figure, and friends had introduced her to the world of Soho. Soho was a strange place; a girl could disappear there, and no one judged you too harshly. It was a world built on transients – people arrived, some stayed but most left. It was ideal for Amanda. All she had were her looks, and good looks and youth went a long way.

She did not claim money from the state, she paid for herself and her boy. The fact she did not accept money from the state meant that her parents could not find her when the fancy took them. Without claiming benefits, or paying tax, she knew she was living under the radar, and that was just how she wanted it. She was just another young girl trying to lose herself, and all she came from, and she had done a good job up to now of avoiding anything to do with the law, the courts, and the social services. She worked for her boy, her little Bernard. He was all that mattered to her.

Now, though, despite her good intentions, she had fallen for Liam Bailey of all people! She was just waiting for him to leave her, waiting for him to let her down. She was willing to enjoy him while she could, knowing that he would eventually break her heart, because even a few weeks of happiness were better than none; they would give her at least a few good memories for the future. She had so few memories of any kind of happiness that she was prepared to have her heart broken just to gather a few more. She was willing to grab any happiness she could from this man because she loved him – she loved him with a vengeance. He affected her in every possible way, from his looks to his voice to his demeanour. She worshipped him.

Liam had woken and was watching her. She looked so vulnerable; he could almost feel the anxiety emanating from her. He wondered, not for the first time, how such a beautiful girl could have such a low opinion of herself.

'Any chance of a cup of tea?'

Mandy physically jumped at his voice. He instinctively grabbed her arm to calm her and, pulling her to him, he said sadly, 'What is wrong with you? You're so nervous all the time.'

She could feel his heartbeat. She loved the feel of him; he was so big he made her feel safe, and she loved that he was so kind, and he *was* kind. It was such a big part of his nature.

Bernard started to cry in the next room, and he felt her stiffen. 'You make the tea, Mandy, and I'll get the lad, OK?'

She nodded, her eyes wide. She had lovely eyes, deep blue and really beautiful, but they were always full of fear.

'Make the tea, love. What does little Bernard have? Milk? Bring him his usual.'

Liam jumped out of the bed, and went into Bernard's room. The flat was so small – only three rooms and a bathroom that was no more than a shower and a toilet. But she had made it lovely. She kept it clean and tidy, and had decorated it in creams and golds. She had good taste he thought, and he admired her for the way she worked for her little lad.

As he picked Bernard up from his cot, he saw how blond the boy was, and he smiled to himself – there was no way anyone would ever believe he was his dad. But he didn't care, he was a nice kid, and he had a fuck-off little mum.

'Hello, Bernie boy, it's Uncle Liam again, and I think your mum is the nuts!'

Bernard Wright grinned; he liked this big dark-skinned man who spoke to him with kindness and who held him so tightly. Bernard snuggled into the man's arms; he felt secure with him. As he looked into Liam's eyes he smiled widely, his huge eyes trusting, and when his arms wound their way round Liam's neck, Liam knew that this was all he wanted; Mandy and her little boy were a team, and he wanted to be a part of that team.

He got back into bed, and he sat Bernard on his lap. When Mandy came back in with the tea, he smiled at her and said seriously, 'All right, Mandy?'

She nodded; as always, she was quiet and grateful, and it frustrated him. She was a fucking diamond, she had no reason to put herself down.

'He's a great little lad, our Bernie boy, and I think he likes me!'

As he said it, young Bernard hugged him tightly and, wrapping his arms around the child instinctively, he smiled happily. He could see the pleasure on Mandy's face, knew that she appreciated he was nice to her little lad. He was saddened that she was so grateful for so little, that she didn't understand just how wonderful she was.

'Listen, Mandy, I want to be with you all the time, and this little fella and all. Do you think you could find it in your heart to love me back, because I love you, darling, and this little fella too.'

Mandy Wright looked at her son's blond head, and watched as he laughed as Liam Bailey tickled him. Putting down the mug of tea, she sat on the bed, and started to cry. She was sobbing, unable to believe what he was telling her.

Liam pulled her into his arms and, kissing her forehead, he said honestly, 'Mandy love, this was supposed to make us all happy.'

Hugging him tightly she said eventually, 'Oh, I am happy, Liam, that's the trouble.'

Chapter Fifty-Six

'Delroy, if you fucking don't tell me the truth, I will kill you stone dead, I swear it.'

Imelda was in one of her jealous rages and Delroy was determined not to let her cause him any trouble; he loved her with a passion, but she knew better than anyone that he could never be completely faithful. 'Stop it, Mel, I *mean* it. This is a fucking stupid enterprise, and we both know it. I love you, and you will always be my number one woman. But if you cause murders for any length of time, I *will* fucking leave – I'll walk out. I love you and my boy more than life itself, but I will not be a part of all this shit. The girl came for a job, no more and no less. If I was on the nest with someone else, do you really think I would be stupid enough to let you know about it? Would have them nearby? Give me some credit, for fuck's sake. Now, please, let this drop.'

Imelda looked at the man she had loved since the first time she had laid eyes on him, and she knew that no matter how she felt, she had to let this go. Delroy would not let himself be dragged into any arguments about his fidelity, he had told her that from day one. She knew he loved her but, as time went on, it was getting harder and harder to overlook his failings. She knew in her heart that if he was seeing someone else, he respected her far too much to ever put her in a position where she might actually come into contact with the person. Oh, there'd been whispers over the years, but never anything concrete. Then, two days ago, she had seen him dropping off a girl at the club in Brixton. It had been like a physical blow. The girl had been young, white and lovely. Imelda had felt so bad because the girl had been fresh and young, and Imelda couldn't compete. She hated herself for letting him know she had seen him, for letting him know how much she cared, but she couldn't help herself.

Delroy understood her fears; he knew Imelda so well, but he was not a man to be curtailed in any way. He loved her but, in all fairness, he had never promised her fidelity and he wasn't going to start now. He wouldn't lie to her either – not unless he really felt he had to. Even so, he hated to see the hurt on her face, the pain of betrayal in her eyes.

'I love you, girl, you know that. You're my woman, the mother of my child, and you know that there ain't no one who can compete with that.'

Imelda couldn't answer him because, for the first time ever, she was convinced that he was lying to her.

Chapter Fifty-Seven

'I want this Communion to be really great, Lena. Tania is our only daughter, and for the first time ever you can pick out a dress. With the boys it was so different, I know – just nice suits and shirts. But this time you get to go over the top! So I will leave you and Ria to sort it out.'

Daniel could sense the strained atmosphere between his wife and his sister-in-law because of the state of affairs between him and Peter, and he knew that his presence would not make it any easier. He needed Lena and Ria to be friends – it gave the illusion to the world that all was well with the Bailey brothers, even if people knew the real score.

As he left his house, he looked around him, and he saw the home he had provided as other people would see it. At the front door he paused and, turning round, he looked at the hallway, saw the tired carpets and the grubby wallpaper. The kitchen door was open and he saw the old-fashioned units, as if for the first time. He wondered at Lena then; she had never really bothered about their surroundings – it was clean and cheerful but it was also dated and cheap. It had never bothered him before; now, though, he felt that his home should reflect him and his success, and a little bit of him resented Lena for never wanting that for herself. She still salted money away, and he had been grateful for her thriftiness in the past, God knew. But now he suddenly felt that his home should have been upgraded a long time ago to befit a man of his standing, and reflect his status.

Peter lived like a fucking king; he had always said that a house was an investment, and he had bought and sold many over the years, so that now he had a seriously big drum. Electric gates and the privacy that only money could buy. Daniel could easily have the same – he had enough legit businesses to cover any costs he incurred.

His mother's words had penetrated and he *was* genuinely trying to look at the world through his sons' eyes. They wanted him to toe the line, and he was *trying* desperately to do just that; it was fucking hard going if he was honest. But he was determined to keep a low profile as such, and listen to the boys' advice and, by doing so, he hoped to eventually fit in with the rest of his so-called peers. He'd cut down on the drugs for a start – he still did the odd line but he felt like he had a clearer head now.

Shutting his front door gently behind him, he decided that he was going to upgrade his living accommodation and his transport. He would also accept the boys' advice on getting new offices – though he would still keep his scrapyard. He would never relinquish those premises for anybody; not only were they ideal for certain types of meetings, but he also knew that he would need a bolt hole from time to time.

As he sat in his car, he looked up at his house, his home, where he had been very happy and contented, and he wondered at how he had never noticed before just how scruffy and unkempt it actually was. No wonder people didn't see him like they did his brother Peter – he must have looked like the poor relation, even though he had earned just as much as his brother.

It had never bothered him before; like Lena, he had never craved the trappings of wealth. Now, though, he finally understood the psychological advantage of being seen as a person who earned a good living. People saw what you had and they then saw you as successful and, because of that, they believed that they could earn through you; they trusted you because you already had what they wanted.

He sighed, wondering why it had taken him so fucking long to understand the Life he was involved in. He was annoyed with himself; he didn't have the nous to see things in the same way other people did – he accepted that, and now he was willing to listen to other people. He was determined to address the problem even though, in all honesty, he was finding it very hard.

He started the car and, as he pulled away from his house, he hoped against hope that he could keep a lid on his temper, and that he could keep up with this new way of life. He was certain of only one thing – that his little Tania would grow up in a home that befitted her, and his Lena was going to have to get onboard, whether she liked it or not.

Chapter Fifty-Eight

'I'm telling you, Petey, it's like he's had a personality transplant. You can assure your dad that we are keeping him sweet.' Danny could hardly believe it himself.

Petey laughed. 'It's mad, ain't it? I keep hearing good things about you all! My old man is amazed at your dad's transformation. He's pleased, obviously, but he is also a bit sceptical, you know.'

Danny swallowed his anger; he could see first hand that his father was really trying to work with them, and he knew just how hard it was for him.

Petey Bailey, his cousin, who he loved dearly, was arsehole-lucky that he had a father who was not a fucking hair's breadth away from the nuthouse. But they had to work together; the fact that they were the go-betweens for their old men was as important as it was sad. That was the way it was, and there was nothing they could do about it.

'I told you I would keep him in check, and I am. Now, what's the score with the new clubs? I know we talked about coming into Essex next, and I have just the place actually. It's as cheap as chips – the bloke who owned it fucking slung most of his profits up his nose. He is a complete cunt. He also owes a big amount of wedge to us and, as luck would have it, he now owes a fair amount to Davey. I got Davey to offer him an out, so he gave him enough money to cover the interest on his original loan, that means now, of course, he has *two* loans that he can't pay. It's just a matter of assuring him that we will forgo the debts if he signs the premises over to us. He will be glad to get shot, I think. He made the cardinal mistake: he opened a club and saw it as his personal hangout, not as a business. It was only a matter of time before he fucked up.'

Petey smiled; he loved Danny's knack of sniffing out a bargain. 'Sounds good to me! Bailey Enterprises are on the up, eh? Where's this place located?'

Danny lit a cigarette and, taking a deep pull on it, he said nonchalantly, 'Ilford High Street. Used to be Colin Farmer's drum, now it's ours. Run properly it could be a gold mine.'

Petey was impressed; Colin Farmer came from a good family – they would have bailed him out if he had asked them to. Evidently Danny had convinced Colin otherwise, and he wondered what he had used to lean on him. It had to be something big – much more than the debts alone.

Danny could almost hear his cousin's brain crunching as he tried to work out the score, and he grinned, deciding to let him in on the secret. 'I pointed out that his coke habit was not something his family would embrace, and that his penchant for young boys might cause a few raised eyebrows.'

Petey was absolutely gobsmacked and his cousin's amazement pleased Danny no end.

'I gave him an ultimatum, so to speak, while he was getting a blow job in the front of his car from a fifteen-year-old Asian kid – not that I have told any of my brothers that, and I expect you to keep it to yourself as well. It will come out eventually, that kind of thing always does, and it is best we have nothing to do with it whatsoever. I have given him my word that I'll keep schtum, and I will honour that.'

Petey Bailey was still reeling. Colin Farmer was a ladies' man – he played the part of the womaniser with gusto. Peter had never had an inkling that the man might be an iron hoof. 'That is fucking unbelievable! How did you find out? His old man would go fucking spare.'

Danny shrugged. 'A little bird told me!' He had no intention of letting on that he had a network of people on his payroll whose only job was to find out anything and everything about anyone and everyone in their world, including his close family, and their cohorts. Knowledge was power, and he knew the value of secrets. He also knew, without a shadow of a doubt, that one day the knowledge he was so patiently gathering would be worth more to him than money alone.

Petey was thrilled that his cousin had got them such a bargain. Like his brothers and his cousins, he was weary of the situation between their fathers, but they knew they had to work around it, and they were doing a pretty good job. They had the family businesses, and they had their separate businesses; somehow they made it all work.

Danny poured them both a large brandy and, saluting his cousin, he said happily, 'To us, cuz; onwards and upwards.'

Petey clinked glasses with him. 'That sounds fucking good to me, mate!' Then he laughed again, his huge head shaking with mirth. 'I can't get over it! Colin Farmer, a fucking shirt-lifter!'

Daniel looked at his cousin then and said seriously, 'Petey, he's a fucking nonce. The boy was a fucking schoolkid, he was barely fifteen.'

Petey digested that information slowly before saying, 'Fuck me, you're right. That's fucking gross.'

Danny shrugged nonchalantly. 'Tell me about it, Petey, but it will all come out in the wash. Until then, the fucker's mine.' Danny drank his brandy, savouring every sip, safe in the knowledge that he now *owned* Colin Farmer lock, stock and fucking barrel. And, before he was finished, he would own a lot more people. He was his father's eldest son; it was down to *him* to bring back some kind of respect and admiration for their side of the Bailey family, and he was going to make sure that happened. They were not going to be perceived as second best any more. All his life he had watched his father go his own very strange and very peculiar road, and he had realised early on that it had not gained them anything of any real value. His father, unfortunately, was a man of extreme but random violence – not something that was seen as a drawback in their world normally. But Danny understood that his father's complete disregard for the moral codes that they lived by, and his inability to see his actions as anything other than justified, had caused them serious problems. His Uncle Peter had ensured that his father's more outrageous escapades had been overlooked, but they were still remembered.

Well, now he and his brothers were grown up, and they were not going to stand by and play second fiddle to anyone; he was working day and night to make sure that the sons of Daniel Bailey were seen as trustworthy and, more to the point, as men in their own right. Petey Bailey and his brothers had *nothing* to prove, and Danny was pleased for them, but he and his brothers had to work twice as hard to prove their worth. They were willing to do that, to bring a good wedge to the table, and show their Uncle Peter that they were more than capable of scratching a good living. And, unlike their cousins, they would achieve it against the odds.

Petey Bailey watched his cousin as he rolled a joint, and he wondered at what it must be like to live in the shadow of a father like his Uncle Daniel – a bona fide fucking nut-job. Petey loved his cousin; he felt sorry for him, because he had a lot to live down, but he was confident that Danny was well able to do the job. And whatever Daniel Bailey Senior was, he was still a man who could terrify the average man on the street. He was still one of the Bailey brothers, and that counted for a lot in their world.

Chapter Fifty-Nine

Lena was delighted with her daughter's Communion dress – it was absolutely beautiful. She was glad that she had let Ria help her with the choice. She felt that Ria had much better taste than her, and would know what material was suitable, and what style would suit Tania; she had a knack for all that. As Lena looked at the finished article, she was absolutely beside herself with happiness. It wasn't simply a dress, it was a gown! The sleeves alone were a work of art, all hand-stitched, and screaming class. Oh, she was so excited about the Communion now. Not that she hadn't been before; after all, it was not a fashion parade – it was a very serious event. Her daughter would be making her first confession, and partaking of the Holy Eucharist for the first time. Lena blessed herself quickly at the thought.

Even so, she could not stop looking at her daughter's dress, and admiring it from every angle. Having a girl meant you could really push the boat out – even the poorest of the families did. Holy Communion was a big event in the Church, and in a child's life. Her Tania would be the most gorgeous child there this year, of that much she was sure.

Lena's big worry was not about the ceremony itself, but about the party they were putting on afterwards at the Shandon Bells, for Tania and Delroy Junior. Peter and Daniel would be properly in the same room for the first time since the 'big falling out' as she called it. She was desperate to make sure that nothing happened to ruin the children's big day. She was relieved that things were back to normal between her and Theresa – that was one less worry anyway.

Tania came into her mother's bedroom, smiling widely; she adored the dress almost as much as her mummy did. She was desperate to wear it and the accessories they had chosen. There was a small diamanté tiara that would hold her veil in place, and a mother-of-pearl Bible that she would hold in her hands – hands that would be covered by white lacy gloves. She was going to look like a princess! She hugged her mother, and they stood together admiring the dress in silence.

Daniel walked into the bedroom, and when both of his girls turned towards him he saw the happiness on their faces. Grinning, he said jokily, 'Is this the dress, then? I thought it would be delivered by the fairies! It looks like a fairy dress.'

Tania was excited already, but her dad's praise was all she needed. 'Do you love it, Dad? I love it.'

He picked her up and hugged her to him. 'I think it is the nicest dress I have ever seen, sweetheart.'

Tania beamed with happiness.

'It is lovely, Daniel, even if I say it myself. She will be the best dressed there, I know that for a fact.'

Daniel was pleased to hear Lena; he wanted his daughter to be dressed as he saw fit. She was a good-looking child, and he wanted her to be perceived as he felt a daughter of his should be – well dressed and a cut above the other kids. He remembered Imelda's Communion years before; Ria had decked her out like a fucking society bride. Peter had told him the price of the dress and, at the time, he had thought they were fucking mad to pay that much for a child's outfit – an outfit that she would only wear once at that. Now, though, he could understand it. A girl was a different kettle of fish when it came to these occasions – they were special because they *could* be dressed up like miniature brides.

He would make sure that his daughter, his *only* daughter, would look expensive and classy if it was the last thing he did. He was learning, at this late stage, how to play the game and he was determined to play it better than everyone else.

'Who wants to hear my good news, then?'

Tania hugged his neck tightly and squealed, 'I do, Daddy! Tell me!'

Lena was smiling happily; she assumed it was about the Communion, it being all she thought about these days.

'I have bought us a new house. A big detached house, and you, my princess, will have your own bathroom! What do you think of that?'

Tania was not sure what to think, and it showed. Laughing loudly, Daniel hugged her once more. 'You will be able to have a bath in your very own bathroom!'

'Really, Daddy? My own bath, just for me?'

'Your own bath, princess, nothing is too good for you!'

Lena was watching him warily now. 'You've bought a house without telling me?'

Placing his daughter on the floor, Daniel nodded. 'Yes, I have, Lena, and not before time. We have the money and I want this little one to have everything we can give her.'

It was the right approach and he knew it. Lena would move heaven and earth for her daughter, she would gladly move if it meant Tania would get the benefit. He wondered how they had coped with the boys in such a small space. But, then again, he hadn't cared in those days, one way or the other.

Chapter Sixty

Tommy Barker was very happy with Theresa – she suited him perfectly. His mother was Irish, and his father had been Scottish, so he had been brought up with the best of Catholic intentions and, as big a rogue as he had eventually become, he had never really left his Catholic upbringing behind.

Seeing Theresa so excited about her granddaughter's Communion was something he had never thought would affect him so much, but it had, and he was looking forward to it as much as she was.

Theresa Bailey was a bit of a girl – there was no doubt about that! He had known her many years ago, and he had admired her then for the way she had worked for her boys, and shrugged off the stigma not only of having two children out of wedlock, but of having a child of colour into the bargain. In their day that had taken a lot of guts, and she had more guts than most of the men he knew. She had been devoted to her boys, which had been apparent to anyone who knew her, and she had never apologised for either of them. He had a sneaking feeling, though, that these days she felt the strain of her younger son more than she let on.

Daniel Bailey, the slippery little fucker, was trying to elbow his way into his affairs, and he was not sure if he was pleased about that or not. A part of him was amenable to letting a younger man take on some of the responsibility – Tommy was not as driven as he had been years ago. But Tommy was in a unique position as the mastermind behind his earn – he laundered money for anyone who was anyone. He could take ill-gotten gains and make them into legal money with the least amount of fuss. That was his forte, and he had a niche in the market. He didn't have a lot of people in his employ, but those he did have, he trusted implicitly. Hand-picked, they were aware of the risks involved, which, although minimal thanks to his forward planning, were still dangerous enough to give the average person food for thought. It was a delicate and intricate business, needing a steady hand and, more importantly, someone who understood economics – of both the global and the criminal variety.

Tommy was a natural; he instinctively knew where to place money and when to withdraw money, he knew where to spend the cash and on what. These days he laundered money for the Russians. They were caked up with money – drug money, he assumed. He had a few tame lawyers in his employ who were more than happy to organise cash purchases of expensive properties in London and arrange large mortgages on them. Subsequently, the owners of these properties now had legitimate cash to spend, invest or just put into high-interest accounts. It was a doddle really, and these days he was bored with it. He would not be averse to Daniel Bailey doing the donkey work, giving him more time to enjoy his old age.

He was feeling older than he cared to admit. It was comfortable being with Theresa – he liked that they were of an age. Tommy's penchant for young girls was long gone – he wanted someone he could talk to properly, someone who understood the Life, who he didn't have to buy with expensive trinkets and exotic holidays. Theresa was still a good-looking woman, and she didn't take any shit. Coupled with her lust for life, and her sense of humour, that made her a diamond. Tommy was, for the first time in years, settled, contented. He realised he genuinely loved her. He still had a good earn, which he valued, but he was ready to hand over the reins. All he wanted these days was a few drinks, a good laugh, and the occasional sexual encounter with his Theresa.

As he listened to her singing along with the radio, he smiled, his mind made up. Daniel could take over his business if he really wanted to; in truth, he would be doing him a favour.

As he walked down the stairs and into the kitchen he was a much happier man. Now that he had finally made the decision to get shot of his businesses, he felt freer, as if someone had taken the weight of the world off his shoulders. Daniel was a hardcase, and that was exactly what was needed in his game; Tommy would teach him, take his cut, and gradually fade into the background.

'You look happy.' Theresa was in a good mood; she was always in a good mood since she had taken up with Tommy Barker.

'That, my darling, is because I am!'

Chapter Sixty-One

'Well, I can tell you now, Liam, Imelda doesn't like her, but she'll get over it. Look, if you're happy, son, I'm happy.'

Liam was embarrassed; he could feel the heat as it washed over him, and he knew that he looked a fool. He'd been confident that his mother wouldn't care about Mandy's profession. She had heard him out, welcomed Mandy and her little lad as if they were visiting royalty, and now he knew she would defend his choice of partner if the need should arise.

'Thanks, Mum; I knew you would understand.'

Ria smiled. Liam was still so young, but he was clearly genuinely enamoured of this Mandy and she seemed like a nice girl. She was a looker, there was no doubt about that – in fact, she was stunning. She was a very polite young woman, and she had a beautiful speaking voice; the fact she was a stripper was something Ria knew she would just have to overlook. She had a feeling Amanda wouldn't be stripping for long anyway, not if her son had anything to do with it. The little boy was well looked after, that much was evident, and Liam appeared to adore him. It was strange really – her Liam, the ladies' man, had been knocked for six by a pretty face. Well, as long as he was happy, that was the main thing. She thought it might do him good to take on a bit of responsibility – Christ knew he needed something to focus on; he was inclined to drift.

The same could be said for each of her boys, she supposed. None of them seemed to want to settle down, but then they were not living the kind of life suited to that. They ran nightclubs, were used to late nights, and they were enjoying every second of it. It was every young bloke's dream, she guessed. But now here was her Liam on a love job, and she really was pleased for him.

'Go in the front room and entertain your girl. I'll rustle us up a bit of grub. Does the little fella eat anything special?'

'Bernard eats whatever you put in front of him. He's a good kid, Mum – funny and all. I've been teaching him a bit of boxing.'

Ria could hear the pride in her son's voice, and for a few seconds she felt the urge to cry. She was proud of her son, proud that he had a heart big enough to love that poor girl's child. It took a lot for someone to do something like that, and not every man was capable of it. But Liam seemed to genuinely care for the boy.

'I can hear your dad. Let him in, will you?'

Five minutes later Peter came into the kitchen, amazement written all over his face. Laughing softly, she said, 'I know what you're thinking, but she seems a good girl, Pete.'

'She's a fucking looker, I know that much!'

Ria laughed again. 'I know, and why not? We have good-looking sons! All joking aside, he is absolutely smitten with her, and her little lad as well. She's had it hard from what Liam's said, and she is very young, but she makes him happy.'

Peter Bailey loved his wife with a passion, and she knew that. Jealousy had never been a feature of their relationship, and he was pleased about that more than he would ever admit. Liam's girl was a real beauty, and there were many women who would not welcome her into their lives. Very beautiful women were rarely liked by other women, he knew that from his years working the clubs. Imelda was a jealous woman, and she had already given her opinion about Mandy to him very vocally. He was sorry about that because Imelda needed to realise, before it was too late, that it took more than good looks to keep a couple together.

'It's his life, Ria! He's a grown man.'

'A stripper! I bet she caused a few heart attacks!'

They were laughing loudly together when Liam came into the kitchen with his ready-made family.

Mandy Wright was nervous, excited and happy all at the same time; she loved the atmosphere in this house, and she felt that Liam's mother liked her and, more importantly, that she liked Bernard. She was daring to hope that she might have finally landed on her feet.

Bernard was crowing with laughter. Seeing his son hugging the blond child as if he was his own flesh and blood, Peter was suddenly reminded of his brother Daniel and how he had looked out for him when they had been kids. Daniel had the same blue eyes as this little lad and, like Liam, Peter had brown eyes. War and Peace was their mother's nickname for them, but they had been so close. For the first time in a long while, Peter missed his brother.

Mandy was sitting at the kitchen table, her son on her lap, chatting away to Ria, and Peter opened a bottle of wine for them. He felt a sudden rush of contentment wash over him. This was what life was about – being together as a family, enjoying each other's company, and appreciating what you had.

Young Bernard put his arms out; Peter Bailey took the child and, smiling happily, he said to his son, 'What are we going to call him then, eh? Bernie boy?'

Mandy watched as a big fuss was made of her little boy; she saw Ria watching her husband and son as they played with the child, and she dropped her head on to her chest as she tried to keep her emotions in check.

Ria placed a hand on her shoulder and, squeezing gently, she leaned down and she whispered into her ear. 'Listen love, relax, you're with friends.'

Mandy looked up, and her eyes were wet with emotion. Ria pulled the girl into her arms and, hugging her tightly, she said loudly, 'This one's a keeper, Liam.'

Liam looked at his father and they smiled together. Young Bernard was in his element being the centre of attention. Liam was happier than he had believed humanly possible. Winking at his mum, he began wondering where would be the best place to buy a property, so he could not only house his new-found family but, at the same time, make a good investment for the future.

Chapter Sixty-Two

Delroy was counting up the divvy. He knew it was light, but he wasn't too bothered – the remainder would be collected the next day by his lads. He yawned loudly.

Imelda came into the kitchen and he smiled at her despite the fact he was still irritated with her. She knew better than to accuse him of infidelity this time. He was a player, no doubt about that, but he would never do anything to jeopardise his relationship with her.

'Is everything ready for Sunday?'

She nodded. She was nervous around him these days, constantly terrified that he would walk out on her and their son. 'It's going to be lovely. Little Tania's dress is out of this world! I just hope my dad and Uncle Daniel don't have a row.'

Delroy shrugged. 'They won't. It's been a while now, girl, and they don't communicate, except through the boys. It will be cool; stop worrying about nothing.'

Imelda felt that he was dismissing her, but she bit her tongue. She had always been of a fiery temperament, and lately she had been feeling uneasy. Seeing him laughing with that young girl had unnerved her more than she would have believed. She *did* believe him when he said there was nothing untoward going on with her; she knew he would never do that to her – not publicly anyway, and not where they were both known. She was lucky he was like that – many of the men in their world had no such qualms, and they took their girlfriends to the same places they took their wives.

But it was seeing him with that girl, so relaxed, laughing out loud at something she had said, that had affected her so much. Who else was he like that with? Was she white? Blonde, with pneumatic tits, and big blue eyes? Was she a typical Rasta boy's Klingon? Did he hold her in his arms? Did he tell her things, private things? Did he compare *her* to his lover?

Even though Delroy kept his women well tucked away, just knowing he had them was enough to break Imelda's spirit. The fact that he *needed* other women was more than she could bear. She had tried never to let it bother her before, but the nightmare of seeing him laughing with that young girl, knowing she wanted him even if he didn't want her, was almost a physical pain. Like someone had wrenched her guts out from inside her and thrown them on to the dirty road.

His job alone made sure he was always around other women. He worked odd hours; he would never be a man she could pin down in any way. He was a man who took a flyer when the fancy took him, but she was tortured by the idea that one of those girls he used would become more than just a sexual pastime. If he left her she would die. She would never recover, of that much she was sure.

'You all right, Mel?'

She forced a smile and, coughing nervously, she said gently, 'Course! I'm always all right. That looks light.'

He grinned. Trust her to notice that. 'It is. I was tired; I just wanted to get home.'

It was what she wanted to hear, and they both knew it.

Chapter Sixty-Three

'It's fucking loud in here.' Noel could scarcely hear himself.

Jamsie nodded his agreement; it was pointless trying to answer his brother. They pushed their way through to the back of the club, relieved to shut the door of the small office; they could still hear the music, but it was muted enough to at least hear yourself think.

'This place is a fucking gold mine! I told Danny a good DJ was worth the money, didn't I?'

Noel was pleased that his ideas had worked out so well. He had argued that a good DJ developed a following, and he had been proven right. Since getting their hands on Colin Farmer's place they had tripled their income almost overnight. They now had monthly guest spots in all their clubs, and they sought the best of the best. Northern soul was big again, so the Northern boys were very popular; the punters were happy to jam the place out on week nights, pleased at the opportunity to hear the DJs they had heard about perform live for them.

It was a great time to be in the club industry. Everything was so easy now – the venues were huge, they had the facilities to put on the bands, and the capacity to make sure it was an earner. The strip clubs were all well and good, but they saw the future in clubbing. Young people were willing to pay for a good night out, a bit of gear, coke, whatever, and as they also supplied that along with the alcohol consumed, they were on a fucking roll.

'I'm fucking knackered, Noel. Cut me a line, will you? I need a livener.'

Noel did not need to be asked twice. As he cut the coke on the desk top with a credit card, he felt a rush of contentment; this really was the life. They were charmed, they had it all.

Jamsie poured them both beers and, after they had snorted a couple of lines each, they toasted each other.

'They are late. If they don't get a fucking move on they can piss off.'

Noel laughed. 'Oh, Jamsie, fuck off. They'll be here.'

Jamsie grinned. He could feel the buzz coming over him, his tiredness was gone, and his brain was active once more. 'That's a good fucking snort!'

Noel laughed. 'I should hope so. Jack knows where to get the good stuff!'

They were both roaring with laughter now.

A knock on the office door heralded the arrival of their guests. Noel opened the door with a flourish, and ushered in two men; both were in their late twenties, from Liverpool. They were the Daly brothers, legends in their own lunchtimes, and as dangerous as they were handsome.

Gerry Daly took in the scene in nanoseconds and said loudly, 'Oh, just what we needed! A snort and a beer. It don't get better than this!'

Paddy Daly took out a notebook and, as Noel was cutting them lines, he explained, in glowing terms, how they were all going to benefit from the bank robbery he and his brother had planned down to the very last detail.

Noel and Jamsie were thrilled; as the youngest of Daniel's boys they were desperate to spread their wings, go out on their own, and the Daly brothers were more than willing to help them achieve their goal.

Chapter Sixty-Four

Little Delroy looked handsome, and he knew it; he was a very confident child. His father laughed as his son walked around outside the church like a mini version of himself. It was funny how seeing yourself in your children made you realise that, through them, you would never really be gone. Those people who said they didn't want children were nutbags; why else would God have created the human race?

Imelda looked gorgeous, but then she always looked good. Not that she would believe a word he said nowadays. She was a difficult female, but Delroy had always been attracted to the feisty ones – he liked a bit of spark in his women.

He saw Daniel Bailey, Tania and Lena walking towards him, and he smiled at them easily, determined to put the dramas of the past behind them today. Little Tania looked absolutely fantastic. She was a good-looking child, and she would one day be a beautiful woman. You could see Theresa in her – she even had her nana's walk. 'Look at you!'

Tania beamed with pride; she knew without a shadow

of a doubt that she looked lovely today. She *felt* lovely as well.

Delroy offered Daniel his hand in greeting. 'You all right, Daniel? What a great day, eh? Your old mum's like a fucking maniac with it all.'

Daniel Bailey smiled tightly, but his attention was not really on Delroy. He was aware that his brother was somewhere in the vicinity, and that they were unlikely to acknowledge each other except with a brief nod.

Lena had made her way straight to Ria, and Daniel felt irritated for a moment, but he swallowed his anger. Ria and Lena were close mates, and their friendship kept up the pretence that everything was OK between the brothers, even though everyone in their world knew the truth.

Danny was watching his dad closely. He was not going to have even one drink today – he would keep as close to his father as humanly possible, without making it too obvious and, if there was even the slightest hint of a problem concerning him, he would remove his father from the premises immediately. Uncle Peter could be relied on to keep his cool, no matter what. His dad, however, could not. He was trying though, and they gave him credit for that, but it didn't change the fact that none of his sons believed he was cured of his angry outbursts. A few drinks, and an imagined slight could easily cause World War Three. It was his little sister's day today, and he was hoping against hope that his father would keep that fact in the forefront of his mind.

Danny glanced around the church grounds; the place was packed out with parents, families and children. He wondered where the fuck his brothers were. Noel and Jamsie were nowhere to be seen.

He saw Liam Bailey arrive with his girlfriend and her little boy; she was a looker all right, and a stripper! He had seen her without her kecks on more than one occasion – they all had. She had been a sight to see, God bless her, all tits and lip gloss. But if Liam didn't give a fuck, why should he? He was well loved-up by all accounts.

Mandy waved at him shyly, and he smiled back at her, amazed at how she could remove her clothes for money yet still be bashful in male company. That was a melon scratcher all right. Liam winked at him and mouthed hello. Liam had never looked so happy, and Danny was pleased for him; he seemed to enjoy playing the daddy, and the kid adored him, anyone could see that.

His Uncle Peter was walking into the church, and Danny watched as his father acted like he wasn't bothered either way. He prayed, please God, let the day go without a hitch. He was not in the mood for aggro, and he did not relish his task as unofficial minder.

Chapter Sixty-Five

Noel and Jamsie were nervous. They had arranged this sure in the knowledge that they would arrive at the Communion in time for the service and the clock was ticking. As they sat in the white Transit van with the Daly brothers, they were sweating with apprehension and anticipation. Noel kept his hand on the pump-action shotgun purchased especially for this occasion. He liked the feel of it, the knowledge that he had it close by. Powerful guns were like expensive cars – they said something about you personally, made you feel good about yourself. He glanced at his brother and they exchanged uncertain smiles.

They were at the top of Green Lane and, at any moment, a Securicor van stuffed full of bank notes would be travelling towards them. It was the monthly run from the Bank of England. The van carried used notes that were on their way to be burned. They were old, tattered, too long in circulation. Only this time, if they pulled it off, the notes would be legal tender once again.

It was a fucking doddle. The only real problem would be getting the doors of the van open, and that was it. The Dalys had a high-velocity rifle that would easily penetrate the windshield and then they'd rip it out with crowbars. The men inside would open the back doors without a second's thought! Any heroes would be despatched easily enough – no one would be shot fatally, but a shattered kneecap was normally enough to ensure everyone's cooperation. At least that was what the Daly brothers had assured them.

The radio was on low, and Queen were singing 'We Are The Champions'. Jamsie grinned. It was a fitting song, considering what they were about to do.

It was a beautiful day, and Jamsie was glad; he wanted his little sister's big day to go well for her. They had lived and breathed this fucking Communion for weeks now. He was feeling sick with excitement, knowing that what they were about to do could easily cause them serious trouble but, like Noel, he needed to prove to everyone that they were capable of doing things on their own.

Gerry Daly put on his balaclava, and they immediately followed suit. Paddy Daly pulled the Transit van out from the kerb and into the path of the Securicor van quickly and expertly.

There was a screeching of tyres and then all hell broke loose.

Chapter Sixty-Six

The Shandon Bells in Ilford was packed out, and Ria and Lena were both feeling the emotion of the day. The kids were running around like maniacs, the seriousness of the occasion long forgotten now that they were away from the church. Tania was dishevelled – her diamanté tiara was askew, and her veil was hanging down her back like a rag – but she was triumphant. She had made her first confession, and her first Holy Communion. It was the beginning of her journey into adulthood, a day she would never forget.

Little Delroy was full of himself, but it was *her* day really. The boys didn't get to dress up like the girls and so didn't get as much attention. She had known she looked gorgeous, and she had liked that feeling.

As she walked through to the toilets, she heard her daddy's voice and, without thinking, she stopped in the small doorway that heralded the men's toilets.

She stood there quietly, her eyes wide. Her father had her brother Noel by the throat, and Jamsie was on the floor with his head in his hands and he was bleeding. Noel was trying to escape from her daddy's grip, dragging and pulling at his father's hands. She could hear him choking, as if he couldn't breathe, his face red and flustered.

Her daddy was shouting at him, 'You fucking idiots! Robbing a fucking security van! Putting yourselves up for a fifteen stretch! You're a pair of useless cunts!'

Jamsie was shaking his head in denial, and she could see Noel's eyes popping out of his head. She was frightened, terribly frightened. Her oldest brother Danny was watching it calmly, as if it didn't mean anything, and Davey, standing next to him, looked appalled.

'I'll fucking murder you both! Don't you ever fucking pull a stunt like this again!'

Daniel Bailey threw his son away from him, and Tania heard the sickening thud as Noel's head hit the tiles.

Davey pulled himself away from the wall, and he stopped abruptly as he saw his little sister in the mirrors above the sinks. 'Dad . . .'

'Stop it, Daddy, stop it.' Tania was hysterical.

Daniel Bailey turned towards his little daughter, shocked that she was there in the men's room.

She heard her eldest brother Danny whisper, 'For fuck's sake!'

As her daddy walked towards her she backed away from him in fear.

'Come here, princess, come here, love.'

His voice was low, full of love and she couldn't believe it was the same voice that had just spouted such hatred, such bile at her brothers.

Tania was white with fear and, as Noel dragged himself up from the floor, she looked from him to Jamsie. She saw that his eye was bleeding, and his mouth was swollen and bloody, and she knew instinctively that her father had done that to him, had hurt him like he had Noel.

He was kneeling in front of her now, her daddy, and she could see the sorrow in his eyes, could feel his panic.

'Listen, princess, you're too little to understand all this, darling. Noel and Jamsie know it's for their own good. Come here, sweetheart, come to your daddy.'

He pulled her into his arms, and she let him, but she was clearly terrified. Daniel could feel the trembling of her little body, feel the pounding of her heart. As he stroked her back gently, she felt her stomach churning and, before she could stop herself, she brought up everything she had eaten that day. All the lovely sandwiches, fairy cakes, chicken drumsticks, and crisps vacated her body in one massive heave. She felt faint, as if she was unable to stand up by herself. Her head was filling with hot air, and she leaned into her daddy for protection.

Daniel held his daughter tightly, sorry to the core for what she had witnessed, angry that his sons had caused him to lose his temper like that, and nervous about how his wife would react when she heard about this particular scenario. He was unsure exactly how much his daughter had seen, and how much of what she had seen and heard she had actually understood.

Noel and Jamsie were both shamefaced and guilty about the trouble they had caused. They had not expected their father to react as he had – they had honestly believed he would pat them on the back and congratulate them on their industry. They had earned a small fortune in less than ten minutes. Surely that had to count for something? Neither of them had thought about the consequences if they had been caught; that possibility had never occurred to them.

Davey watched it in horror; Noel and Jamsie were a pair of idiots, that was obvious, but little Tania was not capable of understanding this.

Tania had vomited all over the floor, and down the back of her father's jacket. He put her down gently and, slipping off his suit jacket, he placed it into the sink nearby. Then, picking his daughter up once more, he left the men's toilet without another word.

There were a few men waiting outside and Tania saw immediately that they were aware of what had gone on. Unlike her, though, they had kept away from it all. She saw the way they avoided her daddy's eyes, and she was reminded of how no one in her orbit, whether at school or playing out in the street, ever said anything detrimental to her or about her. Everyone she knew bent over backwards to please her, and she realised then that was because of her daddy. Because people were frightened of him.

Chapter Sixty-Seven

'Will you just go over and say hello?' Ria had had a few drinks, and she was irritated with her husband and his brother. This was the kids' day, not theirs.

Peter sighed. 'Stop it, Ria, and I mean it. We've done our bit, so let it drop, all right?'

'I think it's fucking ridiculous, but fine, that is my last word on the subject.'

Peter smiled despite himself. 'Well, thank fuck for small mercies.'

Even Ria laughed at that. She glanced over towards Lena and frowned. Daniel was handing Lena little Tania, and he looked fit to be tried.

'Pete, something's happened. Look at little Tania, she looks ill, bless her, and your Daniel looks like someone's nicked his bike.'

Peter sighed theatrically. 'She's probably eaten too many sweets. Remember the boys on their Communion days? Sick as fucking pigs. And, as for Imelda, she puked all over my mum's fur coat.'

Ria laughed again; she had forgotten about that.

Peter swigged his beer and decided to ignore his wife. Actually he knew *exactly* what was bothering his brother, and he would have been as angry himself had it been his boys out on the rob like that. Fucking fools! Armed robbery was not a game for amateurs – it was a fucking serious job and it came with even more serious sentences: twelve to eighteen years for a capture. The judiciary frowned on people taking money from the banks. Rob a poor old fucker's house, take everything they had worked for all their life, even give them a dig, and you were in and out in a year. But, as always in this country, money and property took precedence over people. It was a fucking joke.

The Dalys were now marked men, and so they should be. Treacherous little fuckers, engaging those lads in their fucking affairs – it was an outrage. More so because they should never have dared attempt a blag in London without permission. They had used Daniel's lads as a means of getting their big fat scally feet in the Baileys' doorway.

Noel and Jamsie were nice lads, but they were not exactly a pair of Albert fucking Einsteins, more Albert fucking Tatlock, if the truth be told. Especially after this fucking performance.

What the fuck had they been thinking? No, this was one time he was on Daniel's side. Those lads needed a fucking fright and Daniel was just the man to distribute it, but it wouldn't harm to lend his support. He walked towards his brother.

Chapter Sixty-Eight

Delroy and Davey were smoking a joint together outside. Davey was very subdued; he was more worried about Tania than his brothers – he hated seeing her so upset. Danny joined them and they sat in shocked silence.

Everyone was absolutely stunned by the younger boys' foolishness; how they could even have contemplated a blag without running it past their own brothers was unbelievable. Delroy almost felt sorry for them; he could understand the appeal of robbing a security van – it was a fucking grand adventure for them. But it was *not* something to be attempted without detailed planning and, more to the point, permission.

The Dalys were good at what they did – no one could dispute that – but what had possessed them to rope in Daniel Bailey's sons? They were fucking living on borrowed time now; Daniel Bailey would not swallow this – it was a fucking out-and-out piss-take.

Noel and Jamsie joined them warily. They were all outside on the street when Peter and Daniel Bailey exited the club at the same time. Delroy was amazed; it was a long time since they had done anything together but, at times like this, you put aside personal problems.

Ushering them on to a side street, Daniel came towards them like an avenging angel. His anger was almost tangible – he was obviously seething.

'You fucking morons! Look what you've caused! Not just the fucking robbery but ruining Tania's day as well. Do you even understand the seriousness of what you've done?'

Noel and Jamsie were at least too shrewd to answer him. It was best to let him vent his spleen and get it out of his system; any replies from them would only add to his fury. Daniel Bailey asked questions, but he didn't expect any answers. They just nodded in agreement.

Peter Bailey laid his hand gently on his brother's arm; he knew that at any moment Daniel was liable to attack them again. 'You need to calm down, Daniel. No use hammering them here in public. The last thing we need now is for someone to call the Filth. Noel, tell me now, where's the money?'

Noel looked gratefully at his uncle, aware that his presence would keep his father's famous temper in check. 'It's still in the boot of our cars. We had to get back here in time for the service, like.'

Delroy couldn't help it, he started to laugh. 'Do you mean to tell me that the money's been here all this time? You never even tried to hide it?' The incredulity in Delroy's voice was evident to everyone there, as was the complete disgust written all over his face. 'Are you having a fucking laugh?'

Peter spoke to Delroy. 'Go inside, get my Petey and Liam. Tell them to get on the blower and get a couple of drivers – we need to get rid of the motors and the poke as soon as. Tell them to have everything delivered to the scrapyard, and then they can do the necessary.' He turned to Daniel's boys. 'In the meantime, you lot get back in there and make a point of having a fucking good time. If anything *does* get a bit iffy, I want people to remember you lot at this fucking Communion, all right?'

The younger men went back inside, grateful to be away from Daniel who looked as if he was ready to explode.

'Fucking useless ponces. I can't believe they were that fucking stupid. Haven't they learned anything from us?'

Peter shrugged. 'Well, they are young, and when you're young you think you're invincible, that you won't ever get a capture, and everything you do will miraculously turn out all right.'

Daniel nodded sadly. 'I bet they've still got the guns and the balaclavas in their boots as well. Fucking pair of tossers! My Danny is fucking fuming with the Daly brothers. I told him to keep well away – I know him, he will see this as a personal affront. Neither of them saw fit to mention it to him, and that is what will be really gnawing at him. He feels like they have mugged him off, and I can't say I blame him. I feel exactly the same way.'

Peter Bailey laughed, a long, low, sarcastic laugh. 'You're a fucking piece of work, Daniel. Talk about the pot calling the kettle black! At least they didn't shoot a fucking bloke with his little kid in the car, or batter an old bloke nearly to death. They were trying to get an earn – they thought that the hundred grand they cleared would make you see them as men in their own right. Whereas you nearly fucking destroyed us on a whim on more than one occasion. So get off your high horse. With a bit of luck they are home and dry. Yes they fucked up, but at least they didn't take it on themselves to go on the rampage for pennies and halfpennies. You're a fucking hypocrite, do you know that?'

Daniel Bailey watched his brother as he stormed back into the club, and he stood outside for long minutes, until he stopped shaking and his breathing was once more under control. He consoled himself with the fact that his brother had been watching his back, and his boys' backs. At least he now knew that, no matter what happened, at the end of the day, they were still the Bailey boys.

Chapter Sixty-Nine

Lena and Ria were sitting down watching the goings-on around them. Tania was exhausted – such a shame, Lena thought, that the excitement had made her unwell. Still, they had made it through the most important part of the day unscathed. She put two chairs together, and laid her down there, covering her with a coat.

Ria was keeping an eye on her own daughter. When Imelda had had a few drinks she could be a bit aggressive, and Ria didn't want her to start at her son's Communion. Young Delroy was nowhere to be seen – he was probably up to all sorts with a couple of other boys. She glanced at Tania; the child was white as a sheet. All too much for her, she supposed; it was a long old day for the kids.

Everywhere she looked, people were laughing, having a good time. Ria liked her life, especially at times like this. She appreciated how lucky she was, she didn't take it for granted like other women. She knew that this could all disappear overnight, she wasn't a fool, but that didn't scare her in the way it always had Lena. Ria was determined to enjoy it; if not, what was it all for? Her boys were having a good time; she wondered if Lena had noticed that two of her sons were sporting shiners. Well, she wasn't going to mention anything, they were grown men.

She spotted her grandson sneaking a puff of a cigarette someone had left burning in an ashtray, and sighed with irritation. He was going to be a holy terror, that fucker, and Imelda would have many a sleepless night over him. Young Delroy was not going to be easy to control; he was a born mischief-maker, just like her Jack. *He* had arrived at the church late, and had since gone on the missing list. Peter was far from happy about his youngest son's antics, and she was waiting for them to have words one of these days. Ria had a bit of a soft spot for her youngest – probably because he was her baby. He'd been acting a bit odd recently – very secretive. Worse, though, was the knowledge that he had stolen some of her jewellery. Not the big stuff – he knew his father would notice if that went on the trot – but he had stolen her everyday stuff. He didn't understand that it was the cheaper jewellery, the necklaces and rings that her Peter had bought her when they were young, that meant the most to his mother. Now it was all gone, in an uncle's somewhere. She was keeping it from Peter at the moment, but it broke her heart. She suspected he'd been stealing from Imelda too and wondered if she should talk to her daughter about it. She hoped the situation would right itself. But Jack was Jack, and she feared he wasn't going to change any time soon.

Lena tapped her on the arm to get her attention. 'Your Imelda's just getting to the point of rowing.'

Ria got up a little unsteadily; they'd had more to drink than she thought. She could do without all this. 'Thanks, Lena. Fucking real, eh?'

Imelda was at the bar; her father was talking with a crowd of men on her left-hand side, and her Uncle Daniel was with his friends to her right. Ria wondered at what people really made of it all.

Imelda was pointing a long, manicured finger into her husband's face, and Delroy was not looking too happy about it.

'You look at her again – I mean it, Delroy – and I'll fucking go over there and lay her out.'

Ria stood in front of her daughter. 'I beg your pardon? Who are you going to lay out?'

Delroy sighed, clearly frustrated. He was a handsome man all right, but Ria wondered why her daughter couldn't control herself where he was concerned. She wished Imelda could see herself right at this moment, see how spiteful and vicious she was being. If she could only see herself as everyone else saw her, she would be so ashamed and embarrassed she would never let herself get so upset in the future, not in public anyway.

'This is all about Mandy, Liam's bird. Apparently I am ogling her, giving her the eye, so to speak. I tell you, Ria, I ain't in the mood for this tonight. Talk to your daughter, because if this keeps up I will slap her down.'

Ria watched as he walked away from them.

'I mean it, Mum, I can't do this any more.'

Ria looked at her child. She saw a beautiful girl, with a great bone structure, high cheekbones, and olive skin that looked like burnished copper. She wished Imelda could see how lovely she really was instead of constantly wishing she looked different. She had huge eyes that were framed with thick, dark lashes which, even as a baby, had brought comments from complete strangers. She had a good figure, she dressed well, she had long slim legs, and she was as lovely today as she had been as a sixteen year old. She still had the fresh-faced beauty that Ria had always seen as something really special. Imelda was what her father would call a good eyeful.

Grabbing her daughter by the arm, she pulled her through the crowd on the dance floor and into the ladies' toilets, before saying seriously, 'Listen, Mel, I love you dearly, but you need to stop all this jealousy lark. Liam's girlfriend is gorgeous, and you can't do anything about that, love. Everywhere you go, there will always be good-looking girls, younger girls, prettier girls. That doesn't mean that he is going to go off with them. All men look – your father's the world's worst for it. But that's all he does, and he loves me as much as I love him. I never felt the jealousy you feel. I see how it eats at you, and I've got to tell you, Mel, it's not a pretty sight. It makes you look ugly and mean. You must learn to control it or, one day, if you're not careful, you *will* drive him away. You'll accuse him once too often and he will think to himself, *Fuck it, I'm always being accused of shagging around, so I might as well do it.* Now, I am half pissed and I don't want to argue with you, not today, on little Delroy's first Holy Communion. So, promise me you will let this go.'

Imelda looked at her mother's kind face, saw the love there, and the worry for her and, nodding sadly, she said, 'OK. But he does take a flyer, Mum, I know he does.'

Ria pulled her daughter into her arms and, hugging her tightly, she said sadly, 'So what, darling? As long as he don't rub your face in it, so bloody what! You're his wife, you have his child. You're his first priority. Now, let's get back to the party, shall we?'

Chapter Seventy

Peter and Daniel were both aware of the other. They stood at the bar, no more than ten feet apart, but it might as well have been ten miles.

Tommy Barker stood beside Daniel; now they had finally established some ground rules, they actually got on very well. Tommy was surprised at how much he did like Daniel Bailey; when Daniel was alone, and relaxed, he could be very good company. He knew he was a loose cannon – Tommy had realised early on that Daniel Bailey was not what might be termed the full shilling – but that was part of Daniel's make-up. These days, however, he was also a man who was genuinely interested in other people's lives, who listened to their opinions, and asked relevant questions so he could fully understand what he was being told.

He and Daniel had struck up a friendship of sorts, and he believed that Daniel felt that he was good for his mother.

Now that he was gradually handing his money-laundering operation over to Daniel, he was seeing how shrewd he was where money was concerned. Daniel Bailey knew his maths all right; he could work out any percentage in his head, and he could tell you down to the last halfpenny what was owed where and by whom.

Tommy had underestimated Daniel Bailey's intelligence, and he realised that many other people had made that same mistake. Peter had always been considered as the brains of the outfit; Daniel's rep was just as the hard man. But Daniel was more than that. He was very good at dissecting how a scam worked and, once he had thought it through, nine times out of ten, he could come up with a way of improving on it. He had already proved that by increasing their earnings almost overnight. Tommy Barker's respect for Daniel Bailey's acumen was without question.

'Look at them, Tommy, drunk as skunks, and twice as fucking annoying.'

Tommy smiled. Lena, Ria and Theresa were all singing along to the Irish ballads that were now being played. It was time for the lock-in and, for many of the people there, the night was only just beginning.

'Your little Tania will be all right, Daniel. She won't remember the half of it tomorrow.' Tommy guessed what was bothering Daniel the most about today's events.

Daniel shrugged. 'I hope not. It's funny, you know, Tommy, I realised something today. I realised, for the first time, that I don't want this for her. I don't want my daughter to grow up in the Life. I want her to have a chance. I want her to do something with herself.'

'That's good, Daniel. That's natural, wanting the best for your kids.'

Daniel smiled. 'I want a bit more for her than some fucking oik whose life is dependent on a fucking thieve, you know what I mean? I want her to live in the real world, with real people. I saw her fear today, and I saw myself as she must have seen me. A big, aggressive fucking gangster. What the fuck must my baby have thought? She is seven years old, Tommy! I must have looked like a monster. She was physically sick, you know? She was *that* scared. I had that fucking muppet Noel by the throat, and she saw all that. I have never seen her so frightened, and I never want to see her like that again. You know I've bought that great big drum? Well, Lena doesn't really want to move, but she has a fucking surprise coming to her. We are going, and sooner rather than later. My Tania is going to have a good life, a comfortable life, and she will go to a good school and all. The best that money can buy.' He swallowed down his beer quickly, then motioned to the barmaid for a refill. 'But, as for that pair of fucking prats, Noel and Jamsie, they can fucking whistle for a crust in future. Who does a fucking robbery like that, first time out? They are a pair of fucking idiots. Not a fucking useful brain cell between the pair of them. Still ain't out of the woods are they? Fuck knows what really went down today. Knowing that pair, they left a fucking gas bill behind for the Filth – name, address and fucking phone numbers. Unbelievable, un-*fucking*-believable.'

Tommy Barker couldn't help laughing. 'Still, they got a good wedge, you've got to give them that, Daniel.'

'I ain't giving them fuck-all. That's *my* money now, I think that should teach them a lesson in etiquette. Never go on the rob with strangers. I have told them all, time and time again – keep things in the family.'

Peter Bailey overheard his brother's last words and nodded in silent agreement. He had drummed that into his lads' heads since they were old enough to walk. It was the Bailey mantra. But once they were grown men, they would eventually go their own road. That was human nature.

Chapter Seventy-One

Lena was not comfortable, and she didn't like that feeling. The house Daniel had bought them was lovely, but it was too big, and she didn't like the feeling of isolation it gave her. Even though they were on a road, the drive was a good thirty feet, and the front wall was obscured by great big trees. Once she was inside the house itself, she felt like she was living in the middle of nowhere.

The kitchen was big, and she quite enjoyed pottering in there but, other than that, she didn't like any of the other rooms very much. They were beautifully decorated – whoever had lived there before them had wonderful taste – but she felt like an intruder, like she was in someone else's house.

Daniel, on the other hand, loved it. He walked around admiring things, like the coving and the hardwood doors; the brass door handles were a particular favourite of his. But to Lena, this house was like a hotel, somewhere you visited for a few days and then went back to your own place where you felt safe, secure.

She sighed. She was sighing a lot lately: she had sighed when Ria had picked out the new furniture for her, she had sighed when everyone had squealed with delight over how well it went in the new house. If she lived here for the next twenty years, she had a feeling she would still call it the 'new house'.

As she walked out to pick up the post she saw herself in the large mirror that Ria said would look *perfect*. She wasn't getting any younger, but at least she looked all right for her age.

She picked up the few bills that were lying innocently on the oatmeal-coloured carpet, and walked aimlessly back into the kitchen. She sat at her new glass and chrome table and, picking up her mug of tea, she took a large gulp. Who needed a glass table this size? It was a bastard to keep clean, and she harboured a secret hope that one of the boys would accidentally break it, smash it into smithereens. According to Ria, it wouldn't break like a wine glass, it would shatter like a windscreen. Shatter or smash, she didn't really give a fuck – she just wanted it gone.

She heard her husband coming down the stairs and she automatically poured him a mug of tea.

'The boys already gone?'

'Not yet, they'll be down in a minute.'

Daniel put on the TV he had installed on the worktop. Now, she quite liked that, if she was being honest.

'They are hardly ever here, Dan, I just do their washing and feed them these days.'

Daniel laughed. 'Well, they are grown up now, girl,

thank Christ. All fleeing the nest, it's only natural. Only our little Tania left now, eh? She is a clever little mare, did you see her school report? She is a budding genius, that one.'

Lena nodded. She was tempted to point out that of course she had read Tania's school report – she had read it days before he had in point of fact – but she didn't.

Noel and Jamsie came into the kitchen noisily, but shut up when they saw their father. They both seemed to be nervous around him. Whatever had happened on the day of the Communion must have been serious. Serious enough for her husband to refuse to even acknowledge their presence in any way for months on end.

'All right, Dad?' Jamsie asked warily.

Daniel smiled benignly at them. 'I'm all right. Now, shut up – the news is on.'

He turned up the volume, and Lena poured the boys out mugs of tea. They sat around the glass table, and she took their breakfasts out of the oven and served them quickly and quietly.

The TV was loud, and she was just about to ask her husband to turn it down but, as she opened her mouth to speak, he hushed her with a furious wave of his arm. The newsreader's voice was tinny in the quiet of the room.

'Two men were found murdered last night in East London. They had both been shot, execution style, in the back of the head. Police have named them as Gerald and Patrick Daly, two brothers from the Liverpool area. Police are treating the murders as gangland-related, and have appealed for anyone who might have any information regarding this incident to call them . . .'

Lena saw the way her sons looked at one another, and she knew that the news they had just heard was somehow relevant to both of them.

Daniel had finally turned the TV down and, sitting at the table, he opened his newspaper and started to read it without a word. But the atmosphere in the room was heavy with menace, and she could feel the animosity pouring from her husband. Lena wanted to scream in frustration at the futility of it all.

'You want any more toast, lads? You got enough?'

They both shook their heads mutely, and she felt so sorry for them, but she knew that she could not interfere.

Ten minutes later they left the house, and the atmosphere immediately lightened.

Daniel got up and walked to the back door.

'Look at that garden, Lena; like a painting, ain't it? The gardener says we can expect colour all year round. What do you think of that, eh? He's a nice old boy, knows his onions so to speak!'

Lena smiled dutifully. 'Is everything all right with the boys, Daniel?'

He laughed. 'It is now, Lena, so don't worry about it. I've had to pull them into line, that's all.'

She sighed. As always she chose to believe him, that was always easiest.

Daniel watched her for a few minutes. 'Oh, for Christ's sake, Lena! What the fuck is wrong with you lately, girl? You're walking round like a fucking tit in a trance! Are you feeling all right, love? Are you sickening for something?'

She knew she should say how she felt right this minute, but she couldn't do it. He loved this house so much, he enjoyed it on every level, he even sat on the patio and read his paper, pleased as punch that he was able to do it, that he was learning how to appreciate this new way of life. Why couldn't she do the same?

'I'm just tired, Daniel. The move and everything took it out of me, that's all. It's been a busy couple of months.'

He was happy with her answer, and that irritated her for some reason, even though she knew he believed every word she said.

'Right then, darling, I better get a move on. I need to sort out a few things today.'

He kissed her gently on the lips, and she kissed him back; she did love him still.

Then, placing his hands gently on her shoulders, he looked into her face for a few moments, before saying softly, 'Enjoy this house, Lena, *please*. I got it for *us*, for me, you and little Tania. It's bought and paid for, and it's in your name, so even if I get a capture tomorrow and they give me thirty years, this is still all yours, mate. *No one* can take it away from you. I know you are a fucking hoarder, I know you hide money everywhere, but I swear to you, Lena, we are rich, girl, seriously rich. So stop it, love.'

She was so pleased he had noticed that she was upset, that she smiled widely as she said, 'Oh, Dan, I really thought you didn't know I was missing the old place. I can't seem to settle here.'

'Well, in all honesty, I'm not surprised, are you? Considering Ria chose everything! Go out, go up west, and buy your own bloody furniture – get a proper table, at least. That glass thing is like something from *Tomorrow's World*! I don't like looking at me feet when I'm eating me dinner!'

She was laughing with him now. He was right – she had been so worried about what should go into a house like this, she had forgotten that, no matter what, it was still her home. Her family's home.

'You're right, Dan. I will buy a new table at least – I hate this bleeding thing too; it feels cold, somehow. I like a nice bit of wood myself.'

Daniel Bailey laughed out loud. 'Get what you like, you dozy mare! Just cheer up, will you?'

She beamed, but couldn't stop herself from asking again, 'Are the boys all right really, Daniel? I know you have been annoyed with them, and I hate it when there's a bad feeling in the air, you know?'

He grinned. 'Look, they were out of order, but I've sorted it now. So stop worrying, and just start relaxing and enjoying our new home, eh? They're moving out soon anyway. They've all bought flats – with my fucking money, of course! It's time they started looking after themselves.'

She smiled, but she still felt uneasy. Gangland murders were not something she could overlook as easily as her husband could.

Chapter Seventy-Two

Peter Bailey had heard the news concerning the Daly brothers' demise within minutes of it happening – as had his brother. Peter had made sure that everyone in the family was well within the public arena as it was going down. There was no way it could lead back to them, no matter what people might think. It had not been cheap, but he had not expected it to be.

Everyone assumed the Daly boys had been chastised severely because they had gone on the rob without the Baileys' permission and no one would argue with that. Even their own families had been forced to wipe their mouths; the brothers had disregarded any kind of protocol and that could not be overlooked. The main thing was that no one knew the real reason – that they had involved the younger Bailey boys in their affairs. It was imperative that no one saw that there were any weak links in the family.

It had also been a warning to each of the younger Bailey boys of what could happen if you didn't toe the line. No one worked anything without it being discussed and, more importantly, agreed by them all. That was the only way they could keep themselves safe – the fewer outsiders involved in the big decisions, the better for everyone in the long run.

He sat at his desk and wondered how Daniel was going to move forward. His brother was still fuming over Noel and Jamsie's foolishness, but Peter believed that's all it was – young men being foolish, trying to prove themselves; there had been no malice in it.

Peter felt old suddenly. He'd heard, of course, that Daniel was doing a great job with the money laundering, and he was impressed with just how well his brother had done. Tommy Barker still oversaw the business, but that was a formality really; Daniel was a natural at it. He also had the temperament needed to deal with the Russians – they were like Daniel in many ways; they were violent criminals, who were not only uneducated, but were also devoid of any social graces. A match made in heaven really.

Daniel, like him, was earning more than enough on a weekly basis, and they were both teaching their boys the ropes. The sons were still very close, and that was very important because, as a family – as the Baileys – they were a formidable team.

The fly in the ointment, as far as Peter was concerned, was his youngest, Jack. Something was up with him, but Peter wasn't quite sure what yet. As the youngest, Jack had grown up a bit of an attention seeker. He had plenty of swagger and with his looks had no problem attracting women. He was a natural for the business and Peter had been happy to give him free rein at running his drinking clubs. But Jack had been working less and less recently. Peter's eyes and ears at the clubs reported that he disappeared for long periods and he was very secretive about where he'd been.

Peter suspected that Petey and Liam were protecting him at the moment. But he was convinced that wouldn't last – eventually they would have to confide in him. That was the nature of the game they all played – nothing stayed a secret for long, not from Peter Bailey anyway.

Chapter Seventy-Three

Tania was watching her mum and her Auntie Ria. They were both very quiet and, as usual, her nana was doing most of the talking. Tania sat with her dollies as quietly as possible – she knew that if they remembered she was in the room, she would be sent out. When they spoke angrily like this or if they spoke to each other very quietly, she was always sent out of the room. So she sat by the side of the sofa as still as a statue, her ears on red alert as she listened to what they were saying.

'Dear God, are you sure this is true?' Lena's voice was hushed, little more than a whisper.

Theresa nodded, her face serious, showing every line she had accumulated over the years, making her look old suddenly. When she was smiling, laughing, you forgot her age – now even Tania could see how different she looked and it frightened her. Lena was watching Ria as the words sank into her brain.

'My Jack? Are you sure that this is about *my* Jack?'

Theresa was heart-sorry for the burden she was planting on her daughter-in-law, but she knew that the only person who could deliver this kind of news to Peter was his wife. She would go with Ria of course, but only

Ria's presence could keep him from doing something he would regret for the rest of his days.

'Jack is at my house and Tommy's there with him. He came to me because he didn't know where else to go, Ria. He knew he had fucked up, but he also had the nous to know that he couldn't sort this out by himself, that this would have a terrible impact on the family if it got out. Now get your Peter on the blower, and make him come to my house, OK? And then we can sort it out from there.'

Ria was reeling. She felt sick, as if she was going to vomit everywhere – she had never felt so ill before in her life. She could happily drop down dead right now, right at this minute, and not care in the least. This was monumental, and she was not sure how best to deal with it. Peter would go ballistic, and she admitted that he would have every right. 'He'll kill him, Theresa; he will fucking *kill* him.'

Theresa sighed heavily. 'That's why we have to make sure he sees him at *my* house. Now, get your boys to come as well – they'll have to help Jack if Peter goes for him. I don't care what you tell them, just get them round mine. Daniel has sent Noel and Jamsie to sort out the body, before someone finds it, and it gets out of hand.'

Ria nodded; she understood what her mother-in-law was telling her. Time was of the essence.

Chapter Seventy-Four

Noel and Jamsie slipped the key into the lock and, opening the door slowly and quietly, they listened intently for any sounds that would tell them the flat was occupied. There was silence.

Shutting the door gently behind them, they screwed up their noses at the sour smell that seemed to pervade the whole place. There were bags of rubbish everywhere they looked – dirty nappies had been left on the floor, along with old clothes, and the odd pile of dirty washing. Toys were scattered along the hallway, and old newspapers, yellowed and brittle with age, were strewn around.

It was a typical tower-block flat; it had a long dim hallway with doors that opened off it to the bedrooms and bathroom then, at the far end of the hallway, a door led them into the front room, and from there another door led into the kitchen. The whole place was filthy.

They walked quietly down the dark hallway and, opening each door as they went, they both checked the rooms thoroughly. The first room had nothing in it at all except for a battered, old-fashioned cot. Somebody had once painted it white, but now it was chipped and ingrained with years of dirt and neglect. The mattress was stained and ripped. A single blanket had been folded up and placed neatly at the bottom, and it looked incongruous compared to the rest of the room. The wallpaper was hanging off the walls, the floors were bare and there wasn't even a curtain at the window to say that the child who had once graced that cot had ever had someone who cared about them.

The other rooms were in a similar condition; it was only when Noel opened the front-room door, that the two brothers stopped abruptly.

'Fucking hell, Jamsie, this is mental.'

The girl was lying half on and half off a very dilapidated, dirty PVC sofa. It had once boasted orange nylon cushions but they were now a dull brown – years of neglect had seen to that. The rest of the room was as filthy as everywhere else in the flat. The coffee table and floor were covered with pieces of tin foil, used needles, and all the other paraphernalia and debris that junkies seemed to collect. Amongst it was a dog-eared photo of a smiling baby girl, her deep blue eyes huge in her little heart-shaped face. The dead girl was obviously the child's mother.

Noel and Jamsie looked around them with complete and utter disgust, unable to comprehend how anyone could choose to live their life like this. The girl's body was already going rigid but, even in death, you could still see the girl she had once been before the drugs had taken over her life. Her face was bruised – she had obviously taken a battering at some point in the last few days – her lips were blue and slightly parted, and her eyes were glazed.

They checked the rest of the flat – there was no sign of the child.

Noel opened his coat and took out a whisky bottle full of petrol, and Jamsie followed suit. They poured it everywhere – especially around the sofa – and, as they worked, neither of them said a word.

At the doorway, they paused, taking a final look around to make sure they had not left anything that could be traced back to Jack Bailey. Satisfied, they lit a book of matches and threw it on to the coffee table. They waited for a few moments to see that the fire had a good hold and then they moved carefully along the corridor, starting a fire in each of the rooms, before finally leaving the flat as quietly and as unobtrusively as they had entered it.

Outside they got into an old banger which, contrary to its appearance, boasted a tuned-up engine that guaranteed them speed should the need arise. It blended into the surroundings so well that no one would give it a second glance.

Noel shook his head in annoyance. 'What a cunt! Who in their right mind would take fucking heroin – it's a fucking mug's game. Sell the fucker to animals like her, but keep away from it yourself. Only Jack would be that fucking weak and that fucking stupid.'

The brothers drove away sedately, both relieved that

because of Jack the onus had been taken off them. God certainly did move in mysterious ways, as their old mum was forever telling them both, and today it seemed that she was right.

Chapter Seventy-Five

Peter Bailey was still unable to comprehend what his mother and his wife were telling him. He could hear what they were saying, but he could not bring himself to actually believe any of it.

Not his Jack. Never his Jack. He had known there was something going on with him, but he had never dreamed that it could be anything even remotely like this. His baby, his youngest boy, had beaten a fucking defenceless young girl to death while out of his fucking tree on skag? On heroin? His baby was polluting his body with that shit and no one thought to tell him? None of the boys had thought it should have been brought to his attention? Had the world gone fucking mad?

'Please, Peter, you have to understand that no one thought it would come to this . . .'

Peter snapped his head round and looked at his wife, his Ria, the woman he would have sworn was incapable of keeping something like this a secret.

'Did you know, Ria? Did you know about this?'

Ria was shaking her head vehemently in denial, and he could see she was terrified. 'Of course not! I wouldn't fucking overlook something like that, would I?'

He was nodding, convinced that she was telling him the truth.

In her heart, Ria had had her suspicions – Jack's sleeping patterns, his erratic moods – all had indicated there was something not right. But she had *never* thought it might be something like this.

Petey placed a hand gently on his father's arm, and he was almost thrown into the wall by the strength of his father's reaction; it was as if the human contact had somehow snapped Peter Bailey out of his trance.

'Get your fucking hands off me! Now, where is he?'

Petey sighed. 'Nana wanted him to be here but I sent him away from you. Liam's with him. I don't think you should see him yet.'

Peter Bailey laughed nastily. 'I will ask you once more, son, and only once. *Where the fuck is he?*'

Theresa took a step towards her eldest son.

'And you, Mother, keep away from me. One more step and I swear I will rip your fucking head off your shoulders. Now, for the last time, where is he?'

Chapter Seventy-Six

Jack Bailey was so frightened that he was unable to breathe properly. He could feel every thump of his heart crashing in his ears.

Daniel Bailey watched his nephew with disinterest; as far as he was concerned, the boy was already dead to him. Oh, he might clean his mess up for him, but that was for the family name more than for this fucking oik. Jack was less than a rabid dog to Daniel now. He had stepped over the line in more ways than one. From what he could gather, he had done the girl in while out of his box, and woke up to see his handiwork. He had then shit himself big time, and run to his nana for help – the weak, useless fucking piece of dirt.

Fucking coward! Well, Peter would not swallow this little lot, he knew that even if the others hadn't quite grasped that fact yet. Liam had brought him to Daniel's house while the others tried to talk Peter down. But it was pointless. Jack Bailey was what the Yanks called a dead man walking.

'Did you inject that shit, Jack?' he asked conversationally.

Jack looked at his uncle fearfully; he sounded so

calm, like he was chatting about the weather or asking after his health. Jack nodded.

'Well, for what it's worth, you would have been much better off OD'ing, son, 'cos you're a fucking dead Bailey either way.'

Jack didn't answer – there was nothing he could say.

Chapter Seventy-Seven

Tania could hear her Auntie Ria crying – it was a terrible sound, as if she was struggling for breath. Sitting at the top of her nana's stairs, Tania could hear everything that was being said.

'He will kill him, Lena, I know he will. The boys won't be able to stop him, no one will be able to stop him . . .' Ria was in despair. Peter would out Jack, son or no son, of that she had no doubt at all. Ria, who'd always had her eyes wide open to the Life, suddenly wished for the blissful ignorance Lena had maintained. What had her boy been thinking? Jack must have known from the moment he took that drug how it would be received if his father found out about it all. This wasn't something they would ever countenance, it was something that was seen as a weakness, as a sign of mental incapability. You sold drugs, you didn't fucking take them – not that kind of shit anyway. 'He's my baby, Lena, he's my little boy. Call your Daniel, tell him to hide him, tell him to take him away somewhere . . .' Ria was distraught, desperate, but she knew it was useless.

Lena still didn't answer her friend. She rubbed her

back gently, unable to say anything to comfort her, and feeling guilty that she was grateful it wasn't one of her boys. 'Drink this brandy, Ria. Imelda will be here in a minute.'

Ria didn't answer her and, after a few moments of grief-driven crying, she was suddenly quiet.

As Lena hugged her friend tightly, she wondered at how they were ever going to get past this. They had the money, the prestige and the cars – they had front-row seats in the Life. But this was the downside. The Life was good, no doubt about that, but, as they all knew, it came at a price. At times like this, it was a terrible price, but one that had to be paid no matter what the consequences might be, or who it might hurt. This was the Life at its worst, and poor Ria would have to live with it. They all would.

Chapter Seventy-Eight

'Thanks, Daniel, I appreciate what you've done.'

Daniel nodded at his brother. 'You'd have done the same for me.'

It was strange talking like this, face to face, alone together after such a long time, and they both felt that.

'How's Ria?'

Peter shrugged. 'How'd you think? Women never understand the real economics of this. They think it can all be fucking sorted out. But not this time.'

'You're definitely outing him then?'

Peter nodded. 'What do you fucking think?'

Daniel poured them both a large Scotch. 'Get that down you, Pete. You're going to need it.'

Peter necked it in one swallow.

Daniel saw the pallor on his brother's dark skin, and he felt genuinely sorry for him and his predicament. 'Truth is, Pete, he was dead from the moment he started using that filth. Junkies are dying from the first hit.'

Peter laughed ironically. 'He was dead from the minute I found out he was using. Drink is a dangerous enough game, as we know – makes people too fucking loquacious, as the old woman used to say when we were boys. Coke is bad enough, but at least you can wake up with a relatively sensible head. That brown is a different ball game. It eats at you like a cancer. It steals your soul, turns you into a fucking thief, a liar. It cancels out family, loyalty, everything that is important to most people, but *seriously* important to people like us, people in our game. He is no use to man or fucking beast. He's weak, Daniel, he's shown his true colours.'

Daniel Bailey knew the truth of his brother's words. Junkies were anathema to people in the Life; they were completely untrustworthy and their habit guaranteed that they would betray anyone for a price.

'Look, Peter, I've spoken to a couple of tame Filth. The girl's death is being treated as a tragic accident – the lads did a good job, she was burned to fuck. So no comebacks from that quarter anyway.'

Peter wiped his nose with a huge hand. 'Fucking real, ain't it? Nineteen years old and dead as a fucking doornail. She nicked his stash by all accounts. Like that is supposed to be an excuse or something.'

'If you want, Peter, I can take care of him for you . . .'

Peter held up his hand. 'I will do it, but thanks anyway. This is my shit, and I will clear it up.'

Daniel didn't answer, he would be the same way himself. Somehow his lads' foray into the world of armed robbery was suddenly no more than a boyish prank. At least they were trying to earn for the family. As fucking idiotic as their antics might have been, there was the knowledge that they were only trying to spread their wings, prove themselves. They had more than redeemed their actions by the way they had sorted Jack's problem out, quickly, quietly and without asking too many questions. There was hope for that pair of fucking muppets yet it would seem, they had proved that much. He knew one thing, though, he wouldn't wish this kind of shit on his worst enemies.

'Do you want me to come with you?'

Peter Bailey was actually pleased by his brother's offer. After all that had gone down between them, it was good to know that Daniel was willing to stand by him in his darkest hour.

'No, Dan, but I do appreciate the offer.'

'How's Mother taking it?'

Peter Bailey did laugh then, as Daniel had known he would. 'She will survive. That Tommy Barker is good for her, I think.'

'She is a lot of things, our mother, but, at the end of the day, she is on our side. She will look out for Ria, we both know that, as will my Lena.'

Peter Bailey nodded. He was banking on that.

Chapter Seventy-Nine

'For fuck's sake, Imelda, shut up about it, will you?'

Imelda was going out of her mind with panic. 'You can talk to my dad, Delroy, or take *me* to him. I know you know where he is.'

Delroy almost smiled at his wife's naïve belief that either of them could change the outcome of her brother's situation. 'Listen, Mel. Nothing is going to change your father's mind so get your head round it.'

'But my mum! What about my mum? She is in bits . . .'

'And that's to be expected, but she ain't a fucking fool, Imelda – she knows your father better than anyone. You make me laugh! *You* insisted on being a part of all this, and now you are, and you do a good job. But *this* is a part of the Life too. No one likes it, but it has to be done. Jack has fucked himself, Mel, so get over it. I liked him – we all did, but he cannot be allowed to swerve this. He could have brought us all down – me, you, the whole fucking shebang. There are some things that can't be sorted and, in our world, that is fucking rare, granted. But Jack decided to walk his own road, now he has to pay the price. I'm sorry, but if you want to be a part of this Life, you'd better accept it.'

Imelda could not believe what she was hearing. This was her brother, her little Jack, not some fucking romancer no one gave a toss about, and she said as much, but Delroy held up his hand.

'That's *enough*, Mel.'

He caught sight of his son in the kitchen doorway; he was obviously frightened. Delroy plastered a smile on his face, well aware that the child was picking up on the negativity between his parents; kids were good at that. 'You all right, mate?' He lifted his son into his arms and took him back to his bed. Ten minutes later he was back in their newly refurbished kitchen.

Imelda looked her husband in the eye and said quietly, 'What if it was *him*, eh? What would you do, Delroy?' She was genuinely interested in his answer. Delroy knew that she was asking him to tell her what she wanted to hear, but he couldn't; she had to grasp the seriousness of their life together. Imelda had to understand that this was not a life that you could dip in and out of, once you were in it, you were in it for the duration.

He shrugged nonchalantly. 'The same as your father, Mel. And a bit of friendly advice – don't ask questions you don't really want the answer to.'

Chapter Eighty

Jack Bailey was jonesing in the back of the car and he was jonesing badly. He was sweating, withdrawing and, compounded with his fear, it was worse than he could ever have imagined. He'd never been denied access to his preferred drug before. He needed something to calm him down, but he knew his brothers were not going to provide anything.

'Will Dad be long do you think?' In his mind he thought he would get a good hiding, but once that was over he hoped he might have time to go out and score. Or he could easily call a dealer who might come to him if he was incapacitated. All Jack wanted was all this over with.

Jack was completely unaware of just how much trouble he was in – believing his place as the baby of the family would ensure his father's lenience. He had gone to his nana because she was the only person his father really listened to. His big fear had been his Uncle Daniel – he wouldn't put it past *him* to shoot him and then go and have his dinner as if nothing untoward had occurred. His Uncle Daniel had a reputation for his hard-nosed attitude to other people's problems.

His brothers were subdued, but that was to be expected; he had, after all, fucked up big time. Jack was convinced, though, that his mother's love would provide protection – his dad would never hurt *her*, would never harm her baby boy. His dad loved him – they'd find a way to sort this out to everyone's satisfaction.

Petey and Liam pulled him from the car gently.

Jack looked around in confusion. 'Where are we?'

Liam smiled. 'We're in Essex. Dad owns a lot of warehouses here, and he wants to talk to you in private.'

Jack entered the building willingly, safe in the knowledge that his nana, his mum and everyone in the family who loved him knew about his fuck-up and wouldn't let anything happen to him.

Liam turned on the lights while Petey unloaded a carrier bag, pulling out a couple of bottles of whisky and a pack of children's paper party cups. They looked far too festive in the dimness of the warehouse, far too colourful, and brimming with the promise of good times ahead.

Petey poured a large drink and passed it to his little brother. Jack gulped at it gratefully, all the while thinking that what he could really do with was a joint, something to take the edge off.

'Sit down, mate.'

Liam pushed a chair towards him, and he sat down. The building had high ceilings, and it was chock full of electrical equipment. Jack guessed this lot came from lorry heists; it was a lucrative business, mainly because the lorry drivers were more than happy to be robbed for a price, especially coming up to Christmas. If he had known about this place he would have asked for an in by now; it was a scam for the future anyway, so the night would not be totally wasted.

Chapter Eighty-One

Tommy Barker was sorry about the whole situation, more so because it had hit Theresa harder than any of them, except maybe poor Ria. She had believed that her intervention would be enough to keep her grandson alive, but he had known that was never going to be an option.

The boy had killed a young girl without a care, beaten her to death over a fucking few grams of heroin; nothing could ever wipe out something so fucking outrageous no matter who his father was. Junkies were scum, they were without any scruples, were devoid of even the most basic moral code. All they seemed capable of was treachery, betrayal and, worst of all, the inability to see what they had become. They were fit for nothing in the Life, and they were not to be tolerated.

Jack's death was a necessary evil – sad, tragic, but inevitable. He would have become the weakest link and, through him, the whole family would have been in jeopardy.

'Come on, Theresa, let's go to the Irish club, eh?'

Theresa looked at the man she had found so late in her life and she nodded sadly. 'OK. I know, Tommy, deep inside, that nothing is going to change my Peter's mind, is it?'

He shook his head. 'No, mate. It's going to be harder on him than anyone, don't forget.'

Theresa doubted that somehow, but she didn't voice that opinion. 'He was a beautiful baby was little Jack. A real little darling. Ria ruined him – she could never see him without, you know? He was always a bit of a lad, bless him, but she never chastised him like the others. Spare the rod, eh?'

Theresa had swallowed the situation, she was a hard old bird, but she was also a realist. Nothing was going to stop the events of this night and the sooner everyone accepted it the better.

This was the downside of the Life, one which everyone had to face eventually.

Chapter Eighty-Two

Danny, Davey, Noel and Jamsie were in a club in Manor Park; they were loud, out of control and, as they were all Baileys, no one said a word to them about their behaviour. What no one knew was that they were each determined that tonight would wipe out the horror of the last few days – even if only for a few hours.

The club was packed with revellers and, as the boys looked around them, they were acutely aware of how different their lives were in comparison to everyone around them.

Jack's youth, along with his foolishness, was hitting them harder than they would admit. They were finally aware of how precarious the lives they were living actually were. For the first time, they were understanding just how dangerous the Life could be for people who didn't take it as seriously as it warranted. The weight of their family name and reputation suddenly felt like a burden. It wasn't a game any more.

Peter and Daniel Bailey were men who had fought hard for their positions in the world and, as their blood, their sons were expected to work just as hard. They were expected to be just as cunning as their fathers, and just as capable of making difficult decisions – even if those decisions were about their own flesh and blood. This had brought home to them *exactly* what they were all involved in and, more to the point, what was required of them.

Jack was their blood, their family, but that had not been enough to help him in his hour of need; in fact, it was *because* he was a Bailey that his actions were seen as so heinous. The girl's death was terrible – no one was disputing that – but she was a junkie; it wasn't like she was an innocent. But Jack had also become a junkie, and they knew now that there was *no* excuse for such a monumental fuck-up, no matter *who* you were.

It seemed that they were not as safe as they had always assumed. They were not living the charmed lives they'd boasted about. The Life they took for granted came with its own set of rules, and those rules were harsher than any of them had ever realised.

Noel motioned for his brothers to follow him into the offices of the club, and they went willingly. None of them were really in the mood to enjoy themselves.

Inside the small office, Danny poured them each a large drink and then, holding his glass up, he said loudly, 'To Jack! Cunt that he was.'

They swallowed their drinks quickly, but they each knew that nothing could raise their spirits this night. All any of them wanted was to forget.

Chapter Eighty-Three

Peter Bailey pulled up outside the warehouse in Basildon; he had a heavy heart as he turned off his car engine. He sat in the dark, pleased to see that the lights in the warehouse were muted – his sons had learned well how things were supposed to be done. Petey and Liam needed to be a part of this, he knew that much. They needed to understand that there was always a price to be paid for mistakes, for doing anything that could affect the family as a whole.

He suspected that his eldest boy was at peace with what was going to happen, and that showed him that Petey was sensible enough to understand that sometimes in their world you had to do things that were a necessary evil. Liam was still learning about the Life and, unlike Imelda, Peter had a feeling he would take all this onboard and learn a valuable lesson. Imelda was a good girl, but she was too emotional for her own good. Well, she was Delroy's fucking problem now – not his. She had to understand that there was no way the family could ever be compromised, it was as simple as that.

Jack was beyond redemption; he had no fucking chance of walking away from this. Peter intended this to be a lesson to the other boys – Daniel's too – that they *had* to police each other. One of them *had* to have known what Jack was getting involved in, suspected that he was getting in over his head somehow. This would show them that, in future, it would be more sensible to bring that kind of knowledge to the powers-that-be, sooner rather than later. They would hopefully understand how their actions impacted on everyone around them and what could happen when these problems weren't addressed.

He got out of the car slowly. Walking into the warehouse, he heard Jack's voice, and he felt a momentary pang of genuine sorrow. Jack had been such a lovely little lad, with all the potential to be a son he could be proud of, but his weakness had won out.

As Jack looked at him with his big brown eyes and his crooked smile, Peter saw not only the deep-rooted belief that he would actually walk away from this but, worst of all, he saw the weakness in his son that had finally manifested itself in his addiction. It was hard for him to admit that his youngest son was capable of such skulduggery, but he was.

'All right, Dad?' Jack smiled nervously.

Peter Bailey nodded. 'Yeah, I'm all right, son.' He turned to Petey and Liam, who were watching him intently. 'You done what I asked?'

Petey gestured to the side of the warehouse. 'Yeah, it's through here.'

Peter Bailey pulled his youngest son up from the

chair by the scruff of his neck and, dragging the protesting boy behind him, he forced him bodily towards a large vat of water.

He drowned his son as easily as he would have drowned a litter of kittens.

When it was done, he wiped his hands and addressed the other boys. 'You made sure this water was from the Thames, didn't you?'

Petey nodded.

'He has to have the correct water in his lungs apparently, when he's found floating in the Thames. It has to be seen as a tragic accident.'

Petey was quick to reassure his father that everything had been done properly. 'Don't worry, Dad, it's all taken care of.'

Peter Bailey sighed. 'At least this way your mother gets a fucking funeral for him and no one is any the wiser.'

Liam Bailey was staring at his little brother's body, unable to believe what he had just witnessed. It seemed surreal somehow, as if it was a dream and at any minute he would wake up. Liam was shocked at his father's complete indifference to his actions. He seemed to have no real emotion about what he had just done – Liam could see that. It was wrong, all wrong.

Motioning to his two remaining sons to follow him, Peter poured them each large Scotches. 'Get that down you, Liam, and remember, son, he brought this on himself.'

Liam drank the whisky but he didn't say a word. He was unable to answer the man, but Peter Bailey understood his son's feelings far more than he would ever let on.

'Right, well, you both know what to do.'

Chapter Eighty-Four

Ria was lying in her bed, and all she could think about was her youngest son. Her baby Jack. He had always had a cheeky smile, always known how to get around her, and she had loved that about him.

She could hear Imelda pottering about in the kitchen, and she pulled herself upright in her bed. Lighting a cigarette, she pulled the smoke deeply into her lungs. She had been sick over and over again – Imelda had even had to pull over in a bus stop so she could once more empty her belly of alcohol. Now she was more or less sober, but the pain had not lessened at all.

She glanced at the clock on her bedside table. It was past three o'clock, and she wondered if she would ever again sleep through the night; she very much doubted it. She looked around her bedroom; it was huge, decorated red and gold. Her Jack used to say it was a poor man's Buckingham Palace, and she had known then that he had no respect for how lucky he was.

He had killed that young girl, beaten her to death. It was so hard to believe; he had been her baby – how had he become someone like that? How had he become a man capable of harming a female?

She felt the sting of tears once more, felt the deep sorrow that she would never see her son again.

Imelda came into the bedroom with a mug of hot, sweet tea. Ria sipped at it gratefully, the tears still streaming down her face, the pain of her loss as acute as a knife in her heart.

'Don't worry, Mum, everything will be OK.'

Ria nodded at her daughter, unwilling to talk about it to anyone. Imelda was obviously as upset as she was, and Ria understood that. This was a traumatic time for them.

Imelda sat on the bed and, taking her mother's hand in hers, she held on to it gently, trying her hardest to give her mother some kind of comfort.

Ria pulled her hand away, and held on to her mug of tea as tightly as she could. 'Get yourself home, Mel. You have your own family, love. I'm OK, darling. Your dad will be in soon.'

Imelda looked at her mother in abject disbelief. 'Can you hear yourself, Mum? Do you realise what *he*'s fucking done? My *dad*!'

Ria sighed heavily. 'Stop this *now*, Mel, I mean it, you stop it.'

Imelda was so shocked by her mother's words, and what they actually meant, she was unable to answer her. Unable to believe what she was hearing. 'For fuck's sake, Mum, whatever Jack's done he's still your son! My little brother . . .'

Ria sipped at her tea again, unable to look her

daughter in the eye; she was not prepared to listen to anything detrimental about her husband, it would only add to her pain. 'Go home, Mel, and I mean it. This is about a lot more than you realise, love. One day you will understand all this, believe me. Until then, let me grieve for my son in peace.'

Ria was sorry for her daughter; she knew that she was hurting over her brother, but so was *she* – and far more than Imelda would ever know. But Jack had brought this on himself and, even though she loved him with all her heart, the family as a whole was what was really important.

Imelda looked into her mother's eyes, saw the hurt there, coupled with resignation, and she knew then that her lovely mum was far more aware of the pitfalls of the Life than she would ever be. Imelda understood now that her mother was willing to overlook anything – even the death of her youngest child – if her husband deemed it necessary. Imelda could not believe that she had never understood the true impact that the Life actually had on the people involved in it.

The realisation that her mother was willing to overlook the murder of her own child was an outrage that Imelda was unable to comprehend. That her mother was so entrenched in the Life that she could accept her youngest child's murder as no more than an occupational hazard was fucking outrageous! Imelda was absolutely horrified by the realisation that her own mother could not see how wrong this was, let alone how vicious and cold blooded it proved them all to be. And her own husband more than any of them.

Imelda saw the Life in stunning clarity for the first time and wondered how she could have been a Bailey for so long without understanding it.

Just then, her father returned and she watched as he came into the bedroom, and pulled his wife into his arms. He held her gently as she cried, assuring her all the while that everything would be all right now that he was home, and he would look after her.

Smiling at his daughter, Peter Bailey motioned with a movement of his huge dark head for her to leave them alone together.

Imelda left the room quietly, with a heavy heart, knowing that, after this night, nothing would be the same for any of them ever again.

Book Three

There is power in the blood, justice in the sword
When that call it comes, I will be ready for war

Alabama 3, 'Power In The Blood'
Album: *Power in the Blood*, 2002

You prayed at the holy shrine
Still the guru wouldn't receive you
You've seen so many signs
Still they call you a non-believer

Alabama 3, 'Come On Home'
Album: *Power in the Blood*, 2002

Lousy but loyal

Anon, London East-End slogan at
George V's Jubilee, 1935

Chapter Eighty-Five

1997

Lena yawned noisily and stretched her arms above her head. She was glad to see the sun beaming through her bedroom window. Daniel was already up and about; she could hear him pottering about in the kitchen and, pulling on a dressing gown, she went downstairs quickly.

He looked up as she came into the kitchen. 'You can smell a cup of tea from two miles, you!'

Lena laughed. 'One of my many gifts! I can't believe I slept in! Tania gone off already?'

Daniel nodded as he poured them both mugs of tea. 'She was up and out before I got up. And what a fucking mess she left as usual!'

Lena smiled tolerantly. 'Well, that's our Tania all right. Even the boys weren't as messy as her.'

They took their teas out to the back garden; it looked beautiful. Lena admired her surroundings and wondered for the thousandth time how she could have hated this place all those years ago. Now it was her haven, the place where she relaxed, where she found peace.

'What do you think about tomorrow, Lena? Shall we go or not?'

Lena sipped her tea. 'I think we have to, Dan. Ria is expecting us, anyway.'

Daniel had thought as much. 'Who'd have imagined Petey would be getting shackled! I hope it works for him.'

In all honesty, Daniel had no real interest in going to Petey's engagement party. He knew that it was a sham. Petey was incapable of ever being faithful, as had been proved time and again over the years. He went through women like other men went through underpants. He had the perfect life for a lover of women; from the nightclubs right through to the strip clubs, he had his pick of the fillies, and he was good-looking too. Daniel didn't care what he did but his strict ideas about fidelity in a marriage meant he thought Petey should give all that up once he tripped down the aisle. He knew Peter felt the same even though he had taken the occasional flyer in his day – not that anyone else had ever known that, of course. Saint Peter, as Daniel thought of him lately, had made sure of that much.

'I think Ria wants it at the house to keep it small, Dan, you know. If it was at one of the clubs it could easily get out of hand.'

Daniel turned his attention back to his wife and nodded his agreement, but he kept his own counsel on that point. Young Bernadette O'Toole liked the clubs a bit too much, as he'd observed – and she liked the men who frequented them as well. Not that anyone could actually accuse her of anything untoward – she was just a flirty type – but Daniel Bailey knew a whore in the making when he saw one, and his nephew's intended had 'trollop' written all over her. She had even tried to give *him* the glad eye! She needed to be admired by every man within her orbit. Petey would have more fights than Muhammad Ali once he shackled himself to her, but that was his lookout. He decided to suss Lena out on the subject, saying craftily, 'She seems like a nice enough girl. What do you think, Lena?'

Lena thought about his question for a few seconds before saying, 'To be honest, Dan, I can't take to her, and God knows I've tried. But there's something about her I just can't abide. Do I sound nasty saying that?'

Daniel saw the genuine sadness on his wife's face at the quandary she found herself in and, laughing, he answered her by saying, 'Well, that makes two of us, Lena! I think she is "high maintenance" as they call it nowadays. She has too much to say for herself, and nothing I've heard her utter has been worth a fucking wank. She is a lovely-looking girl – no one can take that away from her – but she has no real substance to her. It's all top show.'

Lena was taken aback at just how accurately her husband had described Bernadette O'Toole. She could not have put it better herself. The girl was stunning, absolutely gorgeous in fact, but once you got past her looks, there was nothing else to keep your interest. She had no warmth to her; she didn't seem to engage with anyone on a personal level – in fact, she didn't even seem to engage with *Petey* properly. They didn't look or interact like a couple somehow.

'I'm amazed at what you just said, Dan, because I think that as well. I know Ria feels the same too, but it's Petey's choice, ain't it? Shame that no one's kids ever think of the fact that the people they bring into *their* lives also have to be a part of the whole family. They should think about that before they inflict their choice on everyone else!'

Daniel laughed out loud at Lena's honesty. But she was right, this generation were all selfish little fuckers. Years ago people had the nous to look at the whole package – this generation just looked at the outside. Looks were so important now – in fact, they took precedence over everything else. But a personality went a *lot* further than good looks in a marriage. His Lena had always understood him, as he had understood her, that was why they were still together. Peter and Ria were the same – they had stood by each other no matter what, and no matter how hard things had got. Look at Ria and her boy Jack! She had understood that Peter had no option but to take that useless cunt out of the family equation. He would stake his last few pence that this O'Toole piece had no idea of that sort of loyalty. She would be on the trot at the first whiff of aggro. Petey Bailey would sup sorrow from a long spoon, as his old mum used to say, and he would rue the day he tied himself to such a female.

'Well, it's his fucking funeral, girl. At least she's

willing to have the full Catholic ceremony – that's something, I suppose.'

Lena laughed with him. 'Ria made *that* as clear as fucking day, don't you worry! Fucking registry office! Have you ever heard the like? Bernadette's a Catholic anyway, Irish as well, about the only thing going for her as far as your mother is concerned.'

'Well, at least that proves the girl has the sense to know what's good for her.'

Lena nodded. 'Good family as well; the O'Tooles are decent enough people.' She could tell Daniel was bored with the conversation now, so she finished her tea and got up. 'Come on then, you. Let me cook your breakfast. Fancy a bit of egg and bacon?'

Daniel nodded. That was what he loved most about his Lena, she knew when to let things drop. So many women were unable to understand the importance of knowing when they were starting to bore the arse off their old men. It was a knack his Lena had acquired very early on in their relationship, and he loved that about her.

Chapter Eighty-Six

Bernadette O'Toole was more than aware of just how lovely she was and, as she studied herself in the mirror of her dressing table, she was genuinely amazed at how, even without a dab of make-up, she still looked absolutely amazing.

Her mother had said to her many years before when, as a thirteen-year-old girl, she was already being looked at by men – older men – that she should understand sooner rather than later that girls who looked like her didn't have to play by the same rules everybody else did. Her looks would open any door she chose to walk through. As she grew up she began to understand the power of her beauty. Neither of her parents were that good looking actually, but she had inherited the best from both of them and, somehow, she had turned out a real stunner.

Now she was about to tie herself to Petey Bailey and, in so doing, ensure that she would have the kind of life that she felt was hers by right. She *liked* Petey well enough – he was a nice bloke. But he was also a Face, and she knew the importance of *that* better than anyone. He could provide her with the world on a plate, and she was determined to make sure that he did just that. She was not going to waste her God-given talents on a fucking no mark, of that much she was sure.

As a teenager she had understood the importance of keeping her reputation; she was determined that the man who eventually got her would know that no one else had been there before him. Petey Bailey was going to pay dearly for her virtue.

She smiled happily. After tonight, her life was settled; she would be a part of the Bailey family, and everything that entailed. It had been a long old haul, but it had been worth it. Soon she would be Mrs Peter Bailey Junior, and that was just about the best any girl could ever hope for. She was going to be the First Lady of the South East, and she intended to make sure that everybody knew that.

Chapter Eighty-Seven

Ria was determined to make this a really good night. True, she had her reservations about Bernadette, but she knew she had to keep them to herself. Her Petey was 'plighting his troth', as Theresa kept putting it in her own sarcastic way. *She* did not like Bernadette at all, but it was Petey's choice at the end of the day.

Liam and Mandy were both helping with the arrangements, and she was glad that he had seen the sense to marry *her*. Mandy was a good girl, and she had become very close to her over the years. Her only sorrow was that they had not yet had their own child, though Liam seemed happy enough as they were. Young Bernard adored him, and he adored Bernard right back. He was a natural-born father was her Liam, and it was unfair really that they had no other children.

She looked around the room, and she was pleased with how it had turned out. She felt that having it in her own home was a way of making it more personal, as well as ensuring that it didn't get out of hand. Her Petey was a good lad, but he did like the clubs a bit too much. Now he was settling down at last, she was hoping that he would take this engagement seriously enough to curb his wild ways. Bernadette O'Toole might not be her first choice where her son was concerned, but she hoped the girl had enough life in her to make sure the man she married would toe the line. Petey needed to settle down, and the sooner that happened, the better. Ria wanted more grandchildren, and she wanted her boys settled, like her Imelda.

As she checked everything was in order, Bernard came running up to her. Now twelve, he was a handsome boy with his blond hair and his big blue eyes, and Ria loved him. He slipped his arms around her waist and she instinctively hugged him to her.

'Nana, Nana, can I stay here tonight?' It was his usual request; he loved staying with his nana and granddad, and Bernard was as much a part of the family now as little Delroy or Tania.

'Course you can! You know you can stay here any time you like!'

Mandy grinned as she followed her son into the room. 'You let him get away with everything! You know he already has his overnight bag packed, don't you?'

Ria laughed. 'He's all right, love, we love having him, you know that.'

'Well, if you're sure. The caterers are already setting up in the kitchen. Shall I help you dress the tables? It's going to be so lovely, Ria. I hope Bernadette appreciates it.'

Even though Mandy didn't realise what she had said, Ria was aware that the fact that she was also unsure of

Bernadette's reaction to everything spoke volumes. Miss O'Toole had not really endeared herself to the women in the family; in fact, she was the kind of girl who overlooked other women, more interested in the reaction she got from the men.

Ria sighed. 'Well, Mandy love, we've done our best – we can't do any more.'

Chapter Eighty-Eight

The engagement party was in full swing, and Peter Bailey watched as his son greeted the guests. He was a good man, of that Peter was confident. Over the last ten years, he had watched his lads grow into strong, trustworthy men, and he had been proud to be a part of their lives. Petey and Liam had both become close to him. After what happened with Jack they all understood the importance of family, and the need to ensure that family took precedence over everything else. That was the strength of the Baileys – they were so tight no one could ever get near them. Even when decisions – tough decisions – had to be faced, they understood that they were for the family's benefit and, as hard as they had been, the choices had to be made.

Things had been better with Daniel too in the last decade. His brother had seen that his sons were more than capable of looking out for themselves, and he had been happy to let them grow into their roles in the family hierarchy. The days of them having to prove their strength were long gone – they were now accepted as the foremost family, not just in the Smoke, but in the whole of the UK. Nobody attempted anything of import without getting their approval first. The Baileys were sensible enough to know that they had to let other people, other families, have a good earn in their name. It was the only way to keep their position, and also the only way they could garner goodwill.

In all that time, they had never once had a serious threat to their empire; everyone in their orbit knew that they were not people who you took on lightly. Peter saw that his reputation, coupled with that of his brother, was more than enough to deter the majority of the people they dealt with from stepping out of line. Plus they were very fair in their dealings, and that went a long way. They also made a point of keeping the peace; when other families had grievances against each other, they mediated between them and they always tried their best to come to a conclusion that was acceptable to both the parties involved. It was important to remember that everyone they dealt with had some kind of involvement with the Baileys.

Peter observed as his eldest son welcomed people with the right amount of respect, making sure that they knew who was the boss. He watched his Ria as she oversaw the waiters as they passed around the champagne; this had had to look 'expensively casual' – whatever the fuck that meant! That was what Ria was aiming for by all accounts; this was her domain and he had to let her do whatever she wanted.

Bernadette O'Toole, who, as lovely as she was, had never had a real fucking wedge in her life, was clearly determined to have the best of everything. Well, after tonight, that was his eldest son's job, not his, and he had a sneaky suspicion that his lad would soon feel the pressure of her insistence on only having the very best. If she had been brought up to all this then Peter would have said fair play to her, but knowing that she had been raised one small step away from hand-to-mouth irritated him. He couldn't help it.

Bernadette O'Toole acted as if she was better than everyone around her. Her looks were enough to make some believe that might actually be so. But as soon as she opened her mouth and spoke, any thoughts along those lines were soon forgotten. Bernadette O'Toole sounded rougher than a Basildon pikey.

Still, Petey was enamoured of her, although the real attraction for his eldest son was the fact that she was a virgin; for a man like his Petey that was a major selling point. He had the kind of personality that made him determined to have everything first, from cars to women. Peter only hoped his son didn't lose interest in this wife of his as quickly as he usually did with his new toys. He still hoped that it all worked out for them, despite his dislike of the girl. Like his wife, he was willing to put up with her if she was what his son wanted.

Bernadette smiled at her fiancé's father, hoping he was as bowled over by her looks as everyone else was.

Peter Bailey smiled back, wondering how long it was before the real food came out. He was starving.

Chapter Eighty-Nine

Imelda loathed her brother's girlfriend with a vengeance. She knew enough about men to understand their preoccupation with a pretty face, but she could not for the life of her comprehend Petey getting involved with Bernadette O'Toole. The girl was gorgeous, no one could dispute that, but she had the personality of a gnat. Even Delroy, who appreciated a good-looking female, could hardly contain his active dislike of the girl. She seemed to rub everyone up the wrong way.

She was not just vain, arrogant and ignorant – which would have been bad enough. The real rub was that she genuinely believed that she was special. In a way, Imelda was more than a little jealous of the girl's self-confidence. Imelda had been forced to suppress her natural nature; as the years had gone on, she had finally admitted that her Delroy was not a man to be challenged, and certainly not a man who was willing to allow his wife to dictate how he lived his life. It had eventually sunk in that her jealousy was not something he was prepared to countenance; it would be the reason he walked out on her. It had been a hard lesson, but she had learned it for the simple reason that she had no intention of losing the only man she had ever loved, or ever would love for that matter.

After her brother's death, she had been forced to re-evaluate everything in her life, and admit that her family and her husband's place in that family were the most important things. Her feelings as an individual were not. Everything was actually about the Baileys as a whole. Delroy loved her, there was no doubting that, but his love came with a proviso, and that proviso was that she did not encroach on him or his livelihood in any way. Her father agreed with him about that, as did her mother, and that had been the hardest lesson of all.

Sipping her champagne, she made her way over to Mandy, who somehow had become a close friend despite their shaky start. Mandy was the only other woman within her orbit who seemed to sympathise with how she felt.

Chapter Ninety

Michael O'Toole was feeling very awkward; he didn't like ostentation, and he knew that he looked as out of place as he felt. The Baileys had been fantastic, there was no doubt about that. The problem was wholly his, and he would have to overcome it sooner rather than later. His daughter had bagged herself a real prize, and that was her prerogative. Hers and her mother's, of course – like a pair of fucking witches the two of them. For all Bernadette's good-girl act, he knew she was just hanging it all out for the main attraction – Peter Bailey the younger. Michael only hoped she realised just what she had taken on; the man wasn't a fool, not by anyone's standards, and she might just find she had bitten off more than she could chew.

The worst thing for Michael was that he felt like a ponce; *he* was the father of the bride-to-be and, by rights, this night should have been organised by *him* and his old woman. If that had been the case, there was no way it would have been anything remotely as upmarket as this. And that was the rub – his own daughter had more or less told him that there was no way she was going to celebrate her engagement on his penny; she had almost laughed in his face when he had suggested it.

Pity she didn't understand the Baileys; they would have respected whatever he had provided – they were decent like that. But his Bernadette was more than happy for her *new* family to foot the bill, and they had done that all right. Smoked salmon! He had to laugh – they had been lucky to have tinned fucking salmon at the best of times. He had provided as well as he could, and his wife and daughter should give him credit for that. They might not have lived in a mansion, but they never went without. Now those two talked about food as if they were suddenly related to the fucking Galloping Gourmet. They disgusted him, the pair of them. Especially his Beryl – all the years they had been married and she still couldn't cook a decent meal, no matter how good or expensive the ingredients might be. Now she talked as if she cooked banquets on a daily basis. The only good thing about prison had been that the food inside was much better than anything he had ever eaten at home!

He observed his daughter as she attempted to play down the sheer size of her engagement ring, while making sure everybody was aware of it. It was five carats, and cut into what she called a baguette-style stone. She held her perfectly manicured hand out away from her body, and let the ring catch the light. Silly cow! He knew that stone had been half-inched from somewhere; there was no way Petey Bailey was going to pay the full price. He was a lot of things, Petey Bailey, but a mug wasn't one of them.

At least tonight was nearly over; then all he had to do was get through the wedding. Bernadette had wanted a registry office do, and then a party in a posh hotel. Well, Petey Bailey had thwarted her there, and that was how it should be. Fancy turning her nose up at the church where she had worshipped all her life! Just more of her snobbery.

If only she could see herself as everyone else saw her. Tonight she was wearing a tight minidress, off-white, or *ecru* as she insisted on calling it. It only fit where it touched and, along with the fake tan, the overabundance of bleached-blond hair, and nails that looked like they had been grown in a greenhouse in Eastern Europe, she looked every bit the poor man's Pamela Anderson. She had about as much class as a fucking Ford Fiesta. Not that she would ever see that, of course – thanks to her mother, she believed she was a cut above. He swallowed down his Chivas Regal, and made his way towards the bar for a refill.

'You all right, Michael?' Peter Bailey was genuinely pleased to see his daughter-in-law-to-be's father.

Michael O'Toole smiled. 'Yeah, it's a grand party, Peter, really lovely. You've done her proud.'

'To be honest, I think this is a bit over the top, but that's kids these days – though my Petey is not a kid any more, not by anyone's standards! He's weighing out for this lot. I told him – you and her want a fucking circus, you can provide one.'

Michael O'Toole relaxed then, relieved that this man

was not paying for his daughter's engagement, and grateful that Peter saw his point of view on the matter. 'I offered, Peter, but she blew me out. Not good enough these days it seems . . .'

Peter heard the bitterness in Michael's voice. 'Fucking kids, ungrateful the lot of them. Anyway, I was wondering if you were available for a spot of lunch this week? Go somewhere we can talk, you know? I have a bit of work I thought I might put your way.'

Michael O'Toole hesitated for only a few seconds before replying easily, 'Sounds good to me, mate.'

Peter smiled, he understood how Michael was feeling; he was clearly a man who had a lot of pride, and that was a trait Peter respected. One good thing about this Bernadette debacle was at least her family weren't expecting to jump on the bandwagon.

Chapter Ninety-One

Davey, Noel and Jamsie had escaped to the garden when the party was in full swing. They were smoking a joint, and enjoying the night.

'That is a puff and a half, Jamsie! Where'd you get it?'

Jamsie grinned. 'Delroy won't like it, but I got it off a young lad in Tulse Hill. I heard about him from one of the strippers. He's a good kid – only twenty-two, and already he has a serious fucking clientele. I'm going to offer him an in; we need to know where he is scoring this gear.'

Davey laughed. 'Fucking right and all! This is amazing. I love it when we find a new avenue, you know? Keeps everything nice and under control. There are so many youngsters out there looking for a new bit of scratch.'

'Well, we can only give him a chance; if he knows what is good for him, he will snatch our hand off. But he seems pretty cool – from what I've heard he has a good little rep. Only problem is, he thinks he's a *gangster*! Fucking morons – they listen to a few rap records and think they are fucking hard men. If only it was that easy!'

They all laughed then.

'What's the score with the Allen family? Uncle Peter invited them tonight, but neither him or Dad have really given them the time of day.' Davey sounded troubled about it.

Noel shrugged. 'I don't know, but I would assume it's serious. They are the nearest thing we have to rivals, after all. I expect the old men have put the brakes on something they want to do. Dad had the arse with them a while back, I know, because I was there when he bawled Terrence Allen out. Dad was fucking fuming.'

Davey and Jamsie shrugged.

'Well, it'll all come out in the wash; it always does.'

Noel Bailey nodded, but he had a feeling this was far more serious than any of them suspected.

Chapter Ninety-Two

Daniel Bailey watched Terrence Allen as he talked, and, boy, could Terry Allen talk when the fancy took him! Years ago they had called him Terry the Tarpaulin because he had a reputation for making people disappear; when they finally turned up they were wrapped in an old tarpaulin. It was Terry's signature; no one could prove it was him, but the people in the know had their suspicions.

Now Daniel Bailey observed as Terry held court. He was a good-looking man, well into his forties, but with a fine head of dark brown hair, and lively blue eyes. Like them, he had an Irish ancestry, and like them he was proud of it. Although, unlike Daniel and his brother Peter, Terry knew who his father was. Tony Allen had been a real force in his day; he had died in prison of liver failure a few years previously, seventeen years into a thirty-year stretch. Prison hootch was a fucking killer. The lads had buried him with the required pomp and ceremony that denoted his standing in the criminal community, and then quietly taken over his role along with his businesses. They had done a good job as well, no one could deny that.

But they were getting a bit too big for their boots. They had been particularly disrespectful about the Baileys, and that had come to Peter's attention on more than one occasion. The Allens were beginning to think that they were above being rebuked by the very people who gave them their earn. Both Daniel and Peter were aware of that, and knew that the Allens had to be cut down to size before it got too far out of hand.

People like the Allens were dangerous; they were intelligent enough to plan a coup, hard enough to carry it out, but not patient enough to bide their time. They had fucked themselves with their own hubris, because they had underestimated the Baileys' reach. The Allens had not foreseen just how many people were loyal to the Baileys, and depended on them for their earn as they had for many years. These were the same people who had no qualms about putting the word into the appropriate ear when they deemed it necessary.

Now the Allens had to be reprimanded – and publicly. They were a real handful, and that was the problem. Both Daniel and Peter were agreed that they were not men to overlook, and definitely not men who you gave any kind of leeway. If they managed to recruit other families they could then become more powerful. The fact that they were the main providers of recreational drugs this side of the Watford Gap was enough to make sure they were taken seriously as a threat.

Daniel saw his brother watching Terry Allen as he mocked the people around him; in his exuberance at telling his story he was slopping drink everywhere, with complete disrespect for Peter Bailey's home. Catching his brother's eye, Daniel Bailey winked at him mischievously, looking forward to taking Terry down a peg or two.

Terry Allen knew very well that his antics and foul-mouthed joking were being observed and, looking at his brother Billy, he said loudly, 'Get us another drink, Billy Boy, I feel a real bastard of a thirst coming on.'

Billy Allen grinned. He knew as well as Terry did that Peter and Daniel Bailey would not appreciate cursing at their little soirée. They were real old fogeys like that – still living by some old fucking moral code that had gone out with the ark. The Allens were confident enough to play up to the gallery; it was what they wanted. It was about time that someone showed the Baileys that they were not the only game in town – they had too much to say for one family.

Billy could hear his brother telling another filthy joke as he walked to the bar to refill the glasses, insisting in a loud voice on a decent-sized drink. 'Fuck me, are this lot on a budget or what?'

The insult was there, and everyone around them heard it.

Chapter Ninety-Three

Petey Bailey watched as his wife-to-be danced provocatively all by her lonesome. She was a good eyeful, no doubt about that, but she was also a first-class prick-tease. He could see most of the men in the room trying not to watch her as she gyrated with a vacant smile on her face, and he wondered why he was putting himself through this charade.

He had vowed to himself that, if he could get in her knickers before the big day, he would out her without a backward glance. He would even let her keep the ring – he could be very magnanimous when the fancy took him. Up until now, her drawers had been harder to break into than the Bank of England; Bernadette was canny – she knew that once she succumbed to his charms he would lose interest. If she held out, he would marry her, but if he *did*, he intended for her to be banging out babies like a fucking machine gun, that was for sure.

Her inflated opinion of herself would not cut any ice with him once the dirty deed was done; he would knock her up and move on to pastures new. She would get what she wanted: the name, a big drum, and a gold card. He would get a family and, if she provided him with that, he would tolerate her.

Petey recognised that he had a lot of his Uncle Daniel in him. Over the years he had learned to be very ruthless; in fact, since his brother Jack's demise, he had found a strength that kept him sane. Seeing first hand just what his father was capable of had been a real learning curve, and it had hit home how lucky *he* had been to escape any stronger punishment for his gambling and his attempt at skimming off the family take.

Walking to Bernadette, he pulled her into his arms in a gesture of possession. As she looked up into his eyes, he appreciated just how stunning her appearance was, and a bit of him knew that many men would envy him his good fortune. Petey was under no illusions that there was anything of any real substance inside the perfect shell. She was like a lot of the girls in their world – useless, without any kind of personality, completely devoid of the work ethic, and on the lookout for a decent pay packet. Bernadette had hit the mother lode with him. As much as that knowledge disappointed him, a part of him didn't judge her. Bernadette had no proper education or understanding of the real world. She had no chance of getting a job – all she had going for her were her looks, and she had used them as her only asset. Unfortunately, looks did not endure; once they were gone, she would be one fucking unhappy person. She would hang on to her youth with the determination of a Japanese tosa and, like that dog, she would fight tooth and nail to make sure she got what she wanted.

She swayed against him, and he felt the usual stirring inside him; he knew she was aware of it too. He grinned at her. 'Happy?'

She nodded, her deep blue eyes sparkling with triumph. 'I am, Petey. I love you.'

He hugged her close, kissing her softly on her glossy pink lips. They were both aware that he didn't say it back.

Chapter Ninety-Four

Ria had observed this exchange with Lena and Imelda and each of the three women felt that the little tableau was all wrong. Petey and Bernadette looked like they were on a blind date, and a disastrous blind date at that. They did not resemble a real couple in any way.

Ria sighed. 'Where's Tania?'

Lena shrugged. 'She will be here, you know what she's like.'

Ria glanced around her home; it was more than large enough to accommodate all the guests, and the DJ who had set up in the conservatory was now, finally, playing the older-style records; the younger people were dancing happily to a bit of Motown. The men were in the kitchen, the older men anyway; it was the time of night when business would be the order of the day. She was tired out, but she was relieved that the party was a good one, by anyone's standards. It was just after eleven, and the whole thing was just taking off; she had hours to go before she could excuse herself.

As she saw Tania come into the room, she smiled in relief. Lena had been watching the door for her daughter all night and, now she was finally here, Lena could relax.

Tania was lovely – not as obviously beautiful as Bernadette O'Toole, but she was a natural beauty. Where Bernadette had learned to enhance her natural assets with make-up, hair dye and expensive underwear, Tania still had the fresh-faced youth that was actually far more appealing, in Ria's opinion. With her reddish-blond hair, and her deep blue eyes, she was the double of Theresa Bailey as a girl; anyone who saw her immediately saw the resemblance. It was uncanny. Being the good girl she was, Tania went straight to where her grandmother was sitting, and she made a huge fuss of her before making her way over to her mother and aunt.

'Where were you? I expected you hours ago.' Lena tried not to sound as worried as she obviously was and Tania laughed.

'Mum! I was doing my coursework with Ellen Sparks. I told you I was going there first. We need to get ourselves in gear if we want good grades. How's it going? Is it all right if I have a proper drink?'

Imelda laughed at her cousin's bravery. 'Come on, Tania, one little vodka won't kill you.' She whisked her away quickly. 'You've already been drinking! I can smell it on you – cider, and cheap cider at that!'

Tania grinned as they pushed their way towards the bar area.

'Coursework, my arse! Where you been really?'

'No, I *was* working, Imelda. Me and Ellen just had a drink while we were studying, that's all. I'm seventeen, for God's sake! My mum and dad act as if I'm twelve.'

'It will never change, you can take that as fact from me. My dad still treats me like I'm a fucking schoolkid.'

They both got double vodkas, and the noise and the heat of the room drove them out into the large gardens. The cool air was just what they needed.

'So how has it been? Has Petey somehow miraculously seen the light?'

Imelda smiled and took a deep gulp of her drink. Tania had a crush on her older cousin, and Imelda knew that she didn't think anyone had sussed that out yet. But Tania looked at him like he was some kind of god, and she suspected that Tania's crush would be there for a good while yet. It didn't help that Petey unwittingly made a big fuss of her – they all did. She was a very lovable person. Clearly Tania hoped that one day he would see her for the woman she was becoming, but that was never going to happen. Imelda had her fingers crossed that the crush would fizzle out naturally.

'Petey is happy, Tania – he knows what he wants. He's in his thirties, he ain't a little kid. We might not like her, love, but he's the one who's chosen to tie himself to her.'

Tania was devastated by her words, and Imelda was sorry to hurt her, but sometimes you had to be cruel to be kind. Tania was growing into a lovely young woman, and Imelda knew that Tania was feeling the ache of her unrequited crush on a daily basis. It was almost painful to watch her at times. She changed the subject. 'Lot of people here; why didn't you invite any of your friends?'

Tania shrugged. 'Dunno. Look at the boys, drunk together as usual!'

All the cousins were halfway down the garden lawn and, if Imelda knew anything, they were stoned as well. Even at fifty feet away she could see the signs. Both of her Delroys were with them, which annoyed her; her son was a handful at the best of times, without his father and the boys making him worse. She secretly hated that he was working for the family already – unlike Tania there was no way that he was ever going to use his brains for anything outside the Bailey empire. Delroy had been pleased at his son's insistence that he just wanted to join the family firm. She had not been able to talk him round; he had decided his own fate from a very early age. She had hoped against hope that he would want to become a regular member of society. She worked the Bailey businesses, and she enjoyed it, but she wanted more for her child; she didn't want the danger of prison hanging over *his* head. But he had known what he wanted, and she had quickly been made to understand that she had no say in the matter. It was early days – he was only sixteen – but he was already getting a name for himself.

Delroy Junior had always been a difficult, wayward child, with a dangerous streak. He had been nothing but trouble at his school – too much to say for himself, his teachers said, and no interest in working for anything. Eventually he had been expelled for fighting, and that was after years of trying to make him see that

359

there was another life out there if he would only look for it. Her husband had dismissed it as natural spirit; he'd been proud of him almost, whereas she had seen it as a recipe for disaster.

'You all right, Imelda?'

'I was just thinking about you and my Delroy as kids – now you're both so grown up. It's hard, you know, to finally accept that you're old enough to do your own thing.'

Tania hugged her, understanding that Imelda was worried for her son. 'He'll be all right, Imelda, everyone looks out for him. Stop worrying.'

Imelda nodded, saddened that even Tania knew that her young Delroy's only real strength against the world he lived in lay in the fact that he was a part of the Bailey family. Except Tania didn't know just what being a Bailey actually entailed – not yet anyway.

'Come on, drink up! I'll get us another one.'

Tania did as she was told. She watched Petey and Bernadette as they slow-danced together – even through the patio doors she could see that Bernadette was moulded to her cousin like a wet T-shirt, and the scene saddened her. Petey was so handsome and so clever – why couldn't he see that Bernadette was not good enough for him, was not worthy of his name?

She walked aimlessly towards the boys; they were loud and their laughter was enticing. They welcomed her into their company happily, and she felt the usual warmth of their love surround her.

Chapter Ninety-Five

Peter and Daniel were in a small room at the back of the house that Peter used as an office. It had once been the butler's pantry, and Peter liked everything about it, from the wood panelling on the walls to the small oriel windows that were still in possession of their original stained-glass motifs. It now sported an antique desk and a large, leather captain's chair; it was a beautiful room, and Peter knew that it impressed people. He had filled the bookshelves with what he saw as important books – anyone who scanned the shelves would assume that an educated man lived there. He had paid a lot of money to ensure that, and he had sworn that one day he would read the books. It was his dream – when he finally retired – to educate himself before it was too late.

Terry Allen stood with them uneasily; he was about to be reprimanded, and he had expected as much. What he had *not* anticipated was feeling so nervous about it. He had to show the Baileys that he was a man of power and strength, let them know that they didn't intimidate him. Now, though, seeing the brothers side by side, he could see why they had achieved so much together. As a team they were formidable, there was no doubt about that; even the knowledge that they were not as close as they once were did not detract from the sheer menace that they exuded. Up close and personal, they were evidently more than capable of looking after their interests. The death of Jack Bailey was still the stuff of legend; there were many people who laid the boy's death at his own father's door. Coupled with Daniel's reputation for maiming, crippling and murdering for the slightest of reasons, the brothers were both seen as men to be wary of.

But the Baileys had been at the top for far too long, and Terry was not going to let old stories and ancient history cloud his judgement. *Everyone* could be taken down; it just needed the proper planning. As in any war, if you used your knowledge of your adversary properly, you could eventually find the right strategy to bring about your enemies' downfall. The Baileys' downfall had to be catastrophic – not only public, but also serious enough to incapacitate them completely. That meant, of course, that the Bailey brothers had to die – quickly and violently. Without these two, the whole family would flounder.

Daniel broke the silence, aware that Terrence Allen was nervous, and wondering what the fuck was going on in his head. 'So, Terry, me and Peter here feel that you need a bit of a tug. Your language tonight and your general attitude has offended us deeply. You see, unlike you, we feel that when in someone's home, a modicum of decorum is to be expected. Do you get my fucking drift?'

Terrence Allen was astounded by Daniel Bailey's sincerity; he truly *did* believe that he had the right to say his piece. Whereas Terrence would have used the behaviour as simply an excuse to pull someone into line, he realised that the Bailey brothers believed that they had an honest grievance. It was like stepping back in time. It made him finally understand just what he was dealing with. These men were fucking dinosaurs, still living by some old criminal code, and they had to be made aware that those days were long gone.

Terry Allen smiled, feigning bafflement. 'Come on, guys, this is a party, for fuck's sake! I've had a few drinks, a bit of gear. If I offended you I can only apologise.'

Peter could tell Terry was far more rattled than he was letting on and he was pleased. Their summoning him away from the party would have been noticed; they had made sure of that. 'You came into *my* home, and you have not shown me or my son an ounce of respect. Listen to me, Terry. If you *ever* fucking disrespect me or mine like that again, I will kill you. *You* don't curse around my family, my wife and daughter, and you do not fucking act like a lairy cunt on my watch, or my brother's. Do I make myself clear?'

Terry Allen was not smiling now. He had made two very dangerous enemies, and his plan of being seen by his peers as a man who had no fear of the Baileys was suddenly moot. Everyone would now know that he had been given a serious tug and, unless he was seen to retaliate somehow, his credibility was basically fucked. He had no intention of causing a tear-up in Peter's house – there were far too many Baileys under one roof to even contemplate such a foolish action. But he could bide his time.

Daniel could almost read the man's thoughts, and he loved that both he and Peter still had the skill to suss out a situation for what it was. This ponce had thought he could use this night as his chance to make the Baileys look weak. Now it had been made clear to him that he wasn't in their league, the humiliation he was about to endure would guarantee that he would not forget this lesson in a hurry.

'Get your brother, and your crew, and get out.'

Daniel's voice was low, almost bored-sounding, and Terry Allen knew that he had no option but to leave.

'Come on, I've apologised, we are mates, ain't we?'

Peter Bailey stood up, and Terrence Allen was reminded of just how big he was; he had misjudged the situation badly.

'What part of "fuck off" don't you get, Terry?'

When he left the office, Daniel and Peter started to laugh, once more in perfect sync. Together they were invincible, and that made them both feel good. They could feel the sheer power of their combined strength, and suddenly they were reminded of the early days, how they had worked so well as a team and taken whatever they wanted. The Allens' departure would be noted, talked about, and they would not forgive them the humiliation in a hurry. But people like the Allens needed to be taken down a few pegs before things got too out of hand.

The Allens were fucking good earners and, if they had used their brains, they would have been given a lot more responsibility. Peter and Daniel had had great plans for them, but they had fucked it all up now. They were mugs of the first water – arrogant, grasping and not prepared to wait for what they believed was their right. Well, they would find their operations seriously curtailed for a while. Let them see who was actually running the whole show.

'Shall we get a drink, bruv?'

Peter grinned. 'You took the words right out of my mouth.'

Chapter Ninety-Six

'Good night or what?' Liam climbed into the car beside his brother.

'One of the best, bruv.'

Petey had actually had a good time at his engagement party last night. The spread had impressed everyone, which was exactly what he had wanted. His fiancée, as she now insisted on calling herself, was well pleased; she had deigned to give him a blow job at the end of the night, so he felt he was winning *that* war. Five carats it had taken, but at least he was making a bit of headway. Funny thing was, while she was blowing him, he was thinking about one of the strippers – a young black bird with relaxed hair, and the softest skin he had ever felt on a woman. She had a neat, tight little body, and when she stripped she could mesmerise even the most jaded of men. It was a melon scratcher all right.

Liam had enjoyed the evening, and now he wanted a huge breakfast, and at least three pints of tea. The brothers stopped outside a café in Canning Town. Inside they were treated like visiting royalty and, once they were settled into their seats, they ordered the full English, lit themselves cigarettes, and finally relaxed.

Sipping his tea, Liam said seriously, 'Those fucking Allens must be on a death wish! What the fuck was all that about last night? Did you see the state of Mum's floor? It was drenched and scuffed – they must have been on something fucking good, because no one in their right mind would act like that if they were normal.'

Petey shrugged dismissively. 'They are chancing their arm, that's all. Fucking wankers. No brains, either of them – a fucking twelve year old has more nous than those two. They were like amateurs putting on a show. They were lucky they weren't ironed out.'

Liam nodded in agreement. 'What are we going to do about them?'

'I'll sort them out, Liam. I talked it over with the old man last night, said I'd pull back their earn for a while, keep an eye out, like. I've got a meet with them later – me and Danny are going to put the hard word on them, and that should be enough.'

Liam yawned loudly. 'I know you always got on all right with them in the past, and they must have pissed you off, but you did the right thing not letting off at your own party. Not worth wrecking your night, is it?'

Petey laughed. 'Imagine Bernadette's face if it went off at her engagement!'

Liam grinned. 'She would have had your nuts!'

'Well, to be honest, bruv, it would have been worth it in that case!'

Chapter Ninety-Seven

Peter and Daniel were sitting in Peter's pub in Essex. Daniel had never been there and he was impressed; it was a really nice place. Country pubs had always been a favourite of his – he enjoyed the anonymity they afforded him. He enjoyed mixing with the locals, as he put it, and not having to talk to people he knew all the time. It was relaxing.

'Lovely drum, Pete, you got a good spot here. From what I hear it gets packed of a weekend.'

Peter Bailey grinned wryly. 'You get your half! You should come here more often, it's a good place. All the lads pop in – I think it's the local talent. There's plenty of strange here on a Saturday night. It's out of the way enough, you know? The Filth are good as gold too. We have a late drink, a bit of music – in the summer it's perfect really. During the day you get the families, so it's a good spot.'

Daniel nodded, laughing at his brother's obvious amazement at the way the pub had turned out. 'I assume your Petey picked the bar staff? What was the main criteria? Bra size?'

'He's like a fucking fourteen year old on his first ride! That Bernadette ain't got enough going for her to keep him at home. At the moment the attraction is that she is a so-called good girl, and he could never resist them. He's a fucking savage really – if he spent as much time on actual work, as he did on the nest . . .'

Daniel felt really happy; this was nice, this was what it had been like before he had fucked up. As the years had passed he had become more adept at curbing his natural inclinations. For example, his instinct last night was to take Terrence Allen outside and shove a broken bottle into his face, and he would only have taken him outside because it was Ria's house, and he wouldn't want to make a mess; years ago he would have demolished that fucker in a heartbeat. But that was then, and this was now. He still thought he was right, though; people respected what they couldn't control, what they couldn't understand. People were still in awe of his reputation as a man who was not only unpredictable, but who was also devoid of emotion when it came to work-related situations. He meted out punishments which were remembered by everyone concerned. He had been swallowing his knob for many years now, but sometimes it was bloody hard to keep a lid on his emotions.

'She will quiet him down once she produces a child or two. When she's the mother of his kids he will finally understand about loyalty to women.'

Peter shook his head. 'I don't hold out much hope, Dan. He has a roving eye all right – probably got it from my father, whoever the fuck that was!'

They laughed together. Neither of them cared that their fathers had abandoned them; they had been lucky enough to have Theresa as a mother and she had been more than enough as a parent.

'I've told him to get your Danny onboard, and come down on the Allen brothers. I think we have to let the lads be seen to be sorting this one. They ain't mugs, and this will give them the opportunity to prove themselves – not only to us, but to the public in general. I think we are best playing this down a bit – I don't think it will gain us anything if we make too much of it, you know? They will be seen to have lost a considerable amount of earn. The thing is, we don't want the other families we work with to think that we are without some degree of restraint.'

Daniel nodded, hiding his annoyance. His brother was asking him nicely not to interfere in his usual way – no public hammerings, no crippling, and no outrageousness. After all his years of good behaviour, he resented his brother feeling as though he had to mention it. Daniel was a lot of things, but he was not a fool. Personally, he thought that where the Allens were concerned, his kind of justice was all they would understand. They were bullies, no more and no less, known for their violent outbursts. But, as usual, he swallowed.

'Fair enough, if that is what you think. But last night we were agreed about the fact they needed a fucking reprimand.'

Peter was expecting his brother to say that. 'And they got one, we made our feelings crystal clear last night – not only to them but to everyone else there as well. We tugged them publicly; they know the score now. Thing is, my Petey thinks we should sit back now, and see how the Allens react. It's a new world, Daniel, and if they are sensible they will take onboard the situation they have found themselves in, and hopefully learn from it. If not . . .' He left the rest of the sentence hanging between them in the air.

Daniel nodded once more. 'For the record, Pete, I think they need a bit more than a fucking slap on the wrist, whatever Petey thinks. This smells all wrong to me. I know they bring in a decent wedge, and I also know that they are well compensated for it. Without us, and our groundwork over the years, that money they spend like fucking water would be in someone else's back pocket. All that aside, I will swallow for you, but I feel that I have to give you my honest opinion.'

Peter Bailey respected his brother's honesty. He had let Petey talk him round about the Allens. He hoped that the lad was on the right track – if he wasn't then Daniel Bailey would once more be let off the leash, and this time it would be with his blessing.

'Let's just see how things progress with the boys, eh? If push comes to shove, we can easily rectify things if they fuck up. I've got Delroy keeping a beady eye out as well, so I think we are well covered.'

Daniel sighed. 'I suppose it is time we let the lads

have a bit more leeway but, as I said, if the Allens fuck up again, then their arses are mine.'

Peter grinned, and Daniel saw how old he was getting; they were both looking a bit grizzled. But that didn't mean they were any weaker, and people like the Allen brothers would do well to remember that.

'How about a bit of scran, then? I hear the steaks here are lovely.'

The brothers ate together contentedly, each pleased that they were once more relaxed in the other's company. Peter had felt such rage towards his brother Daniel over the years but, despite all that, he knew that he could trust him more than anyone else – even his own sons. As mad as Daniel could be – and, on a scale of one to ten, Daniel was a resounding twenty – Daniel genuinely loved Peter, and would never intentionally do anything to harm him.

It was a beautiful day, and the brothers enjoyed their afternoon together more than either of them would ever have admitted.

Chapter Ninety-Eight

Tania was watching her mum, and she smiled at the way she could manage to do three things at once. She adored her mum; all her life she had been there for her, no matter what, and she had always known that her mother's main concern was her welfare. As she had grown older, it had sometimes made her feel like she was being suffocated, even though she realised her mother was only looking out for her.

Tania Bailey knew more about her family and the Life than she let on. She had felt the difference in the way she was treated compared to the other girls she had grown up with. Her friends' parents were the worst offenders, but even at school the teachers had treated her differently; everyone in her class had understood and accepted it.

Tania was aware of the value of the name Bailey, but the knowledge was not something she could share with her mother; her mum liked to think she had shielded her from the worst of it. But the stories about her dad and her uncle were local folklore, and her brothers and cousins were following in their footsteps. Furthermore,

Nana Bailey was very loose-lipped with a few drinks in her, which was often these days.

Her dad knew that she wasn't as innocent about it as she let on, of that much she was sure. Her dad was of the opinion that his lifestyle was something she should appreciate and respect even if she was not an active part of it. As always with her dad, it was a mass of contradictions, which pretty much summed up him and his personality perfectly.

Tania was aware that she was pretty, but there were not many boys in her orbit brave enough to ask her for a date. That hurt. It made her feel different once more, and not in a good way. It was in junior school that she had started to realise that her family were different somehow to those of her friends'. She was always offered the starring role in the nativity play, she was never *ever* picked on, everyone she knew was overly nice to her; if she went to friends' houses, their parents treated her as if her presence was what they had lived for all their lives. When she had started to understand, she had felt awful, questioning if people liked her for herself not just because of her name. Even now, in sixth-form college, she was still treated differently to her peers, but she had finally accepted it; she had no choice. She couldn't change her family. Whereas Delroy Junior had embraced the Bailey name, she had always played it down, making sure that she was never seen as too big for her boots, or spoiled.

She wondered sometimes if her mum knew how she

felt, and that was why she over-compensated. Whatever the reason, she knew that, as mums went, she had one of the best ever.

'Can I help you, Mum?'

Lena smiled and Tania saw sadly that age was finally creeping up on her mum. Her Auntie Ria still wore a lot of make-up, still dressed well for her age, whereas her mum had lost interest. She was happy enough in her house, watching her soaps, and immersing herself in the latest series of *Law & Order* – she loved the American crime programmes especially. Tania knew her mum lived what she would judge to be a good life; she was content.

'You're all right, lovely. I'll be finished in a minute, and we can have a cuppa together. Did you enjoy last night?'

Tania forced a smile. 'Yeah, it was all right. Personally, I think that Bernadette's a moron, but Petey knows his own mind, I suppose.'

Lena sighed and, looking at her daughter, her lovely, innocent daughter, she said lightly, 'Listen to your old mum, Tania. You'll look back on these last few years and laugh about it one day. When you're older and you grow up a bit more, you'll see the crush you've got on Petey as no more than the product of a young girl's fancy.'

Tania could feel her face burning; she was mortified at her mother's astuteness. Lena went to her daughter and hugged her tightly. 'Did you think I didn't know?

Darling, all girls go through it, but he's your cousin, and that is a big part of how you're feeling. All young girls set their sights on an older man – someone they can trust not to take advantage of them. It's like a rite of passage. Then, one day, you will meet a nice lad, and it will disappear.'

Tania felt like she could cheerfully drop through the floor with embarrassment.

Lena knew that it had never occurred to Tania that anyone might suss out her little crush. 'Don't worry, love, no one else has worked it out. I only know because I'm your mum, that's all. It's my job to know these things.'

Tania buried her face in her mother's chest, loving the familiar smell of her. She had always had the same scent – Estée Lauder perfume, Benson & Hedges cigarettes, and Palmolive soap. It was a comforting aroma, and she loved that it had never changed. She was also surprised to find that her mother knowing her secret made her feel a bit better somehow; it just proved to her once more how close they really were.

'Does Auntie Ria know?'

Lena hugged her daughter even tighter. 'If she does, she ain't said anything to me about it, and you know Ria, she was never one for keeping things to herself.'

It was exactly what Tania wanted to hear, and Lena knew that.

Chapter Ninety-Nine

Danny was so drunk he could barely stand up, and Davey, Noel and Jamsie were aware that they would have to keep an eye on him. It was unusual for him; he was not known for heavy drinking. They were at the Electric Lady, the lap-dancing club they had acquired in King's Cross and, as it was early in the evening, the place was half empty.

The head bouncer, an Arab lad from North London, was not pleased with Danny's antics, as they were aware.

'For fuck's sake! He's only had a couple. He came in with Petey about three o'clock. Now he is fucking rat-arsed. You'll have to take him out – we're expecting a private party in at eight.'

A record came on and two semi-naked girls walked on to the stage. They began to gyrate around their poles, neither of them bothering to make much effort; there were no real customers to impress – that would come much later.

Davey was annoyed. 'All right, keep your fucking hair on.'

He checked his mobile for messages from Petey and there was nothing. 'Where did Petey go? Did he say?'

Karim Hussain shrugged. He was a huge speci-
men of manhood, with a bald head, and an expertly
shaped beard. Women loved him. Rumour was that
he was hung like a donkey, and his preference was
for tiny blondes. 'Do I look like his fucking social
secretary?'

Davey had to laugh. Karim was one mad bastard. He
hated drunks and, in fairness, Davey had never seen the
man take a drink; he was strictly a Diet Pepsi man. 'All
right, we will sort him. But you know this ain't like
him.'

Karim nodded. 'If I didn't know better, Davey, I
would say he was under the influence, know what I
mean? And I don't mean the usual recreational.'

Davey didn't answer him, but motioned to his
brothers to remove Danny and place him in the office.
There was a large sofa there where he could sleep it off.
Going outside the club he phoned his cousin, and all he
got was voicemail. He was annoyed; this was no time
for Danny to be dropping Es and fucking around. They
needed their wits about them, and Danny should have
known that better than anyone. He was supposed to
meet with the Allens tonight. He and Petey were
expected to sort out the situation the Allen brothers
had caused. Danny was more than aware of how
important it was, so his getting off his face was not
going to look good for any of them.

Davey was suddenly worried, and he wasn't sure
why. But this all felt terribly wrong. Their old man

would hit the fucking roof if this was to become common knowledge.

His phone rang and he answered it quickly, relieved to see that the caller was his cousin Petey.

Chapter One Hundred

Delroy was in Brixton. He had a few calls to make there, and they were the kind of calls that were better made face to face. He was a great believer in the personal touch; that way you ensured that you kept a proper handle on your business affairs. Delroy, like all the Baileys, never used a mobile phone for more than a few days, never had a contract of any kind, and always used a phone box if there was one available. Mobiles were too easy to trace, and they made it far too easy to get in touch with people. In their game that was always a no-no; the less evidence you left behind the better.

Delroy was meeting his son on Acre Lane. The boy was learning fast that the best way to keep your eye on your earn was to make a personal appearance when necessary.

He pulled over in his BMW, and Delroy Junior climbed in.

'All right, son?'

Young Delroy smiled. 'I'm good.'

'You ready for this?' The boy nodded, but Delroy's heart sank; he could smell the strong aroma of skunk coming off his son's clothes. 'You sure about that?'

Young Delroy shrugged indifferently. 'I'm cool. What's your problem?'

Delroy stopped the car. They were on a quiet road; most of the terraced houses were now flats, and the people who resided there were generally outsiders.

'Why we stopped here?'

Delroy could hear the annoyance in his son's voice. He was already psyched up for the night ahead, of that much he was sure.

'You're stoned.' It was a statement.

Young Delroy grinned foolishly. 'So what, Dad? I had a little puff. I was with company, a few friends, chillin', you know.' It was said with a faux Jamaican accent, something else that always irritated Delroy. He hated the whole Jah Boy image; he thought it was an insult.

His fist hit the boy's head hard, and he followed the first punch with five more, each one harder than the last. 'I told you to use your fucking brain tonight; I told you to keep a sensible head on your shoulders. I will not embarrass myself by taking you with me into serious situations while you are too stoned to work out the fucking score. Now get out the car.'

Young Delroy was humiliated; he deserved his father's wrath – he had known that he should never have taken the first hit, let alone allowed himself to get wrecked. But he had been with friends, and he had not been able to resist smoking with them. He was regretting that now, big time.

'I said, get out of my fucking car.'

The boy did as he was told, knowing it was pointless arguing. He had fucked up, and he had fucked up in the worst possible way as far as his father was concerned.

As his father sped off, he rubbed a hand across his face; it was already beginning to swell up and he knew he would look like he had been hit by a train by the morning. Sighing, he began to walk to the nearest cab rank. His big night – the night when he was going to finally be a real partner with his dad – was over before it had even really begun. He felt the sting of tears and he swallowed them down; he had brought this on himself, and he knew that better than anyone.

Chapter One Hundred and One

Petey Bailey was at the Electric Lady; it was gone two in the morning and the place was packed out. The smell of sweat, perfume and make-up was heavy in the air. The music was loud, and the atmosphere was genial.

As he made his way through the club to the offices, he waved at Karim. Inside, Davey was waiting for him, as expected.

'Where are the others?'

Davey grinned. 'Where do you think? Getting private dances by now. I thought it best to keep them out of this, you know?'

Petey nodded understandingly. He poured himself a drink. Danny was still out cold and, shaking his head with mock severity, he said, 'What the fuck was that all about today?'

Davey shook his head sadly. 'Fuck knows, Pete, but it ain't like him. He is usually a sensible head, my brother. But he is out of his fucking box. Look at him.'

Petey shrugged. 'He was already well gone when I saw him. I knew it was pointless taking him to the meet with the Allens, he could barely fucking talk. All I can

383

think is that he got something off one of the girls here. You know what he's like. That redhead he has his eye on – what's her name? Stephanie, is it? She has been warned about dancing while boxed out on ecstasy. I'm sorry, Davey, but there was no way he was fit to work.'

Davey saw the truth of that. 'My old man will go fucking ballistic.'

Petey took a large sip of his brandy. 'Well I think the best thing we can do now, right, is not tell him, or *my* dad come to that. Keep it between us lot. Even Delroy can't know – you know what he's like; he'll feel honour-bound to let the proverbial cat out. This is a fucking abortion, but if we use our heads we can salvage the situation.'

'What about the Allens?'

Petey grinned nastily. 'Think about it, Davey, they are hardly going to broadcast to the nation that I went round there on my lonesome and put the hard word on them, are they?'

Davey could see the logic in that. 'I don't know, Pete, the old boys have a knack for sniffing out trouble.'

Petey shrugged again. 'Well, personally, I think this is best forgotten, but I'll leave the final word on it up to you.'

'How did it go?'

Petey laughed. 'I let them think Danny was outside with the rest of you, and that he was too wound up to come inside for the actual meet. That put the wind up them, I can tell you. But they were suitably contrite. I don't think they will be showing off any time in the near future, put it that way.'

Davey was quiet; he was in a quandary. His loyalty to his brother eventually won out. 'I'll make sure my brothers know the score, Pete. You're right – this would just cause unnecessary aggro. Fucking Danny, what was he thinking?'

Petey sighed. 'I'm telling you, it was that ponce Stephanie. She was all over him like a fucking rash earlier – the sooner we out that fucking whore the better. Imagine if this was a paying customer! We could end up in the dock. I'll take oath that he's given her all his cash and, let's face it, Davey, it wouldn't be the first time, would it?'

Stephanie had a penchant for E; she said she couldn't dance without it but, as Petey pointed out, this was a step too far. Danny had a little pash on her; he liked redheads, and she had relieved him of his readies on more than one occasion. She had slipped the customers one too many Mickeys in the past, and they had been lucky that the geezer concerned was a weekend warrior, not a man of any substance. If she carried on, they would eventually get a tug.

He sighed. 'I'll make sure she's out on her fucking ear. Like you say, Pete, she ain't worth the fucking aggravation.'

Petey Bailey refilled his glass. 'None of them are – the fact they work here in the first place speaks volumes.

Now, what else has been going down? Anything I need to know about?'

The subject was changed and Davey was glad about that; the night had already been far too fucking stressful for his liking.

Chapter One Hundred and Two

Tania was sorry for her cousin; young Delroy's face had already swollen up like a balloon and she knew it would look even worse once the bruising came out. As he sat in her mother's kitchen, she bathed his face gently with ice water. When he had texted her she had snuck downstairs and waited for him to arrive, already anxious; if he was coming there on the quiet it had to be serious.

'Who did this to you, Del?' Her tone was gentle.

'My dad.'

His response was so low that at first she thought she had misheard him. 'Why would your dad do this to you? Your mum will go mad! What on earth brought that on?' She was scandalised, and her voice was rising because of that.

'Shush, you'll have your mum down on top of us.'

Tania could not believe that Delroy's own father could have hurt him so seriously and, more to the point, that Delroy was so accepting of it.

'Why did he hit you?'

Delroy shrugged. 'I fucked up, let's just leave it at that. Have you got any paracetamol? My head is splitting.'

Tania realised he was not going to tell her any more, but she was shocked; she would never have believed that Delroy's dad could hurt him like this. She also guessed that if Delroy wasn't willing to tell her about it, he must have really fucked up badly. She sighed, and instead made them both a mug of Ovaltine.

Some things were best left alone, and she had a feeling this was one of them.

Chapter One Hundred and Three

Imelda was worried about her son. In the few weeks since his accident, as he insisted on calling it, he had become a different boy. Whoever had attacked him must have been someone from *their* world, and she was nonplussed that her husband didn't seem to be too bothered about it. He should have been hunting the fucker down, making sure they never went near their boy again. A little voice was telling her that he knew more than he was letting on and she was wary of probing too deeply. She had a feeling that she would not like what she might find out – that whoever was responsible was close to her, and her son.

Delroy Junior was so serious now, spending all his time with his father; her husband was giving his son an education about the Life, teaching him how to be a part of it, how to survive. Because when you stripped away the glamour and the excitement that is what it came down to really: surviving. Not just physically, but ensuring you weren't put away for the duration. Imelda had known many men who had gone away to prison still in their prime, only to return years later, older, but not really any wiser. It was such a waste; all that time locked away for years on end. But, if you didn't get caught, the Life could be sweet.

She was worried about her Delroy trying so desperately to emulate his father. It seemed forced lately, as if he was playing a part.

Unlike her brothers and cousins, she wasn't sure that her son had what it took to be part of the Life. She didn't *like* it but she understood it, and that was half the battle. She'd only ever been part of it to keep an eye on Delroy, if she was truthful, but any taste she'd had for it had been destroyed by the circumstances of Jack's death.

At his young age, her son had only seen the exciting part of the Life. But as he was exposed to the actual economics and what it entailed, Imelda could sense that he was nervous. She surmised that he had fucked up somehow and been reprimanded; in the Life it was usually brutal, the only way for a person to understand the enormity of what they had allegedly done.

She wished he was like Tania, and kept well out of it all. He had always been so sure that he wanted to be a part of the Life. Well, now he was a part of it and, as a Bailey, he would be brought straight into the main business.

Young men like Delroy Junior were attracted to the trappings of the Life: the rewards, the cars, the birds, the excitement. They didn't appreciate that it was a *lifestyle*; one you ultimately had to live twenty-four seven. They didn't understand that with the Life came the constant threat of being harmed, murdered, getting a capture, and being banged up for the best part of your youth.

Knowing and accepting this was what kept you at the top of your game. Her boy was only just beginning to understand the real dangers that the name Bailey brought with it, and she hoped fervently that he could cope. Until Jack, this had never occurred to her; she had bowled through life believing that her name gave her some kind of security. But that was all an illusion.

Her confident boy was gone now. Delroy Junior was nervous, frightened of his old man – that really bothered her because she knew that Delroy had always idolised his father. But what bothered her most was that she wondered, in the dark of the night, if his father had been the person who had marked him, and that thought wouldn't go away.

Jack was on her mind a lot these days. Her mother's complete acceptance of his death was something Imelda had never come to terms with. She knew that she would fight hammer and tongs for her child, no matter what the consequences and no matter what he had done. If that meant she had to take on the whole Bailey clan, then so be it. Jack had been a victim of her family, and a victim of the Life. But *her* boy would not go the same way as her brother, not if Imelda had anything to do with it.

Chapter One Hundred and Four

Terrence Allen was finding it very hard to accept that the Baileys had taken away their main earn. The Allen brothers had previously been the biggest supplier of drugs to their Northern counterparts. Now, it seemed, that honour had been given to one Michael O'Toole, a man who had no idea what a fucking gram of coke looked like, let alone a key. It was a fucking joke – everyone knew that the Baileys had just given him the title, but *they* supplied his workforce. Michael O'Toole couldn't broker a deal with a fucking eight year old selling conkers. He had spent more time in stir than a card-carrying Old Bill, and he still thought the Krays were someone, for fuck's sake. It was nepotism at its worst.

The Allens had been forced to stand back like a pair of errant schoolboys as everything they had built up over the years was just given away to a fucking no-mark. The Baileys had taken it away without a thought for the time and effort he had put in over the years, setting the deals up, making sure the people they dealt with were kosher, and not liable to turn at the first glimpse of Lily Law and put them all in the frame for a long stretch.

And that was becoming more customary as the courts handed out bigger and bigger sentences. It was shocking – fucking murder didn't warrant the sentences drug dealing did. Get pissed and take out a whole family in your motor – husband, wife, kids, the lot – and you were looking at a four or a five stretch; be found with three keys of coke, and you were doing a twenty. It was a scandal – especially as most of the drugs confiscated were back on the street within weeks. The Old Bill were not averse to a bit of dealing themselves; if it wasn't for the Filth he wouldn't have half the product needed to satisfy the demand. And, whether people liked it or not, there was a fucking big demand for it. Cocaine was a middle-class drug – he served up half of Canary Wharf, those city boys couldn't snort it up their hooters quick enough.

The Baileys handing it on a plate to Michael O'Toole was the final insult. Although Terry knew he could not show his hand yet, that did not mean he could not show it at some point in the future. It was like a festering sore, not just the drop in wages, and the loss of prestige, but the fact that they had been replaced by a mug like Michael O'Toole, a man who was in no way clued-up enough to run an outfit of such huge proportions. He was a fucking local boy, one step above a gas-meter bandit. He had done a few armed robberies back in the day, when a wages-snatch for twenty grand was still seen as a fucking big event.

Word on the street was that the scallys were not too

thrilled about Michael O'Toole either; that was because, along with the Allens, they had, over the years, devised a method of payment that ensured that they *all* got their money's worth, even if the Baileys didn't.

Petey Bailey knew all about the scam – *he* had been the brains behind it – so it was going to be an interesting few months for everyone concerned. Petey had always had that fucking greed in him, that need to tuck an extra few quid in his back pocket. It was as if he enjoyed having his old man over and, in a way, Terry could identify with that. Like everyone else, Petey had to live by the Bailey credo and, for a man like Petey, that had to burn. He had a personality that didn't take well to being curtailed, and the older Bailey brothers controlled everyone around them in one way or another.

Petey Bailey was not liked or trusted by many of the people in the Life any more. He was tolerated at best by most; he was far too petty in many respects – he had been known to chase a person down for a poxy score. He was a fucking cheapskate by nature, a drama queen who could, and would, cause murders for a few quid. He had no class. Petey was a product of his father – he had lived so long in his shadow he wouldn't last ten minutes in the real world. Alone, without the Bailey name, the Bailey backing, he would be insignificant. The fact he was having his own blood over on a daily basis said all that needed to be said. Now he was panicking, and so he should be; his little scam was in danger of being discovered. Of course, that left the

Allens in a position of power – for all their troubles, they knew the truth of the matter.

So Terry would wait, and he would plan. Petey Bailey had fucked off more than a few people over the years and, like Terry, they would welcome the chance to take the fucker down and with him the whole Bailey family. This was personal now.

His brother Billy was not the sharpest knife in the drawer, but he was with Terry all the way on this. Billy knew that without Terry he would not have anything, and his brother had always looked out for him. If Terry said that something had to be done, Billy never questioned it, he just did as he was told. Terry was more than willing to use his brother for his own ends. Billy would do anything if you asked him nicely: maim, harm, torture. If Terry asked him to chop off his own foot, chances were Billy would do it.

Together they were a good partnership; Terry was the brains of the outfit, and Billy was happy to be led. Terry cared for his brother deeply but, that aside, if he had to sacrifice him, he would without a qualm. The Baileys were not the only people capable of taking out a family member, and the sooner they realised that the better.

Petey Bailey was at panic stations at the moment; unlike his father, he didn't have the brains to think everything through. So Terry Allen was confident that he had the edge; it was just a matter of time until the tables turned.

Chapter One Hundred and Five

'Come on, Danny, you can't keep up this silence indefinitely. You must remember something about what happened the other night. Petey had to go to the Allens alone, for fuck's sake!'

Of all the brothers, Davey was closest to Danny; he'd been like his shadow as a child and now that Danny was heading up operations, Davey was his right-hand man. Davey had no real desire to be a leader; he was a man of few words, who didn't feel the need to prove himself.

Davey knew it was completely out of character for his brother to miss a meet because he was drunk or stoned; he took his responsibilities very seriously.

'Just let it drop, Davey, all right?' Danny sounded as pissed off as he looked.

'Is it something to do with Petey?' Davey was trying to work it out. He might not be a contender for *Countdown*, but he knew when he had hit a nerve. It was always about Petey in the end – he was such a fucking wind-up. Danny could be a lairy fucker when the fancy took him; he sailed quite close to the wind on occasion, but that was Danny, he was a maverick. He used his nous to stretch his earn, but he made sure the earn was shared by them all. But Petey was greedy – he always had been. Even as a kid he had always had to have what *they* had – he would even take their pocket money from them. Like all gamblers he had no real care for the people he hustled. Danny was different, and his brothers were willing to let him call the shots. He was the eldest, he was the man their father trusted to see that everything was running smoothly, and he was more than capable of doing that job.

'Come on, bruv, what's the problem? I know it involves Petey, I just can't work out how.'

Danny sighed. 'The truth is, Davey, I feel exactly the same. I haven't worked it out yet, but there's something I need to find out. I want you to come with me – we need to get to the bottom of this. I think there's skulduggery afoot, as you obviously do too, and if it does involve Petey then the fewer people in on it the better.'

Davey was silent for a few moments, digesting his brother's words. 'I see. It's like that, is it?'

Danny nodded.

Chapter One Hundred and Six

Lena and Ria watched their husbands standing at the bar of the Shandon Bells Irish Club, deep in conversation. It was good to see. It had been a long time since they'd appeared so relaxed in each other's company.

'Look at them two! Like a pair of fucking old women, gossiping away.'

Ria laughed out loud at the simile; the men were a lot of things, but gossips was stretching it a bit.

'Where's Imelda? I thought she was meeting us?'

Ria shrugged. 'Not a clue. Honestly, Lena, she gets on my nerves lately. She's so wrapped up in her own little world. She needs to get over herself, that one.'

Lena sipped her brandy and Coke daintily; she'd known for a long time that Imelda and Ria were at loggerheads, but she was surprised that Ria had actually openly acknowledged that there was a problem between them. Ria was usually proud like that. 'Well, Ria, you know what she's like. Too much time on her hands, if you ask me.' It was what Ria wanted to hear.

Ria nodded and replied sadly, 'I've told her that, ever since Jack. You know, Lena, until that night it never occurred to her that the life she lived was run by our men and their businesses – her old man included, I might add. She thought we could control it, that we had some kind of authority. But I think that night opened her eyes and she didn't like what she saw. *We* are expected to sit back, and take whatever comes our way – the good and the bad. We live with that knowledge every day of our lives, and she doesn't know how to deal with it, especially now her boy's onboard. She can't hack that because she knows too much for her own good.'

Lena placed her hand gently on her friend's arm; she could hear the hurt and the pain in her voice and understood completely why she was worried for her daughter.

'Do you know what I think, Ria? Our generation were geared up for it all somehow. We came from nothing and we accepted what our husbands chose, not just for us, but for our families. I washed Daniel's bloody clothes, and it wasn't *his* blood on them either. I provided alibis and, in the middle of it all, I brought up the kids. We didn't expect as much as girls do today – they think they need to know everything. But sometimes the truth is more dangerous than ignorance. I know that my Tania is just starting to question things – I can see it in her eyes. Despite the fact that I have done everything I possibly can to protect her from the Life, I think she might know more than she lets on – she was always earwigging as a kid.'

Ria had never heard Lena talk so openly before; she'd tried to keep up the pretence of ignorance for so long. Now that Tania was growing up she seemed to be more inclined to admit the truth. 'Thanks, Lena, I know you're right, mate. But I worry about Mel – she can't seem to let things go. She should have had more kids, had something to focus on.' Ria shook her head as if shrugging all the worries away from her. 'Here, Lena, guess what? My Petey is talking about having kids. Can you imagine that? Bernadette with a baby? I can't, for the life of me. I wouldn't trust her with a pet, let alone a child. Petey reckons that if they do produce a child it will be a miracle of modern science – he reckons she is not the type to ruin her figure with a pregnancy.'

Lena laughed with her friend, glad that she was back to normal again. 'If she does produce a baby, it will be a fashion plate, Ria – all designer labels, and expensive prams. Bernadette hasn't the sense of a doornail, the poor child will be round your house or her mother's within a month of being brought into the world.'

Ria nodded; the truth of the statement was there. In all honesty, it depressed her. 'Well, Bernadette O'Toole has a lot to contend with coming her way, as we know to our cost, Lena. The Life soon sorts out the girls from the women, eh?'

Lena smiled sadly. 'I'll drink to that.'

Chapter One Hundred and Seven

Stephanie Carlton was thrilled to see Danny Bailey, and it showed. Her smile was wide as she left the stage and excitedly walked into the dressing room of the Lonsdale Gentlemen's Club. She didn't really like it here; it wasn't as good as the Electric Lady, the club the Baileys owned, where she had worked quite happily until a few weeks ago. That still stung; Karim had outed her with no explanation whatsoever – just told her that her services were no longer required. He had hinted, in a very aggressive way, that her penchant for E had not been appreciated but, as most of the girls were coked out of their nuts, she felt that was a tad hypocritical. Seeing Danny pleased her; she genuinely liked him, and she had believed that he liked her.

She looked in the mirror, and smiled at what she saw; as a natural redhead – both collar and cuffs, as Danny put it – she had an unusual beauty. She had a good body, and it was all natural, which she suspected was why she was so popular with the punters. Unlike the majority of the girls with their fake tits and orange tans, she had pale milky skin, and large natural breasts that seemed to defy gravity. They moved properly, and that was a bonus in her game. She was a trained dancer as well; she'd taken ballet classes as a little child, eventually moving on to modern dance and ballroom. Too short in stature to ever make a career of it, she had used her talent for lap dancing; now she could climb a pole without even concentrating.

She had missed Danny Bailey; she had not expected to see him again. He had waved at her as she danced on the podium, and mimed having a drink, so she was content with that much for the moment.

As she slipped into a short leather skirt and white fitted shirt, she was confident she looked good. A quick spray of Coco Chanel, and she was ready.

Danny and his brother Davey were waiting for her in a private booth and, as she slipped in beside them, she was already buzzing with suppressed excitement. She had dropped half an E about an hour before, so she had a gentle high – just enough to make her eyes look dreamy, and the world around her feel more accommodating. She couldn't dance without a little help; she hated being naked, or nearly naked. It made her feel too vulnerable, and she would never carry off the private dances without a little buzz.

'Long time no see, Danny. You're looking well.'

He smiled at her, and saw the gleam in her green eyes that told him she was under the influence of chemicals as usual. He sighed sadly. He enjoyed a bit of gear – everyone did in his game – but he had never understood the power of E for people who weren't out raving. It was a dance drug. True, Stephanie danced, that was fair enough, but E was also a very unpredictable drug. Not his cup of tea at all.

A young woman in thigh-high boots and tiny hot pants brought them through a bottle of champagne and, slipping the girl a tenner, he opened the bottle theatrically. When they each had a glass in their hands, he said gaily, 'You're looking very well yourself, Stephanie. How's it going here? I hear the money's good.'

She smiled. 'It's all right, but I preferred it when I worked for you. The management here are only interested in the earn, they don't really look out for us. Most girls here depend on the private dances, but they also take a percentage of your earn, so it's not as lucrative as it should be. I'm surprised to see you, to be honest. You couldn't wait to get shot of me not too long ago.'

Danny and Davey could hear the hurt in her voice, and Danny felt inexplicably bad for her. She was a nice girl as lap dancers went. She had a good sense of humour, and without her kit on she was a fucking young lad's wet dream. She was naturally stacked, but she had the face of a virgin – a lethal combination in the lap-dancing world. Most of the girls looked just what they were; the Stephanies were few and far between.

'That was why I wanted to see you. I need you to tell me something, and I want the truth, right? I promise I won't get annoyed, unless you lie to me.'

She nodded; he could see she was genuinely puzzled, but also frightened. 'Why would I lie to you, Danny?' Her voice was quivering with nerves.

'Did you slip me a roofie, or a couple of Es that last night you saw me, without me knowing?'

He was smiling as he spoke to her, but Stephanie could hear the underlying seriousness in his tone, and she was terrified. What was he accusing her of exactly? He was definitely accusing her of something, she knew that much. She could feel Davey's eyes boring into her too, and she felt hot and clammy.

'I ain't going to do anything to you, Steph, I swear, but if you gave me something for a laugh, then tell me. I just need to know.'

She was shaking her head in denial. 'I wouldn't do that, Danny, and I certainly wouldn't do it to you!'

He could hear the truth in her voice, and he was sorry for scaring her. 'Listen, Steph, I was with you, we were having a laugh, and then I was fucked – completely fucked. I wasn't on anything, and I didn't drink that much. So someone must have given me a livener. It stands to reason, don't it?'

She swallowed noisily. Her pleasure at seeing him was gone now, she just wanted to get away. Karim had been especially nasty after that night and suddenly it all made sense. 'Well, it wasn't me, Danny. I wouldn't dare do that to you! Anyway, I just thought you was on it, you and Petey. You were well out of it, don't you remember? You couldn't hardly stand, and you kept asking me my name! I was a bit miffed, to be honest. I'd never seen you like that before. But I take oath, Danny, I never gave you nothing. I wouldn't – I would be too scared. I admit I've roofied a few of the punters, but only enough to keep them in line – you know what the city boys can be like. But never would I do it to anyone like you, Danny. I ain't stupid.'

Davey believed she was telling the truth, and he gulped his glass of champagne quickly. He saw Danny staring into the girl's white face, as convinced as he was about her innocence.

'Look, Danny, I told you, I have laced a few punters, I admit that, it makes them easier to handle, and they tend to be a bit more open-handed, you know? But I would never do that to you, I wouldn't have the front.'

She was nearly in tears now, and Danny felt bad for her. She was only confirming what he had already sussed out. 'All right, mate, calm down! I believe you.' He took out a clean white handkerchief and wiped her eyes carefully; her make-up was a work of art like all the girls who worked the clubs, and he didn't want to ruin it for her – he had ruined her night enough as it was. 'Now drink up, darling, and I'll take you out for a meal, eh?'

She sniffed loudly, and nodded her acquiescence. There was something about him that attracted her, even now when he had scared the shit out of her. She knew she would end up in bed with him before the night was over. She drank her champagne, feeling that somehow she had dodged a bullet. Why did this man have such a hold over her? Because, as nice as he was, she knew he would take her out without so much as a backward glance should the situation warrant it.

Chapter One Hundred and Eight

Michael O'Toole could scarcely believe his luck. The Bailey family had welcomed him into the business with open arms and the best part was he had no responsibility; all that was expected of him was to relay whatever the Baileys told him to his new workforce. It was as easy as having a shit after a hot curry – there was no real effort involved whatsoever, and he was in receipt of over five grand a week.

Now he was convinced that his daughter had done him a favour by getting her claws into Petey Bailey. She'd just better make sure she kept them there. Michael was well aware that Petey's main attraction to Bernadette was that she looked extremely fuckable, but was still intact. He understood Petey's reasoning; in the Life there were far too many females who were willing to drop their kecks for a Face. It was half the fun really.

Michael had been against the drugs trade, seeing it as a fucking mug's game, but now he couldn't fault it. For the first time in his life, he was on a serious earn, and being treated with the respect he had always craved. That was the real clincher for him. He understood that he was no more than a front for the operation, and that suited him; he had no real idea what the economics of the situation actually entailed, nor did he want to know.

The only bugbear was the Allens; *they* were not so happy about the reversals in fortunes. He was aware that there might be a retaliation of sorts, if not now then in the future. They were not men to swallow a blatant piss-take, and that was exactly what this was.

The Baileys were untouchable; the Allens might feel the urge to punish them, but they would not have the guts. *He* was a different story – an easier target. Because of that he was keeping an eye on them; if his incarcerations had taught him nothing else they had taught him the value of knowing your enemy. You couldn't survive for any length of time in top-security jails without learning a little bit about guerrilla warfare, and how to keep yourself safe in the most extreme of violent environments.

He only felt secure in his new position because he was watching them *all*, and none of them gave him credit for having the brains to do that. Another lesson that prison taught you was to never trust anybody. Such was the downside of the Life; too many people vying for the top and no one willing to step away without a fight. It was the way of the world – their world anyway.

As he lit himself an expensive cigar, Michael was feeling very satisfied; he had all the angles covered. But he would not let himself relax too much; after all, his daughter still had to walk that fucker up the aisle and, until she had pulled that off, his position was precarious to say the least.

Chapter One Hundred and Nine

'I want to make sure we know what the fuck is going on around us, and I also want to make sure that we are not paying you for a fucking laugh.'

Daniel Bailey was furious, and Detective Inspector Harry Smith was more than aware of that fact. As usual, Peter Bailey was quiet; he was always willing to let his brother do the dirty work, so no change there. In over twenty years of dealing with the Baileys, Harry Smith had never once felt that he was anything other than the paid help. It rankled, there was no doubt about that, but he knew there was nothing he could do about any of it now. Even the sons of these men were the same – ignorant fucks the lot of them. But they were criminals, so what else could he expect?

Inspector Smith sighed heavily, aware that he was expected to make some kind of protest, and more than willing to do just that. He knew *exactly* how to play the game.

'Listen, Daniel, if I heard anything on the street, you know that you would be the first to know. From what I can see, no one is saying anything detrimental about any of you. Even the paid narks – who I make sure you know about – haven't said a fucking dicky bird. The Allens are not showing their hand. I can assure you that, if and when they do, you will be the first to hear about it.'

Daniel Bailey was still not satisfied. 'You get a decent collar from us and, lately, you have given us fuck-all of any real interest.'

Smith smiled. 'If there's nothing to tell . . .'

Peter Bailey hated this man with a vengeance, as did his brother. Smith was first and foremost a Filth – never a good thing in their world – but, even worse than that, he had never understood that his willingness to sell out his own was the reason they would not, and could not, ever trust him. They paid him, they tolerated him, but that was as far as it went. To them, he was worse than scum.

He had his uses, and that was why they had cultivated him for so long; he was a part of their world now whether they liked it or not. He was a celebrated Filth, he had his so-called creds, and a penchant for women and money. Both weaknesses had been the reasons they'd recruited him in the first place. He sold out anyone within his orbit for a price, a heavy price admittedly, and he still believed he was one step above them. The man was a cunt, as Daniel Bailey said on a daily basis, and a treacherous cunt at that.

'The Allen brothers are keeping a low profile; they have done nothing that would warrant a mention from me. All I can tell you is that I made sure your Northern counterparts were left alone. I have a colleague who is now up in Manchester, and he is more than willing to come onboard.'

Peter and Daniel exchanged a look, and Smith knew that he was skating on very thin ice.

Peter Bailey was sitting behind his desk, and Smith could see the deep-seated resentment in his eyes as he said loudly, 'Would this be a certain DI Brown by any chance?'

Smith was not surprised about the Baileys' intimate knowledge of the police departments around the country; he knew better than anyone that they had ears everywhere. He wasn't the only person they had bought off over the years – they had all sorts on their payroll, from High Court judges, to court-appointed psychiatrists. They recruited from every walk of life – it was why they were still on the outside and also such formidable opponents.

'Well, it seems you are ahead of me. Why am I not surprised?'

Daniel Bailey fought the urge to smack Harry Smith around the room, and instead he grinned nastily. 'Well, to be honest, Harry, he had the sense to tell us about your approach within hours of it occurring. Seems he doesn't fucking trust you either.'

It was a warning, a veiled threat, and Smith was well aware of that. He was also annoyed; despite all the cash he liberally weighed out to his brethren, no one had ever seen fit to tell him that Brown was already on the take. It was a real eye-opener; it just showed him, once again, that the Baileys were one step ahead. He was due to retire in the next eighteen months, which was bothering him. He was too used to the extra cash the Baileys provided – he had seen himself recruiting a few key personnel so he could still be of use to them, still collect his extra bunce, and enjoy his little perks.

Now, though, he wasn't so sure about that. At the moment he had the protection of the Metropolitan Police; the Baileys had believed that to take him out would do them no good; he was, after all, a senior officer. But it seemed that he might actually be wrong about that – they were already making plans that didn't include him. He needed to bring them something solid, something important, to prove his worth to them before he finally bowed out. He needed that last big pay-off; he was depending on it. His pension was not enough for a fucking fortnight's holiday in Benidorm, let alone enough to keep him and his wife in the manner that, thanks to the Baileys, they had become very accustomed to.

Smith had worked out very early in his career that crime, for a small percentage of the population, really did pay. There were certain people who understood the importance of having the enemy close by, even if you couldn't control them. With people like the Baileys, who appreciated the significance of having people like him close, and who made sure that their enterprises didn't impinge on the general public too much, you could at least ensure a degree of safety, know that there would be no civilians caught up in unnecessary violence. That would not be the case, however, if the streets were left to the mercy of anyone who had a shotgun and big ideas. Like the Krays and the Richardsons before them, the Baileys actually policed their own manors; they made sure that nothing untoward went on without their express permission and that everything was within their boundaries and guidelines. In a way, they were as necessary for public safety as the Home Guard in wartime. Families like the Baileys actually made the streets safer for the average person – not that anyone would ever admit that, of course. Without the big crime families taking that control, the pavements would be overrun with wannabes and loose cannons, would be at the mercy of every little crew who felt the urge to go out on the rob; it would be anarchy. The Old Bill all knew that, from very early on in their careers. They hated it but the bottom line was, better the devil you know.

Smith looked at the two men he had been dealing with for over twenty years, and he smiled genially. 'I have my ear to the ground and, be fair, have I ever let you down?'

Daniel Bailey snorted in derision. 'There's always a fucking first time, *Harry*.'

Chapter One Hundred and Ten

Petey Bailey was sitting at a secluded table in the garden of one of his favourite pubs in Hainault. It had a nice outlook, the garden was very well landscaped and, best of all, there was a little clique of young birds in his eyeline. One of them was already giving him the glad eye, and he was more than happy to return the favour. He knew that his dark good looks, coupled with his expensive apparel, were a real pull for a lot of women. He had the brooding appearance of a young Bob Marley, or so he had been told anyway – not that he really gave a fuck. His old nana said he resembled his granddad more than the others. The way she told it, his granddad was a mixture of Kunta Kinte from *Roots*, and Sammy Davis Jr. A mixed bag admittedly, but as long as it attracted the birds, he was happy.

As his cousin Danny walked towards him with a tray of drinks, he smiled widely. He had good teeth; apparently he had inherited those from his granddad as well. If his nana was to be believed, his granddad had been a paragon of every virtue except, of course, loyalty to the woman he had knocked up. He had scarpered as soon as she had told him she was in the club. He had been Jamaican according to her, and Petey believed the man had been a fucking scoundrel. A user devoid of any kind of decency; he had fucked her and left her, end of, no matter how good a spin she might put on it.

Danny sat down opposite his cousin; they both smiled in greeting but there was a coolness between them of which they were both aware.

'Well, well, well, what's all this cloak-and-dagger about then?' Petey's voice was low, bordering on the sarcastic.

Danny didn't answer him at first, sipping on his pint of beer instead. He was a real-ale fanatic, and he savoured the mouthful of Spitfire for a few seconds, before saying earnestly, 'You know why I'm here, Pete, let's not play games.'

Petey shrugged nonchalantly and, sipping his pint of lager, he said with mock innocence, 'I'm all ears, cuz.'

Danny watched his cousin; he had loved him like a brother, but he didn't trust him any more. He couldn't bring his personal worries to the family without there being a major fucking incident, so he just intended to let Petey know he was aware of what was going on.

'I wasn't at the meet with the Allen brothers, as you well know . . .' He let his words hang in the air for a few seconds, making his point, before adding nonchalantly, 'Seems I was a bit worse for wear that night. How are the Allens adapting to their new situation?'

Petey felt relief wash over him. He guessed that he had been sussed but clearly his cousin was not going to make a big drama out of it – if that had been his intention, he would have done it well before now. He was impressed; he had not anticipated Danny working it out at all, let alone so quickly; it just proved that he could never underestimate his cousin. He had really thought that Danny was none the wiser, assuming that when his cousin finally surfaced from his drug-induced haze, he would just kick himself for being so foolhardy.

Petey had obviously misread the situation; a mistake he would not make again. He was suddenly contrite, his handsome face a picture of worry and wide-eyed honesty – he was good at that.

'They were all right, actually – not exactly thrilled with how it had panned out. But they ain't idiots, they know that they stepped over the line. The thing is, though, Danny, I've had my own little earn going with them.'

He watched as Danny took in the enormity of what he was saying. He had learned many years ago that the best way to disguise any real fuckery was to openly admit to a lesser charge. You could disguise the true problem you were trying to hide with an element of truth. It was simple psychology.

'I'm trusting you with this because I realise now I was a cunt to try and keep it on the down low. If you repeat this, Danny, you know I will be in fucking deep shit. I have been creaming off the Allens' take since day one. You know what I'm like – I always have to take things to the extreme. I ain't skanking off the family, though, just taking a percentage of the Allens' earn. They acted so fucking flash, like *they* were doing *us* the favour, you know? So I strong-armed them. I should have told you, but I couldn't.'

Danny Bailey was in a quandary; this was more complicated than he had anticipated. 'If the old men were to find out about this . . .'

Petey nodded eagerly. 'Precisely. But I have guaranteed the Allens' silence. You see, I knew they needed to be replaced. They were getting too fucking lairy for their own good. *I* am the one who dealt with them on a daily basis, Danny, don't forget that.'

Danny could see the fear in his cousin's eyes, and he had every reason to feel scared. Petey was a natural-born con man – it was part of his charm. But Danny had never thought he would be fool enough to instigate a rob against his own family; that was as outrageous as it was perilous. Petey's own brother had been eliminated for less. What the fuck was he thinking?

Danny lost all his self-control in an instant, absolutely sickened by what his cousin was telling him. 'Jesus fucking Christ, Petey, are you on a death wish or what? I *know* that you slipped me a roofie to keep me away from the meeting with the Allens. You fucking caned me. Can you imagine how that makes me feel? Knowing you were willing to fucking disable me? And for what? Because you are a fucking thief? Because you wanted an outside fucking earn? This is fucking unbelievable! I guessed that you had some kind of fiddle going with the Allens. I ain't a complete fucking moron, whatever you might think. And now you have dragged me into it. I *know* about it now – that makes me a part of it.'

Petey was genuinely nervous now; Danny had suddenly become his Achilles heel, and he didn't like it. If he wasn't careful, he was well and truly fucked. This had suddenly got completely out of control. He had underestimated this cousin of his, believing strongly that he was shrewd enough to pull the proverbial wool over Danny's eyes, but Danny was much more astute than he had ever given him credit for. He could hear the terror in his own voice, could feel the genuine panic as it washed over him.

'Listen to me, Danny. I have sorted it, OK? I'm only telling you all this *because* you're my cousin, because I *trust* you. I need you to stand by me on this. I swear I will never step outside of the family again.'

Danny felt sick; knowing what his cousin was capable of was not something he felt comfortable with. He finished his pint slowly, unsure how to play this. It was far too personal for him; he was not capable of such skulduggery – it just wasn't in his nature. His own cousin had spiked his drink, and left him incapacitated, without even the wits to take himself to the toilet. He had been completely disoriented for nearly two days, simply because this man had not wanted anyone to know he was skimming off the family. It was the sheer treachery he couldn't get to grips with. Knowing that Petey had been capable of something so heinous was bad enough, but what was worse was that Petey now expected him to overlook it. Now that Petey had admitted his sin, admitted what he was capable of, Danny would never be able to trust the bastard again. 'You are fucking out of order, Petey, and if you weren't my cousin, I would cheerfully see you demolished over this.'

Petey sighed with obvious relief. 'I swear, Danny, I still can't believe I did it. But it must prove to you how fucking desperate I was! I couldn't hurt you, you must know that. I just saw my chance – I wasn't really thinking, you know?'

Danny didn't answer him for long moments, and when he did he said sadly, 'All I know, Petey, is that I will never trust you again. I won't broadcast this; you're my cousin, and you have painted yourself into the proverbial corner. But it hurts that you didn't think that I had the sense to work out what you'd done to me – you actually thought I was that thick. Well, for your information, Einstein, you're not as fucking clever as you think you are.'

He left him then; Danny knew if he stayed any longer he would physically harm his cousin, so he walked away.

As he watched him go, Petey Bailey knew he had just lost the best friend he would ever have. He felt almost tearful, because he had made himself a serious enemy – one who was far too close for comfort, and far more intelligent than he had ever given him credit for.

Danny had always accepted that Petey liked to be in

charge, and had been more than willing to listen to his opinions and, more to the point, respect them. Now all those years of familial friendship and camaraderie were gone. Like their fathers before them, years of love and affection had been wiped out in minutes.

Petey Bailey also knew, though, that he didn't have the loyalty which came naturally to Danny and the others. *He* was quite capable of removing his cousin should the need arise. He knew too much and that, unfortunately for Danny, meant that Petey would be looking for any excuse now.

Chapter One Hundred and Eleven

'Do you really believe that Michael O'Toole can keep this up for the duration?'

Peter Bailey sighed. 'He knows the score, Daniel, he knows he's just a fucking front. *Everyone* knows he's just a front. But it keeps everything on an even keel. He's so grateful it's pitiful to see really, and we can trust him.'

Daniel looked out of the window at the scrapyard. Unlike his brother Peter, he felt much more secure here than in their new offices. He liked the scrapyard and the whole feel of the place. It was surrounded by a big metal fence, and the night watchman kept his Dobermans here day and night; no one was coming in here without his knowledge. Peter believed they were past all of that now, but Daniel would never feel that way. He still had the gutter in his bones, and he was proud of that.

'I think the Allens could benefit from a personal appearance.'

Peter laughed. 'They don't need that, Dan.'

Daniel could see their reflections in the windows of the Portakabin. Even though they were different races, there was a distinct resemblance. It was their build more than anything, and the shape of their heads. He had missed his brother when they had been at odds, and he was glad they had patched up their differences.

Daniel was of the opinion that the Allens needed to be watched, especially Terry. Billy Allen was basically a fucking moron – a thought in his head would die of loneliness. But Terry Allen was a man whose disposition guaranteed his need for revenge.

If it was left to Daniel he would just take the fucker out; it wasn't like anyone would miss him. But Peter felt differently. Daniel thought his brother was making a big mistake, was becoming far too lenient for his own good. But he kept his own counsel.

'You still on for tomorrow?'

Peter stretched noisily, and said, 'Fucking right I am! The girls are out buying new outfits as we speak!'

Daniel was pleased. It was good to have his brother back in his life.

Chapter One Hundred and Twelve

The whole Bailey clan were together, and they were proving to be a noisy bunch.

Bernadette O'Toole was loving it; they were in the VIP enclosure of the new club in Romilly Street in Soho. Her whole life had been leading up to this moment – she was finally where she was destined to be. She was the main attraction in a nightclub her husband-to-be's family owned, and that meant so would she soon! The icing on the cake was that everyone was staring at her; she had made damn sure she looked good.

Imelda had remarked earlier, in her usual catty way, that soon her name would be Bernie Bailey, as if that was a bad thing. She had pointedly overlooked the barely veiled insult; until she had that wedding band on her finger she daren't start any fights. But once she was married she would cause fucking murders, and enjoy every second of it. Imelda Bailey was a bitch, that was the truth. She seemed to get her kicks from trying to get a rise out of Bernadette, but she was too shrewd to fall for that.

Her dad was on a good earn, guaranteeing that he was in a jovial state of mind, which was a bonus. He was usually such a miserable ponce. Her mum was, for the first time in years, in possession of a decent wage too. All in all, Bernadette had a lot to be grateful for.

The only fly in her ointment was that Petey, her intended, was obviously worried about something. Christ Himself knew that he wasn't the most affectionate of men at the best of times, but tonight he had basically blanked her.

She was not about to cause ructions about it, even if she felt like it. She had to keep everything on an even keel; Petey was a man with fickle tastes.

When she saw him, a few minutes later, looking longingly down the cleavage of a young blonde waitress, she vowed that, when they were finally married, she would take the fucker apart piece by piece. He would finally see that she was not a woman who took kindly to being sidelined, humiliated or ignored. He had a big shock coming to him, and she was already relishing the day when she could finally make her feelings known. Petey Bailey was due a fucking wake-up call, and she was just the woman to give it to him.

Chapter One Hundred and Thirteen

Petey and Danny were studiously ignoring each other. Liam now knew the truth of the situation, having forced it out of Petey. He wasn't worried that Danny would betray Petey – it seemed that this silence between them was as bad as it was going to get for the time being – but it still made him uneasy.

He glanced around the club. It was so packed no one would notice that the cousins were not really engaging anyway. He was still reeling from the revelations. Petey had always been a man of few morals, but until now he could never have been accused of being a complete fucking shithead. But Liam had to admit his brother had really earned that epithet.

The big fear was that the two patriarchs of the Bailey family would find out the *real* reason for the lads' falling out. The boys had had their disagreements over the years – that was human nature – but this time the reason for this latest disagreement was known only to the younger members of the family.

Petey came over to him, and Liam forced a smile; he knew his reaction was going to be noted by everyone in the room. It was not the best smile, and he was aware of that. Personally, he would happily punch his brother out; as much as he loved him, even *he* could see that this time it had all gone too far. Liam was in a quandary. Petey was at fault here, but he was still his brother, and that was the real bugbear. Danny had every reason to be fucked off and if this latest escapade came out it would not be readily overlooked by his father or his uncle.

'You all right, Liam?'

It sounded like a challenge. Petey was drunk, and that was the last thing they needed; a drunk Petey was a troublesome Petey.

'I'm fine, Pete, I'm *always* fine, I just go with the fucking flow. Now why don't you use your fucking loaf, and sober up a bit. This is not the time or the place for you to be getting irate.'

Petey knew his brother was perfectly right to chastise him, but he had snorted a few lines, imbibed a few drinks, and now his natural antagonism was at the fore. He hated being mugged off or overlooked; *he* needed to feel in control at all times, needed to feel that *he* was the one who called the shots.

He pushed his face close to his brother's as he said viciously, '*Bollocks* to you, bruv, you need to fucking lighten up.'

Liam stared into his brother's eyes; he could see the anger there, and he realised suddenly that it had always been there. The thought was so random yet so true, he was deeply affected by it. Petey was an angry person, and his anger wasn't because he was deprived or had problems, it was just a part of him, like eating or drinking. Like Uncle Daniel, he had been born like it. Both had been born without any kind of boundaries whatsoever.

Liam saw his brother as if for the first time. 'Do you know what, Pete? Bollocks to *you*. You're a cunt. Who do you think you are? At the moment I am just about the only person in this whole world who is actually on your side. But if you don't want that, you let me know. Because I have had you up to my back teeth.'

He walked away from Petey before his brother could answer him; if his brother pushed it tonight he would finally retaliate.

Chapter One Hundred
and Fourteen

Lena had a headache, and she felt sick with it. She knew it was the change, and the hot flushes were overwhelming her.

The noise was horrendous in the club; the music was too loud and, in her opinion, without any tune whatsoever. Even showing off her new outfit was not enough to make her want to stay.

She had been quite pleased to get a message from Tania, asking her if someone could pick her up from the house. Like she couldn't get a cab! Lazy little mare. It was because of her crush on Petey; Tania had been worried about tonight. She was still so young, so unsure of herself. If only Lena could make her child understand that the day would come when she would laugh about this. She had a sneaking feeling that her Tania had not really wanted to come and witness Petey with his bride-to-be, the fragrant Bernadette!

She smiled to herself, heart-sorry for her baby's predicament. Oh, to be that young again, and know what she knew now.

A drive was just what she needed, though, some fresh air and a chance to clear her head. She was sweating again; the heat in this club was unbearable. Plus, in all honesty, she didn't like to think of her girl alone at home, all hormones and teenage angst – she needed her mum more than ever tonight.

Lena made her way over to her husband and his brother. She was really feeling her age – not something she was going to admit to anyone here, of course. Ria was like a fucking linty, dancing and drinking. Even her mother-in-law was having a better night than she was, and she was in her late sixties, for fuck's sake. Ria wasn't having as bad a time as Lena was with the change; in fact, Ria was breezing through it without too much difficulty.

Lena smiled up at her husband. 'Give me the car keys, will you, Dan? I feel a bit iffy. I'm going to pick up our Tania. She is late as usual – honestly, she will be late for her own funeral, that one. But I could do with the break anyway.'

Daniel knew exactly what was wrong with his wife; she was nothing if not vocal about her change, and he did feel sorry for her. He could see how much it affected her on a daily basis. He was glad he was a man; women, he felt, certainly got the thin end of the wedge when it came to hormones, or in this case, the lack of them. She was like the Antichrist some days, and he would be glad when it was all over at last.

He put his arm around her protectively. 'You all

right, Lena? You look dog rough, girl.'

Lena laughed; only her Daniel could say something like that and still think he was being nice. 'I'm all right, I just need to get a bit of air, that's all. I want to see Tania anyway. She should have been here ages ago. Give me your car keys.'

Daniel grinned. 'They're in my coat. But hang on and I'll get someone to drive you, love.'

Lena was shaking her head. 'Honestly, Daniel, I don't need a driver; I'd rather go by myself, mate.'

Peter Bailey pulled his brother towards him. 'Don't worry about it, I've got the keys to my Merc here. I won't be driving tonight, young Roy Barber is my designated driver. Have you seen him? He only looks about fucking twelve. I'll get him to drive you, Lena.'

Lena sighed in annoyance now. 'No, honestly, Peter, I'd rather drive myself.' She smiled at her husband sadly. 'I might not come back if you don't mind, Daniel – if Tania isn't in the mood, like. I'll stay at home with her.'

Smiling, Peter said, 'Fair enough.' He handed the keys to Lena. 'Look, it's right outside. You take it, mate. Tell Tania she needs to get a fucking wristwatch. She's worse than my Ria for being late.'

Lena really laughed then. 'I know, Pete, she is on her own time zone, her. I'll make sure the doormen keep your space for you, OK? But if I don't come back, you won't mind, will you?'

Peter shook his head. 'Course not, mate. Fuck me –

if we can't get a lift home then we are doing our jobs wrong!'

Lena hugged her brother-in-law and he hugged her back. Then she kissed her husband on the cheek, and he held her tightly to him. 'Come back, Lena, please? I think me and you have a dance booked later – that's if this ponce ever plays real music, of course.'

Lena laughed once more and, as she pushed her way through the crowded club, Daniel said to his brother loudly, 'Best fucking decision I ever made, marrying her.'

Peter nodded. Both of the brothers were very pleased at how the night was going. The atmosphere in the club screamed success, and it was a legitimate earn into the bargain.

'I know, Dan, we both done well in that way. We knew a good thing when we saw it. Unlike this new generation; they only see the top show, they don't understand there's much more to marriage than that.'

The brothers were still laughing and joking five minutes later when they felt and heard the explosion. The front of their new club disintegrated before their eyes, and pandemonium broke loose.

Chapter One Hundred and Fifteen

Peter Bailey was looking around him at the devastation that the bomb had caused. The front of the club was completely destroyed – there was nothing left except a gaping hole. All around him were casualties, young men and women, cut and bleeding. The glass front they had so lovingly designed had been no more than a weapon in the end.

Imelda was sitting on the dirty pavement, her mother beside her, holding her close, their new clothes forgotten now, both of them looking bewildered.

Peter looked at Theresa and, even now, amidst such carnage, he still had to admit, she was a fucking phenomenon. She was talking to him, trying to remind him and his brother that they mustn't forget the real issue here. He could hear police sirens and fire engines, he could smell the acrid stench of burning, of smoke, and he could see the remainder of his car. The car in which Lena had been butchered.

'Peter, son, get your brother away now. Sort him out before the Filth get here.' Peter knew his mother was right; he had to keep it together for the time being at least. He pulled his dazed brother away from the scene;

they needed to focus on the next few hours. The police would be all over this like a rash, and the papers would be milking it like a Jersey cow. It was a dream story for them: bombs, criminals and Soho. It was the sixties all over again.

'Daniel, listen to me. You have to think straight. The Filth will be all over this, and you can't say anything at all.'

Daniel Bailey was nodding as his brother spoke. Peter knew he was absolutely stunned, unable to take in the fact that his wife had been murdered, blown to smithereens. Daniel looked into his older brother's face and, with tears rolling down his cheeks, he said quietly, 'Peter, *you* listen to *me*, bruv. You don't get it, do you? That bomb was meant for *you*, mate. Not my Lena.'

Peter Bailey stood on the pavement holding his brother's hands, as the reality of his words sank in.

Until now, that had not even occurred to him.

Chapter One Hundred and Sixteen

Tania was annoyed; she knew that her tardiness was a family joke, but she was still irritated that her mum had not even bothered to call her back.

The thought of going to the club and watching her cousin playing happy families was not something she relished, but she knew she had to show her face at some point. The later the better, as far as she was concerned and, even though she'd made sure she looked pretty good, she felt she could never compete with Bernadette O'Toole.

She sighed heavily, and lit a cigarette. She usually only smoked when she was drinking, but tonight she felt on edge, nervous.

It was gone midnight, and no one had even bothered to ring her to see if she was OK and ask if she was going to come to the opening. She was hurt. It seemed that everyone was enjoying themselves so much they had forgotten about her. She felt the sting of tears; apparently even her mum wasn't bothered about whether she went or not.

She put out her cigarette, and made her way up to her bedroom. It was her own fault; she could easily have got a cab – her family owned most of the cab ranks anyway, it's not like she would even have had to pay. Stubbornly, she had not wanted to appear as if she was bothered either way about the night.

Now she was feeling sorry for herself, and it was far too late to turn up on her own. As she undressed, she wondered why her mum had not even returned her call. That wasn't like her.

Lying in her bed, she felt lonelier than she had ever felt before in her life. She had been a fool; she should have gone to the opening with a smile on her face. She had as much right to be there as anyone – more right in fact than that Bernadette O'Toole. At least she really was family.

Picking up her phone from the bedside cabinet she rang her mum's mobile number and, when it couldn't connect, she smiled. Well, that was another mystery solved! Her mum probably couldn't get a signal in the club. That satisfied her; she didn't feel so abandoned now.

As she lay back against her pillows, she wondered if Petey was having a good night. She hoped so. Petey was always making her laugh, always making her feel good about herself; he made life feel exciting. He flirted with her really, and she enjoyed that more than she let on. He teased her, which annoyed her brother Danny, and she couldn't understand why it angered him so much.

She wished she was older, more Petey's age. She often played out a scenario in her head before she went to sleep in which she would accidentally bump into him, and he would suddenly look at her as if for the first time, and then that would be it. He would see her as a woman, as someone of note. She was desperate to be seen as a grown-up at last, not just little Tania. Even if the impossible did happen, though, she knew her father wouldn't allow it, let alone her brothers. It was just a dream and life was so unfair.

She wished her mum would come home; it wasn't like her to stay out this late. After a night out, her mother would make hot drinks for them both and regale her daughter with anecdotes from her night. Tania loved her mum and they were very close. Her mum really understood her, and she was lucky to have her. Growing up, as she had worked out some of the truth of the Life, her mum had always been there to make her feel better when she was frightened.

Well, at least her mother would give her the highlights of the evening, whether she wanted them or not. She really wished she had just gone now, and enjoyed the night for what it was. She knew it would have been a good night out; her friends would all have been jealous that she had even been there, let alone a part of the management, so to speak.

She sighed sadly as the truth finally dawned on her. She had really shot herself in the foot; she had passed up the chance to be treated as a grown-up at last. She had not even had the sense to see that until it was too late.

Chapter One Hundred and Seventeen

Terrence Allen was, as usual, holding court; he knew more jokes than Frank Carson, and he loved nothing more than telling them. He was in a pub on Southend seafront with his brother Billy – a pub that was owned by the Baileys. He had been in there since early evening, a fact that could be corroborated by at least twenty people. Now they were enjoying a lock-in.

He was pissed, but not so pissed he didn't know what he was doing. He was actually having a good time. He was in terrific company; they were all like-minded men and, more importantly, they were Faces. These were men the Baileys would listen to, and they would each swear on a stack of Bibles that the Allens were in their company when the bomb went off outside the club. Peter Bailey would be spread all over the West End like a paper chase before the night was over.

That just left Daniel, who would guess pretty sharpish that he was living on borrowed time. Peter Bailey's son would be shrewd enough to keep Daniel in line until such time as it was safe to remove him as well.

Daniel Bailey would have his suspicions, that was a definite. But it would be a while before he had anything remotely concrete to act on.

Terry Allen was pleased with himself; he had planned this down to the last detail and, after tonight, certain people would know that he was not a man to cross. He was already euphoric. It felt fucking good, there was no doubting that.

As he ordered another round of drinks, he saw Dessie Graham, the landlord of the pub, walk into the bar area and, smiling widely, he said cockily, 'You all right, mate? You look like you've lost a tenner and found a pound.'

The man ignored him and, unplugging the jukebox, he waited patiently for everyone in the pub to stop talking before he said quietly, 'There's been a car bomb in London. Lena Bailey, Daniel's wife, has been killed.'

No one said a word. A few of the women made choking noises as the enormity of the woman's demise hit them, and Terrence Allen could almost feel the genuine shock and horror of the people around him as a physical thing.

But it was nothing compared with the shock and horror that was settling on to his shoulders. This had gone seriously wrong, and he was shaking with fear.

The tragic news would spread like wildfire, as he had known it would, only it wasn't the news he had been expecting. This was news he had not contemplated in a million years. Lena Bailey was a woman of renown – she was respected, she was Daniel Bailey's wife, for fuck's sake! She was not supposed to die like this. She was supposed to die in her bed, years from now. Her untimely death would be seen for what it was – a complete fucking abomination.

What the fuck was she doing in Peter Bailey's car? And, more to the point, why was no one in it with her? This was bad, very bad, for all concerned.

Chapter One Hundred
and Eighteen

Her father's grief was palpable and Tania was unsure how to deal with it.

Her brothers were sitting in the big kitchen, their faces white with the shock, and still she couldn't cry. She knew she should be beside herself, knew she should be prostrate, but instead she was just numb. She couldn't feel anything, she wasn't even sure she believed it. Maybe they had got it all wrong; her mum couldn't be dead. She just couldn't be.

Danny was pouring them large whiskies, and she took the glass he offered her without thinking. As she gulped down the fiery liquid she started to cough, feeling as if it was choking her, burning her throat and belly. Her brother pulled her into his arms, and she buried her face into his chest; she could smell the acrid aroma of burning, knew that it was the aftermath of her mother's death. She had been blown apart – there was nothing left of her, she was gone. It was surreal.

Jamsie was crying quietly, like a baby, and Davey was trying to comfort him. As Danny held her close, she felt herself holding on to him as tightly as she could. Noel was just sitting there, staring ahead of him.

But it was her father who was worrying her; he was wild-eyed, and he looked like he could collapse at any second. Never in her life had she seen him looking so vulnerable, so human. He seemed smaller somehow, crushed.

She could hear her nana coming through the front door and, when she came into the kitchen, Tania flew into her arms, grateful to have a female around. Her nana was the next best thing to her mum – she always had been.

Theresa held her granddaughter in her arms, and she whispered over and over again that everything would be all right. But Tania knew it would never be all right, nothing would ever be all right again.

Tommy Barker busied himself making tea, pouring drinks, and, like each of them, he was wondering who the fuck could be behind this night's work.

And, like each of them, he had his own suspicions.

Chapter One Hundred and Nineteen

Ria Bailey was standing beside her husband; they had been in West End Central for hours, and now they had finally made it to Daniel's home.

She knew that she would never ever forget this night as long as she lived. It was unbelievable. Lena, poor Lena, to die like that.

As they walked into the house, Ria could see traces of her friend everywhere, from her cardigan draped over the banister to her slippers lying by the front door. Cut down in her prime, and by a car bomb that had been meant for *her* husband. That was the real shocker. It was her Peter who should be spread all over the West End, not Lena. She felt guilty because, deep down, she was glad it wasn't him, she was glad he was beside her still. She felt bad for feeling like that, but it was the truth.

Poor Tania – she was just seventeen, and her mum was gone, murdered. It was so fucking unfair, so *wrong*.

Lena had never done anything to anyone, she was the best of the bunch really. Now she was dead, and there was nothing anyone could do about it, nothing that could bring her back.

As they walked into the kitchen, Ria saw Tania. The girl looked awful; she was being held by her nana, and Theresa looked old, so old. It was as if the night's events had finally forced age to creep up on her. Theresa was not as strong as she liked to think she was and this was a blow the older woman would never recover from.

It was one that *none* of them would ever recover from.

Chapter One Hundred and Twenty

Tania wondered if even the weather was coming out in sympathy with her; it was dark and cold and the rain was lashing the windscreen, the sound loud in the confines of the car. The world outside looked grey, scruffy, dilapidated, and that was exactly how she felt.

She was sitting beside her father as they drove through East London. They had been to see the undertakers to organise the funeral. Her mother was to have a glass carriage pulled by four black-plumed horses and her coffin was to be lead-lined – the best that was available.

Her father had just talked his way through the arrangements, not listening to the undertaker or able to comprehend what was being asked. He had simply chosen the most expensive things offered, and he had looked so beaten, so old as he did, that she was heart-sorry for him. In truth, her mother would not have wanted this; Lena had never been comfortable with pomp and ceremony, but her father felt he was doing his wife proud, and so Tania kept her own counsel. He was feeling it more than any of them – herself included. Her father, whatever his faults – and they were legion –

had loved her mother with a passion. No one could ever dispute that he had adored her, and they had been together for so long.

Tania still felt strange; it had not really hit her yet, not properly. She still expected her mum to come into her bedroom with a cup of tea in the morning and tell her it was time to get up, or walk into the kitchen and see her ironing while the dinner cooked and Radio 2 was blaring. But those things would never happen again; she knew she had to accept that. Nothing would ever be the same again for any of them. Her brothers were creeping around their father, as wary as she was about how he was going to react once he came out of his stupor.

She had overheard him the night before; the police had been at the house and it seemed to her that it was her father asking questions and not the other way around. In fact, she guessed her father was somehow involved with them – and not in the usual way either. He was threatening them, demanding that they find the culprits. She had wanted to laugh at that. Culprits! The word sounded so old-fashioned, yet she knew her father was dealing with it the only way he could.

She feared that once the reality sank in her father would be capable of anything. She had heard enough, seen enough over the years to be well aware that her father was not a man to cross. The fact that the bomb which had killed her mother had been meant for her Uncle Peter, had brought home to her just how dangerous the Life was for all concerned. It had taken her cousin Jack, and it had taken her mother. Who would be next?

Delroy Junior had been a diamond. He had really been there for her, even though the circumstances of her mum's death had hit him like a sledgehammer too. It was as if they were each waking up to a new reality; until now it had never occurred to her father or his brother, or to any of the family come to that, that their lives might actually be in danger. Her dad was devastated about her mother but, reading between the lines, she also guessed that he was unable to comprehend the fact that anyone would dare to challenge them – the *Baileys*. *Beyond belief* and *incredible* was how he kept describing it; as the days were passing, he was focusing more and more on that. It was as if he needed to settle this before he could actually allow himself to grieve properly.

Tania guessed there was more Bailey in her than any of them had ever realised, herself included, because she had been shocked to discover that if she found out who the culprits were she would readily take them down herself. The idea that she was even capable of such emotions had really amazed her – that she could lie in her bed, wide awake, and plan her revenge on the people responsible had made her feel sick at first. She had fought against her thoughts. But, like her father and her brothers, she was becoming consumed by them; they actually made her feel better and capable of taking control of the situation. The men who had murdered her mother had no right to be walking around as if nothing had happened, no right to be living their lives when her mother was dead, gone for ever, never again to be held close, never to see her grandchildren or her daughter's wedding. Tania wanted them dead, every bit as much as her father did. Maybe then she could finally grieve too.

'You hungry, Tania?' Her father's voice made her jump. He was being so solicitous. He was like a fish out of water with her; he had always been there for her, but he had believed that a girl needed her mother. Her mother, on the other hand, had done all she could to make sure she was protected from the Life. Now, ironically, she was as much a part of the Life as the rest of them because it had finally drawn her in; the circumstances of her mother's death had guaranteed that. The sheer violence of it, the complete disregard for human life, had meant there was no other choice.

Tania and her father needed each other now. Tania needed his strength and his desire for revenge. She was looking forward to seeing it done.

She shook her head. 'Not really, Dad. I've not got any appetite.'

He placed a huge hand tentatively on her leg; he was so uncomfortable showing affection. He was trying his utmost to do right by her, and it was at times like this she understood just what her mother meant when she had said that her dad might be a man of few words, but was deeper than people gave him credit for. Until now,

Tania had honestly believed that her mother had only said that to make her feel better about her father's inability to show affection. He had never quite managed the knack of actually talking to her, but that had never mattered before, because she had had her mum. If she was really honest she had always been a little bit wary of her father and his propensity for anger over the slightest thing.

She suddenly remembered the day of her first Holy Communion, and what she had witnessed in the men's toilets. There had been other times over the years when she had seen that side of him unleashed on the general populace. Friends at school had heard the stories about her dad. He'd killed a man and his little child. He'd crippled another man for no good reason. Like everyone else, Tania had heard the rumours, but she had a different perspective to the people outside her family – she knew him as a dad. He would move heaven and earth for her if she asked him to. He might not be the most demonstrative man on the planet, but he was still her father and she knew he cared about her deeply.

She'd never let on to her mother that she'd heard these stories. Lena could not have coped with her daughter knowing something so heinous. But the strange thing was, even though Tania knew it was wrong, she had also come to believe that there must have been more to it than people outside the family saw. They were a family of villains, and successful villains at that. But they were also her family, and she was not going to judge any of them, least of all her dad.

He hadn't answered her, he hadn't exactly been eating either, though her nana was ensconced back at their house, cooking like a woman demented. Her brothers were glad of Theresa's presence, and so was she. Her nana knew the score and, over the years, she had tried to give her granddaughter an insight into the Life. In fact, as old as she was, her nana had a brain like a steel trap, and Tania had realised in the last few days just how important her opinion was to her family. She was really getting an education from listening to her talk, and she was glad about that – it gave her something else to focus on. She also sensed that her nana felt it was high time Tania knew the real score of being a Bailey, and exactly what it could entail.

She sighed heavily. Blinking back the tears that were blurring her vision, she said seriously, 'I hope you find whoever planted that bomb, Dad, and I hope you make them pay.'

Daniel Bailey glanced quickly at his daughter; he was so sorry that she had been forced to grow up so quickly, and had lost her mother. But he could hear the Bailey determination in her voice, and it suddenly occurred to him that she was as much a part of the family as the rest of them. That knowledge would break his Lena's heart, but he could see that it was the Bailey strength that would eventually get his daughter through this.

'Don't worry, love. I'm on it.'

Daniel's mobile rang then, and he answered it as

they were waiting at the traffic lights in Stepney. He didn't even say hello to the caller. He never did – he always just listened when he was on his mobile. Tania used her phone as a social tool, as something to keep her in contact with her world and her friends; her brothers and her father used the phone as little as possible and, even when they did, they never said anything of any import. She remembered the times her father had stopped the car, annoying her if he was dropping her off at a friend's, and used a payphone, even though she had a mobile, as he did too. He had always said that he hated them and believed that eventually the people who had them glued to their heads would end up with brain tumours or worse. She had laughed at him, thought he was sweet because of his old-fashioned ways. Now, though, she realised it was so no one could listen in to his conversations and accuse him of anything untoward.

She jumped as her father suddenly barked angrily into his phone, 'I'm on me way.'

Tania was thrown sideways as her father rammed the car into gear and did an illegal U-turn, to the consternation of the other drivers around them.

'What's happened? What's going on, Dad?'

Her father didn't answer her; they sped through the streets, as the evening slowly drew in around them. She sensed that this was something important, and she sat back in her seat, wondering why she wasn't feeling remotely frightened.

Chapter One Hundred and Twenty-One

The scrapyard was quiet, and Danny had made sure the guard dogs were removed from the premises. The old boy who did the night watch had picked the animals up without a word; he knew better than to query anything that concerned the Baileys – especially now. Everyone knew there was a serious crisis in that family, and anyone with even a modicum of brain cells knew better than to interfere or, worse still, question a direct order. Lena Bailey's death was not going to be overlooked, that much *everyone* was agreed on.

No one was allowed on these premises unless they were accompanied by a close family member. Daniel Bailey was old school; he believed that the best form of defence was to be hidden away behind some kind of fencing – he wasn't as enlightened as his older brother or, indeed, his sons. They all thought – wrongly as it had now been proved – that they were immune to retaliations. Daniel had always known that a fortress was better than a fucking office door if things were suddenly to go seriously fucking pear-shaped. Now his sons had come round to his way of thinking – especially his eldest boy, who had begun to appreciate the need for such a structure, and who also thanked God that there was already one in existence. Danny was aware that his father was more on the ball than he had given him credit for. Like the others, Danny had been lulled into a false sense of security over the years, but his mother's murder had disabused him of that notion.

He looked around the Portakabin, pleased that his father had situated it in such a way that there was no chance of anyone seeing what was going on inside it. His father had, over the years, built a wall of iron which encompassed the Portakabin. Because of that, it was not only entirely private, it was also more or less soundproof. No one could hear you scream and, even if by some remote chance they *did*, the fact it was owned by Daniel Bailey guaranteed no one would bother to investigate anyway. Danny had his own suspicions about his mother's murderer, but unless he had something concrete he daren't voice them out loud – not with the family as they were now. He needed to be absolutely sure before he blew them apart.

He looked at Dessie Graham; he could feel the terror coming off him in waves and he forced himself to wink at him in an attempt to put him at ease. He was sorry for him – Dessie was a good bloke, and it would have taken a lot of guts to come here like this.

Dessie Graham, a handsome man in his sixties, was so nervous he felt physically sick. It was nothing to be ashamed of – at times like these anyone in their right mind would be on edge. But he had to say his piece; the Baileys had been good to him, and he was loyal – he prided himself on that. Dessie ran the Baileys' pub on Southend seafront, and he had no option but to come and discuss his suspicions with the men who paid his wage – a good wage at that. When he had come out of the nick after a twelve stretch, Daniel and Peter had given him a good earn; he would never forget that.

He had come alone, a fact that was noted by Danny and his brothers with respect. In the present climate, there were not many men who would come alone to a meet like this. The Baileys – especially Daniel Bailey – would not exactly be likely to be at their most amenable at this tragic time in their lives.

When Daniel Bailey walked into the Portakabin with his daughter, Dessie felt his heart actually skip a beat. He was terrified to the point of virtual apoplexy now, even though he was innocent of any misdeeds against the Bailey clan. Of course, there was the added bonus that anyone with information would also collect a hefty wedge for their trouble. But Dessie liked to think he was doing this for the right reasons; if he was correct and got a reward of some kind that would just be a bonus.

'Dessie. Good to see you, mate.' Daniel Bailey shook his hand firmly, and Dessie felt himself begin to relax. 'I hear you want to talk to me?'

Dessie nodded.

Danny made a face at his father, gesturing towards his sister. It was clear to everyone, including the young girl, that he did not want her in the room.

His father snorted. 'Take her out to the night-watchman's office. Put on the heater and the telly for her.'

'I'm all right! I'm not a kid!' Tania protested.

Her brothers laughed; Davey took her gently by the arm and removed her from the Portakabin. Walking her quickly across the yard, he could sense her annoyance, but he was not too bothered; she would get over it.

As he led her into the office, he said gently, 'You must realise, sis, you can't be a part of this, OK?'

'I am a part of it, though! I'm as much a Bailey as any of you.' She could see the sorrow in her brother's eyes at the truth of her words.

'Look, Tania, this could get a bit out of order. The less you know, darling, the better.'

She sighed in frustration. 'I ain't a fucking kid, Davey!'

He turned to her, and she could see his shock at her choice of words. 'That's enough of that language, OK? Do you think Mum would have let you talk like that, eh? Have a bit of respect.'

He left the small room, and she sat down on the smelly armchair. Gritting her teeth, she wondered how they could still treat her like a child after the last few days. Her mother had been blown apart by a bomb – a bomb meant for her uncle – but she had been coming to fetch *her*, so she had endured that guilt every second of every day since. She wanted to take her revenge on the culprit as much as they did – why couldn't they see that? She finally wanted to cry, but she was not going to.

She stood up and watched her brother as he hurried across the yard once more; the rain was pelting down, and she felt lonelier than she had ever felt in her life.

Back at the Portakabin, Danny poured them large brandies and, as Dessie threw his back in one nervous gulp, Danny said gently, 'Tell him what you told me.'

Dessie nodded. He could feel the men's eyes boring into him, and he hoped he was doing the right thing. If he was wrong, he would be leaving himself open to all sorts of fucking aggravation – and not just from the Baileys either. He was sweating with fear; the tension in the room was almost overpowering his ability to speak.

'I heard a whisper, Daniel, and I didn't know if I should repeat it, you know? I don't want to drop anyone in it. But I felt that you needed to hear it.'

Daniel Bailey just stared at him. Dessie could see the toll his wife's death had taken on him, and he was genuinely sorry for the man. Everyone knew that Lena Bailey was his big love; it was already an urban legend because of the way she had died.

Danny nodded at him, urging him to carry on. 'Just tell him, Dessie.'

Dessie took a deep breath before saying quietly, 'At the time, I didn't think anything of it, it was just

455

something I'd overheard, it meant fuck-all, you know? But after everything that's happened—'

All the boys jumped, as their father suddenly bellowed, 'For fuck's sake, Dessie, just spit it out, will you!'

The man's face turned ever paler; he looked like a statue, he was suddenly so still. Abject terror in his eyes, he struggled to speak. They felt desperately sorry for him, but their father needed to hear what this man had to say and, by all accounts, it was important enough for him to have requested this meet. They were willing Dessie to get it over with.

'I heard something in the pub, it was the night that . . . when . . . you know . . . Lena.' He stumbled once more as he tried to explain himself.

Daniel rolled his eyes up at the ceiling with impatience. 'I assume you mean the night my wife was blown all over the West End, the night my brother was supposed to die instead of her. Is that the fucking night you are referring to, Dessie, or was there another fucking night I don't fucking know about?'

Danny said evenly, aware that his father was at breaking point, 'All right, Dad, let's hear what he has to say, eh?' He smiled gently at Dessie, saying, 'You all right now, Des? Need another drink?'

Dessie nodded, then he cleared his throat noisily. Jamsie started to pour more brandy, as they waited to hear what he had to say.

Daniel Bailey was like a scalded cat, but he knew his

son was right – he had to keep calm, let the man say what he had to say, but it was hard.

'Billy Allen was in the toilet, having a line. I was on the john, I needed a dump, I'd had a gyppy belly all day, so he wasn't aware of me being in there, like. Well, Terrence came in and they were talking the usual coke shite, you know, having a sniff, the usual. But then Billy said to Terry, "I wish we could be there, don't you?" and Terry just laughed with him. Then Stevie Taylor came in and they started chatting about more old shit. I stayed in the stall until they had gone. I knew then that I was best keeping a low profile in case it was about their private business – you know what the Allens are like, especially that cunt Billy. I didn't want them to know I had heard anything that was of a private nature, from what was obviously a private conversation. It was only afterwards that I even remembered it. When I got the call later on saying what had happened at the club, about poor Lena, I went through to the bar and relayed the news to everyone there. We were having a lock-in, and they were all our people, like. But when I thought about it the next day, I remembered that Terrence Allen had looked like he was about to collapse when I said what had actually happened – that Lena had been killed. I was a bit pissed by then, had a few lines myself, but I don't forget things, Daniel, as you know. The more I thought about it, the more I felt I should tell you. I knew that you and Peter had given the Allen brothers a sharp tug recently, and I also knew they were not too thrilled about it. Look, if I'm talking shite, then I apologise, but I just knew I had to tell someone about it.'

Daniel Bailey was staring at Dessie Graham as if he had never seen him before in his life. His face was hard, closed, he looked capable of literally anything. He forced a smile on to his face and, holding out his huge hand, he gripped Dessie's and pumped it up and down quickly, saying, 'You did the right thing, Des. Now, keep this conversation to yourself. Not just because I'm asking you, but also because the Allens would not take kindly to you relaying it to us lot. I thank you for coming here, and I know you are as sound as a pound, mate. If it helps, you will be in line for a fucking treat, OK?'

Danny knew the score and, within a few minutes, he had escorted a much more relaxed Dessie Graham from the Portakabin out to his car. After thanking him once more, and promising him a bonus for his loyalty, he was back with his father.

'I've already got our boys out looking for the Allens, Dad – they are hunting them down as we speak. But I haven't said a word to Uncle Peter or his lads about any of this yet. I felt it best to tell you first, and then let you decide where to go from here.'

Daniel looked at his son and he saw, for the first time in ages, just how like him this boy was. It was like looking at himself when he was a young man.

'I didn't think that pair of cunts would have had the

guts, son. I thought this would be about the Russians – they are notorious for their fucking treachery, as well as bombings. I felt this had to be the work of someone of note, you know? Not a fucking tinpot pair of cunts like the Allens. That ponce Billy couldn't tie his own shoelaces on his own. They are both nothing more than bully boys – they couldn't have kept their game up without us behind them. Surely Terry had to have known that.'

Noel watched his father as he digested the information. The worst thing of all was the insult – that his wife could actually have been murdered by men so far below him and his that they were unworthy even of his notice. He sat quietly, with Davey and Jamsie, knowing that they were a unit now. They didn't need their cousins really. They were all of a like mind on this one – just interested in seeing that whoever was responsible paid dearly for their actions. Until this moment, he had never thought of them as a family without bringing his uncles and cousins into the equation; now he saw that his father was the head of *his* family – of him and his brothers. His dad was a force of nature; he walked his own road, for good and bad, and he would never change. They were the Baileys all right, but they were actually separate entities – the same family, but different sides of the same coin. It had taken his mother's untimely death for that to be brought home to them.

'What do you think, son? Do you think the Allens have the guts to pull off a stunt like this?'

Danny shrugged. He thought about it for a few seconds before lighting a cigarette. Drawing on it deeply, he said honestly, 'Once we get them in here we can ask them what they were talking about, but I think they *are* stupid enough to pull a stunt like this. They have a few creds, Dad, but they forget that their creds are only because of their association with us. That Terry is definitely cunt enough to think he can fucking walk over us. It's the nature of the beast, ain't it? He is a fucking scoundrel; he would con his own mother if he thought it would further his career.'

Davey laughed nastily. 'I don't trust him either, Dad, he is always a bit too slippery for my liking. Always got a fucking snide remark, you know? Acts like he is a fucking hard man, but it's Billy who's the hard nut. Without him, they wouldn't be fuck-all.'

Daniel was impressed by his son's acumen, pleased that Davey had sussed that out.

Danny's mobile rang. He sighed. 'Seems Billy Allen is on his way here. It took four of the lads with a fucking Taser to even get him in the van. He is well pissed apparently.'

Daniel Bailey looked at his sons' faces as he said angrily, 'Fuck him! He ain't as hard as he thinks.'

Danny nodded in agreement, but said seriously, 'I'd rather his brother, though. Terrence is like all bullies – deep down he is a fucking coward of the first water.'

Chapter One Hundred and Twenty-Two

Peter Bailey watched Ria preparing dinner. He was concerned about her. Since Lena's death, Ria had been quieter; she was feeling her friend's absence acutely. They had always been very close, and her friend's death had brought the reality of their lives once more to the fore. She knew, as they all did, that the bomb had been meant for him. Clearly the person responsible had a different agenda to what the outside world seemed to think.

Lena dying in his place had really affected Peter too; the guilt was overwhelming. If he had not given her his keys that night, she would still be here, her daughter would still have a mother, his brother would still have a wife he adored, and his own wife would still have her best friend.

Ria had taken it very badly. Lena's death had brought back memories she had struggled to forget. They had never discussed Jack and his antics in great detail; she had accepted his death, as she had always accepted everything Peter had chosen to do. Like Lena, she was a

461

woman who looked to her husband for guidance and, like Lena, she trusted her husband to keep them safe. Now he was sure that belief had been shaken.

Peter was still reeling from the shock, but like each of them he focused on his suspicions. He did not share his brother's opinion that this was the work of someone with a higher intelligence – he felt this was more on the level of wannabes. It was a botched attempt to take *him* out; according to the police forensics they had spoken to, it was basically amateur hour. Not a professional job as such, but perfectly adequate in the end. Like they couldn't work that one out by themselves! Lena *was* dead. All the fucking money they had invested in the Filth over the years, and that was the only thing they could come up with – the bleeding obvious. Unbeliev- able. Fucking outrageous. Typical fucking Old Bill – clueless. As Daniel had remarked to them, they couldn't find their own homes without a detailed map and fucking Sherpa Tenzing. Well, they were certainly aware now that they had to pull something out of the hat soon if they wanted to keep their earn. They had taken the money quick enough; but now they were expected to earn it they were acting like nervous schoolgirls on their first date. Frightened of their skulduggery being revealed, and finally having to do something for their keep, the Filth were acting far too uneasy for his liking.

Everyone in their orbit knew what had happened; it was only a matter of time before someone somewhere put two and two together, he was convinced of that.

But, as he had remarked to Daniel, they were at the mercy of everyone who looked to them for their crust, and that meant there would always be someone who wanted that bit more, who wanted, ultimately, what *they* had. If he had died as planned, it would have left Daniel without his partner, his closest blood. And the next one to have been outed would obviously have been him.

So now they had their workforce looking for traitors, as well as sniffing round the different organisations they dealt with. Yet Peter still felt in his gut that this was the work of wannabes; those already at the top would have done a much cleaner job.

Chapter One Hundred and Twenty-Three

Billy was the only Allen brother they could locate, and he was even harder than Daniel would have given him credit for. He was acting as if he was there because he *chose* to be, not because he had been Tasered and forced physically into the blacked-out van. His arrogance was so overt, so blatant, as to be an insult in itself.

The boys were standing around, waiting to take their lead from Daniel, as he knew they would. They were good kids.

He could feel the old rage welling up inside him, and he welcomed it. Since Lena had died, he had once again felt it gradually building, hour by hour, until he was only hanging on by a thread. This man, unbeknownst to him, was exactly what he needed – an excuse to let off some steam.

'Get the secateurs out of the drawer there, and tie him to the chair.'

Noel and Jamsie rushed to do what he asked. Danny poured them each a drink, listening with a half smile to the grunts and protestations of Billy Allen as he was forced on to the metal typist chair, and bound tightly so he couldn't move.

'For fuck's sake, Daniel! Surely you don't think you can scare me.' Billy was almost laughing in derision, as if they were fools and he was the only person there with even a speck of intelligence.

Billy Allen was a known hard man, and he prided himself on that fact. His enormous strength was everything to him – it defined him. He had the old-school loyalty as well – something else he felt was important to who he was, and how he was perceived by the people he dealt with. But he couldn't prevent a note of trepidation creeping into his voice. It was strange how the threat of violence was always so much more intimidating than people imagined. Now that he was trussed up like a turkey, the younger Allen brother was finally becoming aware of how precarious his position was. He had assumed he could talk his way out of anything, and now it was sinking in that that was not the case.

Danny stood holding Billy's hand flat against the metal arm of the chair as his father began to remove the first of the man's fingers. Billy Allen steeled himself for the pain, his body tensed, the veins standing out on his forehead. But he was determined to stay silent, not beg as a lesser man would have done.

Outside, Tania had seen the man being dragged from the van which had arrived earlier, and she had waited until the van had left the yard and her brothers had shut the gates, before she slipped out of the small night-watchman's shed. Shivering with cold, she had crept over to the Portakabin, and positioned herself so she could watch what was going on. She saw Jamsie standing in the open doorway, and her other brothers spread around the small office; like them, she watched her father as he went to work. After long moments the man began to groan. Listening to his agony, she was shocked that she had no adverse reaction to what she was seeing.

Chapter One Hundred and Twenty-Four

Peter Bailey told his son Petey about the capture of Billy Allen as they were sitting together in his BMW 6 Series, driving quickly towards the scrapyard. Peter was glad his brother had refused to unload the yard now; he'd been absolutely right – he had always said they would need its privacy one day.

'From what Danny's said, the man is a fucking phenomenon. You have to give credit where it's due – my brother has taken off every finger on his right hand, but he still won't fucking say a dicky bird. He is threatening them with all sorts.'

Petey could hear the genuine admiration in his father's voice, and he knew he had to say something. 'Why have they dragged him in, though? Who grassed him up?'

He saw his father shrug as he answered carefully, 'I don't know yet. All I do know is my brother heard a whisper, and now he wants me there. My guess is Daniel would really much rather sort this himself – it is *his* wife who's dead, after all. But, by the same token, he also knows that I was the intended target. As if any of us are ever going to forget that.'

Petey nodded absently. The fear was growing inside him; he had been less than honest about his dealings, with his greed as usual taking precedence over his common sense. The Allens could easily cause him untold trouble, and the enormity of that fact was finally hitting him. He was thieving off his own – in more ways than one. He was only too aware of his father's opinion about what he saw as weakness of any kind; his father, who in reality should not even still be here, who should be dead, would see his actions as tantamount to mutiny.

'Like a fucking bull, that Billy Allen! I remember years ago he was jumped by about six geezers, and they each said afterwards that they had never had a fight like it in their lives. They battered him in the end, but he made sure they fucking worked for it.'

They were approaching the scrapyard, and Petey felt sick with apprehension. As they waited for the gates to be opened, he saw his father glance at him; he sensed his dad was picking up on his nerves.

Once they were parked up, he had to force himself to walk towards the Portakabin. It was raining hard and, as he followed his father through the maze of man-made iron walls, he was impressed by his uncle's planning. If they were raided right this second, the Filth would have no idea whatsoever how to negotiate this place. It was like a rabbit warren, and the scrap was used as its main defence. It was brilliant how his uncle had thought it out.

As they approached the offices, Petey could hear the animal grunting of Billy Allen and, as they walked up the steps, they saw Noel Bailey in the doorway. He was smiling at them, as if this was just a normal visit between family.

Inside, the place was running blood, and the stench of sweat, blood and urine was overpowering in the confines of the small room. Billy Allen was clearly on his last legs and Petey felt the relief wash over him.

Billy was lying back in the typist chair; one hand was no more than a bloody stump, and his fingers, along with his thumb, were strewn all over the floor by his feet. His right eye was gone – Peter Bailey guessed it had been removed by his brother, probably with one of the teaspoons he usually used when making them a cup of tea. Billy looked like something from a Wes Craven movie, but he was unwilling to admit defeat. He was still fighting it, as he lapsed in and out of consciousness. The amount of blood he had lost would have killed any other normal person by now.

Daniel Bailey looked at his brother and shook his head in a gesture of denial, but Peter could see that he was impressed despite everything that was going on. Billy Allen was intent on playing the hard man, right until the bitter end.

'We'll get nothing from him, Pete. I think he's almost enjoying this – the mad bastard – proving how hard he is.'

Peter knew the man had to be in mortal agony; his brother, when he got started, would have gone for the maximum of pain, especially as this was so personal to him.

Danny said loudly, 'We need that cunt Terrence. I've got everyone out looking for him. Now he *is* a fucking grade-A coward. He wouldn't last a minute, not like this fucking maniac.'

Peter sighed in agreement. 'I take it he ain't said nothing?'

Daniel shook his head in consternation. 'Not a fucking word – forced a few screams out of him, though.'

His brother laughed. 'No brain, no fucking pain! How many times have we heard that one, eh?'

Daniel nodded. Then he went to his desk and picked up the small blowtorch. 'Take his shoes and socks off.'

Jamsie did as he was told, and Petey stood with his cousins, watching the scene with mounting trepidation; even *he* could see the man was beyond help, unable to even keep his remaining eye focused on anything or anyone around him. No one there had any kind of care or interest in the pain he was experiencing, except to see how it might benefit them. Petey saw his family and the Life in stunning clarity then; he was a fool not to have realised the truth before now. He saw his father slip his coat off and fold it up neatly, before carefully walking through the blood and placing it in the other office. Then he walked back towards his brother and, taking out a lighter, he ignited the flame, before lighting himself a large Cuban cigar.

Danny and Davey lifted up the man's right foot, and Petey watched as his uncle adjusted the flame, and then held it an inch away from the man's sole.

The scream was horrendous. Laughing nastily, his uncle said loudly, 'I ain't letting you go quietly, you cunt. Tell me what I want to know and I'll finish you now. Quick and clean.'

Billy Allen was barely conscious, but he still managed to spit out, 'Fuck you, Bailey.'

The smell of burning skin was overwhelming, and Petey felt the food he had eaten a few hours earlier attempting to make its way back out into the world at large. It took every ounce of willpower to stop himself throwing up all over the place. He saw his cousin Danny watching him intently, well aware of what was ailing him; he felt a spark of shame at this obvious weakness on his part. He knew that in the Life it was kill or be killed – you had to be able to do whatever was required to keep not only yourself but your family safe. He had never believed that he was this feeble, though he had always recognised, deep down, that he wasn't as comfortable as his cousins with the more violent aspects of their work. Oh, he could hold his end up, he could do what was necessary, but he had always been a great believer in delegating the less savoury tasks to other people. He was fine with administering a good hiding, teaching someone a lesson, but torture – that was a different thing altogether. Now he saw why his father and his uncle were so revered, respected by so many people. They had no such qualms, and neither did his cousins by the looks of it. He lit a cigarette, more as an excuse to look away from the bloodied mess that had once been Billy Allen, than because he actually wanted a smoke.

Daniel Bailey took the man's pulse and, shaking his head in annoyance, he said loudly, 'He ain't going to last much longer.'

He took a glass of lager from his youngest son and, throwing it in Billy's face, he waited patiently for the man to come round. It took a few minutes before Billy Allen opened his eye. He looked horrendous, but he glanced at each of them. He tried to laugh, but the laugh became a hacking cough, and he was suddenly spewing blood everywhere.

The boys moved away instinctively, but Danny caught a spray of it across his face. His brothers laughed then at his obvious horror; jumping up quickly he picked up an old rag from the top of one of the filing cabinets and, wiping his face, he said in disgust, 'That's all I needed! Fucking wanker! He did that on purpose!'

Peter Bailey looked at his brother and said quietly, 'He's dying, Daniel. He won't last much longer.'

Daniel nodded in agreement. 'Sling him in the boot of the black Sierra out the back; it's next in line for crushing. He will be in a two-by-two metal coffin first thing tomorrow morning.'

'His brother must realise he's gone on the missing list by now. Strange no one's fucking located him yet, don't you think, Dad?'

Daniel looked at his eldest son. 'Delroy's got the whole firm on the case. We'll find him, don't you worry.'

Peter blew his cigar smoke out noisily. They could hear the rattle as Billy Allen fought to take in his last few breaths.

'He thinks he has beaten us – thinks that he's died a fucking hero's death! How thick can he be? The fact he wouldn't talk tells us that he knows more than is healthy. Why put yourself through that?' Jamsie was genuinely astonished at the man's stupidity.

Daniel sighed. 'He died knowing he never grassed no one up and, in many ways, son, he did die a hero's death – not to us maybe, but to him, and to whoever he was protecting. One thing we know now, though: if the Allen brothers weren't the main instigators of the trouble, they definitely know who is. They were in on it.'

Peter Bailey saw the logic in his brother's words. 'Well, let's just hope we find his brother sooner rather than later, before he has a chance to tell whoever he's rolling with that the game is almost up. Though the fact we are hunting the Allens down will be enough to alert whoever they are in league with.'

Everyone was in agreement, talking at once. Peter glanced around the Portakabin, and saw with quiet humour that nothing in there had changed since they purchased the place all those years ago – except for the blood that now coated everything.

'This place will need to be gutted, Daniel. There's enough mess here to keep the old London going on a Saturday night. Everything, from the carpets to the desks, will have to go.'

Daniel nodded. 'Sorted. It's being gutted tomorrow. I've got Delroy's mate, Phillip Harrison, on it. He has an industrial cleaning outfit, and Delroy reckons he's a fucking whiz with blood. Does crime-scene cleaning, by all accounts – earns a fortune, and it's legit. Marvellous really, ain't it, how you can earn a fucking crust these days?'

Peter had heard about the lad and, like his brother, he was amazed at how people could find a niche in such a market, but that was a sign of the times, he supposed. Murder made a lot of money, for a lot of people.

He could hear the rain hammering on the roof; it sounded like a machine gun. He glanced outside. He thought he saw someone outside the main door; it was a few seconds before his brain registered that it was his young niece, looking for all the world like a drowned rat, her face blurred by the heavy rain that was lashing against the Portakabin. At first he had thought it was the lights outside playing tricks on him, until he saw her move. Then he realised that it was really her, that she had been watching everything as it transpired.

She was staring into his eyes now, and he saw that

she did not seem fazed, she was looking at him through the pouring rain as though her being there was the most natural thing in the world. Turning from him abruptly, suddenly she was gone, making her way back hurriedly towards the small office.

Peter Bailey watched her as she ran, his mind racing with the implications of how much she had actually witnessed. He was so shocked that he hesitated for long moments, before turning to his younger brother and bellowing angrily, 'What in the name of holy fuck is our Tania doing out here?'

Chapter One Hundred
and Twenty-Five

Terrence Allen was surprised as well as appalled at how scared he was. Until now, he had believed he was incapable of feeling this much terror; he had perceived himself to be a man of substance, a man of character. He was now aware that he had been completely wrong about that and everything else; he wished desperately that he had never ignored the unwritten law which said you didn't fuck over those who were stronger than you. He had made a fatal mistake believing he was the cleverest of them all.

He cut himself a line on the dirty worktop and, as he snorted the powder deeply, he felt the rush as it hit his brain. He sniffed it up higher, tasting the bitter flavour sliding down his throat, mingled as it was with his snot. He heaved involuntarily, and swallowed the mucus down, taking a deep swig from his bottle of beer to help it on its way.

The only light he could see at the end of a rather long and dark tunnel was his brother's innate loyalty. Billy would not say a word, no matter what was done to him. Billy was a cunt like that – he lived and breathed being the quintessential hard man. As thick as shit, of course, but still a man of certain old-style principles and beliefs.

That wasn't to say, though, that the Baileys wouldn't find a way to break him. Daniel Bailey was known to be a man who could happily torture a subject while eating his lunch. Whatever people's past issues with his style, now anything he did would be applauded by the same people who had formerly whispered that he was a fucking headcase. His actions – taken to avenge his wife's death – would only enhance his reputation.

He looked around the flat, and shook his head at the filthy state it was in, but it was a safe house, and that was what he needed now more than creature comforts. He had beer, Scotch, fags and drugs – the main require-ments of a man on the run, and he *was* on the run. The flat was in Barking, and it was due for demolition, so he was the only tenant. He opened the curtains slightly, and looked out into the darkness; all he saw was rain and rubbish. The only light he had was from a few candles – and they were not exactly illuminating the place – and he was freezing into the bargain.

A Calor Gas heater was on low, but it would not last much longer; he wished he had made proper provision in case something like this happened. But there was literally nowhere else to go – the Baileys knew everything about them, and he didn't know who in his circle he could really trust now. After all, he had fucked up big time; Lena Bailey's death was not something that would earn him brownie points. Unless something drastic happened to the Baileys, he was persona non grata for the foreseeable future.

He tried Petey Bailey's mobile once more, but it was either turned off, or the battery was dead, so he left yet another message, and hoped against hope for the best.

Maybe Billy had convinced the Baileys that they were a pair of innocents. Unfortunately, his behaviour at the engagement party had not been appreciated – he had shown his hand far too soon. Arrogance was his biggest failing. He had believed at the time that he had something to be arrogant about. Now, the people he had been working with all these years would readily serve him up without a second's thought.

Terry dropped down heavily on to the greasy old settee that looked and smelled like it had been purchased some time during the Korean War, and he waited.

It was the waiting that was the worst part.

Chapter One Hundred and Twenty-Six

Petey Bailey looked at his young cousin and smiled. He had not realised how pretty Tania had become, or how much she had matured physically in the last couple of years. Even like this, soaked to the skin and shivering with cold, she looked good.

He had insisted on taking her home, and she had been so grateful, refusing to go with anyone else but him. He had been glad to leave the scrapyard; now he looked like the hero of the hour. His father had been beside himself with anger about her being anywhere near the place. But with everything that was going on, Petey could see how she could be lost in the middle of it. These were not normal times, as he had pointed out to his father and, as such, normal behaviour was not to be expected.

But it was Tania who had really shocked him; she had argued her point with passion and a strength that he had never believed possible of her. She had really let rip, reminding them that her mother was dead and she had every right to know who was responsible. She had

Martina Cole

also pointed out that she had been a Bailey all her life and, as she wasn't deaf, dumb or blind, she had sussed everything out from a very young age. She was nearly eighteen and, like young Delroy, she had as much right as the rest of them to be treated as an adult.

He had left them there, arguing the toss, insisting that she needed to get home and warmed up before she caught pneumonia or worse. He had been the perfect knight in shining armour.

'You all right, Tania?'

She nodded sadly.

'How much did you really see, darling?'

She shrugged, thrilled at his calling her darling; she had imagined him saying that to her so many times. He was such a big part of her life; he didn't know that she thought about him all the time. He was larger than life – her equivalent of a rock star or actor. Petey was everything that she believed it was important for a man to be. It wasn't just his good looks, but the way he treated her; he was the whole package.

The car was getting too hot now, and Petey really wanted to open a window and let some cold air in, but he knew she was probably freezing. She had been a handy little tool tonight, bless her – she had got him away from all the fucking shit.

'I don't know why they think I'm some kind of fragile doll. *I* lost my mum, remember? I don't care who suffers, as long as we find out who did it.'

He could hear the determination in her voice, but it

480

was mixed with a girlish whine that just proved how young she still was. She was trying hard to be strong. Petey guessed, rightly, that she wanted to be a part of the family firm because she needed to feel like she was doing something constructive, rather than just grieving. He understood how she was feeling; she was, as she pointed out, more of a Bailey than they realised. She had the same genes, and her grandmother's strength of character. One day, he was sure, she would be a woman to be proud of.

'You shouldn't have poked your nose in. You should have listened to your brother, and waited patiently like he asked you.'

She snorted in annoyance. 'I thought you were on my side.'

He laughed then, a quiet, exasperated little laugh. 'I am, Tania, believe me I am, darling. But you need to understand that knowledge can be a very dangerous thing, and you know something now that really isn't good for you to know. Suppose the Filth were to pull you in? Suppose they stuck you in a room, and said unless you told them what they wanted to know, you could get banged up, eh? What about that?'

She didn't answer him for a moment. Then she said sarcastically, 'Like that's ever going to happen! Our dads wouldn't let them anywhere near me – you know that as well as I do.'

He was impressed with her logic, and her trust in her family's ability to protect her. 'Fair enough. I'll concede that. But what if Terrence Allen snatched you off the street, and wanted to know where his brother was? And what if this same Terrence Allen decided to use brute force to find that out? Do you think you could keep your trap shut like his brother did? If he threatened to cut your fingers off, say? Would you tell him what he wanted to know?'

She was unable to answer him with complete honesty, because she knew that he was right – she would be terrified. They were silent until they reached the house and, once inside, she turned to him and said quietly, 'I think I would be sensible enough to act the innocent, make him believe that I knew nothing of any merit. But if Terrence Allen was fool enough to come after me, take me off the street or whatever, then I think he would know as well as I would that he could never let me go home again. So it's a moot point really, don't you think?'

Then she started to cry, the truth of his words penetrating her mind, while Billy Allen's screams filled her head. Running to her cousin, she threw herself into his arms, and he held her, impressed with her logic, and aware that she was indeed growing up fast.

As he stroked her hair, he could feel her body as she pushed against him. She was holding him tightly to her, and she was ripe, all right – he knew she was as aware as he was of the reaction she was getting from him. He was excited; she was not only young and up for anything, but she was also dangerous, very dangerous indeed. She was his cousin, she was his uncle's daughter, his baby, and she was offering herself to him. And, even though he knew what he was doing was wrong, he couldn't help himself. He had always loved the chase, loved the conquest, and this was the ultimate forbidden fruit; it would taste all the sweeter because of that. He liked being first, and he liked them young.

When she put her arm around the back of his head, forced his face down to hers, and kissed him, Petey Bailey forgot everything except that she was there, she was willing, and no one would be interrupting them for the next few hours.

Chapter One Hundred and Twenty-Seven

'It's like he's disappeared – no one's seen or heard from him.' Delroy sounded as frustrated as he felt.

Peter and Daniel had expected as much. Now, as Daniel changed his clothes after showering in freezing cold water, he knew they could do nothing but wait. All their lads were on the hunt now – dragging people out of bed, visiting every club and pub they could think of, and offering a reward that was big enough to tempt even the most prosperous of their counterparts. But it was still a waiting game, and that was the hardest part.

'He must have found out we were on the lookout. He'll know his brother's been lifted wherever he is – he must be shitting it.'

Delroy sighed. 'I reckon he has to have someone else in it with him – he wouldn't dare to fucking do this on his own. What we need to do is work out who he might be in league with. It has to be a real Face, someone he feels has the manpower as well as the guts to take us on. There's literally no one I can think of this side of the Watford Gap. Even the Northerners haven't got anyone with that kind of fucking clout behind them. But there *has* to be someone in with him, and it *has* to be someone we know.'

Daniel Bailey looked like a man who was reaching the end of his rope, and Delroy could see that he was barely managing to keep himself together.

Daniel cracked his knuckles loudly, before saying with chilling certainty, 'I think that whoever it is, Delroy, they are closer than we would believe. Think about it – who else would fucking dare to try and take Peter out? Oh, we know them, all right – it wouldn't take a blind dog long to sniff that out. What we need to do now is work out who stands to benefit the most from it.'

Peter nodded in agreement. 'He's right, Delroy – it's got to be someone in the firm. Someone we trust.'

Daniel grinned nastily. 'And when I track the cunt down, they will pay for their fucking sins, I'll take a fucking oath on that. If I have to take each one of our fucking senior staff to pieces with a fucking ball-peen hammer and a pair of pliers, then so be it. But I *will* get to the bottom of this, one way or another, and I don't give a fuck who goes down in the fray.'

Delroy and Peter exchanged glances. Daniel would not rest until he got to the bottom of this. But they understood – the way Lena had died was a good enough reason for any of them.

Chapter One Hundred and Twenty-Eight

Tania was over the moon. She had finally got what she wanted – Petey was lying beside her, and she could feel his heart beating in sync with hers. He had his arm around her, and she had never felt so happy. It was as if her whole life had been leading up to this moment.

She was sore, and she could feel the wetness of him between her legs, but the pain and discomfort just reminded her that she was a girl no longer. No matter what happened to her after this, she would always remember that he had been her first. She had given herself wholeheartedly to this man, and he had taken her gently and slowly, proving to her that he loved her.

She had never believed that anything could feel *that* good. She wondered if her mum could see her; she had known about her feelings for Petey, and she believed she would understand that, after everything that had happened in the last few days, Tania had needed to be loved like this.

She had lost so much so fast; it was only right to take what happiness she could. No one knew better than her how easily things could change, how easily people could be taken from you. She had been empty inside, and now Petey, her Petey, who she loved with all her heart, had made her feel alive again.

'Oh, Petey, I never knew anybody could feel like this.'

Petey, now the euphoria had worn off, was wondering what on earth had possessed him. If she told anyone, his life would be over. Her brothers were bad enough, but if her *dad*, or God help him, his own father, found out what he had done to her, he would be truly finished.

He hugged her gently, but looking down into her lovely, trusting face, he knew he had to get himself away from here, from *her*, tout suite. He must have been off his fucking head! If she told *anyone* there would be murder done. He should have left her alone. What had possessed him? Why did he do these things? It wasn't even as if she was that special. Pretty enough, but nothing to fucking justify the consequences should they be discovered. He had to get away, and he had to make sure she kept this to herself.

He whispered quietly, 'Listen, Tania, this was really lovely. I can't thank you enough for giving me something so special, my darling. But we should never have done it, we should never have let it happen. You're so young and so attractive, but we are fooling ourselves if we think this can go any further.'

Tania looked at him, seeing the face she'd dreamed of for so long right in front of her – his brown eyes, his chocolate skin, the manliness of him. She could smell him on her body, could feel the pain of his loving. She remembered the way he had looked at her as he undressed her, and how she had not felt shy or awkward, believing that he had felt the same way about her as she felt about him.

Now, though, she could see the panic rising in his eyes, feel his sudden need to be anywhere but in this bed with her. She'd already lost him, she knew that as well as she knew her own name.

'Look, darling, I have to go. But you must realise that no one can ever know about this, right? It would cause so much upset, and not just for me either. Remember that.'

He was warning her off, actually trying to frighten her into silence. She knew then, with stunning clarity, that this man had used her, in the worst possible way. He had taken what was offered and now all he wanted was to get away from her. Her dreams and hopes were laid bare, and finally she could see them for the childish desires they really were.

As he got dressed, she watched him sadly. He was clumsy in his haste, and she saw the softness around his belly, and the flab that was settling on his thighs. He was much older than her and, until now, that had not mattered so much. Now she was seeing him as he really was, and she was sorry to the heart that she had wasted something so precious on someone so unworthy.

When he was finally dressed, he knelt by the bed and

looked into her pinched white face. 'Are you all right, darling? Will you be OK?'

But she knew instinctively that he had no interest in her whatsoever – he never had. Not only was she used goods, she was also dangerous to him. The power of knowing that went a small way to assuaging the humiliation of her situation. Seeing the way he was trying so desperately to leave, while at the same time trying to keep her on his side, was every bit as shaming for him as it was for her. He smiled at her, giving her the full force of the Petey Bailey charm offensive.

'Come on, Tania, you're a big girl now. You know it makes sense.'

She looked him in the eye for long moments, before she said nonchalantly, 'Fuck off, Petey. Get over yourself.'

Then, turning away from him, she listened as he crept down the stairs, and when she heard the front door close behind him, she finally let herself cry. In less than a week she had lost so much: her mum, who she missed with a physical pain, and her innocence. She had kissed goodbye to her childhood. She had been too naïve to understand the enormity of what she was doing, and Petey had left her feeling like she was worth nothing – less than nothing. That was the worst thing – the knowledge that she meant so little to him.

She pushed her face into her pillow as she said over and over, 'Oh, Mum.'

Chapter One Hundred and Twenty-Nine

Daniel Bailey couldn't look his daughter in the eye. He knew that he should have made sure she was taken home, well away from the scrapyard. He could see the hollowness in her eyes; she had become very quiet since that night, and he blamed himself for it. She had only just lost her mother, and then she had been witness to such extreme violence, and he had been too wrapped up in his own grief to think about what was best for her. His guilt was doubled by the feeling that he had let his beloved Lena down; she had done everything in her power to protect their daughter from the Life, and he had undone all of that in just a few short days.

He missed his wife so much. The hardest thing for him to deal with was that she was gone because of *his* lifestyle. Lena had been frightened for so long that the Life would be the death of *him* – none of them had thought, even for a second, that it would one day be the death of *her*.

Daniel felt tears welling up, and he swallowed the urge to howl out his pain; it was crippling him. He was scared for the first time in his life – scared of being alone. Once Lena was buried, once he had avenged her death, he would be bereft; he knew he would not be able to cope, because he didn't know how he was going to carry on without her. She had been his life, his companion, his lover, the only person to know *every-thing* about him – the good and the bad – and she had still loved him, no matter what. Now he was left with the responsibility of caring for their daughter and he wasn't sure what to do or how to make things right for her, but he owed it to Lena to try.

First, all he really cared about was finding out who the fuck had been behind his wife's murder and, therefore, who felt they were hard enough, powerful enough, to try and take out his brother. He couldn't sleep, eat, or shit without those thoughts constantly playing on his mind. Knowing she was gone and how she had died was eating at him like a cancer. He hated being in his home, he hated being in his bed, he hated that he woke up every day and she was not there beside him. Every morning when he opened his eyes, the first thing he thought of was his wife's terror as the bomb had gone off; she had to have known what was going on, even if only for a split second. It tortured him. Now, though, he had to try his best for their daughter.

'Come on, Tania, eat your breakfast, darling.'

He had cooked them both eggs and bacon and, as he poured them both mugs of strong tea, he wished once more that his wife was there with him. He knew what she would say if she was – she would tell him to be himself. Lena had always believed that he was a good man at heart.

'I'm not that hungry, Dad. I'm sorry.'

He smiled gently. She was a lovely girl, and he knew she had the same capability for love as her mother had. She needed him to be patient with her. 'Just have a few bites, eh? For me, for your old dad.'

Tania knew this was unfamiliar territory for her dad and appreciated that he was trying. It proved that he loved her, and she needed to feel loved now more than ever before in her life. Her mum had always enveloped her in love and kindness; she had guided her, advised her, stood beside her. What would her mum think of her now? She was so ashamed of what had happened with Petey. It was as if losing her virginity had somehow opened her eyes to the brutal truths of the world. She had been used, she knew that now – he had seen his opportunity, and he had taken it.

She was utterly ashamed at how easily she had allowed it to happen; in fact, *she* had instigated the whole incident – that was the worst part. She had orchestrated her own downfall, and given him something of which he was not worthy – that was clear. She was his cousin, and he was old enough to be her father. Petey should have known that she was hurting over her mother's death – he should have held her, comforted her, and made sure she was safe. But instead he had taken advantage of her youth and vulnerability.

She had been no more than another conquest and this knowledge was destroying her.

God knew, she had heard the boys talk about Petey over the years – what a womaniser he was, how he was known to dog a girl until she gave him what he wanted, how he would then lose interest in them. She had heard them talk about Bernadette O'Toole – even her mum and her Auntie Ria had said her only advantage was that she wouldn't sleep with him without the benefit of holy matrimony. Yet, despite knowing all this, she had still harboured her childish illusions and refused to believe anything bad about him.

Now she knew why her mum had kept such a close eye on her; she wasn't interfering as such, she had just understood that there were people in this world who were capable of causing great hurt as well as great sadness for young girls. During her teenage years, boys had been scared of asking her out, because her family name was Bailey, and the Baileys were renowned for their violent reputations and criminal connections. No boy she had met had been brave enough to take that on and she couldn't blame them.

Her mum had warned her of the pitfalls of falling in love – how you needed to be clever and use your brain, not your body, to get someone who would really love you for yourself. She told her that most young men were only after one thing – the very same thing a girl needed to keep for the man she loved, because once it was lost, you could never get it back again. How ironic then that it was a Bailey who should be the one to use her and throw her away like a used Kleenex, rather than the nameless, faceless young lads that her mother had always warned her about.

Many of her friends had already slept with their boyfriends – even gone on holiday with them; Tania had felt so green in comparison. Now look where she was: she was used goods. She was still sore, it stung when she passed water, and the reminder of him was more than she could bear. It was only a day since it had happened, and it was still raw in every way.

Daniel Bailey sipped at his tea, watching his daughter, unable to tell what she was thinking. He took a deep breath, then said carefully, 'Look, Tania, about the other night. You should never have been anywhere near that. I'm not in my right mind, or I would have known that then, darling. I should have protected you. But I'm a bit confused – I don't know how you are supposed to cope with something like this. I don't know what the protocol is.'

He was nearly crying, and she was heartbroken for him; she knew better than her brothers just how much he had loved her mum. *He is a good man*, was what her mother would tell her constantly. *No matter what you hear, Tania, in the future, always remember that your father is a good man*. Tania could see how contrite he was and unsure how to make this better. He believed that he had let her down and, more importantly, that he had let her mother down. But, even after witnessing first hand exactly what he was capable of, she wasn't frightened of him in the least. In fact, she understood him and his actions. She had cared nothing for Billy Allen or his suffering; she had never realised how much of a Bailey she was. She grasped her dad's hand in hers; it was huge and rough, a hand that made you feel safe, despite also being a hand capable of great violence.

She could never tell anyone about Petey; this hand she was holding would be used to happily choke the life out of him. Her father would see it as a personal affront, and Petey Bailey would be a dead man – of that much she was sure. It would destroy the whole family.

She only wished she had been sensible enough to see this before. She was seventeen years old, but she had been a very naïve and immature seventeen year old. Every time she remembered Petey's haste to get away from her, every time she relived the whole episode, she knew that if her mother had been alive it would never have happened. She had best put it behind her, but that would not be an easy task; the shame of it was still too real. But this man, her dad, was the only parent she had left, and she just wanted him to feel a bit better and take away some of his worry if she could.

'I promise you, Dad, I didn't see very much – it was pouring with rain, remember? But I understand that you were only doing what you felt needed to be done to try and resolve this upset. Please, Dad, let's just forget it, eh?'

Daniel was proud of her; she was trying to make him

feel better, comforting *him*. His little girl was growing up, and he truly believed that she would be one hell of a woman. She had much more of his mother in her than she knew, but it was tempered with Lena's innate kindness. He hoped he would do right by her; it was the last thing he would ever get to do for his wife.

Chapter One Hundred and Thirty

'You took your fucking time!'

Petey Bailey laughed at the man's obvious annoyance. 'All right, fucking relax! I'm here now, ain't I?'

Terrence Allen looked awful; he was hungry, tired, and he stank, but there was nothing he could do about it. He was stuck in this shithole for the foreseeable future – at least until he could find a safe place abroad somewhere. He was in seriously deep shit, and there was no way out for him at the moment.

Petey looked around the flat; it was a junkie's dream. He saw the remains of wasted lives and wasted dreams. These flats had been nice once with face brickwork, Georgian windows, large airy rooms, and what were now classed as antique fireplaces. They had even sported beautiful ornamental ironwork on the balconies. Built after the war as homes fit for heroes, they were now condemned. They would have been sought after if they had been private instead of council.

Seeing Terrence Allen reduced to this was actually quite enjoyable, he decided. The man was still being a grade-A arsehole even though he was so deep in the shit a taskforce of Irish navvies couldn't fucking dig him out of it.

'This place is worse than a fucking tip. Even the stairs stink of piss as you walk up them. You would think animals had lived here, not human fucking beings.'

Terry was in no mood for chitchat, especially when it reminded him of how low he had sunk. 'What are you doing, Petey? A GNVQ in stating the fucking obvious?'

Petey laughed; he could be very funny at times, could old Terry.

'Is Billy all right?'

Petey guessed he had already sussed out the answer, but he accepted the question had to be asked. 'Your brother was a fucking diamond, Tel. He was tortured – you know my Uncle Daniel – he does enjoy a nice family torture, bless him. He cut Billy's fingers off, put a blowtorch to his feet, the whole shebang, and that brother of yours never uttered a fucking word out of place. Even my dad and my Uncle Daniel were impressed with his stoicism. Though, as you can imagine, his attitude did rather aggravate the situation. But, the main thing is, we are in the clear.'

Terry was nodding; he had known Billy would not break. He had been a man of few brain cells, but an overabundance of front. He had been worried for nothing. He was only sorry the news of his brother's death had not really affected him more. Terrence knew that his brother had always been loyal to him;

unfortunately, he had never returned that particular favour.

'Where's his body?'

Petey smiled. 'He was crushed. They slung him in the boot of an old Ford Sierra. A fitting end really – he was never a car man, was he? Drive any heap of old shit, him. No class. He looked what he was – cheap and nasty.'

Terry knew that Petey was baiting him; that was Petey's biggest failing – he never knew when to shut his big trap. But Terry needed Petey more than ever now that everything had fallen so spectacularly out of bed. He took a deep breath to control his anger, before saying, 'So, what's the next step then, Pete? Have you sorted me out a refuge until such time as we can put plan B into action? I don't think we should look towards Spain or the Algarve. I think there's too many people we know there. But how about Southern Ireland?'

Petey smiled easily. 'It's sorted, Terrence. I've got you somewhere no one will ever get to you.'

Terry grinned; this was more like it. 'I knew I could fucking count on you, Petey. Once your dad and his brother are out of the way, we can fucking clean up.'

Petey laughed with him. 'True, but that's also the bugbear, ain't it? I mean, how am I going to explain *you* away to the boys? Liam, my brother, *maybe* might swallow, but I doubt it very much. He's never liked you – thinks you're a cunt actually. But my cousins won't be so easily persuaded of your innocence. Their old mum died, remember? My Auntie Lena, the East End's original Pat Butcher. If nothing else, at least no one will have to witness her fucking appalling dress sense any more. Every cloud, eh? But, back to my cousins. *They* will not be willing to forgive and forget, will they? Dessie from the pub put you two right in it, I'm afraid, so, basically, you have no fucking chance of redeeming yourself – not as far as I can see anyway.'

'But they don't know that as gospel, do they? Surely they would listen to you?'

Petey sighed theatrically. 'I'm not sure they would, Terrence. That's the melon scratcher really, don't you agree?'

Terrence Allen was tired, wired and half pissed, but the general gist of Petey's conversation was not lost on him. He felt the sick dread wash over him; *this* was the only ending that Petey Bailey had ever envisaged. Now that he was without a use and knew far too much for comfort, Terry was no more than another job to be done. He had left his weapon in his coat, and his coat was in the kitchen. He looked at Petey Bailey and said honestly, 'Just do me one favour, Petey – let my body be found. At least my mum will be able to bury one of her sons.'

Petey nodded; that seemed more than fair to him. 'Consider it done, mate.'

Petey took out a sawn-off shotgun from a long pocket his tailor had sewn especially into the lining of his overcoat. It was almost undetectable to the naked eye – unless you knew what you were looking for, of course.

Terry knew it had been all over for him a long time ago.

'Look on the bright side, Tel – at least this will be quick. Not like your poor brother who died in fucking agony. Small mercies, eh? You should be found on Monday morning. I understand that's when the council crew is coming in to rip out the fireplaces and the boilers.'

Terry nodded. He felt strangely calm; he had no choice but to accept the inevitable.

Petey shot him twice – once in the belly and then, standing above him, he watched him squirm for a few seconds before he pumped the second round into his head.

The spray went everywhere; Petey had brains and bone all over his overcoat. He was annoyed because he had liked this coat – it had cost a fucking arm and a leg. He had made this look like a gangland hit, so everyone would assume that Terrence Allen had mugged someone else off; his death would, hopefully, put a line under the last few days. The Baileys would be pleased that the Allens were gone for good. They would speculate, of course, about who the Allens had been working for or with, but they could speculate all they fucking liked. They couldn't prove a fucking thing, and that was the main objective as far as Petey was concerned.

If the plan had come off, he would have taken the Allens out anyway; all he had wanted was his father and his uncle out of the frame. He was sick and tired of them both – fucking dinosaurs, the pair of them.

He placed the gun back inside his coat and, walking from the room, he shut the front door quietly behind him. He placed his coat and the gun in the boot of his car. Then he took out a pack of wet wipes and cleaned himself up as best he could.

He was whistling light-heartedly as he pulled away from the kerb. It was a shame that Lena had got in the car that night; if she hadn't his father would have been dead and, within days, his brother would have followed suit. Then Petey would have been able to take the reins and, finally, he could have come into his own. But best laid plans, as his old dad would say. There would be other opportunities, he would make sure of that.

Until then, he would just bide his time and keep a beady eye out for the next big opportunity to come his way. He wasn't too bothered; there was always another Terrence Allen around the corner – it was what made the Life so interesting.

As his dad had once said to him, getting to the top was the easy bit, it was staying there that took the hard work. He was in his thirties, and he was no Prince Charles – he had no intention of waiting around for fucking years to get what was rightfully his. He wanted it now, while he was still young enough to enjoy it.

Chapter One Hundred and Thirty-One

Danny Bailey and Delroy were eating breakfast in a café in Manor Park. They were both tired out.

'I went *everywhere*, Danny. I tell you, Terry Allen was nowhere to be found. Now his body turns up in a fucking squat in Barking? It stinks.'

Danny was inclined to agree with his friend, but he didn't say that. Instead he said nonchalantly, 'How so?'

Delroy grinned, he knew this fucker so well. Danny Bailey wouldn't commit if the Pope himself requested it. 'You know exactly what I mean. Whoever shot Terrence would be crowing about it. Whoever it was would know that there was a price on his head. A fucking hefty price at that.'

Danny agreed; this did stink. Anyone with half a brain would happily put their hand up to Terrence Allen's murder. 'Maybe, though, whoever ironed him out was behind the bombing? And, be fair, it would be in their interests to keep that quiet, wouldn't it?'

Delroy nodded; that made sense. 'But think about it this way: how would we know about that? We have nothing, so surely it would make more sense to own up, and concoct a fucking feasible story about how the Allens had them over? I'm telling you, this feels wrong. No one seems to know *anything* about the bombing and, let's face it, Danny, we have exhausted every fucking avenue open to us. Even the Filth can't come up with anyone who the Allens might have been in bed with. Half the Faces in the Smoke were in the club the night it blew – they wouldn't fucking put themselves in the firing line, would they? Suppose the gas main went with the bomb – that would have taken out everyone in the fucking club. It's all wrong. We are missing something or, more to the point, *someone*.'

Danny was aware that his uncle and his dad were both thinking along the same lines. It had to be someone they knew and knew well. He shrugged. 'I want them. I want them for what they did to my mum – she was an innocent, like most of the people in that club. They were after my Uncle Peter, and that means this had to be the work of someone who has enough clout to follow it through.'

Delroy nodded his agreement. 'That's exactly what I've been saying all along, for fuck's sake!'

Their breakfast arrived, and they both tucked in with relish. Danny was surprised at how hungry he was – since the bombing he had been almost on autopilot. Like everyone in the family he had been so shocked he had not really been able to think properly. He missed his mum; she had been a good woman, and she had cared for them deeply. It was still too raw to take in.

He sipped at his tea and, as he chatted idly with Delroy, he had an idea. He hoped that it might give them a clue as to who they were to look out for.

Chapter One Hundred and Thirty-Two

Davey and Jamsie were both watching over their sister, and Tania knew they were under orders from their dad. She wished they would both go away and leave her in peace; she loved them dearly, but neither of them could ever be accused of being scintillating company. She did appreciate that they were trying to look after her. It hadn't occurred to them until their mother had died, just how little contact they had with her on a regular basis. She'd been closer to Davey than any of them growing up but, as he'd become more a part of the business with Danny, they'd spent less time together. There was a large age difference, after all. Their clumsy attempts at comforting her were sweet, but after the last week all she really wanted was to get the funeral over and attempt to pick up the strands of her life.

None of her college friends had been near; she understood why. Her mum's death had been plastered all over the papers and, in those same papers, her family name had been linked with violence and crime – alleged, of course. It had still hurt – it was hard being a Bailey sometimes.

She wished her nana and her auntie would hurry up; then her brothers could go out with clear consciences, and she could go through the funeral arrangements and make sure they had not forgotten anything.

She went to the kitchen and, putting the kettle on, she looked around her and made sure everything was shining and clean; it was the least she could do for her mother. Lena had always prided herself on her home, and she knew it was up to her to carry that on. Tania was the lady of the house now whether she wanted to be or not. At least while she was scrubbing and washing, she wasn't thinking too much – that was something, she supposed. But she had to face her cousin Petey at some point, and she was dreading it. The shame she felt was still eating away at her.

Chapter One Hundred
and Thirty-Three

'She looks awful. She shouldn't be on her own so much.' Imelda was worried about her young cousin; she felt so helpless that there was nothing any of them could do to make her feel better.

'She's stronger than anyone gives her credit for.' Theresa sounded sure of that, and Imelda hoped she was right.

Ria shrugged. She agreed with her daughter, but it was a difficult situation. Lena's death had been so horrendous – it wasn't as if she had died of an illness or a tragic accident, she had been *murdered*, and that was something no one would ever really get over.

Poor Tania would have to live with it for the rest of her life, as *she* would have to live with the guilt that she was still relieved that it was not her husband who had died; Ria hated herself for that. But Peter was her life; she would lose her own children first – *had* lost one – that is how much she loved him. The knowledge pained her, but she was more than capable of this kind of selfishness, that was the truth.

Tania walked into the kitchen, and she could tell that her aunt, cousin and grandmother had been talking about her. She wished she had the words to tell them that she appreciated their concern; she was lucky to have so many people looking out for her.

'The police are still reluctant to release your mum's remains, but they have assured me it won't be long now.' Ria's voice was choked with emotion.

'We'll give her a real good send off, Tania. She would want that. I remember when you were born, she was so happy. She really wanted a girl, and you were everything she had wished for in a daughter. She loved you dearly.' Theresa's voice was strong, and Tania was glad she had her nearby. Her nana was a character, there was no doubting that, but she was very loving in her own rough way. She had a knack of putting things into perspective, and that was exactly what Tania needed now.

Everyone pussyfooting around her was wearing her down; they meant well, but there were too many Baileys being far too solicitous for her liking. She just wanted to grieve in peace – and not just for her mum, but for herself as well. Petey had destroyed her confidence and her faith in herself. All her long-cherished hopes and dreams had been demolished in the most humiliating experience of her life to date. Her nana used to say, *be careful what you ask for, you just might get it*. Never was a truer word spoken.

The back door opened and Petey Bailey came bowling into the kitchen as if her thoughts had conjured him up. Tania was so taken aback she nearly choked on her cup of coffee. He kissed them each in turn, and Tania felt him squeeze her shoulder; his touch made her skin crawl.

He looked down at her, his face a picture of concern as he said gently, 'How are you, darling? Looking after yourself, I hope?'

Unable to speak, she didn't answer him, but she could feel herself blushing with embarrassment. She was willing the floor to crack open and swallow her up.

Petey was clearly nervous, terrified of her opening her mouth, but she couldn't do that without putting herself in it as well. She could still see him, naked and sweating, hear his grunting as he lay on top of her, and she tried to block out the images. For the thousandth time she asked herself what she had been thinking. She could only tell herself that she had been grieving, and incapable of rational decisions.

'Come on, Mum, I'll drop you and Mel home. Dad's taken your car – he's got a bit of business.'

Ria was irritated. 'Why couldn't he go and pick his own car up? I wanted to go to the supermarket.'

Imelda said quietly, 'He can't use the same car all the time, Mum – think about it.'

Ria didn't answer, but she understood her daughter's meaning. Peter needed to keep well away from his usual routines; whoever had planted the bomb could be waiting for their next chance. Her husband was all over the place these days, and he chopped and changed cars two or three times a day. She sighed heavily; the Life could be very dangerous, but it was also the only life any of them knew. It was far too late to change now. 'Come on, then, let's get this show on the road.'

'You go on. I'll stay for a bit with Tania.' Theresa was watching everything with her beady eyes – she missed nothing.

Tania sat there unable to do anything as they bustled about, putting on coats, and chatting about this and that. When they finally left she sighed with relief.

Theresa was aware there was something going on between this girl and Petey, and she was wise enough to know that it wasn't anything good. Petey was her grandson, but she knew he was capable of taking this young girl down, relative or not. He was a womaniser and, like all womanisers, no female was safe around him. That Bernadette was never going to change him, no matter how hard she might try to convince herself she could. He was incapable of fidelity, and her granddaughter was ripe for the picking. She hated that she could think such thoughts about her own grandson, but she was nothing if not a realist – even where her family was concerned.

Tania was her own double in looks, from her full breasts and tiny waist, to her thick wavy hair. She was also as green as the proverbial grass, and that was something that needed to be remedied sooner rather than later. Theresa grasped her granddaughter's hand in hers and, smiling, she said, 'Things will look better one day, Tania, it just takes time. Time is a great healer. I should know that. I looked at young Petey today and I saw his granddad – he is so like him! And he doesn't just look like him – he has the same ways as well. He's a fucking nightmare around women, as was his granddad.'

She grinned, and Tania could see the remnants of her former beauty in her smiling face.

'I'd never seen a black man until I came to London, can you believe that? Let alone spoken to one! But when I met him that night, I thought all my birthdays and Christmases had arrived at once. He could charm the birds off the trees. Well, he charmed my drawers off anyway!' She was laughing at the memory. 'I was young – younger than you – in a strange city, and I was so lonely. He homed in on that, and I was happy just to have the attention. He left me with a belly full of arms and legs, and nothing more than a few good memories. If I hadn't have met him, I would have married a good Irish boy, banged out a squad of children, and the Bailey boys wouldn't have existed.'

Tania was pleased that her nana felt she was old enough to understand about life. 'Did you love him, though, Nana?'

Theresa blew her lips out in derision. 'What's love? I was too young. I just mixed up sex and love, darling, and I won't be the last young girl to make that mistake, I'm sure.'

Tania smiled tremulously. 'Did you miss your family, Nana? I know they never acknowledged you again.'

Theresa thought about it for a few moments before she answered her granddaughter. 'I did, at first. But my father once called your Uncle Peter a sunburned Irishman and, after that, if they had ever tried to get in contact – which they didn't – I wouldn't have wanted anything to do with them anyway. My baby boy was everything to me, you see – he was my blood.'

Tania felt an enormous sadness for her nana; she had been alone from such a young age, and that must have been so hard.

Theresa kissed the girl's soft hand; she saw the nails bitten down to the quick, and the sadness that was in her lovely face. This was a young girl who had far too much to cope with, and who was far too young for what life had dished out. 'Listen to me, Tania. You're all over the place at the moment. You've had a terrible shock to your system, and you're vulnerable. You keep that in mind, my little darling, and please don't do anything you might regret. There're a lot of men like your cousin Petey out there in the big wide world, and they are only out for themselves – don't you ever forget that. They should have a government health warning stamped across their arses!'

Tania looked at her nana and, smiling slightly, she said quietly, 'I'm nearly eighteen, Nana; I'm not a child.'

Theresa nodded in agreement. 'I know that, but you're still a child to me. I just don't want to see you get hurt, that's all.'

Tania sensed her nana had her suspicions, and she wondered how she would react if she told her outright that her advice had come just a little bit too late.

Chapter One Hundred and Thirty-Four

Danny and Davey were in a private drinking club in Soho. The family had taken the place over a couple of years before in lieu of a debt they were owed by another crew. The money borrowed had been used to purchase drugs – unfortunately, the river police had got wind of the daring escapade and put paid to the new business venture. The debt still had to be honoured though – that was the harsh reality of the Life. There was no insurance in their game, so the crew had signed this place over to the Baileys. They had refurbished it, re-opened it, and it was now a popular haunt for minor celebrities and London Faces. It had been a good money-spinner for them, and it was legitimate. They could launder money through there too – another handy advantage.

As they sat in the small office, drinking expensive coffee, they were chatting about their father and his behaviour.

'I'm worried about him, Dan. I could hear him talking to himself last night. He was making a cup of tea, and I came out of the toilet, and I thought he had someone in the kitchen with him, but he was all on his tod.'

Danny knew his father was gradually losing his grip on reality but, then again, he had never been that rooted in the real world anyway. It was over a month since the bombing and he had watched the man deteriorate day by day. He believed his father would eventually conquer his grief but, in the meantime, it was almost too painful to witness. He only acted normal with Tania, and that was because he was trying to make up for the loss of her mum.

'He's just missing Mum, that's all, Davey. Like we all are.'

Davey nodded, but he wasn't so sure. He changed the subject. 'Who do you think ironed Terrence Allen out, Dan?'

Danny shook his head. 'Who knows? He wasn't exactly Mr Popular, was he? Whoever it was, they don't seem willing to take the credit, do they?'

Davey sighed. There had been a big price on Terry's head, so why was nobody claiming it? Another mystery to add to the pile.

'Listen, you get off, Davey. I've got a meet with a Filth in a minute. You go and round up the lads, make sure they have collected all the debts. Since the trouble, a lot of people have been taking the piss. I'll meet you at the Electric Lady later on.'

Davey laughed. 'That Richard Casey is a cunt. Did I

tell you he tried to fucking shake down our Jamsie? Said he had already weighed out the day before. When Jamsie asked him who he had given the poke to, the idiot said some geezer with brown hair.'

Danny laughed at the man's front. 'What did Jamsie do?'

Davey grinned and, as he slipped his leather jacket on, he said craftily, 'He kicked the living shit out of him, and when he had finished, he took his Rolex off his wrist, and smashed it to smithereens. Jamsie is a natural-born enforcer; he has just the right amount of tact and force – know what I mean?'

Danny laughed with his brother. 'I know. He is coming into his own, our Jamsie. Not the brightest bulb on the Christmas tree, admittedly, but he has the right temperament for collecting.'

Davey hugged his brother and, as he was taking his leave, he stopped by the doorway, and said seriously, 'Do you think that whoever was behind the bombing might be lulling us into a false sense of security? I mean, why ain't they fucking following through? Even the Russians have said as much to me. That big one, Sergei – who, incidentally, I personally think is gayer than a Mexican tablecloth – said that a bombing was generally a first strike, that it was about confusing your enemy, and while they were regrouping you then had the opportunity to do even more damage.'

Danny could see the logic; the same had already occurred to him, but he was keeping his own counsel for the time being. He wasn't willing to share his thoughts until he had some kind of proof.

'I think that is something we should bear in mind but, until we have a name, or at the very least a fucking reason for it, there's nothing we can do.'

Davey sighed in frustration. 'I suppose so, but it's fucking doing my head in, I know that much.'

Danny laughed. 'Join the fucking club.'

When his brother left, Danny Bailey opened the desk drawer and, taking out a large wad of money, he placed it in an envelope. Then he waited patiently for his guest to arrive.

Chapter One Hundred
and Thirty-Five

Theresa was tired; the last few weeks had taken more of a toll than she was willing to admit. She wasn't a spring chicken any more, that was for sure. She loved her little house and her boys had always looked after her – she was a fortunate woman in that respect. Tommy Barker was still with her, and they made a good couple – they both liked a few drinks, a good meal and, more to the point, they were both of a like mind about most things. She was sad that her days of wild coupling were over, but there was more to life than that. She and Tommy still had their moments; they were few and far between but, as he said, there was life in the old dogs yet! Most importantly, they were company for each other, and she felt she was lucky to have found someone like him to end her days with.

Lena's death had hit her harder than she let on – that she had outlived her daughter-in-law was difficult to comprehend. Her Daniel was a man bereft; he had worshipped that woman, and he was not coping well.

He had cried in her arms the night she died, and she had held him like a child for the first time in over fifty years. It had been so painful to watch – he had tried to get to the car, or what was left of it anyway. He had acted like a man demented.

As she held him that night, the years had rolled back and he was just her boy again, the boy she would protect with her own life if needed. It had been hard for her, seeing him so distraught, so broken. Even though he was a grown man, he was still her youngest son, her baby.

She glanced at the clock and, hearing a car door slam, she made her way out into her kitchen. As she put the kettle on, she heard the front door open, and she called out, 'I'm in the kitchen.'

Petey Bailey came into the room; he filled the space up with his bulk. He used his size to his advantage at every opportunity. He was nothing like his father – her son had never needed to prove anything to anyone.

'Where's Tommy?'

'He's gone to the club. You know him and his bloody poker!'

Petey grinned. 'He's a game old fucker, Nana, you've got to give him that.'

She nodded happily. 'True. Actually, that was why I wanted to see you.'

He sat down at the small table, and waited until she had poured out their teas before saying, 'Come on then, what's the big secret?'

She opened the biscuit tin, and placed it in front of him before sitting down opposite him and saying, 'You're gambling again, ain't you?'

Petey sipped his tea before answering her. 'Who told you that?'

She shrugged easily. 'Tommy, of course. He was in a big game over in Ilford last Friday, and your name came up.'

He didn't answer her, instead he concentrated on his tea and waited for her to carry on. He was fuming, but he wasn't going to let her know that.

'I know you won't appreciate me bringing this up, but you know what your father thinks about it, and it's better you get a tug from me than him. Because he *will* find out – especially the way you carry on. Twenty-five large in one night? It's no wonder you're being talked about! Use your loaf, Petey – that kind of money brings attention you don't want.'

'I can handle it.' He was defiant, like a little kid, and she felt the urge to slap him across his face. He was weak and arrogant.

'I hope so, because your father will go fecking ape if he hears about it.'

Petey sighed heavily. 'I'm not a kid, Nana, I'm a fucking grown man in case you haven't noticed.'

She raised her eyebrows.

'It's my own money, hard-earned money at that. I ain't fucking stupid.'

She had said her piece; it was pointless to labour it.

521

And anyway she had something else she needed to get off her chest.

She looked at him shrewdly, and said just two words: 'Young Tania.'

Petey felt fear tighten his stomach muscles, and he looked at her warily. 'What about her?'

Theresa knew straightaway her suspicions were correct. 'She has a crush on you, God help her.'

She watched his shoulders relax at her words. 'There's not a lot I can do about that, Nana. It's the old Bailey charm.'

'*Bailey* being the operative word. She's your cousin.'

Petey looked at his nana; she was as shrewd as she was brutally honest and she was warning him. He shook his head in disbelief. 'Give me a fucking break, Nana! I know I'm not exactly Mr Faithful, but my own cousin? Shows what you really think about me, don't it?'

She nodded. 'It does. Yeah.'

She saw him narrow his eyes, and she knew she had hit the nail right on the proverbial head. 'You leave her alone, Petey. I know you better than you know yourself. What's bred in the bone, comes out in the blood. You're what we used to call in Ireland a cock man – you see a hen at every opportunity, and you live for the chase.'

He laughed, trying to diffuse the situation. 'I hold me hands up! I like the ladies, but I know where to draw the line. She's my fucking cousin! Give me some credit, will you?'

Theresa let it drop; she had made her point, and he was aware that she was on to him. It pained her to admit that, as much as she loved her eldest grandson, it had been many years since she had actually liked him.

Chapter One Hundred and Thirty-Six

Detective Chief Inspector Christopher Williams was a strange man, but Danny Bailey liked him. He was as bent as a corkscrew, and he had the mentality needed to differentiate between certain crimes. He would hunt down a rapist or a nonce, with the tenacity of a Rottweiler, but he was quite happy to turn his eyes away from certain other criminal activities. He was never backwards in coming forwards, especially when it came to his price – and he priced himself highly. But he was a man who could find out literally anything. He was not that tall, but he had bulk and, coupled with his bald head, deep-set blue eyes, and pock-marked skin, he looked more like a villain than a Filth.

'Hello, Danny. My condolences.'

Danny nodded, and poured the man his usual – a large neat Grey Goose over ice. The man sank it in two gulps and held his glass out for an immediate refill.

'Hit the fucking spot, I tell you. Traffic is murder out there. Fucking hours to get through the congestion! I've seen babies born quicker.'

Danny placed the bottle of Grey Goose vodka and the ice bucket on the table; experience had told him that was the best thing when dealing with Williams. He was a functioning alcoholic, and he was actually quite proud of that fact – he brought it into conversation at every opportunity.

Williams poured himself another large drink before saying, 'So, young Danny, I am assuming this ain't a date. What do you want?'

Danny sipped his brandy delicately. 'I need some information, but it has to be between me and you – a private transaction. The family can't know about it.'

Williams laughed. 'Like that, is it? Has this anything to do with your recent problems?'

Danny nodded.

'I hear your family have been on to every bent Filth they own – but no one came near me. So why now? I deal with nonces and murderers, the occasional high-end drug dealer or blagger. I am a legend in my own lunchtime, as you well know.'

Danny laughed; this man was a riot. One arrogant ponce, as his father would say. 'I want you to get me copies of all the fingerprints and all the forensics from the bombing. Could you do that?'

Williams frowned; he was genuinely puzzled. 'But your family have already got all that, or so I heard anyway. West End Central was buzzing afterwards.'

Danny grinned. 'It was damage limitation, that was all.'

'I guessed as much. I can't see terrorists really bothering about you lot, but the papers do love a fucking good story, don't they? How much did it cost to set that rumour abroad?'

Danny shrugged. 'Enough. But what I want now, Chris, is *everything*. I want copies of everything pertaining to the bombing, I want all the paperwork connected to it and I want copies of the original documents.'

Williams was genuinely perplexed. 'Are you saying you were short-changed?'

'I'm saying I want you to do this for me as a personal favour, and I want you to buy the necessary papers from someone who my family has never dealt with before. There's a hundred grand if you can deliver. Two hundred if you can deliver within three days.'

Williams poured another Grey Goose, and he swallowed it quickly. He was running names through his mind, working out how he could accomplish what had been asked. He was ticking off possible candidates he could approach, working out what he had on certain people, and how much it would cost him to buy their services.

Finally, after what seemed an age, he smiled at Danny Bailey and, raising his glass in a toast, he said confidently, 'Consider it done.'

Danny nodded. 'I also want everything they have on Terrence Allen's death.'

Williams sat back in his chair; he was aware there was

a hidden agenda here, and he respected that. He was sensible enough to know that this man had his reasons, and they did not concern him. 'As I said, Danny, consider it done.'

Chapter One Hundred and Thirty-Seven

Liam heard his brother before he saw him, and he was relieved that they would be alone in the office. As ever, Petey was all noisy, good-humoured bonhomie, hailing everyone he saw, from the lowest waitress to the Faces propping up their bar, and it irritated Liam. His brother was the sole reason for his discontent. Petey believed that he could do and say what he wanted without fear or favour. He needed to be knocked down and reminded that he was only there because he had the name Bailey.

Petey came into the room acting the archetypal London criminal, the old-style Face. He even dressed the part and, nine times out of ten, he could pull it off. Petey had more personalities than a fucking chat show, but Liam knew that none of them was the real Petey Bailey. His brother was a fucking fake, albeit a good one; he could talk his way out of a snake's belly.

Petey laid a package on the table between them, and said jovially, 'Here you are, bruv. You can stop pissing your fucking pants now like a big girl's blouse. I told you I could replace it, didn't I?' It was said as a statement – no answer required; he was just proving a point, as always.

Liam picked the package up warily; he had been here too many times before. 'You can't just act like this is fuck-all, Petey. You do realise you nearly buried us both?'

Petey grinned that handsome grin that made the women's hearts melt and the men think he was one of the original good guys. 'Give it a rest, Liam! You know as well as I do, we *earn* our crusts, mate. We do our jobs but, in reality, we are still no more than fucking bus boys. The old man ain't going to ever let us have our fucking due. We have the right to take it.'

'We don't do that bad, Petey, and you know it.'

Petey laughed; Liam could be a real pain at times. 'Face it, he still treats us like kids, for fuck's sake.'

Liam could see the truth of his brother's argument, but he could also see his father's side. They were getting a good wedge, but when you weighed it up with what they actually brought in for the family, it looked like a pittance. It *wasn't* – it was a fucking good earn and, unlike Petey, Liam understood that money had to be invested and he didn't spend every penny he had as soon as it hit his wallet. He had a family to support – Amanda and Bernard relied on him and he took that responsibility very seriously.

Petey was greedy, always had been. He spent his whole life trying to catch up with himself, whereas the other boys managed to live within their means. Even fucking Jamsie could balance his chequebook, and that was no mean feat for him; Jamsie had the brain power of a fucking politician – he listened and repeated anything he thought sounded sensible. But he still managed to pay his bills and spend his earn wisely.

When Petey gambled he bet huge amounts because he was convinced that there would always be more money coming in – he was a Bailey, after all. But even a Bailey could push certain people too far, and that was what was happening now. Petey had run up bills, and bills had to be paid. Petey should know that better than anyone – he had hammered enough people because they owed the family; it was a part of the job description: thou shalt not shaft the people you owe money to. People were demanding their poke, and they had every right to do that.

'Well, clever bollocks, I think you need a reality check. I've had three different families ask me to have a word with you on the quiet about your mounting debts. Do you not see how that looks to outsiders? You are running up bills all over the Smoke because of your gambling, and you don't think the people concerned are going to ask for what they are owed? Are you that fucking stupid? I've batted them off, but if they go to the old man next time, do you honestly think he will just pay them, and then forget about it?'

Petey shrugged nonchalantly. 'I always pay me debts – I just needed a bit more time, that's all. It's not like we can't afford it, is it? For fuck's sake, if *we* can't be trusted then who can? So I like a fucking flutter now and again? So fucking what? In case it has escaped *your* notice, gambling is actually fucking legal in this country – unlike the majority of our other businesses.'

Liam was aware that his brother was actually serious; he could hear the exasperation in his voice. Liam closed his eyes; it was like talking to a brick wall. 'It's not just about the gambling, Petey, and you know it. It's about you running up enormous fucking slates, slates you know you will have trouble clearing, so you go somewhere else, and then start the whole fucking thing again. I had the Bowes brothers in here last night. I know you don't want to hear this, but Jimmy Bowes is more than capable of shooting you if you cunt him off. He is a man of morals, and if he thinks you have mugged him off, he would see his actions as perfectly reasonable. I paid him, Petey, but he told me to tell you that you are not welcome in his clubs any more.'

Petey laughed; he could not for the life of him understand why his brother was making such a big deal about this. 'So what? Fuck him! The Bowes! I'm shaking in my fucking boots! Shall I organise a minder? Jimmy Bowes couldn't shoot his way out of a wet paper bag. He's a fucking idiot.'

Liam shook his head, and bellowed, 'Well, for your information, the old man loves him! He sees him as a good bloke – just like everyone else does! He's never been late with a payment in his life, and he always pays up with a smile but, more to the point, he understands the importance of keeping a low fucking profile. Whereas you are the talk of London lately, and it's a fucking miracle that no one has mentioned it to the old man. He has a lot on his mind at the moment so you've had a swerve, but he won't relish hearing that you are back to your old ways.'

Petey didn't answer his brother, but he knew he was right. Liam was only trying to help him, and that just made it worse. He hated being reminded of his failings, but he prided himself on not being as docile as the others – they would still be tugging their fucking forelocks at sixty if they weren't careful. He wasn't going to wait around for fucking years until his old man, or his cunt of an uncle, either died of cancer or, knowing his luck, fucking advanced old age; he wanted what he was due *now*. Petey felt he was already getting on; he had decided it was time to settle down, to convince his old man that he was finally getting his act together. But he felt like a fucking idiot – he was no better off than when he had been a teenager. He would spend his whole life in his father's shadow if he didn't take matters into his own hands.

He resented the fact that he had no real authority; his father and his uncle still had the final say on everything. Dumb and fucking dumber – and they still had the fucking world by the gonads. They gave fucking Delroy more clout than they gave their own sons! They were like a pair of fucking Duracell batteries: they went on and on. It was ridiculous. They were never going to retire; in his opinion they needed shooting like a pair of knackered old horses. His father was still giving him orders – it was outrageous. He was stuck in his father's shadow – he was the heir-in-waiting, but he had waited far too long already.

Petey realised he had to try and placate this brother of his; Liam was a good bloke, but he was too weak to see that they were being taken advantage of, that they were being fucked over on a daily basis. *They* took all the risks, while the old man creamed in the money.

'Look, Liam, I know I sail close to the wind at times, but I've always had your back, and I can't help my personality, can I? I always pay what I owe eventually, and you know that.'

Liam looked at his elder brother, and fought the urge to smack him right across his face. If he paid what he owed they wouldn't be having this conversation! Petey Bailey had always travelled on a different bus route to everyone else. He was a liability, an accident waiting to happen – it was just a question of *when*.

'Do you know what? Fuck *you*, Petey! Do what you like, but don't say I didn't try and help you. Jack's long gone, and the old man loved him, but he was still willing to take him out for the good of the family. I don't think you understand the old man at all. I don't think you can see that being a Bailey means a lot more to Dad than just fucking acting the part. He is beside himself with guilt over Auntie Lena's death, and I think you know that he will not be thwarted. You're my brother, and I love you, Petey, but I'm sick to death of you – you need to remember that. I ain't covering your back any more – in future you sort your problems out yourself. Oh, and one last word. You better talk to the Patels before they go to the old man for restitution. The East-End Asian boys are a fucking big outfit now; they are not averse to chasing up money owed – and they don't give a fuck who you are either. And, from what they told me last night, you owe them a small fortune, bruv.'

Petey Bailey looked at his younger brother, and he did appreciate that he was trying to help him. But Petey was, as always, in possession of a completely different opinion to everyone else; he believed that *he* was in the right.

Liam was like their cousins – happy to toe the line, and be grateful for everything; well, *he* wasn't. The Patels and the Bowes were nothing to him. If his old man would just stand aside and give him his due, he wouldn't need to fucking creep about. The Bailey family *owned* fucking casinos; they were the sponsors for big-money poker games, and he was reduced to this.

He had waited long enough for his chance, and he was fucked if he was waiting any longer. His old man and his uncle were due a reality check, and he was going to make sure they got it.

He sighed in frustration. 'You do whatever the fuck you want, Liam. But leave me alone, all right?' For all his bravado, he still felt a small frisson of fear; if Liam knew this, then the chances were so did his cousins, and it was his cousins he was worried about, Danny especially. He was in possession of a quick brain and, more to the point, a short temper. He was also a dyed-in-the-wool Bailey; Danny believed that the name was worth protecting – as if anyone these days gave a fuck! It was a different world, a whole new ball game, and it was peopled by men just like him, who knew that to get on you had to do whatever was necessary to achieve that objective, and you had to use whatever means possible to accomplish it. Liam and the others would see that one day.

Chapter One Hundred
and Thirty-Eight

Ria was watching her husband carefully; it was becoming like a sport to her lately. She recognised how guilty he felt about Lena's death, and that he worried that whoever was after him might bring their war to his home. He had kept the Life outside their front door whenever possible, but this latest aggro was not the usual. This was something he could not completely control, and that was really bothering him. Even after all this time they still had nothing concrete. She saw that it was eating at him like a cancer.

'Any news about the funeral yet?'

Peter shook his head slowly. He still had the handsome looks that had attracted her all those years ago. Men were lucky – they had kids, but didn't give birth, and they aged differently as a result.

'Next week maybe – at least that's what they told Danny today, but you know the Filth. Not exactly reliable, are they?'

Ria sat beside her husband and, kissing his cheek gently, she said, 'Be honest with me, Peter, what do you really think happened? I need to know if we are in any kind of danger.'

Peter looked at his wife; they were both getting old, and he was wondering if it was finally time to retire. He had been on the verge of it many years ago, before Daniel had fucked up and murdered that kid; it had not been viable after that. Now, though, he wished he had just thrown in the towel.

His Ria was so lovely, so loyal. She had deep lines around her eyes, but they suited her. He had always thought of her as young, he *still* thought of her as the young girl he had married many years ago. But it was impossible to deny that time was marching on. In a way, he could see that the Life was much harder on the women – unlike the men, they spent their lives at the mercy of fate. He was lucky to have her; she had stood by him every step of the way, and there were very few women capable of that.

'Come on, Peter, please tell me the truth. What do you really think this is about?'

He hugged her to him, and she felt the love he had for her – had always had for her. 'Truthfully? I don't know. I have my own suspicions, but they are no more than that – suspicions. All I do know for certain is that poor Lena got what was intended for me.'

Ria sighed heavily; she knew that nothing she said would make any difference to how her husband was feeling. 'Let's just retire, Peter. I mean it. I think this is a wake-up call, reminding us that life's too fucking short. Let the boys have it all – let's me and you enjoy our lives while we still can.'

Peter Bailey understood exactly where his wife was coming from, but he couldn't do anything until they knew who was behind the murder. Plus, this was not the time to leave his boys alone; Liam he could trust, but Petey was a different story. He was nicking money left, right and centre – Peter knew all about that as well as the fact that Liam was covering for him. He had hoped that his eldest son would have grown up, used his brains and grasped that their only strength was as a family – the Bailey family. But no, Petey was a fucking waste of space, and that was the truth. Peter had worked far too hard for too long to leave it all in the hands of a man who was still incapable of understanding even the basics of the Life and what it entailed.

'We will, Ria, but first there's a few things I need to sort out.'

She was content with that; in truth she had expected as much. 'I was so frightened when I realised I could have lost you, Peter. This has brought home to me how precious life really is.'

He hugged her tightly again. 'I know, darling, I feel just the same. I look around me, see the houses, the cars, the fucking life we lead, and now it all means nothing, does it? It means fuck-all. I'd happily give up everything to have Lena back, but that's the thing, ain't it? She *can't* come back; that is something we can't arrange or pay a fee for; we can't bargain with death.

I have spent my life getting what I want by any fucking means. I have a lot on my conscience, Ria, and I could live with it all, but Lena's death has left me wondering if any of it was really worth it. Daniel is like a ship without a rudder – she was as precious to him as you are to me. He won't survive this unless I stick by his side. He needs me, and I have to be there for him, no matter how long it takes.'

Ria understood. 'Well, as long as you promise me that once this is over we can both walk away, I'll be content.'

Chapter One Hundred and Thirty-Nine

Daniel Bailey looked at the young girl standing in front of him, and wondered at a world where a young lass like this – pretty and amiable – could sell herself so short. She was all of twenty, if that. His wife had not long been murdered – was not even buried – and yet she seemed to think he would be up for a liaison of some description. It was disgusting. She could be his daughter. She could be his fucking daughter's *mate*; though he had a feeling that his Tania would have a bit more fucking sense than to attach herself to a piece of shit like this – at least he hoped so, anyway.

Carmella Carmichael, who at twenty-two years old had recently become the proud owner of a pair of 34Ds, was doing everything in her power to snare Daniel Bailey. He was old, admittedly, but he still had the aura of a hard man, and Carmella recognised the power of that. Daniel Bailey was a real catch for a girl like her. He was a serious Face and he owned, amongst other places, the Electric Lady, the club where she worked. Now his poor wife was out of the picture, he was on the market for a girl like her. It was well known that he had never been a man who felt the lure of strange. He had been a faithful husband, and Carmella thought that was quite sweet. Now, she could see herself as his consort; the thought appealed to her on so many levels. She was sick to death of lap dancing for a start, and she was even sicker of parading herself in the meat markets that passed as nightclubs in the south-east. She had a lot to offer, and she was more than willing to offer *all* of it to Daniel Bailey. If she had a baby with him – and it would *have* to actually be with him, DNA tests being the norm nowadays – then she would be set for life. He was worth a good few quid, and she would be happy to get a piece of that.

Daniel was looking at her incredulously, as if he had never seen a woman before in his life. Carmella saw that as a positive; she had clearly made an impression. She hitched up her enormous chest, and treated him to her widest smile.

'It's such a privilege to meet you at last, Mr Bailey.'

Daniel Bailey stared at the girl before turning his back on her. He motioned to the bouncer nearest him and shouted, 'Oi, do me a favour, mate, get this young lady a cab, will you?' Then turning back to the girl he said quietly, 'Listen to me, darling. Girls like you are ten a penny, and the sooner you realise that, the better off you'll be. All this, the clubs and the money, it's an elaborate fucking sham, darling. It means *nothing* at the end of the day. You couldn't hustle me, love, and the fact you've tried is why I wouldn't touch you with a fucking barge pole. Now get out of my sight. You won't be dancing here ever again. One day, hopefully, you'll thank me for that.'

Carmella left the club without another word; she knew when she'd dodged a bullet. She'd seriously misjudged that situation – Daniel Bailey was one scary man.

Davey had witnessed the exchange and, going to his father, he said sadly, 'That was a bit harsh, Dad. She was one of our best earners.'

Daniel laughed, but it was a tired laugh; he was so sick of everything. 'Fucking young girls selling themselves like pieces of meat. She would happily shag me, and she don't even know me! What has happened to the world? When did youth become nothing more than a commodity?'

Davey grinned ruefully. 'When people like us opened places like this.'

Daniel knew the boy was right, but times had changed. Young girls had options now, opportunities – look at his Tania. He was aware, though, that his wife had made sure that his daughter had those options, and he had never even given it a thought until now. He owned this place and others like it, and they earned a fucking fortune. They had strip joints, peep shows – sex had been a big earner for them for many years. So why was he so bothered?

Maybe it was because he had appreciated that Lena had never liked any of this, and he had kept it from her as much as possible. She had been uncomfortable with the clubs – she was a decent woman like that. He was a hypocrite, but admitting that didn't make him feel any better. He was just trying to justify the Life, the very same Life that had been the cause of his wife's death, the same Life that was losing its attraction for him day by day.

He wanted out. But without his Lena, what would he do? Without her, he had nothing – nothing except his work.

Chapter One Hundred and Forty

Tania was tired out; she wished she could sleep, but she couldn't. Until now, she had always welcomed slumber, had slipped easily into its oblivion. She had enjoyed it; cuddled up warm in her bed, she usually dropped off without any trouble. She had never before experienced the trauma of insomnia, and the way it left you utterly exhausted and so depressed.

Now she was at the church, waiting for her nana. She loved six o'clock Mass; she had accompanied her mum so many times, and they had appreciated the quiet of the church, enjoyed the ritual of the Mass and the feeling of being a part of something big. She had sat here so many times in the chill of the early morning, and been happy because her mum was by her side. She should have cherished those times more, she knew that now. But she had taken so much for granted back then. She recognised now, without a shadow of a doubt, that her mother's daily attendance at Mass was to atone for her father's sins – her mum had prayed for her father's salvation, dragging herself here every morning to ask God to forgive him.

Her mum had always insisted that she make an

offering for her father and brothers to the Immaculate Conception. Her mum had put a lot of store in the mother of Jesus, had trusted her to take good care of them. She had believed that Mary, mother of God, would understand her fears; after all, she was a mother herself. Her son had been imprisoned, her son had been tortured, and He had died for His beliefs.

Tania closed her eyes wearily, and prayed to Our Lady. She begged her to give her mother peace at last, some kind of heavenly reward; she deserved it.

The police were finally talking about releasing her mother's remains to the family, so they could hold her funeral. It was surreal knowing that there wasn't even a body, as such, to bury. She had read in the papers that there had been nothing left of her mother to identify; her mum had been plastered all over Soho. It was a terrible thought, and she tried to stop herself dwelling on it, but it was impossible. Knowing that her mum had been reduced to no more than lumps of bloody meat haunted her. She wouldn't even be able to see her in her coffin and say her goodbye face-to-face. They would be burying what was *left*.

Tania felt her nana slip into the pew beside her and, glancing at her, noticed how much she had aged since her mum's death. She had joined Tania and her mum many times over the years for the early Masses, and Tania knew now that, like her mum, Theresa had also been praying for the salvation of her sons. She could see how seriously her nana took this routine; like her mum, her nana embraced the Mass, felt the power of its message, felt the age-old belief of their religion deep inside her, and Tania finally understood it now herself.

As they took Holy Communion together, Tania felt the familiar security that the sacrament had always engendered inside her. She knew she was, for those few moments, once again clean and without stain.

There were fewer than twenty people in the church; it was cold, it was dark, and yet Tania felt, as always, that she was a part of something much bigger than the world she inhabited. She sensed the authority that this religion commanded in its followers.

She sat with her nana and looked around the church. She focused on the Stations of the Cross, the statues of Christ and His poor mother, the beautiful crucifix that hung above the altar depicting the last moments of Jesus before He died to save them, and she felt a brief moment of peace at long last.

Tania and Theresa sat together after the Mass was over, enjoying the silence of the church, and the atmosphere of calm serenity.

'Are you all right, Tania?'

She nodded. 'I'm getting there. I just wish we could bury my mum. I think once we can do that it will be a bit easier, you know?'

'It's hard, I know, lovely. But you're right, once we lay her to rest, it will bring about a bit of normality. It's like being in limbo. We need to get back to reality.'

'I miss her so much, Nana. I wish she was still here, I

wish I had not taken her for granted, had known we didn't have long left together. I would have made sure we didn't waste a second of it.' She was crying, the tears running down her face.

Theresa smiled sadly. 'Listen, child, we all wish that – it's natural. Death is as much a part of life as living. We will all die, sweetheart, that is the only definite thing we will ever know. It's hard, especially for the people left behind but, beggar or king, it comes to us all – no one can prevent it. That is why you need to enjoy your life while you can. The death of a loved one just reminds us of our own mortality. It reminds us that one day death will come for us too.'

Tania knew her nana was right, but it still didn't make her feel any better; she had far too much on her mind. 'I hope she's happy, Nana, wherever she is. I hope she is at rest.'

Theresa laughed loudly then and Tania could hear the humour in her nana's voice as she said gaily, 'Course she is! We're Irish Catholics, for feck's sake! We believe we have the edge over everyone else when it comes to dying! We *live* to die, and we die leaving others to carry on our names, and we pass those names on for generations, so we can never be forgotten. Why do you think we can't use contraception? We are conditioned to procreate at every fecking opportunity. Populate the earth with more good Catholics! Children are the greatest gift God could give to anyone, and they are the future. Like you, now. Your mum is gone, but you are a part of her legacy – while you live, she will never really be dead. You have her blood in your veins, and her wisdom in your mind. Your child will be a part of her even though she is gone.'

Tania had never thought about it like that before, and her nana's words made her feel better, that in some way her mum was still with her. Then she realised what her nana had just said.

Theresa took her granddaughter's hand in hers and, smiling sadly at her, she asked gently, 'Now, tell me the truth. Are you pregnant, child?'

Chapter One Hundred and Forty-One

Christopher Williams had already spent his hundred grand in his head. He was due to retire in the next few years, and it would be a very welcome bonus. He liked and trusted Danny Bailey; he was a chip off the old block – like his father, if he promised something, he delivered. Williams had been happy to go that extra mile for him. He had done his homework, and he had procured everything Danny had requested.

Another plus was that he had found himself a nice little ally in the forensics department – a dumpy little scientist, with good teeth, nice hair, and a serious coke habit. She was not averse to earning a bit on the side, and he was willing to cultivate her, knowing that she would be very useful to him in the future. Even after he retired, he would keep his hand in. Being the kind of man he was, he had played the long game and, over the years, he had made a point of befriending all the people who would one day be responsible for padding out his pension.

He was pleased with himself; he knew better than anyone that his collars – his knack of finding and removing from society the scum that preyed on women and children – far outweighed his extra-curricular activities. That was the real bonus of being a detective – the force were always loath to accuse people like him of anything dodgy, no matter how much evidence they might have to the contrary. If they *did*, and if they won the case, every collar he had ever felt, every fucking ponce he had banged up, would be lining up round the block, screaming for a retrial. A bent copper caused all sorts of aggro for the powers-that-be. No one wanted the expense or the bother of a new trial; it was far easier and cleaner to offer early retirement to any officers who were found lacking. It was simple economics.

He was very happy as he walked into the pub in Rainham where he'd arranged to meet Danny Bailey. He liked Essex. The females were always well groomed, always smiling. Essex women were born with an instinctive knowledge of how to make the best of their attributes; they were very smart and savvy. Essex men, however, were a different ball game; *they* all seemed to have been born with a natural belligerence that caused more fights than John Wayne, and a biological need to become villains. Like the Liverpudlians, they were capable of serious skulduggery from a very early age.

As Danny Bailey ordered their drinks, Williams wondered for a few seconds just how this young man would use the knowledge he was about to give him.

But that was not his problem; he had simply performed the task requested of him, and what this man did with the information provided was none of his business.

Chapter One Hundred
and Forty-Two

Peter and Daniel Bailey were both very quiet as they drove into the scrapyard.

Peter hadn't seen the renovations to the Portakabins and he was very impressed with the new offices; no one would ever imagine that they were as old as the hills. They had been refitted so well the whole fucking place looked brand new – no way would anyone believe that a gruesome murder had occurred there recently.

'Fucking hell, Dan, these look better than the offices at Canary Wharf!'

Daniel laughed. 'I told you – he's good, the kid, and do you know what, Pete? He wouldn't take a fucking bean off me. He said it was payment for us looking after his old man while he was away. I tell you, I was choked.'

Peter was relieved; no forensic lab in the world would find anything remotely sinister here. The boy knew his job – the only thing left of the original building was the fucking outer shell, and that was probably just because his brother had insisted it be kept. As far as Daniel was concerned, nothing had really changed – he still wanted his security and who could blame him?

'So, Daniel, what do you think this is about?'

Daniel shrugged. 'I don't know, Peter. My Danny asked to meet us here, just us two. That is all I know.' He could sense the worry coming off his brother in waves. 'You all right, Pete?'

Peter nodded, but he couldn't fool his brother. He feared what was coming, and he was powerless to prevent it.

Daniel poured them each a drink and, handing his brother his whisky, he said quietly, 'You know, Peter, that no matter what happens, I won't be taking any prisoners.'

Peter nodded, but he didn't speak. He couldn't.

Danny arrived twenty minutes later and, as he looked at his dad and his uncle, he wished with all his heart that he was not the bearer of such bad news. He had no option – this had to be sorted, no matter what the consequences. But it was still a very hard thing to do.

Chapter One Hundred and Forty-Three

'Is it anyone we know, Tania?'

Ria was as shocked as her mother-in-law at the news. Theresa had insisted on her presence – she had been adamant, in fact. Ria was glad she was here; Lena would have wanted her to look out for her daughter.

Tania was still not saying a word to anyone about who was responsible for her predicament. Theresa had hoped that Tania might have opened up to her. She had an inkling of who the father was but she wanted proof, so she could make her grandson pay for this; she wanted him to be exposed, even though she knew it would cause ructions.

As they sat in Lena's kitchen, and looked at Lena's only daughter, Ria knew she had to help this girl in every way she could, for Lena, as well as for Tania. One thing Ria knew for sure was that whoever was responsible for the girl's condition had taken advantage of her; the Tania she knew had been greener than the grass of Ireland. To her knowledge, she had never been kissed, let alone anything else. Ria had racked her brains, and she could not think of one lad who had been sniffing round her; in fact, the girl had never even had a boyfriend that she was aware of.

Ria leaned forward in her chair, and asked gently, 'Were you forced in any way, Tania? Did someone make you do anything you didn't want to?'

Tania just wanted them both to go away and leave her alone. She was *pregnant*! She had only done it once! If she told the truth, there would be murder done, and her child would never have a chance. It would suffer from the very start. No, this was a secret she would have to take to the grave. She shook her head.

'Look, child, you have to talk to us at some point. We just want to help you. Your dad will want to know, your brothers will want to know – you can't hide something like this.'

Tania still didn't answer.

Ria sighed in exasperation. 'Do you want to get rid of it, lovely? No one would ever know, I promise. If that's what you want, then we can arrange it.'

Theresa was more shocked than she thought possible; she was completely against abortion, believing that a child was a gift from God Himself. All the same, she would stand back and keep quiet, if that was what this poor girl wanted. If her suspicions were correct, it would not augur well for any of them if the truth should come out. But it was Tania's choice – whether she wanted to name him or not was her prerogative.

Tania shook her head once more. 'I can't, Auntie

Ria. I can't get rid of it. All that I can say is, I'm sorry.'

Theresa was glad that her granddaughter was going to keep the child, even though she was sorry for her because life as she knew it was over. Like her, she would be a young mum and, like her, she would be tied to her child for the rest of her life. It was history repeating itself.

Chapter One Hundred
and Forty-Four

Peter Bailey could see his brother's face out of the corner of his eye, and he knew he believed everything that Danny was saying.

Deep inside he believed it too, but he had already lost one son and he was loath to lose another, to believe his first born was capable of such treachery. His Petey was a gambler, and he would never change. He was no fucking better than the people they fleeced on a daily basis, who spent their days dreaming about the big win, the big payout. They could never see that they lost far more money to the bets over time than they could ever recoup. His son had so much already, all of which had been handed to him on a plate. He didn't *need* to gamble; he had a fucking good earn – an earn that most people would have got down on their knees and thanked God for. But his son had a sickness; like his Jack, young Petey was a waste of space.

Peter blamed himself; he had protected his eldest boy, given him chances he wouldn't have allowed anyone else. That this child of his, who he had trusted, seen as his heir, could be capable of such hate was beyond him. His boy had been there the night of the bombing, he had been celebrating in the club with them. And all the time he had been waiting for his father to go out to his car and die.

It was one of the few times in his life that Peter Bailey wanted to cry. Treachery was always worse when it concerned a blood relative; it was hard for a parent to admit they had bred someone so heinous and disloyal.

Danny was heart-sorry for his uncle, but he was adamant that the truth had to be revealed no matter how much it might hurt. It would be far more fucking dangerous if he kept his trap shut – that was the bottom line. There was far too much at stake here, and not just money-wise.

'I can't believe this, Daniel, it's too much.' Peter looked at his brother, hoping that he would come to his aid, tell him that it was a mistake and his son loved him, and could never hurt him. He tried another tack, clutching at straws now. 'I saw all the police reports, and so did your father, didn't you, Daniel? They said nothing about any of this.' Peter Bailey could hear the desperation in his own voice; he knew that he had to face this head on, but it was so much harder than he would ever have believed.

Danny wished with all his heart that he didn't have to be the bearer of such awful news. But, unlike these two, he had been suspicious of his cousin for a long while now, ever since he'd drugged him. He looked his uncle in the eye, and said honestly, 'All Petey gave you, Uncle Pete, was what he *wanted* you to see. He edited everything he had gathered from the Old Bill – he had to. He has been cultivating a lot of Filth over the last couple of years and, from what I can surmise, they worked for him – not us. Not the Baileys, as a family. He was just looking to cover his own arse. He must have been at fucking panic stations when he realised that you were still . . .' He didn't finish the sentence; he knew how hard this was. 'This lot cost me a hundred grand, and that was my *own* money I used. I was willing to lose all that if I was proved wrong, and I *wanted* to be wrong – I never wanted this. But it's the truth. Your Petey was behind the bomb that killed my mum. The bomb that was meant for you. There's no easy way to say that, no fucking way to sugar-coat it, is there? It's a fact. And more than that, a fucking disgrace, a fucking diabolical liberty.'

Daniel Bailey was looking at his brother with fury. The enormity of what he was hearing was just sinking in. That he had been harbouring the fucking piece of dirt, the man who had planted a fucking bomb that had taken his Lena away from him, was unbelievable. He had loved that fucker like a son. He knew as well as his brother that his Danny would not *dare* to accuse anyone of this – let alone a close family member – without absolute proof.

Daniel looked around him at his new offices, all matt paint and designer fabrics, and he yearned for the old days when this had been no more than a common-or-garden scrapyard, and the kids had been far too young to hurt anyone. Peter Bailey had inadvertently produced their own nemesis; he had loved and nurtured that cunt, and for what? Daniel was his godfather; he had stood in the church and pledged to God to look after him if needs be. He had been given *everything*, yet Petey had grown up to be nothing more than a fucking traitor, a man who would plan his own father's demise. He had somehow been born with all the weaknesses that they, as brothers, loathed and manipulated to earn their coin. Petey was a gambler, a womaniser, a traitor, a user of everyone around him. Peter had been harbouring a viper, a liar, and a fucking thief.

It was ironic really, considering how hard his brother had come down on Daniel in the past. Peter never felt the urge to hold back when pointing out that he had caused a major fuck-up. But, whatever Daniel might have done, he had never once been disloyal to his own. Peter had always held himself up as a beacon of fucking respectability, yet he had bred a fucking junkie as well as a fucking traitorous cunt to boot; two of his sons had been slayers of women, had been men without any kind of moral fibre. That his brother could have bred children who were capable of such crimes was beyond Daniel's belief. The fact that his brother believed it so readily told him that Peter had obviously had his own suspicions for a good while. Daniel knew that, deep down, his brother had to have had at least an inkling about his eldest son.

He said as much, furious that his wife's death was

being laid at the family's door. 'You must have fucking had some idea about young Petey. I know you; there ain't much that escapes your fucking notice.'

Danny understood where his dad was coming from. He lit a cigarette, before saying quietly, 'I requested the forensic reports over and over again from Petey, but he never gave us anything worth having. He was always treated like the heir to the throne, and I swallowed that – we all did – but I knew from the get-go that we should have been privy to any information pertaining to my mum's death. Uncle Pete, you know as well as I do that you didn't pursue the culprit as forcefully as you should have. You were frightened of what you were going to find out, weren't you? Well, your son was in league with the Allens. He left a fingerprint in the squat when he took Terrence out. He paid a lot of money for that to go away – he knew the Filth that we didn't own would have been all over that like a rash. Because for every Filth that we have made a point of cultivating, there's always two more we can't get to.'

Peter Bailey felt, for the first time in years, real fear, real panic. The knowledge that his son was capable of planning his own father's death was something he could not get his head around. Petey had been willing to take his own father out so callously, so violently, and had mourned his auntie's death, all the while *knowing* that he had been responsible for it. It was too much to take in. It was the sheer effrontery of it that was the hardest to comprehend.

He looked at Daniel, and saw hate mingled with pity. He was grateful to him for that; knowing his brother still had the capacity to feel his pain was a small measure of how much he really did care for him.

'Does Liam know anything about this?'

Danny shook his head. 'I don't think so. What I do know, though, is that he has been cleaning up his brother's messes for a long time now. Petey owes money everywhere; he has been skimming the takes since day one. But that is just him, ain't it? We accepted his so-called *foibles*, his inability to see the big picture, his need to find that extra con, earn what he felt was his private wage. He always needed to feel he was getting more than the rest of us lads. The sad thing is there would never be enough in the pot for him. He is a fucking shyster, a common fucking thief.'

Peter could hear the deep bitterness in Danny's voice. His son should have been fucking put down long ago. He should have followed his instincts but, after Jack, he had not wanted to believe he had another son devoid of decency and strength. He had not wanted his Ria to have to live with the knowledge that *another* of her children was gone from her. He had seen how hard Jack's death had been on her. He had been so amazed at how strong she had been for him then; she had hidden her real feelings because she had known that he would never have done what he had without good reason. But it had taken its toll; she was a mother, first and foremost. Women loved their babies from the second they pushed them into the world; they were programmed to love them, feed them, and protect them, no matter what. Poor Ria. She would be heartbroken at Petey's death. She couldn't know the circumstances though – she would never forgive herself if she thought a son of hers was capable of anything like this.

He was pulled out of his reverie by his brother's voice.

'I'm sorry, Pete, but you do know that he's got to go, don't you?'

Peter nodded; he accepted this was inevitable. 'Of course. Can I ask you one last favour?'

Daniel shrugged. 'Sure.'

'Make it look like a fucking hit, like he was ironed out by strangers. Ria can't know the truth, she couldn't live with it.'

Daniel nodded.

Danny could see the logic in that; no one wanted the women upset. 'Liam might know more than he's letting on, Uncle Pete – he's been carrying him for a while. Shall I bring him up to speed or what?'

Peter didn't know what to say. He didn't know what to do. He was devastated; he would have only one son left out of three boys, three handsome boys. He had done everything physically possible for his children – he had always done what he believed was the best for them and, at the end of the day, what had he been left with? What had it all been for?

Yet here was Daniel, a fucking bona fide looney by

anyone's standards, a man who could murder on a whim, and yet *his* kids were all fucking diamonds. Daniel's kids were worthy men, and they were absolutely loyal to him – each and every one of them. They were *all* men to be proud of.

He had no choice but to wipe his mouth and look to what he still had; his Liam was a good lad and his daughter Imelda was a strong and capable woman. And, ironically, Delroy, who was not even his flesh and blood, and who he had disliked for no real reason, had proved to be the most loyal, hardworking, and trustworthy of men. Life was a funny thing.

Petey was living on borrowed time. He had warned him on so many occasions that he knew he was on the worst kind of rob – stealing from his own. Yet his son had never had the nous to see that his actions would eventually lead to his downfall.

Peter Bailey was feeling old suddenly, old and decrepit. The Life, as good as it could be – *had* been to him and his family – was now the instrument of his eldest son's destruction. It was the reason he would be minus two sons, and why his wife would never again know true happiness.

He stood up abruptly. 'Come on then, Daniel, let's get this over with.'

Daniel sighed. 'No, Pete, you get yourself home. Ria will need you beside her.'

Chapter One Hundred and Forty-Five

Petey Bailey was buzzing. Bernadette was looking good, and she had impressed him with her choice of decor for their new house; it occurred to him that she might very well be an asset to him one day. The house looked fantastic, and he knew it would impress anyone who walked through the door. His only worry was that he owed a hefty wedge to the mortgage company, and they were already chasing the debt. Unlike in *his* world, they were a faceless corporation, and they didn't give a fuck if they upset you in the course of their negotiations. His name meant fuck-all to them; they were operating well within the law and, if he lost this house, he knew he would never get over the shame of it. He had not put down a huge deposit, so the payments were astronomical, and he had the added stress of paying the decorators as well. He had to find the cash, and he would; he had always managed before. He would have to take a bit of a breather from the cards for a while, recoup some money, and he had a few scams on the go that would bring him in a good earn. He would sort it;

he wanted this place badly, and so did Bernadette.

He was really pleased with his choice of wife-to-be. For the first time in their relationship, he felt as if they were on the same wavelength and that they might have a fighting chance. He wanted this as much as she did; he needed the validation of owning an expensive property. It was all top show to them both, all about what you had, and they wanted the best.

Petey Bailey recognised now that he was as shallow as she was and that, like him, she was only ever after the main chance. If she managed to bang out a few sons, Petey thought she might just be worth the effort.

He felt good today; life was on the up. He had one last meeting and then he was looking forward to having a good night out. He had to start cultivating Liam; he needed him now. He would start his campaign tonight – he knew how to grovel when he needed to. Liam was a good, loyal man, there was no doubt about that, especially when it came to the family.

'Give us a kiss, Bernie, I'm running late.'

She kissed him chastely on his cheek. He smiled as he left; unbeknownst to her, once they were married, she was going to get a big shock. He would ride her hard, and she would not be in a position to call the shots any more. He was quite looking forward to it.

Chapter One Hundred and Forty-Six

Noel and Jamsie were already at the scrapyard, waiting for their dad to meet them there. They knew that he was on his way, and they were hoping that they could be out of here sooner rather than later. They had arranged to meet a few mates in Canning Town, and were going to have a few drinks there, before going on to the Electric Lady.

When their cousin Petey drove into the yard, they let him in and closed the gates behind him, before following him into the offices. Petey, as always, was on his high horse. He looked around the small office pointedly, before saying sarcastically, 'No one here yet?'

Jamsie shrugged. 'Not unless they are hiding under the desk, no.'

He was not bothered in the least about Petey's attitude; Jamsie knew that he would not dare act up like this if his dad or his uncle were in the vicinity.

'My old man's on his way. Do you want a drink, mate?'

Petey nodded warily; this felt off, there was clearly

another agenda going on. He wondered if his uncle had found out about his taking cash from the safe at the betting offices. He had always placed bets *after* races had been run – he had a few little girls who he worked the scam with. His Uncle Daniel had queried the size of the debts and the frequency of them recently. He had a feeling that he had worked out what was going on. Petey was suddenly all smiles, putting on a front. 'Yeah, why not? I'll have a beer. I've just been to the new house – fuck me, it does look good, lads. I must be honest, I was sceptical initially of letting Bernadette loose on the place – let's face it, she is a lot of things, but fucking classy ain't one of them! But she did a really good job. For the first time, I'm actually looking forward to marrying her!'

They all laughed.

Noel saw a car pull up at the gates, and he rushed out of the office to open them.

Petey sipped his lager. 'Do you know what this is all about, Jamsie? Bit cloak-and-dagger, ain't it?'

Jamsie didn't answer him; he was too busy watching his father as he walked slowly towards the Portakabins. He had a shotgun in his arms, and Danny and Davey were walking slowly behind their dad. He felt a sudden sorrow envelop him. It looked like his cousin Petey was actually for the high jump; he didn't know what this was about, but obviously it was serious. He saw Petey looking at his dad, seeing the gun; he could only imagine how scared he must be.

Daniel Bailey saw his nephew watching him through the window of the office, saw the fear on his face. He was surprised at how calm he felt. Long gone were the days of him acting first and worrying about the consequences later. He was finally able to channel his anger and make it work *for* him as opposed to against him. Lena was the reason for that, he supposed. He missed her so much.

Petey Bailey knew immediately that he was finished; his uncle was coming for him and there was nothing he could do about it. Petey was gutted, even though he knew, on a very basic level, that this had been coming for a long time. He was just sorry that it had to be now when he was feeling so good about himself and his coming marriage. He had been so certain that he had covered his tracks. He wondered briefly if his father knew about this, if he had sanctioned it. Who was he kidding? He was probably the instigator of it. Peter had never suffered fools gladly, and his son was a fool – he saw that now. Hindsight was a wonderful thing.

Jamsie saw his father stop outside the Portakabin; he was waiting patiently for his nephew to come outside.

Petey Bailey smiled a crooked, sad little smile. 'I assume he is here for me?'

Jamsie nodded.

'I suppose there's no way I can sort this all out, is there?'

Jamsie raised his eyebrows. 'What the fuck do you think?'

Petey felt strangely calm. He was glad it was his uncle coming for him and not his father or brother – that would have been much worse. Jamsie opened the door and, as the cold air blew in, he said to his cousin, 'Let's get this over with, shall we?' Petey couldn't deny the fear inside him, but he was determined that if he achieved nothing else in this life he would have a good death. No one would be able to say he had been a coward and had tried to run.

He walked slowly outside. It was a dark night, and the stars were out; he wished he had bothered to notice things like that before. The scrapyard was bathed in moonlight, and he knew this was the last scene he would ever witness. It was cold, so very cold. Winter was on its way.

'Get down here, you treacherous piece of shite.'

As he walked down the steps, he said quietly, 'It was never anything personal, Uncle Daniel; it was just business. Auntie Lena was a fucking accident. No one could have foreseen that.'

Daniel Bailey stared at his nephew, noting his fear, but also his resignation.

Then Petey smiled suddenly, a wide beaming smile, and he said craftily, 'But your little Tania, now that *was* deliberate. I took her cherry, and she fucking *loved* it. You know me, Uncle Daniel, I always liked to be the first.'

He was still laughing as Daniel Bailey blew his head off.

Chapter One Hundred
and Forty-Seven

Liam was trying to get his head around his brother's dilemma. He had always feared that this was on the cards; Petey had to have known that he would eventually be found out. Liam himself had been tempted at times – he admitted that. It was hard living in the shadow of two men who were both unable to take a step back in favour of their families. But Liam had also understood that *he* would be exactly like that if he was in that position of power. The Life was so seductive, it was a great way to live.

Petey had never been content; he had always wanted more. Well, tonight he was going to be taken down a peg or two if Danny's phone call was anything to go by. Liam was ashamed that a small part of him was gloating, glad that his brother had finally been seen for the piece of shit he actually was. He wished he could see Petey's face when he realised that he had been fucking sussed.

How could he have even entertained the notion of plotting his own father's death? The whole ethos of the Bailey family was that they were just that – a family, and their true strength lay in that fact. You took on one, you took on them *all*.

His older brother had never understood that – he was a man who saw nothing more than his own wants and needs. Now he had nothing – he was a fucking pariah, and he was finding out the hard way that, eventually, everyone had to pay the piper.

In this case, it seemed, the piper was his Uncle Daniel, a man who, when roused, made Mad Frankie Fraser look like a Girl Guide.

Chapter One Hundred and Forty-Eight

Daniel Bailey was having lunch with his daughter, and he was watching her closely. He loved this girl, she was all he had left of his Lena. He sadly believed that Petey had been telling the truth. Lena had confided in him their daughter's crush on her cousin; they had even laughed about it together, never believing for a second that Petey Bailey would take advantage of Tania. But he had done just that. Worst of all, Daniel knew that Petey would have *enjoyed* taking her down as a means of getting one over on *him*. Tania had been just another fucking way to spread his poison, another excuse for him to take what he wanted. But Tania had not said a word to him, and he could never let on that he knew the truth. Tania would need to keep that to herself more than ever now. Petey was dead and gone, and Daniel would have to draw a line under the whole fucking situation.

Peter and Ria arrived at the house as they were finishing their meal. Tania knew immediately that there was something radically wrong with her auntie. She stood up abruptly and went to her, and Ria put her arms around her niece, as she said in a broken voice, 'My Petey, my boy. He was murdered last night. They shot him, they shot him dead. He was dumped in a skip in Walthamstow.'

Tania felt as if she was going to pass out; the news was so unexpected. She wasn't sure if what she was feeling was relief; all she knew was that she couldn't really take it in yet.

Petey was dead, and she was carrying his baby.

Petey was dead, and she would never have to face him ever again.

She was relieved. She could feel it washing over her in waves. Her secret was safe.

Daniel Bailey went to his brother and, hugging him gently, he said seriously, 'I'm sorry, Pete, I'm so very sorry.'

And he was. They both knew the truth of that.

Epilogue

She got a compact mirror
Stole it off her mother
She got her daddy's overnight travelling bag
Always been told 'If you wanna leave home,
honey,
You ain't ever, ever welcome back'
And now she's down at the station, baby in her
belly

Alabama 3, 'How Can I Protect You'
Album: *Outlaw*, 2005

Woke up this morning
Got *herself* a gun
Mama always said you'd be,
The Chosen One
You're one in a million,
You've got to burn to shine . . .
Born under a bad sign
With a blue moon in your eyes . . .

**Martina Cole & Larry Love, George & Dragon pub,
July 2012 (Lyrics changed to fit with the book!)**

Chapter One Hundred and Forty-Nine

'He'll be all right with me. I ain't in me dotage yet, for feck's sake!'

Tania laughed; her nana was a real hardcase at times. 'Imelda will be here soon. He's staying the night at hers, but I need to get into work early – my dad's expecting me.'

Theresa picked up her great-grandson; he was a beautiful child, and the apple of everyone's eye, including her youngest son. Daniel took far more notice of this child than he had ever taken of his own squad, that was for sure. Tania had named him Daniel – that would have pleased her mother. Lena, God rest her, would have adored him.

Theresa had been worried for a while that the child's looks might give away his parentage, but he was blond and blue-eyed. All he had of his father was his build. At two, he was tall for his age and strong as an ox. He was already very independent, and whatever he decided he wanted he went after with a tenacity that belied his age.

Tania had certainly grown into herself; since the baby arrived she had become a very beautiful woman. She worked in the family business now; Daniel had taken her under his wing and he had been pleasantly surprised at how quickly she had adapted to her new role in the Life. She was his right-hand girl, and she seemed to be enjoying it. She still lived at home with her dad, and Theresa knew that Daniel couldn't imagine his life any other way now. He needed this girl and her son – they were what kept him sane. He still missed Lena so badly it was painful to witness.

Tania kissed her little boy, and he hugged her tightly. 'You be good now.' She kissed her nana on her wrinkled cheek and said lightly, 'Thanks, Nana, I'll see you tomorrow.'

Theresa grabbed her arm; she was smiling as she said smugly, 'Before you go, lady, how's things going with your fella? I like him, and I think we can safely say that he likes you! Your dad thinks the sun shines out of his arse. You do realise that, I hope.'

Tania could feel herself blushing now. 'We're OK, Nana. It's still early days.'

Theresa looked at the girl she loved like her own child, and she said softly, 'If you want my advice, Tania, grab happiness every chance you get. Life is so fucking short, girl.'

Tania smiled happily. 'I'll see you tomorrow, OK?'

As she left the house, Tania felt a wave of contentment wash over her; she was finally living her life, and she was enjoying it. After the last few years, she had not believed that she would ever feel like this. She was happy, really happy, and it felt so good.

Chapter One Hundred and Fifty

Imelda was running late to pick up little Daniel; he was staying with her tonight and she was looking forward to it – he was the apple of her eye and she loved looking after him when Tania was working.

She scanned the ledger before her; as she expertly tallied up the different columns, it was clear that the Baileys were earning far more than ever before. As a cash business, they still did everything important by hand; all the money was still accounted for in old-fashioned ledgers. This was the era of software, yet her family still insisted on doing it the old way. Only the taxable incomes were put on to the computers. She realised they were probably right, and she actually enjoyed doing it; there was something very calming about numbers and working them out. Imelda prided herself on keeping the books she dealt with neat and tidy. It was soothing to see the lines of figures – they made sense, they could be resolved. Being so close to the money in this way made you far more aware of it, and where it was going. She was good at it, and she knew that.

She sat back and sipped her drink – a vodka and tonic, with ice and a slice.

Imelda had relaxed as much as she could in the past few years. She still worried about her son, but she had come to accept she couldn't do anything about it. He was long gone from her; he was a part of the family, and that was all he really wanted. He was another Bailey boy – the Life was ingrained in him, and she had to accept it.

She finally understood her mother's choices and, like her mother, she had decided to put her son's life into her husband's hands. She now realised the futility of trying to change him. The only thing she could do was hope and pray that nothing happened to him. He was his father's son, and his mother's darkest fear.

She truly believed that if she had known how it would all turn out, she would have grabbed her son, and taken him as far away as possible from her family and the Life. But it was too late to change anything now. Like her mum, she was involved in the Life, her husband and son had made sure of that, and she could never walk away and leave them. The only thing she could do now was hope against hope that her son never had to pay the price for his family's mistakes.

Chapter One Hundred and Fifty-One

Liam was shattered, but pleased with his day's work. As his cousins came into the club, he grinned – they were like his brothers now, and he was glad about that. He enjoyed their company, and he was so much happier now he didn't have to deal with his brother and clean up after him. Petey's death had caused more than a few ripples in their world, but no one had really mourned him – except for his mum, of course, but that was to be expected.

Even Bernadette hadn't been that bothered. She had been given the house – all paid for – she got to keep the car Petey had bought her – a Mercedes Sport limited edition – and she was now married to a civilian she met on holiday in Tenerife. She was living there running an upmarket restaurant and bar with him, having decided that the Life wasn't as appealing as she had first thought.

Danny was laughing as he motioned to the barmaid to get them all drinks. 'How'd it go, Liam?'

He was excited, and Liam knew that his news would be celebrated for the best part of the night.

'It's a mover.'

'Fucking blinding news! I knew you could pull it off.'

He wished he had been as sure as his cousin. 'I told them we could cover the distribution, all they needed to do was guarantee the product. They were a bit wary at first but fuck them, we are the ones calling the shots. I've got to be honest, Danny, the Albanians are funny fuckers, but they are good at what they do. Very professional, albeit very fucking volatile.'

Danny didn't give a fuck about that; they were safe as houses – the Albanians needed them far more than they were willing to admit. 'This gives us the exclusive rights to the whole of the European market! It's a fucking seriously big earn.'

Liam knew that better than his cousin – he had worked out the deal after all. 'The coke they provide is really fucking top grade, and they seem to have an endless supply. I reckon we can start distributing within weeks. I've also warned them that if they sell to anyone else, the deal's off. I did labour the point for effect, but they ain't cunts – they know the score.'

Danny shrugged. 'Fuck them. If they push it, we'll just fucking demolish them. There's plenty more where they come from.'

Liam laughed. Since Petey's untimely death, the remaining boys had toughened up, and pulled together. They had realised that the main thing for them now as a family was to be seen as tighter, more impenetrable, than ever before. A lot of people in the Life believed that Petey Bailey had been taken out by his own family, and that suited them. None of them would ever confirm or deny the theory, but the whisper about town had given them an even more fearsome reputation; after all, if the Baileys were capable of taking out their own flesh and blood they were basically capable of anything. No one ever got a second chance – one fuck-up and you were gone. It was a new regime, and it was working better than anyone could have expected.

The Baileys were now not just the premier crime family, but also responsible for the most lucrative business in the game. They now had a stake in almost every activity that occurred in the British Isles. They had a workforce that could rival any major car manufacturing company, and they prided themselves on paying far better wages. The Baileys had never been so popular, and they intended to make sure they stayed that way.

Chapter One Hundred and Fifty-Two

'You sure about this, Tania?'

She nodded. 'Course.'

She heard her father sigh and she smiled. 'You know what, Dad? You make me laugh. You asked for my opinion on this, and I researched it and got you all the figures you requested. I know as well as you do that this is everything you thought it was – and more. It's also completely legit, but if we use our heads, we can organise it in such a way that we will have another avenue to launder the dirty money. It's perfect really.'

Daniel Bailey was very proud of this girl of his; she was in possession of a natural talent to exploit every situation to the family's benefit. He was amazed at just how quickly she had adapted to the Life. He had given her a job to keep her happy, get her out of the house, and so he could watch over her. She had wanted to earn her own crust and he respected that. But he had never believed she would be as shrewd as she had turned out to be. She was only twenty, and she was already turning over a good profit. Furthermore, she was crafty, ruthless and hard as nails if the situation warranted it. She was a true Bailey, all right.

'I'm going to go and make us a cup of tea. You look over the figures again, Dad – I know you will bite my hand off for this.'

He watched her as she left the room; she was a very different girl to the one who had buried her mother. Having her son had changed her too – she had seemed to grow up overnight, but children could do that to a woman. Daniel had never let on that he knew the truth of his grandson's parentage – she had never offered a name, and he had never demanded one. He had also made sure that none of the boys revealed it either.

He had been surprised at his feelings for his grand-child; from the first moment he had laid eyes on him he had adored him. His only regret was that Lena had not lived long enough to see him. The child had brought life back into a house that he had believed could never again know happiness. But he had been wrong. The child had united them all – even Ria had brightened when the child arrived. She had needed something to focus on, and little Daniel had fit the bill. She had filled the role of grandmother that should have been Lena's.

Daniel had taken Tania into the Life because he needed her near him, and he knew that she had needed to be near him just as much. They were a good pair, and he was proud of how she had coped with everything that life had thrown at her. Now she was trying to branch out on her own, and he saw that he had to let her, just as he had been forced to let his boys have their freedom.

Petey Bailey's treachery had brought home to him and his brother the danger of not letting go, of not accepting that there was more than enough to go round. He picked up the file and opened it, but the truth was he had already perused it, digested it, and made up his mind to pursue it. He just hoped that he wasn't doing the wrong thing by giving his daughter so much responsibility. But he was convinced that she was more than ready to tackle it.

As she came back into the small office with two mugs of tea, he said nonchalantly, 'You can have this, but you keep me in the loop, OK?'

Tania grinned happily; like him, once she decided on something there wasn't a lot anyone could do to persuade her otherwise. She had taken to the Life like a duck to water. She was a natural really – even her brothers treated her as an equal now. But there was a small part of him that was sad because his Lena would be mortified to know that her efforts to keep her daughter away from the Life had been in vain. 'You look pensive, Dad. You OK?'

He smiled and nodded. 'You've done a good job, Tania. I'm proud of you.'

Tania Bailey didn't answer her father, but she knew he was right – she *had* done a good job, and she was looking forward to doing an even better job now he was willing to finance it. She had quickly adapted to earning serious money and had slipped easily into the family network. She was determined to make her mark, and prove to everyone just how much of a Bailey she really was.

She had a child who was more Bailey than anyone knew, and she wanted him to have that legacy. Without a father, the only legacy she could eventually leave to him was her own. So she would work night and day if necessary to make sure that he would be seen to be as much a Bailey as any of them.

Chapter One Hundred and Fifty-Three

Stephen Doyle was a big man whose size could intimidate people, so he made a point of always having a cheerful countenance – he had learned at a young age that it put people at their ease. At school he had been the class giant, and his family's name had not helped either. The Doyles were well known as a family to be wary of. His father was a powerful man, prone to drunken rages if he was thwarted, who could smash their home up on a whim. He also, however, had a reputation for being more than capable of orchestrating a good earn for anyone who requested it.

His old man had always been a broker, and Stephen Doyle had inherited his father's knack for finding out everything about everyone, and using that knowledge to his advantage. He put people in contact with each other – people who were looking for a partner in certain enterprises, or who had a product needing a viable distributor or backer. These were people willing to pay a percentage of their earnings to the broker who had found them a perfect match. It was a lucrative earn and one of the few specialist occupations in the Life.

The Doyles were approached by anyone who needed a partner; they brokered deals for new business ventures by marrying up the money-people with the ideas-people. The real knack lay in being able to create partnerships between those who could actually work together. It was important to understand who you were dealing with and to ensure that they could get along. In their game, that was imperative – especially as so many of the people he dealt with settled any differences with a firearm.

Now that Europe had opened up, Stephen was more in demand than ever, regularly approached to broker international deals. He was respected because he never underestimated the people he dealt with, and he would always ensure that everyone concerned received an accurate assessment. There could be no hidden surprises that might cause problems down the line.

Stephen Doyle was thirty-seven years old and, for the first time in his life, he was falling in love. From the moment he had laid eyes on Tania Bailey he had been smitten – until then he had always been happy to play the field. Now he was actually courting a girl of twenty, whose father was a man only a raving fucking lunatic would cross.

But he didn't care. She was like him – intent on living the Life to its fullest. He understood even better than her exactly what that meant. Together they had the potential to be the dream partnership – they could pool their resources and eventually they could own this fucking town.

He could sense the same ambition and desire in her that he had. She had a child and she wanted the best for him. Like him, Tania Bailey had an instinct for achieving what she wanted and, like him, she knew that they were destined to be together. She was so young and so lovely, and he had never wanted anybody as much as he wanted her.

Tania saw him standing by the bar of the new club the Baileys had just opened in Soho. She stood in the doorway watching him for a few moments; he was a lot older than her, but that didn't bother her as much as it did him. She really liked him, and she was confident that he felt the same way.

Her son's birth had brought home to her the Bailey need to earn and make sure that you were capable of keeping yourself and your own. She was a Bailey all right, she had realised that when she had held her son in her arms.

She had been the victim of so much heartache, but it had made her stronger, she could see that now. You had to toughen up, and learn how to deal with whatever life threw at you. Her mother's death had catapulted her into the Bailey world overnight and, from that moment, she had walked into the Life with her eyes wide open. She was so different now; the young girl she had been three years ago was long gone. Her mum had paid the ultimate price, and her uncle had paid a high price as well – he had lost two sons. Her Auntie Ria had never got over Petey's death, and her cousin Imelda spent her life watching her son's submersion into the Bailey franchise. They were all fucking full of regrets.

But Tania wasn't going to end up like them. She wouldn't live off the proceeds of the Bailey name, while distancing herself from what the Bailey name really stood for. She knew better.

Her brothers had grown up in the Life, they had known the pitfalls from an early age but they had never been given a choice. Her mum had tried to protect her from it, but Tania had seen glimpses from a very early age, and when her mother had been taken from her she accepted it could not go unavenged. She had learned there was no getting away from the Life, not for a Bailey. And when she had given birth to her boy, she had sworn to herself that he would never go without.

The Bailey name was her ticket to independence, and the Bailey name would ensure that never again would anyone take advantage of her. In the future *she* would be the one using other people, *she* would be the one to exploit other people's weaknesses. Tania had embraced the Life and thrown herself into it wholeheartedly.

Now she had Stephen Doyle. He was a very dangerous man – she knew that about him, but she didn't care. She wasn't frightened of what the Life had to offer her – for her, the Life offered its own attractions. She had chosen this, and she had no qualms about it whatsoever. Furthermore, she would stop at nothing to get what she wanted. And she wanted *everything* that the Life had to offer, starting with Stephen Doyle.

He smiled as he saw her walking towards him. Tania Bailey had the aura of a woman with power. She looked for all the world like a woman who knew exactly what she wanted from the Life, and who knew *exactly* how to get it.

To find out more about Martina Cole and for an exclusive glimpse of life in London's underworld, visit www.martinacole.co.uk.

Lyrics Acknowledgements

'Hypo Full Of Love'
Music and lyrics by Jake Black/Simon Edwards/Piers
Marsh/Robert Spragg
Published by Chrysalis Music Ltd © 1996
Used with permission. All Rights reserved.

'The Night We Nearly Got Busted'
Music and lyrics by Simon Edwards/Piers Marsh/Robert
Spragg/Charles Harrison
Published by Chrysalis Music Ltd © 1997
Used with permission. All Rights reserved.

'Power In The Blood'
Music and lyrics by Jake Black/Simon Edwards/Piers
Marsh/Robert Spragg/Charles Harrison/Mark Sams/Jon
Delafons/John Jennings/Alexis Worrell
Published by Chrysalis Music Ltd © 2003
Used with permission. All Rights reserved.

'Come On Home'
Music and lyrics by Jake Black/Robert Spragg/Jon
Delafons/John Jennings
Published by Chrysalis Music Ltd © 2003
Used with permission. All Rights reserved.

'How Can I Protect You'
Music and lyrics by Piers Marsh/Robert Spragg/Jon
Delafons/Alan Downey/Anthony McGuinness/
Christopher Dignam/Joseph Jewell/William McGuinness
Published by Chrysalis Music Ltd/Copyright Control
© 2005
Used with permission. All Rights reserved.

'Crazy World'
(Dignam/McGuinness/McGuinness/Jewell/Downey)
Published by Elevate Music Limited
Lyrics reprinted by permission.